SECOND CHANCE

It had always amazed her, how Noah handled his tools so effortlessly, as if they were extensions of his hands . . . strong, well-shaped hands that had once grasped hers and gently stroked her cheek.

Noah turned as though he'd read her wistful thoughts. His dark brown hair framed his suntanned face in a mop of unruly waves. Even though he wasn't Sunday-best clean, Deborah longed to touch him, to coax a boyish smile to his lips.

"Hey," he murmured. He took a deep breath. "I'm sorry if I bumped your ladder—"

"It was my fault!" Deborah insisted as she hurried toward him. "I was watching *you* instead of paying attention to how far I'd reached—how the ladder was swaying. You're always so intent on your work, and so *gut* at what you do, Noah. It's a joy to watch you."

On impulse, she flung her arms around him. "I'm sorry if I've been a bother," she murmured. "I just had to tell you I was wrong—to see if we couldn't patch things up and be together again. *Please,* Noah?"

**Don't miss any of the Seasons of the Heart books
by Charlotte Hubbard**

Summer of Secrets

Autumn Winds

Winter of Wishes

An Amish Country Christmas

Breath of Spring

Harvest of Blessings

The Christmas Cradle

PROMISE LODGE

Charlotte Hubbard

ZEBRA BOOKS
KENSINGTON PUBLISHING CORP.
http://www.kensingtonbooks.com

ZEBRA BOOKS are published by

Kensington Publishing Corp.
119 West 40th Street
New York, NY 10018

All Kensington titles, imprints and distributed lines are available at special quantity discounts for bulk purchases for sales promotion, premiums, fund-raising, educational or institutional use.

Special book excerpts or customized printings can also be created to fit specific needs. For details, write or phone the office of the Kensington Sales Manager. Attn.: Sales Department. Kensington Publishing Corp., 119 West 40th Street, New York, NY 10018. Phone: 1-800-221-2647.

First Printing: March 2016
ISBN-13: 978-1-4201-3941-9
ISBN-10: 1-4201-3941-X

eISBN-13: 978-1-4201-3942-6
eISBN-10: 1-4201-3942-8

10 9 8 7 6 5 4 3 2 1

Printed in the United States of America

*In memory of my dear friends
Jim Smith and Fern LeMasters.
Miss you both.*

ACKNOWLEDGMENTS

Thank You, Lord, for Your guidance as I begin this new series!

Thank you, Neal, for our wonderful marriage of more than forty years.

Many thanks to my editor, Alicia Condon, who embraced this series idea, and to Evan Marshall, the fabulous agent who keeps my writing career rolling. I'm ecstatic that we three are working together on this new series.

Special thanks to Vicki Harding, innkeeper of Poosey's Edge Bed and Breakfast in Jamesport, Missouri. Your assistance has been invaluable! Thanks and blessings, as well, to Joe Burkholder and his family, proprietors of Oak Ridge Furniture and Sherwood's Christian Books in Jamesport. Mary Ann Hake, your help with all things Amish and Mennonite has been a blessing, as well.

Psalm 121 (KJV)

1 I will lift up mine eyes unto the hills, from whence cometh my help.

2 My help cometh from the LORD, which made heaven and earth.

3 He will not suffer thy foot to be moved: he that keepeth thee will not slumber.

4 Behold, he that keepeth Israel shall neither slumber nor sleep.

5 The LORD is thy keeper: the LORD is thy shade upon thy right hand.

6 The sun shall not smite thee by day, nor the moon by night.

7 The LORD shall preserve thee from all evil: he shall preserve thy soul.

8 The LORD shall preserve thy going out and thy coming in from this time forth, and even for evermore.

Prologue

Rosetta Bender stepped out of the stable with a bucket of fresh goat milk in each hand, gazing toward the pink and peach horizon. Sunrises felt special here at her new home. She was grateful to God for helping her and her two sisters jump through all the necessary hoops to acquire this abandoned church camp. Its name alone—Promise Lodge—made Rosetta feel hopeful, made her dare to dream of a better life for her family and for the other Plain folks they hoped to attract to their new settlement. Even so, she let out a long sigh.

"You sound all tuckered out and we've not even had breakfast yet."

Rosetta turned to smile at her eldest sister, Mattie Schwartz, who'd just come from the chicken house with a wire basket of fresh eggs. The sun's first rays made a few silvery strands sparkle in her dark hair, which was tucked up beneath a blue kerchief.

"There's no denying that we set ourselves up for a lot of work when we bought this property," Rosetta replied wistfully. "I wouldn't move back to Coldstream for love nor money, but I wish I could join the gals who'll be cleaning at the King place this week, helping Anna get their house ready for Sunday's service. And I'd like to be at the common meal with everyone after church, too."

Mattie looked away. "So I'm not the only one who's been missing our *gut* friends?" she asked. "In all the hustle and bustle of selling our farms and shifting our households to Promise, I hadn't thought about leaving everyone we've known all our lives. Takes some getting used to, how *quiet* it is out here in the middle of nowhere, ain't so?"

"Is this a meeting of the Promise Lodge Lonely Hearts Club?" their sister Christine demanded playfully. As she stopped beside them, she shifted a bouquet of colorful irises so she could shield her eyes from the sun. "That gorgeous sunrise comes with the reminder that the heavens declare the glory of God and that we should, too—and I for one will *not* miss plenty of things about Coldstream. Every time I saw that new barn out my kitchen window, it reminded me of how my Willis died because someone set the old one on fire," she declared. "I—I'm glad to be leaving those ghosts behind. Focusing forward."

Rosetta nodded, because she'd sold the house where Mamm and Dat had died, too—but Christine's tragedy was far worse than the passing of their elderly parents. The Hershberger family had returned home last fall to discover their barn in flames. When Willis had rushed in to shoo out the spooked horses, one of them had kicked him against a burning support beam and part of the barn had collapsed on him.

"And I won't miss the way Bishop Obadiah refused to allow an investigation into that fire at your place, Christine," Mattie stated. "God might've chosen him to lead our church district—and I understand about Old Order folks not wanting English policemen interfering in their lives. But Obadiah turns a blind eye whenever his son's name is connected to trouble."

"Isaac Chupp and his *dat* know more about that barn fire

than they're telling," Rosetta agreed. "And while I miss the company of our women friends, I do *not* want to endure another of Obadiah's lectures about how you two should get married again and how *I* need to get hitched now that Mamm and Dat have passed on."

Christine chuckled. "*Jah,* he's not one for tolerating women off the leash—"

"Or women who don't submit to husbands anymore, and who don't keep their opinions to themselves," Mattie added with a sparkle in her eyes. "If I live to be a hundred, I'll never forget the look on his face when he heard we'd sold our farms so we could buy this tract of land."

"I thought Obadiah's eyes would pop out of his head when Preacher Amos declared he was coming to Promise Lodge with us, too!" Rosetta chimed in. Just thinking about their last chat with Coldstream's bishop made her laugh out loud. "We broke a few rules, leaving our old colony to start a new one, but I believe the pieces wouldn't have fallen into place had the Lord not been urging us to break away and start fresh."

Mattie glanced toward the barn, where Preacher Amos and her two sons were milking Christine's dairy cows. "Don't expect Roman and Noah to agree with that," she said. "My boys don't like it that I sold the farm where they'd figured on living out their lives and starting families. But I believe they'll have a whole world of new opportunities here—"

"And chances to meet a bunch of girls, as well, when other families join us," Christine pointed out. "That's how my Phoebe and Laura see it. They're both relieved that Isaac Chupp's not pestering them to go out with him anymore. And so am I."

"It should be easier on Noah, too, now that he won't be seeing Deborah Peterscheim wherever he goes," Rosetta remarked. "I was sad to hear that they broke their engagement. They'd been sweet on each other for most of their lives."

"Oh, there's more to that story than anybody's telling." As though she sensed her sons might finish their milking and come out of the barn at any moment, Mattie started walking toward the lodge. "Noah would never admit it, but I have a feeling he did something stupid and Deborah decided she'd had enough. But don't quote me on that."

"And we all know that Preacher Amos really came along to look after Mattie," Christine murmured, smiling slyly at Rosetta. "She's pretending he doesn't make eyes at her when he thinks we're not looking."

As the three of them laughed and strode toward the timbered lodge, Rosetta's heart felt lighter. Was there anything deeper than the love she and her two sisters shared? The surface of Rainbow Lake reflected the glorious sunrise, and as they passed the tilled plots that would soon supply produce for Mattie's roadside stand, Rosetta gazed at the rows of newly sprouted lettuce, peas, and green beans that glistened with dew.

That's how it is with us, too, Jesus, she thought. *You planted us here in Promise, in fresh soil and sunshine, so we can grow again.*

"What'll we cook for breakfast?" Rosetta asked. Her old tennis shoes were saturated with the grass's wetness, so she toed them off. Could anything feel better than walking barefoot in the cool green grass? "We could make French toast with the rest of that white bread in the pantry."

"And fry up the ham left from last night's supper," Christine added as she grabbed Rosetta's wet shoes.

"And nothing's fresher than these eggs," Mattie declared. "Your hens are laying as though they like their new home—even if the chicken coop needs a few new boards and some paint."

Rosetta gazed at the lodge building ahead of them, thinking a double coat of stain and a new roof would be welcome improvements. "Did we bite off more than we can chew?"

she asked softly. "It's going to take a lot of money and elbow grease to convert this lodge into apartments. Every time I turn around, I see something that needs fixing. I didn't notice so many problems before we decided to buy the place."

"Are you saying we got a little too excited before we plunked down our money?" Christine replied as she slung an arm around Rosetta's shoulders. "Don't you dare admit that to the men."

"Are you forgetting that once the Bender sisters decide to make something work, nothing and nobody can stand in their way?" Mattie challenged, slipping her arm around Rosetta's waist. "I'm the big sister, and I say we'll handle everything that comes along."

"You'll feel better after you eat a *gut* breakfast," Christine assured her. Then one of her eyebrows arched. "Have you had your coffee yet, Rosetta?"

Chuckling, Rosetta shook her head. "I filled the percolator but I didn't want to wait for it to finish perking—and didn't want to leave that old stove burning while I milked the goats."

"There's your answer!" Mattie crowed as the three of them climbed the steps to the lodge's porch. "Everything'll look perkier after you've had a shot of coffee."

"And if the caffeine doesn't kick you into gear, I will," Christine teased. "You were born the youngest so Mattie and I would have somebody to boss around, after all."

"*Jah,* Mamm and Dat knew what they were doing when they made you last, Rosetta," Mattie agreed. She held Rosetta's gaze, her expression softening. "And they couldn't have had a better caretaker in their later years, either. They'd be so tickled to know that the three of us are starting up a place for all kinds of folks to call home—folks like us, who need a fresh start and something to *hope* for."

Rosetta smiled as goose bumps rushed up her spine.

Mattie had always been good at seeing the rainbow behind life's storm clouds—and good at pointing out what others did best, as well.

"It's my fondest hope," Christine murmured, "that amongst the new families we'll meet is a fellow who's just right for *you,* Rosetta. A fellow who's been waiting for the best cook and the sweetest soul and the prettiest smile he could ever find."

"Amen, Sister." Mattie squeezed Rosetta before opening the screen door for them. "How about if Christine and I cook breakfast so you can freeze your milk? I think our new families—and the renters in your lodge—are going to feel mighty special when they use the soap you make from it, Rosetta."

"*Jah,* I love your rosemary and mint bars," Christine remarked as she led the way inside the lodge. "And the boys really like the cornmeal soap you make for scrubbing up. It cleans their grimy hands without making them smell girly."

Rosetta smiled. It was part of her dream, when the Promise Lodge Apartments were established, to welcome new tenants with samples of her handcrafted soap and to sell it in her gift shop, too. As she imagined the smiles and appreciative comments the colony's new residents would make about her lovely, simple rooms and her special soaps, she once again believed she could accomplish all the necessary preparations to make her dream a reality.

"You girls are the best, you know that?" she asked softly. "And you're right. With the three of us Bender sisters helping one another, our dreams will all come true—because we won't quit until they do."

"We'll make it happen," Christine agreed.

Mattie's laughter echoed in the high-ceilinged lobby in which they stood. Hours of scrubbing had cleaned the soot from the stone fireplace and their intense efforts with polish and rags had made the majestic double wooden staircase glimmer again. "We can't fail," she reminded them playfully. "Too many men are waiting for that to happen, and we can't let them say *I told you so*."

"*Jah,* you've got it right—and you'll not hear another peep of wishful thinking from me," Rosetta stated. "We'll make do, and we'll make it all work out, and we'll make new friends. Right after we've had our breakfast and a pot of coffee."

Chapter One

Deborah Peterscheim stood at the roadside entrance to Promise Lodge, her pulse pounding. Her English driver was heading back along the county road with her last dollar. As she cradled a cookie tin in her arm and gripped the handle of her old suitcase, she hoped the three-hour trip from Coldstream hadn't been a huge mistake.

But it was too late for doubts. *"This is the day the Lord has made. Let us rejoice and be glad in it,"* she reminded herself as she raised her face to the warm June sun. It felt good to let the breeze ripple her clothing as the trees whispered their welcome—such a comfort compared to the final, harsh words her *dat* had flung at her as he'd pointed toward the door. If only she hadn't spotted the flames coming from the Bender barn. If only she hadn't called 9-1-1 . . .

One more time, to reassure herself, Deborah read the ad she'd torn from *The Budget*: *New settlement in north-central Missouri. Ample land. Lodging available while homes are being built. Limited number of apartments for single women. Old Order Amish and Mennonites welcome. Contact Amos Troyer, P.O. Box 7, Promise, MO.*

Surely Preacher Amos and the other friends from Coldstream who'd started this new colony would understand her need for a fresh start. First and foremost, she hoped to win Noah Schwartz's heart again, after foolishly calling a halt to their engagement last month. *Just one of several stupid moves,* she thought with a sigh. *But don't let on about why Dat sent you away. Not until you absolutely have to.*

Deborah blanked out the painful parting images of her parents' faces and instead focused on the handwritten sign at the roadside.

WELCOME TO PROMISE LODGE
OPENING SOON
THE PROMISE PRODUCE STAND
THE PROMISE LODGE APARTMENTS

She recognized the clean, precise printing as Noah's—he had an eye for arranging things, and a steady hand when it came to wielding a paintbrush or a welding torch. Did she dare believe that Noah was welcoming *her* to Promise Lodge? Or would he reject her apologies—her request for his forgiveness—before she could convince him her pleas were sincere?

There was only one way to find out.

Deborah walked beneath the arched metal Promise Lodge sign, which was positioned between trees that formed a canopy over the entryway. Their leaves rustled in the breeze, allowing splotches of sunshine to dapple the dirt driveway. When she stepped beyond the colorful trumpet vines at the entrance, she stopped to gaze at what she hoped would be her haven. Maybe her new home.

Ahead, Deborah saw a tall, timbered lodge building with a wide porch and a grassy yard surrounding it. Several cabins nestled in the shade of ancient trees behind the lodge. In a fenced pasture beside an old red barn, black-and-white dairy cows grazed and goats munched on weeds as they watched Deborah. Off to her right, about an acre away, the surface of a lake shimmered in the sunlight.

To her left, a large garden plot had been tilled and hoed. Leaf lettuce, peas, and other early vegetables grew in neat, straight rows, their leaves shining a vibrant green against the dark soil. Beyond this planted plot, another garden was being plowed. When a Belgian came around from behind the fragrant honeysuckle hedge, following the contour of previous rows, Deborah's heart stopped.

Noah was driving. She would know his lean silhouette and the dark, wavy hair fluttering beneath his straw hat anywhere, for she'd memorized his handsome features all through school and during their yearlong engagement. This was the man she'd planned to spend her life and raise her children with—and when he fixed his eyes on her, even from a distance, Deborah stopped breathing. He gazed long and hard, his expression indiscernible as the horse plodded along and the plow blades churned up the black soil.

Deborah dropped her suitcase and ran toward him, clapping a hand over her *kapp* so it wouldn't fly off. Such hope—such joy!—danced in her heart. Surely he would feel compelled to give her another chance. She *had* to find a way to make amends. "Noah!" she called out. "Noah, it's so *gut* to see you!"

As he halted the horse and stepped down from the plow, Deborah stopped at the edge of the plot to catch her breath. Noah took his time, stepping carefully over the uneven, furrowed earth. His green shirt clung to his damp chest and his old Tri-blend pants flapped in the breeze as he walked. He'd lost some weight—

But I can fix that! Maybe he's missed me as much as I've longed for him! Deborah thought as Noah crossed the last several feet between them. He mopped his face with a bandanna and then stuffed it back into his pocket.

"Deborah."

She savored the sound of Noah's voice, the way he made her name sound so much sweeter than anyone else could, even if a wary silence stretched between them. When Deborah realized he wasn't going to say anything else, she offered him the cookie tin. "I—I brought you some of those brownies you always liked," she said with her best smile. "The kind with the peppermint patties in them."

Noah took the tin but he didn't open it. Sweat was dribbling from beneath his straw hat down his cheeks, but she didn't dare wipe it off the way she used to.

"Why'd you come here?" he asked. "It's a long trip from Coldstream."

Deborah winced. He was asking the questions she didn't want to answer—but she might as well state her case. "I made a big mistake, breaking off our engagement, Noah," she murmured, holding his intense brown-eyed gaze. "I'm hoping we can—hoping you'll give me the chance to make up for my impulsive decision. I'm sorry for those things I said. Can you forgive me? *Please?*"

His eyes widened. When someone asked for forgiveness, the Old Order ways demanded an answer, or at least an effort toward reconciliation. "I'll have to think about it," he replied tersely. "Why would I want to court you again, after you shot me down like a tin can off a fence?"

Deborah turned so Noah wouldn't see her eyes filling with tears. Their conversation wasn't going well at all, but she had to get past this roadblock. She had nowhere else to go, and no way to get there. "I was wrong to doubt you, Noah," she whispered. "I got too impatient, wanting answers—that house with a rose trellis we'd talked about—before you were ready to provide them."

"How'd you get that bruise on your neck?"

As her hand flew to the mark her collarless cape dress

couldn't conceal, Deborah realized how guilty she must look. "I fell."

She closed her eyes against the memory of how Isaac Chupp had grabbed her in anger because she'd called the sheriff. It wasn't a lie—she *had* fallen after the bishop's son had shoved her into a ditch.

But she couldn't start down that conversational trail yet. Noah would want nothing more to do with her if she told him of the events that had led to her leaving Coldstream this morning after her *dat* had ordered her out of the house.

Noah cleared his throat as though he didn't believe her. He glanced at her suitcase. "How long do you figure to stay?"

Deborah swallowed hard. She hadn't been here ten minutes, yet Noah sounded ready to be rid of her. "This is such a pretty place," she hedged, gazing out over the grassy hills that were dotted with trees and wildflowers. "And you're planning to provide apartments? And open a produce stand? Your *mamm* and aunts are the perfect women for running those businesses."

Noah let out a humorless laugh. "Mamm, Rosetta, and Christine *love* it here," he replied. "Me? I'm not seeing Promise Lodge as the Eden they made it out to be when they declared we were all moving. But there's no going back."

Deborah closed her eyes. Noah's impatient tone suggested that he'd already written her off.

"There's no lack of work to keep me busy here, and to keep my mind off how things went sour between us." He let out a long sigh. "I suppose that's one *gut* thing."

The pain in Noah's eyes sliced into Deborah's soul. She'd had no idea how badly she'd hurt him, or of the bridges she'd burned by so recklessly ending their engagement. "I'm so sorry," she said in a tremulous voice. "I—"

"*Jah,* so you've said."

"—had no idea what I was tearing apart when I thought I wanted to—"

"It was my whole life you tore apart, girl," Noah blurted. "It'll never go back together the way it used to be. Why would I take a chance on getting my heart ripped out again?"

Deborah hung her head. Noah's words sounded so final. It seemed her best option was to use a phone here at Promise Lodge to call that English driver's cell phone before he got any farther down the road. But she had no way to pay him, and no place else to go now that her *dat* had cast her out.

"I've got this plowing to finish," Noah said, gesturing toward the Belgian that was standing in the partially tilled garden plot. "You'd best go on up to the lodge. At least Phoebe and Laura will be glad to see you."

As Deborah trudged toward the buildings, her shoulders slumped and shuddering, Noah's heart thudded. She'd never been much good at lying. Her cheeks flushed and her pretty green eyes clouded over —not that she'd ever really *lied,* that he knew of. But she'd dodged his questions a time or two during their courtship, and she hadn't told him anything he needed to know just now.

In that respect, Deborah was a lot like Mamm and his aunts. They minimized problems and forged ahead without thinking everything through, as they'd done when they'd sold their three farms, pooling their money to buy this abandoned church camp. Women were good at getting themselves into situations men found totally impractical. So now he was plowing and painting at Promise Lodge instead of continuing his welding apprenticeship with Deborah's *dat,* Preacher Eli Peterscheim—not that he'd wanted to remain in Coldstream after Deborah had broken his heart.

Excited barking made Noah sigh. His Border Collie, Queenie, was running up from the pasture to greet Deborah as though the prodigal daughter had come home. "Traitor,"

Noah murmured, watching the dog wag her fluffy tail while Deborah stroked her black head and ears.

Instinct told Noah to set the canister down, but his wistful memories were stronger. As he lifted the lid, scents of mint and chocolate brought back the days he and Deborah had spent together planning their future. Three brownies later, he kicked himself for caving in to sentiment, to the idea that Deborah had baked them just for him. Her brownies were only a temporary fix, a Band-Aid on a gaping emotional wound.

"We've got a long row to hoe, Buck," he muttered to the Belgian as he stepped up onto the plow platform. "Geddap, fella."

As the muscled horse pulled him around the end of the plot, Noah watched his cousins, Laura and Phoebe Hershberger, rush out the lodge door to greet Deborah. Their happy cries drifted out to him and he envied the way they took her into their arms, welcoming her so excitedly. Once upon a time he'd hugged her with the same enthusiasm, believing he could find no finer young woman on God's earth—believing the Lord had created Deborah Peterscheim especially for him. He'd loved her all his life. He'd never had eyes for anyone else.

But Deborah's cruel, unexpected words still rang in his head. *It's been more than a year, Noah. I thought we'd be married by now, in our home and starting our family. Maybe you don't love me enough. Maybe our engagement is a big mistake.*

How could he possibly have responded to those words? What was the right answer, when the young woman to whom he'd given his heart had implied that he *didn't love her enough* and couldn't make her dreams come true fast enough? Hadn't she realized that he couldn't support a wife and a family before he finished his welding apprenticeship and found a steady job?

It made no sense. And to add grease to the fire, a short time later his *mamm* had announced they were pulling up stakes in Coldstream to move to Promise. While he agreed with Mamm and her sisters that Bishop Obadiah Chupp's attitude had become intolerable, he'd obviously underestimated the depth of their disagreement with the bishop's opinions. And who had ever heard of *women* starting a new colony? Why had Mamm and her sisters ever thought they could make it work?

Noah exhaled to release his rising resentment but then his anger came at him from a different direction. Who had grabbed Deborah's neck hard enough to leave a bruise in the shape of a purple handprint? True enough, her *dat* had a temper when he got frustrated, but had he slapped her around? If so, what had gentle Deborah done to provoke him?

What if it wasn't her dat*? But then, why had she been standing close enough for any other fellow to touch her? Unless . . .*

Noah finished the plowing. His stomach churned with suspicion as he unhooked Buck and led him behind the stable. What if Deborah had ended their engagement because another guy had caught her eye? And if that was the case, how long had *that* been going on? Had she fled Coldstream to kiss up to him because she'd been mistreated? Or had she gone astray?

Noah led the horse into the corral and topped off the water trough. The steady pounding coming from the barn told him that either his brother or Preacher Amos was inside. Until new families arrived, they were the only three men at Promise Lodge, and he felt more like talking with one of them than subjecting himself to the hens in the lodge—not to mention facing Deborah again so soon.

As Noah entered the shadowy structure, where cracks in the weathered lumber allowed some daylight through, his older brother, Roman, looked up from the stanchion he was

constructing. When this property had been a church camp,
riding horses, tack, and hay had been stored here, so he and
Amos were renovating it into a dairy barn for Aunt Christine's Holstein herd. After her husband died last fall, Roman
had taken over the milking and the care of the cows.

"Problem?" Roman asked. "By the look on your face,
your mouth was open when a bird flew over."

Noah grimaced. "Deborah's here. Begging for my forgiveness."

His brother's eyebrows shot up. "And you said—?"

He thrust the canister at Roman and then walked around,
checking out the progress on the remodeling. "I told her I
wanted no part of courting her again."

"*Gut* answer! Amos brought five more letters from the
post office this morning, from families wanting to come to
Promise Lodge," his brother said in an excited voice. "Three
of those families have *daughters*. They're looking for affordable land and fresh bloodlines to marry into. So here we are,
brother. The answer to their prayers, right?" Roman pried off
the canister lid, inhaled deeply, and then stuffed a brownie
into his mouth.

Noah sighed, allowing the thrum of the agitator in the
bulk milk tank to fill the silence. Before fall, they needed
to construct a separate stable for their horses, and within
the next week or two they'd have to build a roadside stand
where the girls could sell their produce. So much work, so
little time.

"Still can't argue that Deborah's brownies are the *best,*
though," Roman remarked. "Looks like you've eaten a few."

"*Jah,* they were a peace offering. But once the sugar wears
off, you're only hungrier for something more substantial."

Roman chortled. "That's where these new girls might be
just the ticket. But if Deborah has asked you to forgive her,
you know Mamm and the aunts will side with her," he
pointed out. "And Preacher Amos'll be reminding you about

that seventy-times-seven thing, when it comes to letting go
of old grudges. Even if you don't want to marry her anymore,
he'll tell you to forgive and forget."

It was true. Preacher Amos was an admirable man, even
if he'd come to Promise Lodge mostly because he was a widower and he had his eye on Mamm. He was more laid-back
than Preacher Eli or Bishop Obadiah Chupp, but he insisted
on following the rules Jesus had taught. There would be no
wiggling out of forgiving Deborah, no crying foul just because she'd jilted him. Forgiveness was the cornerstone of
the Old Order faith. They had both joined the church last
year, so he couldn't ignore Christ's most important com-
mandment: *Love one another.*

But he couldn't forgive Deborah. Couldn't let go of the
pain that gave him a reason to get up in the morning. If he
was hurting this badly, he was still alive, right? It was proof
he hadn't curled up in a ball and rolled into a hole.

He intended to move on. To love again and marry someday.

But Deborah no longer figured into his plans.

Chapter Two

As Deborah hugged Laura and Phoebe Hershberger, her two best friends in the world, the sound of their voices healed some of the pain Noah had inflicted with his tough talk. She had really missed these girls since they'd moved away from Coldstream to make a fresh start with their widowed mother.

"Deborah! What a fine surprise," Laura said.

"Just yesterday we were talking about you, wishing we could see you again," Phoebe chimed in, "and here you are! The answer to our prayers."

They all laughed as Queenie yipped in agreement, prancing in a circle around the three of them. Deborah clutched the girls' shoulders, savoring their togetherness. Why ruin this happy moment by telling them the real reason she'd come to Promise Lodge? There would be plenty of time to share the disturbing news of what was happening in Coldstream. "This is quite a place," she said. "I can't wait to see it, and to hear about what you've been doing."

"Oh, we haven't had an idle moment, what with planting the garden plots and fixing up the guest cabins," Phoebe replied. She was twenty, and her slender face and angular body closely resembled her deceased *dat*'s.

"And you can be our first guest." Laura, the younger

of the sisters, had the sunnier disposition. Her blue eyes glimmered as she gestured toward the nearest cabin. "Mamm's finished the curtains and we've put a new mattress on the bed in the cabin closest to the lodge. You showed up at just the right time."

"Come on inside," Phoebe insisted. "Mamm and the aunts will be glad to see a face from back home."

As they stepped up to the lodge's wide front porch, Deborah could tell the building needed some maintenance, yet she knew immediately why her favorite neighbors had fallen in love with the place. Large old trumpet vines grew on either end of the porch, loaded with bright orange flowers. The shade from enormous maple trees felt twenty degrees cooler than the garden, and the homey creak of the screen door welcomed her into a lobby that rose two stories high. Curving stairways framed the spacious room, with sturdy bannisters that joined to form the railing of an upstairs hallway. Above her, a huge chandelier of antlers gave the entryway an aura of rustic elegance.

"Look who's here!" Laura called out as they hurried past a massive stone fireplace. They entered a dining area filled with long wooden tables and chairs—enough to seat nearly a hundred people, Deborah estimated. The lingering aromas of fresh bread and fried chicken reminded her that she'd missed dinner while she'd been on the road. When Rosetta Bender peered out from the kitchen, however, Deborah forgot how hungry she was.

"Oh, but you're a sight for sore eyes!" Rosetta cried as she rushed toward Deborah with a dish towel flapping in her hand. "Mattie and I were just saying that we should write to you and your *mamm*—"

"But hearing the news from you in person is so much better," Mattie Schwartz joined in from the kitchen doorway. "Did you eat along the way? We've got chicken and some rhubarb cake left—which is a miracle, considering how my boys and Amos are packing away the food these days."

Once again Deborah gloried in the warm hugs and smiles from friends she'd missed. Both women's aprons were smudged with flour and their cape dresses of brown and gold felt damp from spending time in a hot kitchen, yet their smiles were as refreshing as lemonade on a summer day. Deborah was grateful that Noah's *mamm* and aunt had never seemed to hold their broken engagement against her.

"A piece of chicken would hit the spot," she replied. She smiled at Laura and Phoebe, who were already fetching her a plate and pulling out the chair at the worktable. "Wow, this must be three times the size of our kitchens back home. I've never seen such big stoves and refrigerators."

"They're perfect for feeding the families coming to our new colony, and for the apartments I hope to open this fall," Rosetta replied. She plucked bread from a covered basket and placed it on Deborah's plate. "You'll hear the fellows talk about how decrepit the buildings are, but all these appliances are gas and they work just fine."

"We're lucky because the church that owned this place left all the utensils, furnishings, and linens, too," Mattie said. "With time and hard work, we can salvage most of those items and save a lot of money, which we can spend for the repairs and new buildings we'll need."

Deborah closed her eyes over a crispy chicken thigh that was still warm. Her heart swelled with Mattie and Rosetta's can-do attitudes, the firm belief that they'd made the right decision when they'd sold their farms to start a new life. "Have you had any response to your ad in *The Budget*?" she asked as she buttered her bread. "Some of the folks in Coldstream are still surprised at how quickly you left, saying maybe you leaped before you looked."

Mattie and Rosetta exchanged a smile that suggested they'd heard this sentiment before. "We Bender sisters have stuck together through thick and thin by the grace of Jesus," Mattie replied without a moment's hesitation. "He wouldn't steer us wrong."

"And with Mattie and Christine losing their men, and our parents passing on to their reward last winter," Rosetta took up the thread, "we all thought it best to look forward rather than letting our losses hold us back. 'In my Father's house are many mansions,' the Bible tells us. Our lodge and cabins aren't as grand as God's dwelling place, but with His help we'll create a little section of Heaven in this old campground for folks who need to set down new roots."

That would be me, Deborah mused as she bit into her chicken again. She was happy to let the two women keep talking so she didn't have to reveal her predicament yet.

"The letters are coming in, from folks interested in buying plots of our land," Mattie replied as she checked a pan of something in the oven. "Amos has called a few of them, and we think we'll see new families by the end of June if they can sell their farms quickly."

"That's only a few weeks away," Deborah murmured.

"We've got a lot of fixing up to do before then," Laura remarked.

"But we'll have plenty of time to chat about our plans for Promise Lodge and show you around while you're here," Rosetta said. "How's your family, Deborah? What's the news from Coldstream? While we don't regret leaving some of the recent goings-on behind us, we sure do miss our friends."

Deborah swallowed hard, her half-eaten chicken thigh poised in front of her face. No matter which question she addressed, these two women wouldn't want to hear her answer. "Oh, you know how it is," she hedged. "Things don't change a lot in Coldstream from one day to the next."

Mattie frowned doubtfully.

Rosetta raised an eyebrow. "Why is your face telling me

something different from your words?" she asked. "Has there been more trouble, Deborah?"

The bruise on Deborah's neck throbbed. Before she could reply, Preacher Amos Troyer came in through the back kitchen door, followed by Roman Schwartz, Mattie's older son. The minister's bearded face lit up in greeting. "I heard we had a guest," he said as he headed toward one of the large stainless steel refrigerators. "Welcome, Deborah."

"And thanks for these brownies," Roman said as he set her tin on the counter. "Too bad we didn't save enough for you ladies."

"We've just asked Deborah what's been happening in Coldstream," Mattie said as her gaze intensified. "And I'm guessing it's not so *gut*."

Deborah was cornered. Sooner or later these dear friends would receive the bad news in a letter from someone, so there was no point in stalling. "The um, barn on the Bender home place burned down."

When Rosetta and Mattie grabbed for each other's hands, Deborah sighed. She'd been here less than an hour, and already she'd distressed half the people she'd seen.

"Dat built that barn when he and Mamm moved onto the place, when they were first married," Mattie recalled sadly. "In the winter when the leaves were off the trees, I could see it from my kitchen window, across the fields."

"*Jah,* more than sixty years it sat on our hill, like a guardian angel for the farm," Rosetta said with a hitch in her voice. "I'm awfully glad our parents weren't alive to witness this."

"Why do I suspect Chupp and his English buddies were involved?" Roman muttered. "Their names came up after Aunt Christine and Uncle Willis's barn caught fire. And with the new owners not yet living on the Bender farm, those guys probably figured they could hang out there and no one would be the wiser."

"Don't go repeating gossip as gospel, Roman," Mattie said sharply. "It's one thing to have our suspicions, but another thing to speculate about these fires without knowing the facts."

"After catching Isaac snooping around at *my* place a while back," Preacher Amos joined in, "I tend to agree with Roman. And although I stood firm against getting the county sheriff involved when the Hershbergers lost their barn—and the man of their family," he added with an apologetic glance at Phoebe and Laura, "I felt we gave the bishop a very convenient opportunity to look the other way. Every time his son's name has been connected to trouble, Obadiah has claimed that Isaac's in his *rumspringa*—sowing his wild oats—so he's exempt from the rules church members must follow. That's the main reason I left his district."

Deborah knew quite well how Obadiah Chupp covered for his errant son. She had also understood why her father, Preacher Eli, had decided that her missing *kapp*, her tumbledown hair, and her muddy, scraped knees told of activities too sinful to speak of in front of her younger siblings. So he'd sent her away. . . .

"And what have *you* heard about the fire, Deborah?"

Rosetta's question brought Deborah out of her painful thoughts. How much did she dare reveal? Would these friends accuse her of overstepping the rules—taking matters into her own hands by calling 9-1-1—the way Dat had? Would they send her packing if they knew what Isaac and his redheaded friend, Kerry, had done to her? She didn't want to lie, but she didn't want to humiliate herself again, either.

"It was Isaac," she murmured.

"See there?" Roman crowed. He grabbed glasses from the cabinet so Preacher Amos could pour them some cold tea. "If we were still living in Coldstream, maybe we'd have caught Isaac with—"

"It's best that we moved on," his mother insisted, silencing him with a purposeful look. "We thank God that Rosetta's horses, goats, and chickens were out of the barn and here with us, and that the house was spared. It was, wasn't it?" Mattie asked in a strained whisper.

Deborah sucked in a deep breath, hoping the topic of conversation would remain on the Benders' property rather than on her, personally. "*Jah,* the house is fine, and so are the other buildings."

"And for that we give thanks," Rosetta replied as she quickly wiped her eyes. "I feel bad for the family who bought our farm, though."

"Something tells me the men will hold a barn raising for the new owners, like they did for the Hershbergers," Preacher Amos remarked.

"But how many times will they do that?" Laura blurted. "It's just *wrong* if Isaac Chupp's causing these fires and—and nobody's holding him responsible."

"You're absolutely right," Preacher Amos agreed. "We must keep our Coldstream friends in our prayers, asking that God's will be done—and that His justice be carried out, as well."

Deborah quickly finished her snack. She felt bad for Laura and Phoebe as memories of that fateful night brought grim expressions to their dear faces: the Hershberger family had returned from an uncle's funeral last November to discover their barn in flames. Other men from around town were rushing over to help put out the fire, but as Willis Hershberger was urging his frantic horses outside, one of them had kicked him into the flames. Part of the barn had fallen in on him, and there'd been no way to save him.

"Is this a *gut* time to look around Promise Lodge?" she asked the girls in a hopeful tone. "Or, if you've got work that needs doing, I want to help."

"But you're company, Deborah," Laura protested. "Sure, we've got more garden to plant, but—"

"This is *me* you're talking to," Deborah teased as she rose from her chair. "Those seeds will go into the rows faster with six hands than with four."

"And maybe if you're out there where Noah can see you, it'll put him in a better mood," Phoebe suggested as they rinsed Deborah's dishes. "He's been mighty cranky since he left you behind in Coldstream."

As they headed out the back door, Deborah's brow furrowed. "But *I* was the one who broke off the engagement, remember?" she murmured. "I've already asked for Noah's forgiveness—begged him for a second chance. But he turned me down flatter than a pancake."

"*Ach,* that's not so *gut,*" Laura stated.

"I thought he was missing your company enough that he'd reconsider," Phoebe remarked. "He's hardly been talking to anybody. Goes through each day with a black cloud hanging over him."

Isn't it just like Noah not to talk about what's on his mind? Deborah thought as they approached the cabin nearest the lodge. A few bright new shingles stood out on its green roof and a new coat of chocolate-brown paint made it appear fresher than the other cabins down the row. It was small, yet she hoped it would be a haven where she could pull her life together again—

Unless the truth is more than these folks will tolerate.

Phoebe swung open the door and gestured for Deborah to go inside. "We figure to have new families stay in these cabins while their homes are being built," she explained. "Everybody'll eat in the dining room and get to know each other while they settle in."

"We're living in the lodge, along with the Schwartzes and Preacher Amos, until enough men arrive to start building houses," Laura piped up. "From our room, we can see Rainbow Lake and the pasture where the cattle graze—right, Mamm?"

Christine Hershberger snapped a curtain rod into its bracket and turned. Her slender face brightened and she rushed over. "Look at you, come to visit us here in Promise!" she said as she embraced Deborah. "Nothing's so sweet as the face of a longtime friend."

"It's *gut* to see you, too. You're making such a nice new home here," Deborah replied as she returned the hug. The longing in Christine's voice told her to keep the conversation light. No need to reveal the tragic details about the fire at the Bender place yet.

Christine, however, eased away to gaze into Deborah's eyes. "I couldn't help overhearing the bad news when your voices drifted out the kitchen windows," she murmured. "While I would love to visit our friends in Coldstream, I doubt I'll ever go back there. I—I couldn't bear to see another burned-out barn. It's best for us to remember the Bender farm—and our own place—as they were in better days."

"Oh, Mamm, we didn't mean to upset you," Phoebe insisted as she slung her arms around her mother and Deborah.

"We'll focus forward, like you've told us to," Laura said staunchly. She joined their huddle and shared in a collective sigh that filled the little cabin.

Deborah realized then that her recent tribulations were an ant hill compared to the mountain of misery the Hershbergers had climbed these past several months. "Whatever I can do to help, you tell me, all right?" she insisted. "We've shared so many things over the years—the fun stuff as well as the work—and I'm ready for some more of those *gut* times. Nobody makes me laugh the way you three do."

Their grateful smiles told Deborah she'd said the right thing. *Maybe you can give as much comfort to Laura, Phoebe, and Christine as you were hoping to receive. Maybe you were led here to be a blessing.*

Deborah gazed around the homey one-room cabin. A lingering lemony scent suggested a top-to-bottom cleaning.

Two cozy old chairs flanked a simple table, with a braided rug between them on the wood plank floor. The double bed was made up with a colorful quilt and fresh sheets. Through an open door, she saw a small bathroom with a toilet, sink, and a shower. The cabin reminded Deborah of the one her family had rented during a family reunion in a state park.

"This is really cozy," she murmured. "If you've got new families coming in, though, I don't want to be in the way when—"

"This is *you* we're talking about!" Laura interrupted. "You'll never be in the way, silly goose. This is the smallest cabin—too cramped for a family with kids. So stay as long as you want!"

"Let's show you around. Then we can catch up on what's going on back home while we plant a second patch of sweet corn," Phoebe suggested. "With all the time it took to move here, we're late planting some of our vegetables for the produce stand. But it'll all work out—especially with you helping us, Deborah."

As her friends showed her the rest of the cabins and the grounds, Deborah's spirits lifted. The Hershbergers were hoping she'd stick around Promise Lodge for a while, and she had no doubt that she could be useful. Everywhere she looked, walls needed painting and windows needed curtains and floors needed scrubbing.

When the three of them reached Rainbow Lake's freshly mowed shoreline, several frogs hopped into the water. The lake sparkled with sun diamonds as it lapped gently around an old wooden dock that extended toward its center. A fish jumped out of the water and splashed back in. As the trees swayed in a refreshing breeze and Phoebe pointed out the overgrown apple orchard they hoped to revive, Deborah felt the tension easing out of her shoulders. Everything about Promise Lodge seemed so peaceful, so welcoming, that she dared to believe she might recover from being cast out of her home.

A movement caught her eye near the entry to the grounds, where Noah was leading his Belgian from the plot he'd finished plowing. Even from this distance, he appeared forlorn, lacking the exuberant energy Deborah recalled from their childhood and courtship.

I did that to him. I had no idea how much he loved me.

Deborah sighed. How could she convince Noah to forgive her, to trust her again? And where could she go if he didn't?

Chapter Three

At supper that evening, Noah focused on his ham and beans to keep from looking at Deborah. It was no accident that his *mamm* and aunts had seated her directly across the table from him, probably figuring he'd get lost in her green eyes and gaze at the glossy brown hair she'd tucked neatly beneath her *kapp,* the way he used to. He buttered a square of corn bread, considering where he'd go after he'd finished eating. Someplace she wouldn't follow him, pleading again for his forgiveness and affection.

"Noah, now that you've finished plowing the produce plots," Preacher Amos said, "I'd like you to putty the windows in the cabins and then paint the windowsills. You've got a steadier hand with a trim brush than I do."

"*Jah,* I can do that," Noah replied as he drizzled honey on his corn bread.

"And, Deborah, your *dat* once told me you'd made quick work of painting the kitchen and bedrooms at your place," Amos went on from the head of the table. "If you could help us out by painting the cabins' interior walls while you're here, I'd really appreciate it. I've got rollers and paint all ready to go."

When Noah glanced up, he couldn't miss Deborah's

pleased expression. Was she tickled because Amos had complimented her, or because the preacher was arranging for her to work alongside *him*? Noah's temples pulsed when he clenched his jaw against a protest.

"I'd be happy to help," Deborah replied with a lilt in her voice. "Mamma has always said that Dat taught me how to paint when I was a kid so *he'd* never have to do it again."

As laughter rang around him, Noah's frustration rose. Everyone had conveniently forgotten how Deborah had humiliated him. Rejected him. Beside him, Roman reached for the bowl of wilted lettuce with a chuckle. "There's no escaping her, little brother," he murmured near Noah's ear. "You might as well make your peace with her."

Noah glared at him. "Who asked for *your* opinion?" he muttered.

As the chatter continued around the long table, Noah quickly finished his supper and excused himself to tend the livestock chores. At least the horses, Christine's cows, and Rosetta's goats wouldn't mock him as he filled their water troughs and put out their evening feed. When he stepped down from the lodge's porch, Queenie met him eagerly with her rubber ball, so he threw it hard, releasing his pent-up tension. Watching his dog chase the ball and catch it after the second bounce made him feel better, so when she brought it back to him Noah lobbed it down the driveway again.

A distant high-pitched yipping made him stop to listen. *Coyotes.* Dusk was falling, and they were on the prowl—reason enough to put Rosetta's chickens into the shed along with the goats. When he'd fed and watered all the stock, Noah took his rifle from behind the barn door and went out to the edge of the woods where they'd stacked their firewood beneath tarps. He fetched some cans from the recycling bin and spaced them across the top of the woodpile.

Ping! Ping! Ping!

Noah shot without having to think about it, watching the

cans fly with rhythmic precision. At the sound of distant female voices, he turned to watch his cousins bid Deborah good night on the lodge porch before she went to her cabin. When a lamp flickered in her window his heart quivered, but another round of target practice restored his resistance to her presence. She would be getting ready for bed . . . and as early as the sun rose on these summer mornings, he should be heading inside, too. He strolled to the lake and sat on the dock for a while, however, scratching Queenie between the ears as the frogs began their nightly chorus.

When Deborah's lamp went out, only two squares of pale yellow light remained in the lodge windows. The darkness deepened into a velvety indigo spangled with stars. Noah breathed easier, relieved that this eventful day had finally ended. Once again the coyotes called to each other, sounding closer now. Although his mother didn't like having Queenie in the house, he decided to slip her into his room. His Border Collie was feisty and fast, and she would dutifully defend the livestock, but she was no match for predators if they outnumbered her.

"Come on, girl, let's go in," he murmured as he started toward the lodge.

When Noah reached the porch, he saw Roman leaning against a support post, shadowed by the dense trumpet vines. Even in the darkness, it seemed clear that his brother had been waiting for him. "You're not planning to use that gun on our guest—or to scare her off—I hope," he teased.

Something inside Noah snapped. After dealing with Deborah's surprise arrival since early this afternoon, he really didn't care to discuss her any further. "Enough already," he muttered, resting the butt of his gun on the ground. "Not so long ago my ducks were in a nice row— I had a fiancée, a farm, and a future—until Deborah ditched me, and then Mamm and the aunts got their half-baked idea about starting a new settlement out here in the middle of nowhere," he ranted. "At least it got me away from Coldstream and the Peterscheims. But why on God's *gut* earth has she showed up *here,* of all places?"

Roman's eyebrows rose. "Better adjust your attitude before Amos starts preaching at you," he warned. "It's no secret how you feel about Deborah—or about being here at Promise Lodge, little brother. Get a grip."

"I'll get a grip, all right—around Deborah's neck," he muttered. "This wagonload of *manure* started rolling downhill on account of her, you know."

Roman's expression confirmed what Noah already knew: his frustration had gotten out of hand. In the eyes of the Amish, such anger was every bit as sinful as the activities Deborah had attributed to Isaac Chupp. "Now you've lost all sense of perspective," his brother stated. "Maybe Deborah had *gut* reason to break up with you when—"

"Stifle it, Roman. Is it a gift from God to be *right* about everything?" Noah exhaled in exasperation. "Sorry. I'm all wound up—"

"Tighter than a top," his brother agreed.

"—because nothing's going right in my life anymore. And now Deborah's shown up to rub my nose in it," Noah blurted. Then he sighed loudly. "Even Job cried out to God when he'd had too many troubles heaped on his head."

The two of them stood in silence, except for the reedy whine of the cicadas and the croaking of the frogs. Noah inhaled deeply, hoping the cool night air would settle the fire and brimstone burning in his gut. He'd always been able to keep a lid on his feelings, even during Dat's nastiest rants when he'd been so sick near the end of his life. Lately, however, his emotions seemed to boil over at every little thing— not that moving away from everyone and everything he'd ever known was a *little* thing.

"What do you suppose happened to Deborah that she's not telling us about?" Roman asked as he watched the fireflies rise from the grass. "There's a story behind that bruise on her neck."

"She dodged the issue when I asked her about it," Noah remarked gruffly. "I doubt the women'll quiz her about that handprint. They probably figure Eli got peeved and grabbed her."

He didn't like the path his suspicions were following, but what would it solve if he kept them to himself? "Personally, I think Isaac Chupp did that to her . . . maybe because Deborah saw him in the Bender barn," Noah speculated. "You'd think she'd know better than to tangle with the bishop's boy. But then, I suspect Isaac's the reason she walked out on *me*."

Roman scowled. "From what I've seen, Isaac flirts with *all* the girls. That doesn't mean it's right if his drinking gets out of hand and other folks lose their barns—or a husband—because of it."

"*Jah*, there's that." Noah closed his eyes against a fresh welling-up of resentment. Why did one bad thing lead to another and another, like lined-up dominoes falling in succession? Truth be told, Deborah's rejection had been just one in a series of disasters. "Seems like the trouble started early last year when Dat's diabetes took him out, and then Mamm's parents succumbed to the flu, which left Aunt Rosetta alone in that big house. And then Uncle Willis died fighting his barn fire, which left Aunt Christine a widow. That's a *lot* of trouble in our family lately."

"Let's not forget how Bishop Obadiah kept harassing Mamm and the aunts to get married, practically before Uncle Willis was cold in the ground," Roman reminded him. "It was only a matter of time before any one of them snapped. They felt God was leading them to this place, so they found a way to afford it."

"And you agree with that? You *like* it here?" Noah challenged. After living in Promise for three weeks, Roman was discussing their life-altering move in a tone that sounded downright happy rather than stoically accepting of the hand God had supposedly dealt them.

"You could've stayed in Coldstream," Roman reminded him. "You had a welding apprenticeship, a *gut* opportunity to—"

"And why would I want to work in Eli Peterscheim's shop, where I'd see *her* all the time? And where would I live?"

Roman shrugged in that exasperating way he had. Because he was three years older than Noah, he thought he was so much wiser. "Even the Lord's will allows us to choose. Frankly, I made the move because none of the Coldstream girls interested me," he admitted. "Sure, Mamm would've fussed if either of us had stayed behind, but she was determined to make a go of this place. While other families buy these lots and repay the initial investment Mamm, the aunts, and Amos made—and they get Rosetta's apartments and the produce stand going—I figure to keep managing Aunt Christine's dairy herd and selling the milk. I think we'll get that old orchard producing again someday, too."

"You really believe this Promise Lodge thing's going to fly?" Noah challenged. "I see a lot of opportunities for falling flat on our—"

"Since when did you become such a naysayer?" Roman countered. "Mamm's willing to try something new instead of struggling to keep up a farm in Coldstream. Plenty of folks have expressed their doubts, but she and Rosetta and Christine refuse to believe them. Maybe we should be taking notes."

Noah kept his mouth shut. There was no use in trying to talk Roman out of his high-flying ideas. In the silence that stretched between them he heard a singsong yipping, maybe from the orchard.

"I'm going to stay up for a while. Teach those coyotes a

lesson," Noah remarked. "If they keep sniffing around Rosetta's chickens, we'll never be rid of them."

His brother went inside the lodge, and a few moments later the lamps went out. Noah gazed out into the night. The darkness that stretched endlessly in every direction was broken only by an occasional glimmer of heat lightning on the horizon, the sign of an oncoming storm that might bring some welcome rain.

But what of the storm in his soul? *What if Roman's right and I should be making amends . . . making my own choices instead of whining about Mamm's? After all, Deborah chose to come here— chose to move beyond whatever happened in Coldstream, and to be near me.*

And what did that say about God's will at work in his life?

Deborah curled into a tight ball as tears trickled down her cheeks. Even though the cabin's bed with its new mattress was far more comfortable than the one she shared with her sister at home, and the sheets smelled sweet and clean from drying in the sun, she couldn't fall asleep. The male voices that had drifted through her window had spelled it out: Noah believed she was romantically involved with Isaac Chupp. That idea sickened her almost as much as the resentment that had edged Noah's conversation with his brother. He sounded very near the breaking point. Not at all like the happy, easygoing young man she'd been engaged to.

Should she go ahead and tell the rest of her story? She *had* gone against the *Ordnung* and the long-established understanding that Amish folks handled their own disasters without involving local law enforcement. She was certain, however, that hearing the exact details of that fiery night would only depress poor Christine more, not to mention upsetting Mattie and Rosetta, as well.

And what if she told the truth and no one here believed her? Dat certainly hadn't.

Deborah stared into the darkness. For better or for worse she'd come here, and she'd told Preacher Amos she would paint tomorrow.

Help me out, Lord. I don't know what to do.

Chapter Four

"All right, Gladys, you can go first, girlie," Rosetta murmured as she coaxed the black-and-white doe onto the milking stand. "We're getting an early start this morning because I couldn't sleep for thinking about your old home being set afire."

When the goat stood contentedly, eating from her feed bin, Rosetta began to milk her in the back stall of the old stable. As the milk splashed rhythmically into the stainless steel bucket, the four other goats munched their ration nearby, unconcerned about the topic of conversation. Queenie, ever the herder, had ushered the chickens out into the fenced area after Rosetta had opened the door, and now the dog watched from her perch on a bale of straw. She was happy to have Rosetta's company—at least until Noah and Roman came outside.

The morning milking ritual soothed Rosetta, yet a tear dribbled down her cheek as she once again envisioned the barn she'd played in as a child being consumed by flames. Had it happened the way Deborah and Preacher Amos had suggested? And if Isaac Chupp was indeed responsible for two of her family's barns burning, why wasn't Obadiah taking his wayward teenage son to task—and why weren't the other leaders of the church demanding that he punish Isaac, as well?

"Thank God you babies weren't inside when it happened," she said in a low voice. "You can bet I would've demanded an explanation from the bishop if our barn had burned while we were still living there—and I've got to wonder if Deborah's connected to this disaster somehow. She's scared. She knows things she's not telling," Rosetta murmured earnestly. "I so badly wanted to ask her who put that handprint on her neck, but—well, I didn't want to embarrass her. Especially if that print fits her *dat*'s hand. And I didn't want to upset Mattie, either. She didn't say anything to Deborah's face, but I could tell she had plenty of questions when she saw Deborah's nasty bruise."

Rosetta shifted the bucket out of the way and released Gladys from the head gate. She vividly recalled the night Mattie had come to their parents' house with a bloodied broken nose after her husband, Marvin, had been in one of his moods. His untended diabetes had drained the life out of their marriage long before it had finished him off. Mattie had been expected to endure such abuse in submission to her husband and to God's will.

Rosetta and their *mamm* had reset Mattie's nose as best they could and Mattie had spent the night. But once Marvin came for her, Mattie had remained sequestered at home for nearly a month until her face had healed and her black eyes were gone, maintaining the code of silence about such episodes. The women around town had whispered about what had happened, but the men had accepted Marvin Schwartz's behavior—just as they believed he had the right to refuse medical attention as he deteriorated from his diabetes.

"Your turn, Betsy. Step on up here," Rosetta said to the gray speckled doe. "You girls know how it is—having a buck around just makes life messier. So we'll all be happy with our *maidel* lives, right, Queenic? Not that anybody's banging the door down to court a gal who's thirty-seven."

The dog let out a low *woof* and met Rosetta's gaze.

Chuckling, Rosetta fastened the head gate around Betsy's neck and repositioned her milk bucket. As she milked Betsy, Bernadette, Gertie, and Blanche, she continued chatting in a low voice because her goats were more likely to stand still if they heard her speaking or singing. It was akin to prayer, this early morning time of airing her concerns or talking her way through a project for the day.

"After breakfast I'll be mixing up a few batches of soap, so the bars will be dried and ready in a couple of months," she continued. "By then I hope we'll have new families here, and we can welcome them with a gift you girls helped me make."

Queenie's ears perked up and then she dashed out the door, a sure sign the boys were heading to the barn to milk the cows. Rosetta picked up her two pails and walked outside, careful not to slosh any of the goats' milk. "*Gut* morning, Roman!" she called to Mattie's older son.

"*Jah,* back atcha, Aunt," Roman replied as he slid the barn door aside on its track.

"Your brother's not helping you today?"

Roman shrugged. At twenty-four, he was tall and lanky, a conscientious manager of Christine's dairy herd. "He must've slept outside last night, maybe keeping the coyotes away from your chickens. He'll be along eventually."

Rosetta sighed and headed for the lodge. Mattie's younger son had seemed sullen and uncommunicative since they'd moved here—and he'd appeared none too happy about Deborah's arrival and the work assignment Amos had given the two of them. She suspected Noah still had feelings for his former fiancée, even though she'd broken his heart. All of them were probably in for a bumpy ride as the young couple reconciled—or didn't. When Queenie loped past her, heading toward the cabins behind the lodge, Rosetta stopped to stare. The dog had gone to her master, who sat propped against the first little cabin, his head lolled to one side as he dozed.

Why is Noah holding his rifle?

When Queenie circled Noah a couple of times and then plopped down to put her head in his lap, Rosetta refrained from rousing her nephew—and possibly startling him into firing his gun. It struck her how much Noah was beginning to resemble his father, especially when he wasn't smiling the way he had when he'd been living in Coldstream, courting Deborah.

Will the sins of the father be visited upon the son?

Startled by this thought, Rosetta hurried around the lodge's back door and set her pails on the counter inside the mudroom. Noah had witnessed the way Marvin had mistreated his *mamm* many times—had been a teenager when his *dat* broke Mattie's nose. What if Noah considered it his right to behave the same way when he married? What if he believed Deborah *deserved* the nasty bruise on her neck, because he'd grown up in a home where the woman had to take whatever the man dished out?

"Oh, we can't have that," she muttered as she took her soap-making equipment from the cabinet. "Not here at Promise Lodge."

"Are you still talking to your goats, Rosetta?" came a teasing voice from the kitchen. "Or has dear old Mamma come back to us?"

Rosetta had to chuckle, because Mattie had once again brought up her penchant for talking to herself, just as their mother had done in her later years. The topic that had filled her thoughts this morning was no laughing matter, however. Rosetta entered the kitchen, where her two sisters were rolling out the sweet dough she'd taken from the fridge before she'd gone out to milk.

"We've got to help Deborah and—and stand up for her," she stated as she went to stand beside Mattie and Christine at the kitchen counter. "That hand-shaped bruise on her neck's gotten me all riled up. Surely God does *not* intend for His daughters to suffer at the hands of His sons. It goes against everything Jesus taught us about loving one another—no matter what the men of our faith believe."

Her sisters' eyes widened, yet they nodded solemnly. With a sigh, Mattie said, "*Jah,* when I saw that bruise I right away figured Preacher Eli had lit into her, so she left home. He and Marvin were cut from the same bolt of cloth in many ways."

"And with him being her father, there wasn't anything Alma could do about it," Christine pointed out sadly.

"That's exactly the attitude we've got to stop!" Rosetta cried. "I can make soap from now until Kingdom Come and it won't wash away the pain and humiliation after a woman—or a girl—gets smacked around. We can't let those attitudes—those male beliefs—from Coldstream contaminate what we stand for at Promise Lodge. You of all people should be willing to end that cycle of violence, Mattie."

Her eldest sister's face fell. When Mattie looked the other way, Rosetta noted the bump in the bridge of her nose, which hadn't been there before Marvin broke it. "I wish I knew how," she said in a tremulous voice. "I've vowed never to marry again, so as not to subject myself to another heavy-handed man. But I guess that's not much help for Deborah or the other gals who'll be coming here, is it?"

"How do we ask Deborah who grabbed her neck, without upsetting her?" Christine said in a low voice. "Maybe she'll open up to my girls when she feels settled in, or—"

"This is mighty solemn talk from three sisters who usually tickle my funny bone," Preacher Amos remarked as he stepped into the kitchen. "And it sounds like a topic best discussed by *all* of the founders of the Promise Lodge colony."

Rosetta's throat went dry as she and her sisters exchanged a startled gaze. Amos Troyer was a skilled carpenter whose talents were badly needed as they repaired the lodge, the cabins, and the outbuildings—not to mention when it came time to build homes for the people who answered their ad in *The Budget*. No matter how vehemently opposed she and her sisters were to domestic violence, they couldn't afford to alienate this man . . . not that he would leave just because their independent attitudes irritated him. Amos had invested all of his money in this tract of land, just as they had.

Rosetta prayed for the right words. "With all due respect for your position as a preacher," she began softly, "we were saying how Deborah's nasty bruise brings up all the reasons we left Coldstream—and Obadiah Chupp—behind. We don't believe men should be allowed to—to abuse their women," she went on in a rush, "or to condone such violence when other fellows carry it out in the name of order and discipline as the heads of their households."

"If we're going to let heavy-handed men have their way in our new colony," Christine chimed in, "we might as well go back where we came from. I might've gotten a new barn after Willis died in that fire, but I got no justice. And I couldn't watch Mattie remarry because the bishop insisted on it, and then suffer at the hands of another mean-spirited husband while the church leaders support him and the women have to keep quiet about what he might be doing to her."

Mattie quickly turned back to the counter and began slicing the long roll of dough into inch-wide segments with her knife. Her cheeks turned bright pink and she sniffled loudly.

Amos let out the breath he'd been holding. His weathered face softened as he went to stand beside Mattie, stilling her knife by covering her hand with his larger one. "I'm a day late and a dollar short saying this," he murmured, "but when I heard that you'd not been coming to church because

Marvin had broken your nose, I confronted him about it. Took him before Preacher Eli and the bishop on the grounds that his violence went against our faith."

Mattie was standing absolutely still, except for the way her nervousness made the skirt of her rust-colored dress flutter. "I never heard anything about that."

"Probably because Eli and Obadiah were of the opinion that a man may discipline his family as he sees fit," Amos replied apologetically. "I was outraged, because had *I* been allowed to marry you, Mattie, you would've been treated with love and respect. I couldn't tell you that while you were Marvin's wife and my Anna was alive, so I'm telling you now. I'm sorry about the way he let his illness—and his temper—get out of hand."

The kitchen rang with silence. Rosetta closed her eyes, hoping Preacher Amos had just responded to their plea for a change of attitude at their new colony.

Mattie sighed, patting Amos's sturdy hand. "*Denki,*" she murmured. "For what it's worth, Dat later admitted he'd been wrong to encourage Marvin's courtship after he bought the farm next door. Water under the bridge."

"*Jah,* but water's what we use to baptize souls into the faith, and to wash away sin," Amos replied as he turned so he could look at all three of them. "It remains to be seen who will become this colony's bishop—God will decide that when a bishop moves here, or if we draw lots amongst the preachers to select a new leader. But I'll support your idea that Promise Lodge is to be a place of peace. Jesus spoke of turning the other cheek, of praying for those who persecute us, and above all, of *loving* one another," he insisted in a low, clear voice. "It was the last command He gave His disciples before He died carrying out God's will—and we should follow Him rather than clinging to man-made attitudes that have prevailed for too long."

"Amen. And *denki,* Amos," Rosetta replied as she beamed at him. "I was wrong to doubt you."

"So how shall we handle Deborah's situation?" Christine asked earnestly. "We all know she's not telling us everything about—"

"But I believe she will, in time," Amos said as he stroked his gray-streaked beard. "Let's allow her love for Laura and Phoebe—and Noah—to restore her confidence, her trust in all of us. Meanwhile, we can offer her a safe haven until her folks come for her."

"You think they will?" Rosetta asked. "If Preacher Eli smacked her—"

"Ah, but we don't know that. Yet." Amos blessed them with a smile that made the skin around his eyes crinkle with mirth. "Now we see in a mirror darkly, but then—well, all will be revealed in God's *gut* time. I'm going out to speed up the milking so we'll be finished by the time those cinnamon rolls are baked. You gals are taking wonderful-*gut* care of me, and for that I'm grateful."

When Preacher Amos was halfway out to the barn, Rosetta slipped her arms around her two sisters' shoulders. "Well, *that* chat went better than I expected," she said with a relieved grin. "Let's make Deborah feel welcome and enjoy her time with us. We'll all be blessed by her company."

Chapter Five

Deborah awoke with a start to discover that the sunrise was already a bright pink blush on the horizon. The salty-sweet aroma of bacon mingling with the fragrances of coffee and cinnamon told her that breakfast preparations were well under way, so she splashed her face at the sink and dressed quickly. Her body felt heavy from lack of sleep and her eyes stung from crying, but she couldn't let her worries overwhelm her.

I will lift up mine eyes unto the hills, from whence cometh my help. My help cometh from the Lord, which made Heaven and Earth, she reminded herself. *If God be for me, who can be against me?*

Deborah arranged her *kapp* over her freshly wound bun and resolutely smoothed its long strings down the front of her lavender dress. She could do this. She could make herself so useful—could paint so carefully and efficiently—that Preacher Amos and the others would be glad she was here even if Noah wanted nothing more to do with her.

She swung open the cabin door and shrieked, nearly tripping over a body. And then she saw the *gun*. "Noah! I didn't know you were—"

Queenie sprang up from Noah's lap, barking loudly, as though to insist she had *not* fallen asleep on the job.

"Sorry," Noah muttered as he rolled away from Deborah, into the grass.

When he stood up, with his hair sticking out in clumps and his shirt half untucked beneath his suspenders, Deborah realized he'd slept in the clothes he'd worn yesterday. But why did Noah have a rifle? Had he thought she might steal away in the night—or steal from the lodge? Had he lost all trust in her?

"Coyotes," he rasped in a voice heavy with sleep. "Come on, Queenie, let's go. Enough of your racket."

Noah hurried toward the lodge with his dog at his side, leaving Deborah at a loss. Of all the places where he could have positioned himself last night, why had he fallen asleep outside her door? Rosetta kept her chickens and goats in a shed on the other side of the lodge, so wouldn't coyotes have been prowling over there rather than near her cabin?

Deborah started toward the kitchen door at the back of the lodge, wondering if she would ever understand how Noah's mind worked. She used to think she knew him inside and out, but either he'd changed dramatically since moving to Promise or she had totally misunderstood him when they'd been courting.

Her unsettling thoughts disappeared as she entered the kitchen. Rosetta stood at the stove, turning strips of bacon that sizzled in a cast-iron skillet while Christine set a table in the dining room and Mattie pulled a large pan from the oven. Deborah didn't want to interrupt their snappy rendition of "Simple Gifts," but she couldn't help exclaiming over the largest cinnamon rolls she'd ever seen.

"I'd intended to help you make breakfast," she protested as she gazed at Mattie's rolls. They were baked to puffy perfection, spiraled around a filling of raisins, cinnamon, and nuts, and they smelled *so* good. "What's the occasion, that you've made such luscious rolls—surely you haven't been up since the wee hours to bake these for an everyday breakfast," Deborah stammered.

Mattie chuckled as she set the pan on a rack. "*You* are the occasion, Deborah!"

"I was looking for a reason to try this new recipe—testing it for when we have new residents eating with us until their homes are built," Rosetta explained. "And what better reason could I have than you? We made the dough last night and kept it in the refrigerator, which shortened the process this morning."

"You can stir up the glaze, if you'd like," Mattie said, gesturing toward a bowl of powdered sugar with a measuring cup of milk beside it. "We'd never think you were shirking, Deborah. You're not made that way."

Deborah was so stunned that she could only gawk at them. "You—you baked these rolls for *me*?"

Rosetta grinned as she placed crisp strips of bacon on a platter. "I call it planning for happiness," she said, her brown eyes sparkling. "We've been so busy, working to keep everyone clothed and fed while we're putting our new settlement together, that it's time to celebrate our progress—and your visit! All work and no play will make us dull girls."

"And cranky," Mattie added with a laugh. "We were all getting a little crisp around the edges, so it's time to ease up. To count our blessings."

"*Jah,* God didn't create His world without taking a break, and neither should we," Christine reasoned as she spooned coffee into the percolator basket. "And now we've got a head start on tomorrow's breakfast, too."

"*If* you hide some of these rolls where the men won't find them," Mattie added with a laugh.

As the three sisters gazed fondly at her, Deborah's heart swelled with gratitude. "It's so *gut* to see you all again," she murmured. "Things haven't been the same at home without you and the girls."

"We've missed you, too, dear," Mattie said wistfully. "While we believe we've done the right thing by starting a new colony, it's been harder than we anticipated to leave our friends behind."

Deborah nodded. It touched her deeply that these women were celebrating her arrival. She stirred the glaze and then drizzled it over the warm cinnamon rolls, watching it soak into the center coils of cinnamon and raisins. Her mother was a good cook, but she seldom created such lavish treats as these. *And what's Mamma doing this morning? Does she wonder where I've gone, or is she focused on the younger kids . . . keeping the peace with Dat by keeping my name out of their conversation?*

As Laura, Phoebe, and the men came in for breakfast, Deborah set aside her gloomy thoughts. She was sharing fabulous food with good friends, and a day of painting and visiting awaited her. *Planning for happiness* seemed like a fine idea. If these folks could rise above unexpected setbacks and the heartaches in their past, she could, too.

Noah strode quickly toward the cabin he was to work on today, a container of putty in one hand and a scraper in the other. He'd wanted to indulge in a second cinnamon roll and another strip or two of bacon, but that would've meant spending more time across the table from Deborah and her wide green eyes. Did she have nothing better to do than gawk at him?

"Noah, hold your horses!"

Noah ignored Preacher Amos's call and walked faster. As he passed the cabin where Deborah had slept, he kicked himself again for dozing on its doorstep. What had he been thinking? After the coyotes had turned tail, spooked by the shots he'd fired into the dirt, Noah had decided to take in some refreshing night air before turning in. He'd been recalling their courtship days and must've gotten too comfortable, leaning against the cabin as he stroked Queenie's soft fur.

"You can't tell me you're *that* eager to work on windows!" Amos teased behind him.

Noah sighed, wishing the preacher had stayed at the table to gush over the cinnamon rolls a few more times. Amos Troyer seemed a lot more bright-eyed and bushy-tailed now that he'd left Coldstream. Noah felt haggard and unkempt in comparison—but maybe if he ignored his appearance for a few more days, Deborah would keep her inquisitive gazes to herself. Maybe she would see that he no longer cared about looking presentable for her.

Liar.

Noah blinked at this telltale thought as the screen door of cabin number four banged shut behind him. He cared more about Deborah's opinion than he wanted to believe, or he wouldn't be hoping that the smell of her paint would camouflage the ripeness of the clothes he'd slept in. He really should've taken a quick shower and grabbed a fresh shirt.

Behind him, the cabin door opened. He turned to see Amos chuckling as he tossed Noah's forgotten straw hat at him. Deborah came through the door after the preacher, holding a plate with some more of those fresh, warm rolls on it. The aromas of cinnamon and sugar wafted around him.

"Thought you might enjoy a little more breakfast," she said softly. "You're looking awfully thin."

Noah swallowed hard. He didn't want Deborah's pity, but he knew better than to tell her so in front of Preacher Amos. His insides tightened at the sight of those rolls with their glossy glaze . . . at the strong yet feminine hands that placed the plate on the built-in shelves near the stone fireplace. "We've been working awfully hard. Burning off more food," he remarked as he pulled the plastic tab on the new container of putty.

"I could tell it was you who puttied and painted the windows in the cabin where I'm staying," Deborah replied with a smile. "Nobody else gets the edges of the putty and the paint so perfectly straight."

Noah's jaw dropped. What would make Deborah notice such a detail—or care about it? He assumed her compliment was intended as a kiss-up—until he caught the flicker of sad regret in her eyes before she looked away from him.

You did that to her. Or did Isaac Chupp? There's no denying that she's lost her sparkle.

"I've had a lot of practice," Noah remarked. He kneaded a wad of putty between his fingers until it became as pliant as modeling clay.

Putty in her hands, he thought as he pressed the off-white material along the edge of a windowpane where it met the wood. *That's what you used to be, but no more.*

Deborah took the hint and poured pale beige paint into the tray Amos had given her. Even though she wore a faded old work dress he recognized as his cousin Phoebe's, with a kerchief tied over her hair, she looked clean and neat—eager to tackle the task Amos had assigned her. She positioned the old wooden ladder at the wall to his right, climbed it, and began spreading the paint with firm, even strokes of her roller, as far as she could reach in both directions.

Amos was replacing the corroded faucet on the bathroom sink, whistling under his breath as he worked. Noah had resigned himself to the preacher's tendency to hum or make some sort of *joyful noise,* as he called it. He was glad Amos didn't expect him to make small talk, even though it meant the hours could get awfully long as they worked. If he hadn't already joined the Old Order, he'd still have the CD player he'd enjoyed during his *rumspringa*—but that was just one of the gadgets he'd given up in preparation to marry

Deborah Peterscheim and follow the rules of the church as a responsible adult.

Noah focused on drawing his scraper straight across the putty he'd applied, keenly aware of Deborah's presence. And why wouldn't he be? The creak of her ladder told him she was climbing down to paint the bottom section of the wall, and then the steady *swish swish* of her roller made him envision the stretch of her body as she covered the area in front of her with fresh paint, crouching to reach the baseboard.

No need to glance at her. You know exactly what she looks like, he reminded himself. The old crank-out window he was working on had six small panes of glass, each of them with four sides. He would repeat his puttying procedure a total of twenty-three times before he needed to focus on anything other than the window.

Noah kept working, trying to pay more attention to Preacher Amos's whistled rendition of "The Old Gray Mare" than to Deborah's creaking ladder . . . her methodical repetitions of painting a section of the upper wall before climbing down to cover the area beneath it. He envied her constant movement, because she seemed to be making more progress than he was as he stood in one spot.

Finish this window and then eat another cinnamon roll. You'll go nuts trying so hard not to look at her.

Noah worked faster, inspired by the thought of unrolling a sweet, frosted spiral of pastry and raisins. *Knead, press, scrape. Repeat.* By the time he snapped the lid on his container of putty, he could practically taste the cinnamon and feel the nuts crunching between his teeth. He pivoted, determined to pay no attention to Deborah as he fetched his snack—

"*Ach!* Oh, phooey!" she cried out.

Noah jumped back just as the roller fell from Deborah's raised hand, bounced wetly on the top of her head, and then tumbled down the back of her dress.

"Are you all right?" Amos asked as he hurried over to help her.

Noah watched helplessly as Deborah planted a hand on the wet wall to keep from falling. How had she come clear around the room so quickly? Why hadn't he been aware that she was reaching up to paint the top of the wall, only a few feet away? Had he spun in such a wide circle that he'd bumped the ladder—or had Deborah stretched too far on the wobbly old thing and lost her balance?

"I'm okay. I—I was stretched way out and wasn't expecting Noah to move," she replied in a breathy voice. She descended the ladder on shaky legs. "Oh dear, I've splattered paint everywhere and made a mess of the floor."

"If you're not hurt, there's no harm done. Latex wipes up with water," Amos assured her as he shot a questioning glance at Noah.

When Noah saw how the beige paint had saturated Deborah's kerchief and was about to dribble onto her face, he grabbed his rag. He quickly pressed it against her head to catch the paint—and then realized he was standing close enough to feel her trembling. She was breathing shallowly, her eyes wide and her lips parted as she struggled to recover from her mishap.

Noah almost kissed her—almost hugged Deborah to comfort her—but he caught himself. Such gestures belonged to bygone days when Deborah had loved him as much as he'd adored her. The handprint on her neck was fading from purple to greenish-yellow, yet another reminder of why he shouldn't succumb to her. He thrust the paint-soaked rag into her hand. "Sorry," he mumbled as he headed for the door.

Once he was outside in the shade, Noah sucked in air. Now *he* was shaken, rattled by Deborah's distress. Her expression had suggested that he'd made her lose her balance, yet he'd truly been unaware that her ladder had been so close behind him. Voices drifted out the cabin's open windows.

"You'd better wash your hair before that paint dries," Amos suggested gently.

"*Jah,* and I've made a mess of Phoebe's dress, too," Deborah replied. Then she chuckled. "Truth be told, I think Noah was more startled than I was. I'll be back after I get cleaned up."

Noah strode to the shed to fetch a can of the white enamel they were using for the cabins' windowsills and trim. Deborah sounded a lot calmer than he felt. She'd apparently regained her sense of perspective, too—no finger-pointing, and no tears as she set herself to rights again.

You, on the other hand, are skittering away like a whipped pup, Noah thought as Queenie bounded across the lot to greet him. As his Border Collie wagged her bushy tail, seeming to smile at him as her tongue lolled from her mouth, he knew he should apologize to Deborah now rather than letting the tension between them fester. Yet as he came out of the shed with the paint, some rags, and a bucket of water, Noah waited for her to disappear into her cabin before he returned to number four.

Amos, crouched beneath the sink to finish installing the faucet, looked up as Noah entered the cabin. "So did you bump her ladder, son? Or did she reach too far with her roller?"

"I have no idea," Noah replied with an exasperated sigh. He plunged a rag into the bucket, wrung it out, and began wiping the paint from the floorboards. "I finished my window and was going to eat another cinnamon roll. Next thing I knew, Deborah was squawking like a bird about to fall from its nest."

"Would it be all that hard to apologize? Even if you weren't to blame?"

Noah sighed. It was just like Amos to foster goodwill and positive communication—especially when folks were least inclined to initiate such things. "I suppose not."

Preacher Amos stood up to run water into the sink, testing the faucets. "Would it be so difficult to grant her the forgiveness she's asked for?" he went on in a low, purposeful voice. "I was hoping I wouldn't have to prod you about this matter, Noah. No one expects you to court Deborah again if that no longer feels right, but ignoring her request for forgiveness flies in the face of Jesus' teachings."

There it was, the bigger issue he hadn't dealt with. Noah kept wiping the floor and rinsing the paint out of his rag. There was no denying what Amos had said, so he saw no point in responding.

"Why did you two split up, anyway?" the preacher continued. "You're both fine young people, entering adulthood with your faith intact and as much potential for success as any couple I've seen."

"Breaking up was *her* doing," Noah blurted, scrubbing harder. "I have no idea what came over her. If you want the details, you'll have to ask Deborah."

"I believe I will. At least she'll give me an answer."

Noah felt about an inch tall. Amos Troyer had been the preacher his family had respected and relied upon all his life, especially after Dat had passed last year. Although Noah had been apprenticed to Preacher Eli Peterscheim, he'd always maintained a cautious emotional distance from Deborah's father. With Eli, it was strictly a business relationship, even though they'd nearly become related by his marriage to Deborah. In contrast, he considered Amos a good friend.

"If she tells you anything interesting, let me know," Noah said more flippantly than he'd intended to. "Far as I was concerned, our courtship was going just fine—until she informed me things were moving too slowly to suit her."

Amos shut off the faucets with a twist of his wrists that suggested he was finished with this conversation. "Don't let the sun go down on your anger, Noah," he warned as he collected his tools. "And don't forget that anger is not our way.

It's a sin as grievous as whatever has come between you and Deborah. Deal with it."

The preacher left the cabin, whistling under his breath. Noah finished wiping the floor, wondering if he should paint the final section of wall for Deborah as an apology. Or would she assume he'd completed her job because he didn't think she was doing it right?

Why do women have to be so complicated? So unpredictable? A guy can fly high one minute and land facedown in the mud the next.

Noah decided to putty the other window in the cabin's main room, as that was his assignment—and finishing the windows would get him out of Deborah's presence sooner when she came back to work. He eyed the cinnamon rolls but left them on the plate. His mission was to prevent further confrontations, simple as that.

So why do you feel as frustrated when you avoid Deborah as you do when you're in the same room with her? Figure that one out.

Chapter Six

Deborah turned on the shower in her cabin and stepped aside as the water spurted out. She removed her dress and stuck it under the water as it warmed up, scrubbing vigorously to remove the trail of beige paint down its back. After she hung up the dress, she washed the saturated kerchief and draped it over the shower stall's door. Phoebe had been kind enough to loan her these clothes, and even though they were old and faded, Deborah was determined not to ruin them.

Lord, I'm grateful for latex paint that washes out and for polyester blend fabric that'll dry without wrinkling, she mused as she unpinned her hair. *And I'm thankful You kept me from falling off the ladder while I was gawking at Noah.*

Deborah rubbed her scalp briskly with her fingertips and lots of shampoo to remove the sticky paint. She was glad to have this time away from Noah and Amos to collect herself, to recover from her embarrassing mishap. Laura and Phoebe were on the other side of the campground planting more of their garden, or they'd be hooting and laughing when she admitted how she'd made such a mess.

It *was* funny, the way she'd squawked and Noah had run off as though she'd been chasing after him with the roller.

Deborah sighed as she turned off the water. Once upon a time she and Noah might have engaged in such play with the paint, not caring how messy they got. What could she do to make him smile again? She missed the sound of his laughter, and the love he'd so gladly shown her.

But that was before she'd made the biggest mistake of her life by becoming too impatient with him.

Deborah dried herself and wrapped the towel around her waist-length hair, tucking it up turban-style. She put on her oldest dress, knowing she'd have to be careful not to splatter it when she resumed to her painting—she hadn't brought many clothes. After she arranged her hair in a bun, she tied on the wet kerchief and returned to cabin number four.

Preacher Amos was stretching a new piece of screen across a wooden frame that went in the door. "Back for more?" he asked with a smile.

"*Gut* as new," Deborah replied.

"I tightened the bolts in that old ladder. I'm sorry I didn't fix it before you started painting," he remarked. "You're doing a great job. Who knows how many years it's been since these cabins have seen fresh paint?"

"I'm happy to help. It's the least I can do while I'm here."

Deborah stepped inside the cabin and paused. She couldn't see Noah, but the squeak of a crank-out window told her he was in the far bedroom. Silently crossing the main room's plank floor, she peered in to watch him work. It had always amazed her, how Noah handled his tools so effortlessly, as if they were extensions of his hands . . . strong, well-shaped hands that had once grasped hers and gently stroked her cheek.

Noah turned as though he'd read her wistful thoughts. His dark brown hair framed his suntanned face in a mop of unruly waves. Even though he wasn't Sunday-best clean, Deborah longed to touch him, to coax a boyish smile to his lips.

"Hey," he murmured. He took a deep breath. "I'm sorry if I bumped your ladder—"

"It was my fault!" Deborah insisted as she hurried toward him. "I was watching *you* instead of paying attention to how far I'd reached—how the ladder was swaying. You're always so intent on your work, and so *gut* at what you do, Noah. It's a joy to watch you."

On impulse, she flung her arms around him. "I'm sorry if I've been a bother," she murmured. "I just had to tell you I was wrong—to see if we couldn't patch things up and be together again. *Please,* Noah?"

As she hugged him, Deborah wondered what had gotten into her. Why was she behaving so boldly? No matter what Noah might think, however, she couldn't let him take the blame for the painting incident.

She felt him softening, returning her affection. Maybe this impulsive hug would bring her closer to becoming his wife. . . .

Noah's arms tightened around Deborah's waist before he realized what he was doing. She smelled fresh and clean. Even though her hair and kerchief were damp, he felt a rush of warmth and longing that made him close his eyes. He'd forgotten how perfectly she fit against him, how firm and strong her body felt . . . how her voice teased at him and could convince him to do just about anything.

For a few blissful moments he savored an embrace that took him back to happier times. *Why is it again that you can't allow Deborah back into your life?* Noah nuzzled the damp hair above her ear, noting how the kerchief set off the line of her jaw—

The bruise on her neck brought him back to reality. The

handprint was less distinct, blurring from purple into a greenish yellow, but it was still the mark of another man.

Noah touched the bruise lightly with his fingertip as he eased away from her. "Did your *dat* do this to you?" he whispered. He couldn't help himself. Deborah's injury held the key to his feelings for her.

Her face clouded over. Noah reminded himself that she'd never been much good at fibbing, even as doubt and pain furrowed her brow and her cheeks turned splotchy and pink. "No," she finally murmured.

Noah took another step away from her. "Wrong answer."

"Wrong question!" Deborah shot back. She crossed her arms tightly, as if to hold herself together when she turned away from him. "Why did you have to ruin—why can't you trust me? Don't you understand that I didn't go *asking* for trouble when—"

"You didn't come to Promise Lodge just to see *me*, either. *Did* you, Deborah?" he countered in a harsh whisper. "Why would I want you back if you're really here to get away from somebody else?"

When she rushed off, he had his answer, didn't he?

A few moments later Noah heard the *swish* of Deborah's roller in the front room. He squeezed putty between his fingers, considering the possibilities. Isaac Chupp still appeared to be the likely culprit, and Noah got a nasty tightness in his gut when he envisioned the details of the encounter. Deborah claimed she had no feelings for the bishop's son, yet she'd been within arm's reach of him. The Bender barn had been on fire, so why hadn't she run in the opposite direction to alert the men in town? Once she'd known Isaac and his English buddies were drinking in there, why had she gotten involved?

In his mind Noah saw the old red barn with its gambrel roof standing staunchly on the rise behind the Bender family's white farmhouse—except now it would be a charred shell, a testimony to the trouble that had festered like an untreated wound in Coldstream. Noah had always wondered how Isaac Chupp could afford beer and cigarettes when the only job he had was occasionally clerking for his *dat*'s auction company. What was wrong with this picture? Why hadn't Bishop Obadiah insisted that his son take up a trade?

Why doesn't Deborah tell you exactly what happened? That was the real question, wasn't it? If she was so innocent, it would seem the easiest, most natural thing for her to tell everyone here the details—the truth—rather than letting them assume the worst.

Noah glanced at the putty in his hand. He rolled it between his palms to form a rope and then pressed it into the crevice between the wood and the glass with his thumb. Life would be a lot easier if he could press this situation with Deborah into a tight, controlled space, as he was doing with the putty.

Preacher Amos came into the room and stood beside Noah. "Better luck next time, son," he murmured. "The fruit of the Spirit is love, joy, peace, long-suffering, gentleness, goodness, faith—to name a few of the benefits God grants us if we live in Him. *Long-suffering* is an old word for patience," he pointed out. "And patience is a virtue."

"I'm not feeling very virtuous." Noah sighed and drew his scraper down the vertical line of putty he'd just applied. "*Long-suffering* fits better right now. Accent on the suffering part."

"This, too, shall pass. Don't give up on her."

When Amos left, Noah wished he had more than the preacher's platitudes for reassurance. For those few shining moments when he'd held Deborah, he had imagined becoming her husband again—had envisioned the house with the rose trellis he'd promised her. Now, however, he seemed more in touch with the thorns than the blooms of the vision they'd once shared.

Noah rolled another rope of putty. Old Order members believed the best antidote for any misfortune was hard work and prayer. If he worked hard enough, long enough, he could put his troubles behind him, couldn't he? The praying part would have to wait. He wasn't in the right frame of mind for that now.

Chapter Seven

Rosetta opened her bedroom window Friday morning and inhaled the fresh scent of rain. The patter on the roof made her smile as she looked out over the garden plots that would benefit greatly from the first real moisture they'd received since Christine's girls and Mattie had planted them. The wet weather brought a welcome day of indoor work for everyone: Roman's hammering rang out from the barn, where he was building more stanchions and stalls. Noah, Preacher Amos, and Deborah continued their painting and repair work in the cabins.

Phoebe and Laura were cleaning out a large storage room on the main floor of the lodge, seeing it as a sort of treasure hunt, while their mother and Mattie polished the paneled walls of one of the large rooms that had once served as a conference area. Preacher Amos envisioned that room as a place to hold church services when more families came to Promise Lodge, while the women considered it the perfect area for quilting frolics and other social gatherings.

Rosetta smiled as she looked around the large room she'd chosen as her own. Located beside the back staircase, which led downstairs to the pantry and kitchen, it was the perfect dwelling place for an apartment manager. Her sisters had also chosen rooms on this side of the house as their new homes, because it seemed so much simpler than managing houses and property. This novel concept had inspired Rosetta to create more apartments in the lodge building for other unattached women who wanted to start fresh here, as well.

Her room, with its dormered ceiling, a private bathroom, a fireplace, and space enough for a sitting area as well as her bedroom furniture, had probably been the camp director's apartment. From the various windows she could see Rainbow Lake, the orchard and the hiking trails beyond it, the barn and other outbuildings, and the arched metal entryway sign at the road. Did God feel as fascinated and pleased with His domain when He surveyed it as she did when she gazed out over this parcel of rural Missouri?

Rosetta laughed at this notion. She would never compare herself to the Lord, but it gave her a heady feeling when she beheld the trees and rolling hills that she and her sisters had purchased. From this vantage point, Rosetta could see for miles and miles—a much grander view than she'd had while living in the downstairs bedroom of her parents' house.

A loud rumbling drew her attention beyond the woods to their only visible neighbor—who was driving a large truck out of a metal-sided warehouse building. Rosetta and her sisters intended to go over and introduce themselves, but that visit could wait until working on the lodge didn't feel so urgent. Old Order folks weren't eager to initiate contact with English, nor did they want to attract curious outsiders to their settlement.

Rosetta was pleased, however, to see that the white house on the hilltop above the warehouse appeared well maintained. Its wide front porch, lush lawn, and profusion of flowering bushes suggested that these neighbors shared a lot of her interests. The grassy lot behind the house was surrounded by a white plank fence, and a couple of horses grazed near the barn.

Someday I'll find out who those folks are, she thought as she approached the wooden chest at the end of her bed. *But today I'm taking a different sort of journey. Help me do this with grace and confidence, Lord.*

Rosetta lifted the lid of the cedar-lined chest Dat had made for her thirteenth birthday, just as he'd given one to Mattie and Christine when they'd reached that age. The pungency of cedar and sachets wafted up from the quilts she'd made and the linens she'd embroidered, looking toward the day when she married. Such high hopes and sweet dreams she'd had while she'd stitched these pieces—

And it's time to fulfill my intention for them, Rosetta thought as she picked out two quilts and sets of sheets that would go with them. With a resolute smile, she carried the linens to the adjacent rooms, where her parents' bedroom set and the nicest pieces of their guest room furniture had been arranged. Someday soon, new residents could enjoy the cozy ambiance these hand-crafted pieces gave to their rooms while their apartments were being remodeled. As Rosetta made up the double bed in the smaller room, her spirit felt light and happy. When she'd stitched this quilt as a teenager, her tastes in color and design had run contrary to traditional Amish patterns—

The clatter of footsteps and her nieces' happy voices made Rosetta straighten to her full height. She prayed she could answer the girls' questions with wisdom and a positive attitude.

"Aunt Rosetta! Look what we found!" Laura called out when she'd topped the stairs.

"You won't believe the boxes of awesome—" Phoebe stopped midsentence when she spotted Rosetta. "And where did you get *that* quilt?"

The girls set aside some planks of wood they'd carried upstairs, and Laura chuckled as she approached the bed to look at it. "Those are butterflies! Made from folded hankies—

some of them with cool crocheted borders! I can't see Grandma working on a bright, flowery piece like this one."

"*Jah,* she tried to talk me out of using prints, saying they'd be impractical when I got older," Rosetta replied as she gazed fondly at the quilt. "I was maybe fifteen when I made this one, from hankies that had belonged to my mamma's mother and her sisters when they were in their *rumspringa.* Can you tell I really loved pink back then?"

Phoebe ran a reverent finger over one of the butterflies. "So you folded the hankies to make their wings, and then embroidered the body and their antennae—"

"And stitched them onto pale pink squares before you put them together with this bright pink calico," Laura finished with a grin. "What a wonderful way to save these hankies— and they're in prettier prints than the ones you find in the catalogs now."

Rosetta smiled, pleased that her nieces shared her love for family pieces that would otherwise have grown yellow with age in the attic. "I thought it was time to use these linens instead of hiding them away in my chest," she said, hoping her voice didn't waver. "I won't be getting married, but I *will* be welcoming new renters—"

"Oh, Aunt Rosetta, you can't mean that!" Laura blurted.

"You should never give up hope that the right fellow will come along," Phoebe insisted as she held Rosetta's gaze with her blazing blue eyes. "I've been praying for that, and I believe it will happen now that we've moved away from Coldstream!"

Part of Rosetta wished she hadn't gone down this conversational trail, because she recalled feeling the same romantic fervor, the same endless hope, when she'd been her nieces' age. But it was time to let the girls know that she felt happy and fulfilled with the *maidel* life God had granted her—time to explain that the single life offered opportunities rather than a reason to feel shame or loneliness.

"Truth be told, the right young man was courting me when I was twenty—your age, Phoebe," Rosetta replied with a wistful smile. "Tim was helping my *dat* take down a dead tree. He was climbing up high to saw off some of its branches, and the top section of the tree gave way. When Tim hit the ground, his neck broke—and the accident broke our spirits for a while, too."

Laura's face fell and tears filled Phoebe's eyes. "I—we had no idea," she murmured.

Rosetta smiled sadly. "We didn't talk about it much. You were a wee little girl when it happened and Laura wasn't yet born," she explained. "A few years later, both Mamm and Dat started having health problems, so it was the natural order of things for me to stay home and look after them— not that I wanted to get serious about anybody after Tim passed away. I was sure he'd been the man God intended for me to marry."

Rather than get into a theological discussion about why God had allowed her beau to die, Rosetta smoothed the butterfly quilt beneath the two pillows with their embroidered cases. "Mamm and I enjoyed sewing together, so I cherish the pieces we made because we passed many happy hours," she remarked. "Several of those quilts are still in my trunk, and now I've got the perfect place to use them. Come and see my other wild quilt!"

Rosetta playfully steered the two girls into the next room. She grabbed the edge of the quilt she'd left on the unmade bed and shook it open. "Can you tell your grandma didn't make this one, either?" she teased.

Laura laughed while she and Phoebe straightened the colorful coverlet to get a better look at its oddly shaped pieces. "What *are* these? Why did you cut the fabric skinny at one end and pointy at the other?"

Rosetta smiled. "Those are neckties that English men wear for dress-up," she explained. "I cut them in half and then positioned them with the narrow end of one against the wider end of another one."

"And then you sewed them onto long fabric panels and joined the panels with this bright blue fabric," Laura said. "Where did you get so many neckties? There must be dozens of them here, with so many colors and patterns my eyes don't know where to focus first!"

"*Jah,* it was a fun quilt to put together. I was still in my *rumspringa,* so Mamm allowed me to have a *gut* time with it—especially since the ties didn't cost me a cent," Rosetta went on. "Somebody English dropped bags of neckties into the thrift store's collection box and the lady who ran the place had no idea what to do with them all. She said they were so out of date, nobody would ever buy them."

"I like it!" Phoebe declared.

"I'm glad you're getting your pieces out and using them," Laura said. "These rooms will look really special with your quilts and embroidered pillowcases—and who knows? Maybe some of the ladies who rent your apartments won't have much bedding or furniture to bring with them."

"I thought I'd be ready to provide anything some of them might not have," Rosetta replied with a nod.

"And maybe you'll want to use these, too." Phoebe fetched the dark wooden plaques she'd left in the other room. "We found a whole bunch of them in the closet we're cleaning out."

Rosetta's eyes widened. "Kids must've made these while they were attending camp," she speculated. "Think how much time it took to spell out the Lord's Prayer with alphabet soup letters, and then glue on the words and the macaroni trim around the edges!"

"And this one is the Twenty-Third Psalm," Laura said, holding another plaque so Rosetta could see it. "We found plaques made with different colors of dried beans and corn, too."

"Pictures of chickens and roosters and flowers," Phoebe elaborated, "along with a really large one of the Last Supper."

"And we found a big angel hanging that somebody crocheted with tiny white thread, but it's got some brown spots. Mamm thought they might be water stains." Laura's whole face lit up with her smile. "We threw away a lot of dried-up glue and melted crayons and faded construction paper, but finding the plaques and pictures was even better than discovering some of the stuff in our attic when we were packing to move here."

Rosetta smiled as she imagined the items the girls had described. "Let's go downstairs and take a look at those pictures. Wouldn't it be fun to display them in some of the common rooms or hallways? Maybe we can soak that crocheted angel in some vinegar water to remove the stains."

As the three of them left the room, Phoebe paused in the doorway for one last look at the necktie quilt. "I bet it took some nerve to get out the linens you'd made for when you got married, Aunt Rosetta," she said softly. "I'm glad you showed them to us and explained about why you've stayed a *maidel*. I've never believed you didn't have guys wanting to court you—"

"But now that I know you chose not to marry," Laura chimed in, "the whole picture of your life makes more sense. You've been piecing your path together the way you wanted it, like you did with your unusual quilts."

The whole picture of your life . . . piecing your path together . . .

Rosetta hugged her nieces' shoulders. "I'm so glad you girls understand what I've told you," she said softly. "Your *mamm* and your aunt Mattie and I are getting our second wind now, after we've lost important people in our lives. And you know what? We're finding out that unattached women don't have to follow so many *rules*," she pointed out. "It's not a bad thing, being single. But don't say that to

Preacher Amos. Bless his heart, he wants us to be happy in the traditional way."

"He wants Aunt Mattie to cook and keep house for him, too," Laura remarked.

Rosetta chuckled. "They were sweethearts for a long time before Dat steered Mattie toward marrying Marvin," she said. "After the way he treated her, though, your aunt is determined not to marry again. We'll see who wins—your aunt, or Amos."

Phoebe frowned, stopping before they descended the back stairway. "Why was Uncle Marvin so mean?" she whispered. "We loved playing with Roman and Noah when we were kids—but not when their *dat* was home. We never knew when he might get cross with us, or with Aunt Mattie."

"Mamm always told us not to gossip about it," Laura chimed in earnestly. "She said we shouldn't talk about the Schwartzes' personal business, nor quiz Aunt Mattie about any bruises we might see."

Rosetta listened to her nieces with a sad heart. Their words confirmed the way folks in Coldstream—and in most Amish colonies, she suspected—looked the other way when a man mistreated his wife. If she and her sisters were to end the cycle of abuse here, they would need younger women of Phoebe and Laura's generation to help them carry out their vow.

"Part of Marvin's moods had to do with his diabetes—and the fact he didn't want a doctor telling him how to manage it," Rosetta replied. "But I always believed that he could've controlled his sharp tongue and his temper, had he wanted to. Unfortunately, Mattie had no way out of their marriage until he died. And we all wonder how Deborah got that big handprint on her neck, too, don't we?"

Rosetta gave the girls a moment to consider what she'd said. "Your *mamm* and Aunt Mattie and I are determined not to keep looking the other way now that we're starting fresh here in Promise," she continued earnestly. "We probably shouldn't quiz Deborah about that bruise, but we can encourage her to talk about what's been going on in Coldstream. We want her to stay as long as she needs—"

"But won't her parents wonder where she's gone?" Phoebe interrupted. "Why hasn't she called home?"

"Deborah's *never* been in trouble," Laura said with wide eyes. "I can't believe her *dat*—or anyone else—would grab her neck so hard."

Rosetta sighed. "I agree. And I suspect that within another day or two we'll know more about it," she speculated. "Meanwhile, we're glad Deborah came to us when she was running from trouble. *Jah?*"

Both girls nodded again.

"Shall we go downstairs and see those treasures you found?" Rosetta asked in a more cheerful tone. "We'll keep Deborah in our prayers. And we'll keep believing that God knows the truth and that He'll reveal it when we're ready to understand it."

As they started down the narrow wooden steps, Laura's chuckle echoed in the stairwell. "We learned some truth about *you* today, Aunt Rosetta," she teased. "No matter what you think, I'm not giving up on Mr. Right finding you here at Promise Lodge."

"Me, neither," Phoebe insisted in a lighter tone.

Rosetta laughed as they reached the bottom of the stairs. "Meanwhile, I'm moving ahead with my plans for these apartments and my new life," she told them. "Hanging around and waiting for a man to show up? Not my style!"

Chapter Eight

"How long can you stay with us, Deborah?" Laura asked as she cracked eggs for the cookie dough.

"It's so *gut* having you here. Just like old times," Phoebe chimed in. She stopped cranking the egg beater long enough to flash Deborah a bright smile. "I bet your *mamm* really misses your help, though."

Deborah concentrated on putting peanut butter into a glass measuring cup. This rainy Saturday morning marked her fourth day at Promise Lodge, and she'd known that sooner or later her friends would start asking such obvious questions. The cool, wet weather meant that again they couldn't work in the garden today. Amos and Noah were helping Roman with the dairy barn renovation, so Rosetta had suggested that the women could spend the day baking breads, cookies, and pies for the deep freeze.

The kitchen had become very quiet. Deborah could feel Mattie, Rosetta, and Christine watching her as they awaited the answer she didn't have. After her run-in with Noah, she'd been wondering when he would tell her that she'd worn out her welcome—and that he had no intention of taking her back. But where else could she go if she left Promise Lodge?

"Even after I nearly ruined your dress, you want me to stick around?" she teased Phoebe.

"*Puh!* That's why I loaned you an old one to paint in," her friend replied. "I can see why you'd want to keep after Noah, though. He's basically a *gut* fellow—"

"Even if he's clueless," Laura added with a laugh. "All the more reason he needs you in his life, *jah?*"

Deborah glanced up in time to see Noah's *mamm* exchange a glance with her sisters. Mattie put a damp tea towel over her big ball of pie crust dough and crossed the kitchen to join the girls. Deborah's heart beat faster. Something told her she wasn't going to get by with hedging any longer.

"I have a little confession," Mattie said. She leaned against the big stainless steel sink as though she might rest there a while. "I didn't want to ask about the bruise on your neck, Deborah, because I recall how awful I used to feel when Marvin took out his frustrations on me," she began quietly. "But I left a message on your family's phone saying we'd heard about the Bender barn fire—figuring your *mamm* would know who'd told us about it and call me back. And she did."

Deborah's breath caught. "I—I *meant* to let her know I was here," she said in a tiny voice. "But I was afraid if Dat or one of the kids went to the phone shanty and heard the message before Mamma did, everyone would get upset all over again."

Mattie smiled sadly. "Alma waited until your *dat* was gone on a welding job to call me. She was relieved to know you were here with us, Deborah," she said gently. "She was worried about where you'd gone after he cast you out."

As the friends on either side of her gasped, Deborah's face prickled with humiliation.

"What happened?" Laura demanded, slinging her arm around Deborah's waist.

"Why did your *dat* grab you hard enough to make that

handprint?" Phoebe murmured, shaking her head. "I was so happy to see you, I didn't want to ask about it."

Once again the scenes from that fateful night at the Bender place flashed through Deborah's mind. For a few painful seconds she relived the horror of being shoved out of Isaac's buggy and then retrieved by his English friend, Kerry, only to discover that the lanky redhead was drunk enough to have all the wrong intentions. "Um, what did Mamma tell you?" she cautiously asked Mattie.

Mattie's eyes darkened with concern. "She said you got crosswise with your *dat*—and now the bishop's upset with you because you called nine-one-one when you saw the Bender barn was afire instead of ringing the big bell so the local men could douse it. And—like you told us when you got here—Obadiah's denying his son had any part in it," she added. "But you made it sound like you saw Isaac there, with your own eyes."

"*Jah*, I did." Deborah lowered her head. Her throat was so tight she could barely get the words out. "He and his English friends were in the barn smoking and drinking. I suspect one of them tossed a cigarette into the hay or kicked over the lantern— maybe by accident."

"Or maybe not!" Laura blurted.

"Let's don't go speculating about that, young lady," Christine warned her daughter. She and Rosetta came over from the stove, wiping their floury hands on towels. "What else did Alma say, Mattie? Maybe some new facts have come to light since Deborah came here."

"*Jah*, she said Sheriff Renfro came looking for Deborah, wanting to talk to her—"

Deborah gripped the countertop while her friends sucked in their breath.

"— on account of how they traced the nine-one-one call to the Peterscheims' phone shanty," Mattie went on ruefully. "Eli told the sheriff he couldn't talk to you. And he told a reporter from the Coldstream paper the same thing. Alma says you've really upset the apple cart back home, even though she knows you didn't intend to cause any trouble."

Deborah blinked, determined not to cry. The women gathered around her were her closest friends, and they wanted the best for her. "I didn't intend to deceive you when I came here, either," she murmured with a hitch in her voice. "But I didn't know what else to do about Rosetta's barn, knowing how Isaac Chupp always wiggles out of the problems he causes. I was afraid you wouldn't let me stay here if you knew—"

"Oh, Deborah, *we* know you don't go looking for trouble!" Laura insisted as her hug tightened. "If you say you saw Isaac and his friends in the barn, they were there."

"And your *mamm* suspects those boys got rough with you," Mattie went on in a strained whisper. "She was mighty worried when you didn't come home until nearly dawn the day after the fire, and you looked like you'd been in a bad scuffle. Are—are you *all right*, dear?"

Deborah wanted the floor to open up and swallow her, even though she knew Noah's mother had her best interests at heart. Mattie wasn't coming right out and asking, but she was wondering just how *involved* Isaac and his friends had gotten with her. Laura and Phoebe were holding their breath. Christine's hand fluttered to her heart and Rosetta's eyes widened with concern as they awaited her answer.

"Isaac shoved me into his buggy when he heard the sirens, to get us out of town before the sheriff and the fire engine got to the barn," Deborah began. "And then after we went down a lot of dark back roads, he—he started touching me and kissing me. Said I'd better let him do whatever he wanted, to make up for calling nine-one-one about him and his buddies." Deborah hung her head, still stinging with fear and humiliation.

"When I slapped him, he made me get out of the rig.

Then he grabbed my neck and shoved me into the ditch beside the road," she rasped, covering the bruise with her hand. "It was pitch-dark and I had no idea where I was. Somewhere along the line I'd lost my *kapp*. My stockings got muddy and torn up when I landed in the ditch and scraped my knees. It took me a long time to find my way back home."

"And your *dat* took that to mean that Isaac and his friends had . . . taken advantage of you?" Christine asked in a horrified whisper. "And that you'd allowed them to?"

Deborah felt as limp as a balloon that had lost all its air. "He said I'd had no business going over to a burning barn, and that any virtuous Christian girl would've run the other way when she'd seen a bunch of boys drinking in there."

Before she could draw another breath, the three women and her friends huddled around her. They took her into their arms, murmuring their comfort and apologies. While it felt wonderful to have the support of these lifelong friends, Deborah still felt sick at heart. Was it a sin if she didn't reveal the rest of the story, about how Kerry had caught up to her and—

"Your *mamm* was afraid your *dat* had jumped to such conclusions," Mattie's voice cut into her dire thoughts. "And when the bishop claimed his son wasn't anywhere near the Bender barn that night, Alma said Eli went along with him to keep the law from getting further involved. Then when you got home in the wee hours, your *dat* made you leave—as though you were to blame for the condition your clothes were in."

"It makes no sense for Eli to say Isaac wasn't in the barn and then to suspect his daughter was stirring up trouble with him," Rosetta muttered. "I'm so sorry it happened this way, Deborah. Thank the Lord those boys didn't hurt you right off and leave you in that burning barn."

"*Jah,* you're here with us now, and you're safe," Phoebe said with a nod.

Even as relief washed over her, Deborah sensed this nasty situation wasn't behind her. What if Isaac found out where she was and came after her? Would he sneak in and set fire to the buildings at Promise Lodge, just for spite? Or was she letting her imagination run amok now that she could finally discuss what had happened on the night of the fire?

It did no good to worry about such what-ifs, however. She had more immediate problems to consider. "Please don't tell Noah," Deborah pleaded. "For some reason he thinks I ended our engagement so I could be with Isaac, and—and I can't seem to convince him that's not true."

"Oh, my," Mattie murmured. "I had no idea. Noah's refused to tell me anything about why you two broke up."

"Anybody with any sense would know better than *that,*" Laura declared vehemently. "Isaac's got such a high opinion of himself, what girl could compete?"

"*Jah,* he's cute, but I don't know any girls around Coldstream who'd put up with him," Phoebe remarked. "He tried to get Laura and me to go out with him, but we both told him to hit the road."

"I know you girls mean well, but promise me you'll keep quiet about this whole business with Isaac on the night of the fire," Christine insisted as she gazed at her daughters. "Now that we know the truth—and now that Deborah's gotten herself out of harm's way—it's best if we let her and Noah work this out between them."

Laura glanced doubtfully at Deborah and then drew her fingers across her lips as though she were closing a zipper. Phoebe did the same, and then she murmured, "This is so sad. So confusing."

"And *scary,*" Laura whispered. "If Isaac can cause all this trouble and get out of it scot-free, what's to stop him from doing anything he pleases? To anyone's property?"

"We'd best leave God in charge of that," Rosetta replied. "We'll keep the Peterscheims in our prayers, and we'll pray for the Chupps, as well—and for all the folks in Coldstream. And we'll thank God again for leading us to Promise Lodge."

"We've been blessed, for sure," Mattie affirmed as she gripped Deborah's hand. "Your *mamm* was thankful to hear you're with us, dear, but maybe you could drop her a note soon. She misses you something fierce."

Deborah nodded sadly. "*Denki* for calling her. And for taking me in, too."

Rosetta glanced out the kitchen window and put a purposeful smile on her face. "Back to our baking, girls. The men are coming in from the barn and they've got another fellow with them."

As Noah listened to Truman Wickey tell Amos about his landscaping business, he exchanged a glance with his brother. Roman was smiling as he tossed a stick for Queenie. Did they dare hope that Truman, the Mennonite neighbor who'd come over to introduce himself, would help them with the tree trimming and brush removal around the campground? He, his brother, and Amos were hard-pressed to keep up with such work until more men came to live at Promise Lodge.

"I'm real glad to see you Amish folks taking over this property," Wickey was saying as they reached the back entry to the lodge kitchen. "I was concerned that a big-city developer might construct a bunch of condos—or that the place would sit empty another year and sink further into disrepair."

Amos chuckled as he opened the door. "I'll let the ladies tell you about our plans for the place," he said. "You picked a great day to come. The rain's kept them inside, busy in the kitchen."

"I could smell the pies baking all the way to my place," Wickey teased as he removed his straw hat.

By his quick count, Noah saw three pans of cinnamon rolls cooling on the counter, along with half a dozen fruit pies and some loaves of bread on one of the dining room tables. The girls had just finished baking cookies, and the aroma of sugar and spices made him realize how hungry he was.

"This is our neighbor, Truman Wickey," Preacher Amos said in a jovial voice. "He and his *mamm* live on the other side of the orchard from us—the place on the hill with the nice white board fence. Our cookie bakers are Laura, Phoebe, and Deborah," he went on, gesturing to each girl, "and these three sisters are the brains behind the businesses we aim to operate. Christine Hershberger owns the dairy herd you just saw. Rosetta Bender's going to manage apartments here in the lodge building. Mattie Schwartz will be opening a road-side produce stand as soon as the vegetables are ready—and she's overseeing the sale of property to folks who want to join us in our new colony."

"Those are impressive undertakings," Truman remarked as he nodded to each woman in turn. He grinned at Amos, including Noah and Roman in his glance. "So what do you fellows do, then?"

"Mostly what we're told," Amos quipped without missing a beat.

The laughter that erupted lifted Noah's spirits. He already liked this guy Wickey. His straw hat had seen better days, and his striped shirt and suspenders were smudged with con-crete because he'd come along just in time to help them set some fence posts for a new corral behind the barn. The farm Truman owned was as neat and pretty as a picture postcard, and he just seemed *happy*.

"I'm not prying, understand, but I noticed electricity out in your barn, and of course this lodge is electrified, too,"

Truman remarked. "Our Mennonite district allows us to use electricity and drive cars and such. Will you folks have to remove all the wiring to comply with Old Order ways?"

"Here in the lodge building, we're going to install solar panels and cover the electrical outlets," Rosetta responded as she checked the pies in her oven. "And since these big stoves and ovens are gas, we'll only need to replace the fridges and freezers with gas ones—when I get the money to cover that."

"And the government requires dairy farmers to have electric bulk tanks to store their milk in," Roman remarked. "The Old Order bishops have had to go along with that so a lot of their members can make a living."

Truman nodded as he gazed up at the pots hanging from hooks in the ceiling. "Plain folks have to deal with a lot more governmental regulations these days."

Preacher Amos was nodding. "When we start building houses, though, the Amish places won't be electrified. Most buggy sheds will have solar panels with plug-in adapters for charging the car batteries that run their buggy lights, and small businesses might use the solar panels to operate cash registers and such. But make no mistake," he added emphatically, "we Amish still stay off the grid, far as electricity in our homes goes."

Truman was peering into a pot on the stove—and then admiring the pies Rosetta and Christine were taking from the oven. "Seems to me these old campground appliances are working just fine for the food you ladies are whipping up, though," he remarked. "You've really got this place shined up. I wish you all the best as you get your businesses going."

"Can you stay for dinner so we can get better acquainted?" Noah's mother asked. "Might be half an hour before the meal's on the table, if you've got that long."

Truman's grin lit up his entire face. "I'd be crazy to refuse an offer like that, considering how *gut* it smells in here."

"Why don't we look around outside, and you can tell me if we've got the right ideas for plotting out small farms," Amos suggested. Then he snatched a double handful of the cookies that were cooling on racks nearby. "Here—a little something to tide us over until dinner."

Noah hung back as the other guys went outside, noting that besides the frosted molasses cookies Amos had grabbed, the girls had baked chocolate chip cookies and—did he dare believe his eyes? Before he could reach for a peanut butter bar, Deborah placed three of them on her palm and extended it toward him.

"These are one of your favorites, as I recall," she murmured.

Noah's stomach tightened. When they'd been courting, *any* cookie Deborah had baked had been his favorite. There was no missing her hopeful gaze, her shy smile, as she waited for him to accept her gift. With the Hershberger girls and the three women looking on, he figured he'd better behave graciously. "*Jah,* these'll do," he murmured as he plucked the cookies from Deborah's hand. "Nice of you to think of me."

Noah closed the kitchen door behind him and then stuffed an entire bar into his mouth. The sweet peanut butter covered his tongue and the crispy cereal and crunchy peanuts gave him something satisfying to chew on. Before he'd caught up to the other fellows, he'd devoured every last crumb of the other two bars. Noah wasn't ready to think about how Deborah was working to win him back, but he had to admit she knew her way around a kitchen—and she also knew that the way to a man's heart was through his stomach.

"Would you like me to trim these trees?" Truman was saying as he gestured toward branches that were dragging the ground. "I could make short work of that with my cherry

picker and saws, and I've got an industrial chipper, too. No
reason you couldn't spread the mulch in flower gardens— or
beneath your apple trees, to keep the weeds down," he added
as he pointed toward the orchard. "I'm so pleased that you
Plain folks have plans for this land, I'd even give you a
gut-neighbor discount on the work I'd do."

Thank you, Lord! Noah thought as he listened to more
of Wickey's ideas for improvement. Truman also chatted
about belonging to the Mennonite fellowship a few miles
down the road, which explained how he could own and
operate the heavy equipment for his landscaping business.
Preacher Amos was happier than Noah had seen him in a
long time, because this fellow and his machinery could
make their settlement take shape a *lot* faster than Amish
horse-drawn plows and chain saws.

"So am I right, thinking none of your women are married?" Truman asked as they headed away from Rainbow
Lake, back toward the house. "Not trying to be nosy, understand. But a man likes to know these things before his
mind wanders too far down the wrong road."

Amos laughed, clapping Truman on the back. "You've
figured us out, Truman. We could just as well call this the
Promise Lodge Singles Colony—not that Christine or Mattie
or I planned on losing our spouses so early in our lives."

Truman's expression sobered. "You've all seen your share
of heartaches, then. I didn't mean to make light of your
situations. Please accept my apology and condolences."

"Accepted," the preacher said. "But I'll tell you right off
that I came here partly because Mattie and I were childhood
sweethearts before we married other folks."

Noah rolled his eyes at the way Amos was staking his
claim on Mamm.

"I see what you're saying. And what of Rosetta then?"
Truman asked.

"Never married. As the youngest of the Bender sisters,

she stayed home to look after their elderly parents until they passed on," Amos replied. He stopped several feet short of the house, lowering his voice. "Rosetta's a member of the Old Order Amish church, however. So that means there won't be any mixing and matching with Mennonite fellows."

"Ah." Wickey sighed as he glanced toward the kitchen window. "Guess I'll just enjoy all you folks as new friends then, and leave it at that."

"Could be the right gal will come along to Promise Lodge to join our colony, though," Preacher Amos remarked. "We've advertised for Amish and Mennonites alike, knowing the two different groups benefit from partnering together. The boys and I are already grateful for your offer to help us with the trimming and the orchard."

"And some of the families coming to Promise Lodge have daughters looking to marry," Roman chimed in. He went over to the pump to refill Queenie's water bowl and wash his hands.

"I'll keep that in mind." Truman gazed out over the campground again. "Come time to build your new houses, I know fellows with equipment for digging foundations and water lines and such," he said. Then he grinned, his eyes alight. "Maybe I can earn a few meals in exchange for bringing them around, eh? My mother's not inclined to cook a lot for the two of us anymore, you see."

Amos chuckled as he went toward the back door of the lodge. "I think we can arrange that. Might not hurt to drop a hint at dinner and see where it gets you."

Truman removed his straw hat and smoothed his sandy brown hair before entering the kitchen. He gave Noah a pensive look. "While I recall running the roads at your age, thinking the bachelor life was mighty fine, I'm still kicking myself over the girl that got away," he mused. "It was a stupid misunderstanding. I insisted on being *right* because I was the man. So now she's got a nice little family, and—well, you don't want to hear my bellyaching. I've got a *gut* life and a prosperous business. No room to complain."

Noah didn't miss the knowing look that passed between his brother and Preacher Amos as the four of them filed through the hot, fragrant kitchen. At least they had the decency not to say *I told you so* as everyone took seats around the table that was set for ten in the dining hall.

Was Wickey just shooting the breeze, or could he sense Noah's romantic difficulties with Deborah? Could be he'd told the story about the lost sweetheart because he'd learned Rosetta wouldn't be able to date him—or maybe it was just coincidence. Maybe the incident had come back to haunt him because the aromas of Rosetta's fruit pies, mingled with the savory scents of meat loaf, fried potatoes, and creamed peas with onions reminded Truman of what he'd lost out on.

Not my circus, not my monkeys.

As Noah recalled that slogan from a T-shirt his friend had won at the county fair, he had to bite back a chuckle as they bowed their heads for a silent prayer. Wickey's problems weren't his problems. It was best to pass the platters and eat rather than to dwell upon Deborah—or to fume over what she was telling him and what she wasn't.

Noah felt the weight of her gaze from across the table. When he looked at her, Noah realized she'd heard Truman's lovelorn tale—or at least the end of it—when they'd been coming inside. Deborah's rueful smile pricked at him. It suddenly seemed that romantic relationships *were* a lot like a circus, with several little dramas going on simultaneously and the constant potential for falling off the tightrope without a moment's notice or a net.

And you are a monkey, Noah.

He sighed at this random thought. Was his conscience working against him, too?

Was it his imagination, or did Amos smile with particular sweetness at Mamm during the meal? "It's a big day for

Promise Lodge," he said as he filled his plate. "Truman's not been here an hour and already he's offered to do some earth moving and tree trimming for us—heavy work the boys and I would be hard-pressed to accomplish expediently. Now *that's* neighboring!"

Wickey looked embarrassed by Amos's praise. "It's the sort of landscaping work I do every day," he said with a shrug. "And we agreed to a fair hourly compensation—"

"At a reduced rate," Roman pointed out. Then he raised his eyebrows at Aunt Rosetta. "And maybe with some pies thrown in to sweeten the deal."

Aunt Rosetta's cheeks turned a pretty shade of pink. It occurred to Noah that while she'd been caring for his grandparents over the years, apparently contented to remain a *maidel,* she'd never seemed interested in winning the favor of a fellow. Or had he merely assumed that? The smile she flashed at Truman Wickey made her look several years younger.

"Baked goodies seem like a fine way to pay you forward," Rosetta said as she gestured toward the items that were cooling on the table behind her. "Figure on eating with us whenever you're working here, Truman. We really appreciate your helping us."

"You've got a deal!" While Truman answered their questions about the best places to buy supplies and groceries in the nearby towns, he heaped his plate with second helpings of everything. When Aunt Christine cut a coconut custard pie and a peach pie for their dessert, their neighbor was easily coaxed into taking a slice of each—and after dinner he left with an entire cherry pie as well as a loaf of cinnamon bread and some cookies.

After they saw Truman off, Noah returned to the dairy barn with his brother to finish the stalls they'd been building earlier. The rain had stopped. As he gazed across the expanse of the sunlit lawn, he noticed that every blade of grass glistened with a single drop of water on its tip. Why had he never noticed such a sight before? Surely the yard at the Coldstream farm had held pearls of moisture in this same breathtaking way, yet the sheer beauty of it held his attention for several moments.

A movement caught his eye near the fence where Rosetta's chickens and goats ambled about. Preacher Amos was cutting some of the irises that bloomed alongside the stable. He carefully cradled the flowers in the crook of his arm, a mix of deep purple, yellow, and white ones, then carried them toward the house. Before Amos reached the door, Mamm hurried outside to meet him, her pleasure evident in her voice and face as she accepted his gift. Their silhouettes were backlit by the sun, Amos taller and leaning slightly forward while Mamm gazed up at him.

Had she ever looked so happy when she was with Dat? Not that Noah could recall—but then, he didn't remember his father ever bringing her a bouquet, either.

Why are older guys like Amos and Truman winning the attention of women while you feel like you've been hung out to dry? Even Roman is looking forward to dating the girls who will soon be moving here.

The thought nagged at him. Just a few months ago he'd been head over heels in love with Deborah, sharing her thoughts and kisses and laughter. She'd come back to him— or at least she wanted to—yet he'd hardened his heart, afraid of having it broken again. Now he was also burdened with suspicions about her involvement with Isaac Chupp.

This is your circus. And you'll continue to be the monkey until you stop acting like one.

Noah glanced at the horses grazing peacefully in the pasture. Tomorrow was Sunday, the day he'd often taken Deborah for buggy rides after church. When it had been just the two of them, with the breeze in their faces as they rolled down the back roads—or when they'd stopped in the shade to enjoy a snack she'd packed—his future had seemed as bright as those irises growing by the shed, and as breathtaking as the expanse of grass blades adorned with beads of rain.

A smile crept over Noah's face. He now had a plan for dealing with Deborah.

Chapter Nine

Deborah liked the coziness of the Sunday church service arrangement. With only nine of them at Promise Lodge, and Preacher Amos being the sole ordained member, they moved dining room chairs into the lodge lobby for their worship. As tradition dictated, the women sat on one side, facing the men—which included only Noah and his brother, because Amos had centered his chair in front of the fireplace. It was much more comfortable than sitting on the pew benches in Coldstream because the chairs had backs on them.

"We have hymnals on order, and as more folks come to live here, we'll build pew benches to accommodate everyone over in the big conference room," Preacher Amos explained to Deborah as they took their seats. "And because I'll be the only one preaching until we get another minister and a bishop, our service runs quite a bit shorter than normal. Not that I've heard anyone complain."

On either side of her, Laura and Phoebe chuckled. In keeping with the tradition of having the eldest in the district seated in the front, Deborah and her friends sat in a row behind Mattie, Christine, and Rosetta. Amos shared a weathered hymnal, the *Ausbund,* with the boys and the women grouped themselves so they could sing from the two copies they had. Most Amish families had their own copies, which were often given as wedding gifts and passed down through the generations, even though each district kept a large supply of them for Sunday services in members' homes.

Amos announced the hymn number and then sang the first note in his rich baritone voice. As she joined in the familiar German words, Deborah could easily distinguish between Roman's reedier tone and Noah's more confident way of carrying a tune. Someday Noah would probably lead their hymn singing, for his hesitation in expressing his thoughts disappeared when words were set to music.

Deborah glanced up and lost track of the song. Noah was looking at her over the top of his hymnal, his brown eyes aglow. His clean-shaven face appeared more relaxed, more inviting this morning, and as he continued singing about the love of Christ for His church Deborah wondered if his heart was shifting closer to the forgiveness she'd asked him for.

Phoebe elbowed her, fighting a smile. Deborah realized she'd gone silent—and in a group this small, everyone else would know she'd been distracted—so she rejoined the music with fresh energy. Could it be that Noah had reconsidered? Did he want to be with her again?

Deborah's heart beat happily, filled with hope. Roman acted as Deacon, reading the scripture passage from the big King James Bible—the chapter from Matthew that included the Lord's Prayer. Then Amos stood up to preach.

"As we move through the days of the lives our Lord has granted us," he began, "we run across situations that befuddle us—and people who get our hearts out of kilter. We in this room are prime examples of folks undergoing major change," he pointed out. He spoke without notes, looking at each of them. "And even though we *initiated* our change of location, we know that once the apple cart's been upset, some of the apples get bruised. And maybe our cart won't fill up again the way we'd hoped and prayed it would."

The three sisters in front of Deborah nodded their agreement. Across from them, Roman sat with a faraway look in his eye while Noah, his arms crossed tightly, continued looking directly at Deborah.

"It behooves us to recall that in the prayer our Lord taught us," Amos continued earnestly, "we are to petition God for His kingdom to come, for His will to be done, and for our daily bread. We ask Him, as well, to forgive us the trespasses—the sins—we have committed. But then comes a stinger."

Although Amos was speaking to them in a quiet, conversational tone, his voice carried up into the high ceiling of the lobby. "We are to forgive others their trespasses in the same measure that God forgives us," he stated emphatically. "Matter of fact, we can interpret this part of the prayer to mean that if we do *not* forgive others, God will not forgive us our sins, either. We walk a dangerous path if we allow the differences between us to fester."

Preacher Amos glanced at the women's side, and then focused on Roman and Noah. "What if God calls us home before we've reconciled with those whom we feel have done us wrong?" he asked eloquently. "How will we answer Him on the Judgment Day, if He says that the unforgiven sins on our earthly record translate into black marks against us in the Book of Life, in the hereafter?"

Although Amos was looking right at him, Noah kept his face carefully composed. He was still focused so intently on Deborah that she felt her face growing hot. She shifted in her chair, hoping Christine's body would block her from Noah's view—but Noah moved, too, enough to keep her in sight. His lips flickered.

Was Noah fighting a smile? Trying not to reveal his

improvement of mood, his change of heart? Or was he making light of the sermon?

Deborah looked down at her hands, which were clasped in her lap. Perhaps it was better not to encourage Noah's attention by returning it. It was a relief, half an hour later, when Amos ended his sermon and they bowed their heads in silent prayer.

Lord, I feel something important—maybe something life-changing—will happen today. Guide my mind and my heart. Help me to be still and know that You are God, and that You watch over us in all of our comings and goings.

Deborah didn't peek, but she sensed Noah might be peering at her even as his head was bowed. During their courtship they had occasionally engaged in this sort of playful eye contact during church, to relieve the monotony of a service that typically lasted three hours. After another hymn, Amos pronounced a benediction and they all rose from their chairs.

"*Denki,* Amos," Mattie said as she picked up her chair. "Your message was thought-provoking, as always."

Following the others' example, Deborah started toward the dining room to return her chair to the table. As she and Phoebe and Laura headed toward the kitchen to set out the food they'd prepared yesterday, however, Noah grasped her elbow.

"How about a buggy ride after dinner?" he asked in a low voice. "It's not going to be like our common meal in Coldstream, where we had dozens of other folks to visit with for an entire afternoon. I—I could show you some of the places around Promise and out in the countryside."

Deborah's heart thumped like an excited puppy's tail. "I've missed our rides," she said, aware of how his warm hand still cupped her elbow. "Shall I pack us a picnic, like we used to take?"

"*Gut* idea. Never can tell how long we'll be gone."

Deborah's breath caught. While her hopes rippled like flags in a breeze, she realized that their afternoon jaunt could either turn out to be too short or way too long, depending upon how the conversation went. She had no doubt that the focus would be on her, and on her Coldstream story. *What if Noah has the same nasty plan as Isaac Chupp, when he took you out into unfamiliar countryside and dumped you?*

Noah was still watching her, awaiting her response— although while she'd been standing this close to him, Deborah had forgotten where the conversation had left off.

She would have to trust him once they were alone in the buggy, as she had during their long courtship. And Noah, in turn, would simply have to believe what she said about the night that had so drastically changed her life. Deborah knew she'd need to plead her case persuasively, without the support of her friends. There would be no second-guessing and probably no second chances to reconcile with Noah if pertinent details slipped her mind while she was under pressure.

Deborah put a smile on her face, hoping she appeared more confident than she felt. "I can't wait," she replied. "I'm so glad you asked, Noah."

Preacher Amos stopped in the kitchen doorway to gaze at them. "It's a sight for sore eyes to see the two of you talking to each other," he said. "Noah, I commend you for making your peace with Deborah. I almost insisted that you apologize to her—forgive her for breaking your engagement— right after I pronounced the benediction, but the Spirit whispered in my ear to leave it up to you." He flashed them a bright smile. "As always, God knew what He was doing."

Deborah considered the preacher's words. If she trusted that God indeed had the perfect plan for her life, maybe someday she would look back on the ordeal she'd gone through in Coldstream and see how every frightening, humiliating detail had contributed to her growth in the Christian faith.

For now, though, she was on pins and needles.

* * *

As his mare clip-clopped along the county highway, Noah concentrated on the curves and hills that surrounded the tiny town of Promise, trying not to let Deborah's nearness weaken his resolve. It was just like old times, having her beside him in the open buggy, sitting so close that their elbows rubbed. But he couldn't let memories of happier days distract him. Even though she lifted her face to the sunshine in a mesmerizing way—even though she looked so kissable with her eyes closed as her *kapp* strings fluttered in the breeze—his mission wasn't to romance her again.

He needed the truth.

"It's hillier here than it is around Coldstream," she remarked as they passed a small farmstead. "More wooded areas, too. You probably have to watch for deer and wild turkeys crossing the road."

"Lots of those around," Noah agreed. He suspected Deborah was making small talk to distract him, although she'd always been more talkative than he was. Couldn't she sense how difficult it was for him to ask questions that might have answers he didn't want to hear?

"A lot of the places we've passed make me think the owners are hard-pressed," she went on, gesturing toward a barn that looked ready to collapse. "Truman Wickey's farm is by far the prettiest place I've seen. He must be doing really well."

"Anybody who owns the big equipment Truman uses has to have a chunk of change to back up his business," Noah replied in a rush. "But, Deborah, I—"

When she focused her soulful green eyes on him, Noah lost track of what he'd intended to say. And then, when he hesitated a few moments too long, Deborah's eyebrows rose in bewilderment.

"What is it, Noah?" she murmured. "Say it out loud. I can't read your mind."

Resentment flared within him. How many times had she said that during their courtship? Deborah *had* to know what he was stewing about today, yet she insisted on pointing up his flaw, his inability to articulate ideas as readily as most folks did. At tense moments like these, he wished for just half of Preacher Amos's eloquence.

Noah steered the horse onto an unpaved side road so he wouldn't have to be as aware of traffic. "So—what happened the night the Bender barn burned down?" he blurted.

Deborah looked up the road, as though she wanted to avoid his gaze now that the subject matter had gotten serious. "What exactly do you want to know?"

Frustration made Noah grip the leather lines. The horse stopped in the middle of the road, which was just as well. "Start at the beginning."

A sigh escaped her. "I looked down the road from our house and saw flames coming out the back of the Benders' barn, so I rushed to our phone shanty. I called nine-one-one and then—"

"Why didn't you alert the menfolk by ringing the fire bell, instead of involving the law?" Noah demanded. "You *knew* you'd be getting yourself into hot water by—"

"Because all the men were at Bishop Obadiah's place!" Deborah shot back. "They were practicing hymns so new fellows could become song leaders—they wouldn't even have *heard* the bell. By the time I could've hitched up a horse and driven clear across the district to tell them, the barn—and maybe the house and the sheds—would've been gone. And with the new family who bought the Bender place not moved in yet—"

She paused, throwing up her arms in exasperation. "Noah, if you're determined to criticize everything I say, why not just take me back to the lodge?" she asked plaintively. "Do you have any idea how upsetting it is that my own *dat* wouldn't hear me out—and now *you* won't, either? Why can't you believe I did the best I knew how?"

Noah let out the breath he'd been holding. When Deborah got riled up, there was no reasoning with her.

Maybe reason isn't what's needed here. Maybe patience is the better approach, because this is your future at stake, as much as Deborah's.

Noah wondered how Preacher Amos's voice had taken over his thoughts, but he probably stood a better chance of understanding Deborah's situation—not to mention the bruise that had almost faded away—if he approached this problem the way he thought Amos would.

"Okay. Sorry," Noah murmured. "So you called the emergency number. Then what?"

Deborah looked away, as though recalling the details upset her. "I ran down the road to the barn," she murmured. "I saw Isaac and some of his English buddies drinking and smoking in there."

Noah scowled. "But how could they not know the place was in flames? Why did they stick around—"

"How would I know what Isaac was thinking?" Deborah interrupted. "There were a lot of empty beer bottles on the floor. Maybe he and the others were so drunk they didn't notice the fire—or maybe they weren't smoking um, regular cigarettes. Or maybe they *set* the fire, seeing who could stay there the longest on a dare."

Noah had no trouble imagining such a thing. Isaac Chupp was all about pushing trouble to the limits, seeing what he could get away with. "And they would've known the men were miles away," he speculated. "And maybe they figured that since nobody was living at the Bender place, they could be long gone before anybody caught them."

"That's how I see it, *jah*."

"But why'd you stay there, Deborah?" Noah asked as he turned to face her. "You had to know Isaac would—he's got a reputation for getting too fresh with—"

"When somebody hollered that sirens were coming, the guys rushed out the door," Deborah rasped. "Isaac saw me outside, stepping out of the way when his friends scattered toward the cars they'd parked out back. He grabbed hold of me—started hollering at me for calling the cops—"

Deborah's anguish made Noah's throat tighten, but he couldn't let her off the hook. Couldn't let the wetness shining in her eyes inspire his pity. "You surely could've broken away—or slapped him, or—"

"*Really?*" she blurted. "If *you* got a grip on my arm, how far away would I get? Isaac's taller than you, and—and maybe stronger."

Noah didn't care to be reminded—especially by Deborah—of all the ways Isaac Chupp was superior to him, even if he didn't understand how the bishop's lazy son could be physically stronger than he was. Already the images in his mind were too vivid, and Deborah wasn't nearly finished with her story. "And then?" he asked, struggling to lower his voice.

She blinked fiercely to keep from crying. "He shoved me into his rig. Said we'd get away from the cops and then he'd set our story straight—tell me what I was to say if anybody asked about the fire." Deborah sighed deeply. "I realized then that I'd gotten myself in too deep, and that when Dat found out what I'd done—and who I'd been with—there'd be no right way to explain my situation. But I was already along for the ride, and it was getting dark. I had no idea where Isaac was taking me . . . or what he might do to get back at me."

Deborah's desperation made Noah's heart shrivel. He didn't really want to know any more, yet he had to hear her out. It would be one thing to forgive her, as his Christian duty, but it was another thing altogether to consider courting her again if she'd been . . . compromised.

"So he kept urging his poor horse along the back roads, going too fast in the darkness," she continued in a resigned voice. "When he finally stopped, I didn't have a clue where we were. He told me I was to deny any knowledge of him and his friends being in the barn—and if Sheriff Renfro came nosing around his place, he'd know it was *me* who'd tattled," Deborah added emphatically. "When Isaac said he wanted to seal the deal with a—a kiss—"

Noah clenched his jaw. The mere thought of Chupp kissing his Deborah made him crazy.

"—I slapped him, as hard as I could," Deborah went on doggedly. "That made him really mad. He threw open the buggy door and hopped out. Told me I was getting out, too—which was fine by me, until he grabbed hold of my neck and shoved me down into the ditch. And then he drove off."

Noah could hardly breathe. He was grateful that Deborah had avoided Isaac's advances, but there had to be more. Preacher Eli hadn't banished his daughter on the basis of what Deborah had said so far. Had he?

Resisting the urge to take Deborah's hand, he gave her a moment to collect herself. "So how'd you get home?"

Deborah's expression turned bleak. "Started walking," she replied heavily. "But I'd scraped my knees on some rocks in the ditch, so my stockings were torn, and once I finally reached a paved road, I still had no idea which direction to go. It's really dark out in the middle of nowhere, in the middle of the night. I got so scared I cried out for God's help."

Noah looked away. Why was he putting Deborah through this ordeal again? Why couldn't he just take her in his arms and comfort her?

"And then a car came along. It slowed down."

Deborah's voice had gotten so soft he could barely hear her. Noah decided he'd better withhold his affection until he'd listened to the entire story.

"It was that redheaded kid, Kerry," she said.

"The one Isaac runs the roads with in that noisy old car?"

Deborah nodded. "He offered me a ride home. Said he'd been following the buggy from a ways behind us, figuring Isaac might . . . hurt me."

"And?" Noah really didn't want to hear anymore, but maybe it would do her good to clear her conscience by confessing the whole truth.

A tear dribbled down Deborah's cheek. "I knew that as a member of the church, I wasn't supposed to get into his car, but—but I didn't know what else to do. I thought maybe God had sent Kerry to help me." She sighed bitterly, swiping at her eyes. "Turns out he had the same ideas as Isaac, about how I could repay his favor. He—he got grabby in the car. I tried to open the door—"

"While the car was moving?" Noah's eyes widened as he imagined this scene.

Deborah's dejected gaze told of a desperation he couldn't fathom. "Well, *jah*," she rasped, "but I couldn't unlock my door. Then we swerved off the road on my side. Kerry was so drunk he cranked the wheel hard to get the car back on the pavement, but it went too far. He hit a guardrail."

"*That* made him mad," Noah murmured.

"He tried to back up, to steer the car off the guardrail, but it didn't move. When he shut off the engine, I jumped out. Ran as best I could, until I could see Kerry wasn't following me," Deborah went on breathlessly. "I must've still been a couple miles away from Coldstream, and I couldn't walk very fast. I was coming up the lane at home when Dat was heading to the barn to tend to the morning horse chores. He took one look at me and assumed the worst."

Noah had no trouble imagining Preacher Eli's reaction. With Deborah's *dat,* things were either black or white—not much tolerance for shades of gray or for teenage boys who drank too much.

"He saw that my *kapp* was gone, and my hair had fallen down. My stockings were tattered, too," she went on in a raspy voice. "Sheriff Renfro had stopped by the evening before to ask about the fire and the nine-one-one call, because they'd traced it to our phone, so Dat knew I'd made the call. He told me that was the *first* of my bad choices. Said I was setting a bad example for my younger brothers and sister, so—so he ordered me to leave."

Deborah looked away, as though searching the woods for a solution to the mess she was in. "If Mamma hadn't stepped in, Dat wouldn't even have allowed me to clean up and pack, he was so mad at me."

"So you hired a driver—Dick Mercer, most likely—and came to Promise Lodge."

"Mamma called Dick and slipped me some of her egg money for his fare. She gave me that tin of brownies from the freezer, but—but she didn't try to change Dat's mind." Deborah hung her head. "She didn't ask me where I was going, or give me any ideas. It was Dick who suggested Promise Lodge, because he'd helped you folks move some of your furniture and stuff."

"Which means you didn't really bake those brownies for *me,*" Noah muttered.

When Deborah looked at him with her red-rimmed eyes, he kicked himself for saying that.

"So on top of my other mistakes—my *sins,* as Dat saw them—you think I lied to you about those brownies and about why I came here," she remarked ruefully. "I'd baked them a while back, hoping to find a way to win your heart again—but then you moved away without even saying *gut*-bye. And now you don't believe me. You think everything I've told you is one big lie—a story I made up so you'd feel sorry for me."

Noah kept his mouth shut. Not that it improved the situation or Deborah's mood.

"Maybe you should take me back—to the lodge, I mean," Deborah clarified in a shaky voice. "Now that I've told you what happened, and I've heard it out loud for myself, I can see why you wouldn't want to court me again, Noah. What a mess I've made. What a stupid fool I've been."

Noah cringed. Until he'd initiated this gut-wrenching conversation, he'd been assuming all the wrong things, and *he* had been the fool. It was serious business when an Amish girl's father cast her out because he believed she'd been compromised. Folks would question Preacher Eli's effectiveness as a parent—and as a church leader—and Deborah's reputation would be ruined, as well. She had come to Promise Lodge because she believed she had nowhere else to go.

The defeat in Deborah's voice told him she now believed that the events she'd confessed had been all her fault, as well. He searched for the right thing to say, because the tables had turned. Now Deborah was placing the blame on herself while he was left in utter amazement that she'd escaped her ordeal with only a bruise and two scraped knees—

Get real. The physical scabs will heal, but her heart—her soul—will be scarred for a long, long time. Unless you help her.

Once again it was Preacher Amos's persuasive voice Noah heard in his head, trying to help him out of this awkward conversational corner he'd painted them into. After all, Deborah had been smiling when they left the campground.

"Deborah, I—I'm really sorry about what happened to you," Noah murmured. He reached for her hand, but she tucked it under her arm, hugging herself as though she were trying to hold body and soul together.

"*Jah,* well, *sorry* isn't going to fix anything," she murmured. "Maybe when the others hear everything I've done, they won't even let me stay."

"That's not true! We're your friends, Deborah—*all* of us," he insisted as he wrapped his arm around her shoulders.

Deborah bowed her head and shut her eyes, too dejected to respond to his reassurance. Noah wished he were better at coming up with the right words. It seemed she'd become so lost in her depressing thoughts that she'd forgotten he was sitting beside her.

After several more painful moments, Noah released Deborah and took up the leather lines. "Geddap, Jane," he murmured to the mare. He saw no point in prolonging their agony by sitting out here, not talking to each other.

Chapter Ten

As Deborah slouched on her bed later that afternoon, staring at the cracks in the cabin's floor—believing she was as deeply, unfixably flawed as the old boards—someone knocked briskly on the door.

"What're you doing in there all by your lonesome?" Laura asked through the screen.

"What on earth did Noah say that's upset you so badly?" Phoebe demanded. "We're about ready to have some sandwiches, and we didn't want to eat without you."

If you knew all the things I've done . . . "Go ahead with your supper," Deborah insisted. "I couldn't eat a bite."

"Now we *know* something's wrong," Rosetta teased, but her voice was gentle and caring. "Can we come in and talk about it? Misery loves company."

"And if Noah's the reason you're so upset, I'll certainly be giving him a piece of my mind," Mattie stated.

"Remember how you came over after Willis passed, bringing us little gifts and cheering us up?" Christine asked without missing a beat. "It's our turn to listen now, Deborah. What're friends for, if not to help each other along?"

Deborah sighed. If all the other women at Promise Lodge

were peering in at her, there would be no dismissing them until she'd satisfied their concerned curiosity. Like it or not, she'd have to repeat what she'd told Noah—finish the story she'd started for these ladies a while back—and endure whatever they dished up. And if it meant they no longer wanted her here, she'd have to go. She'd known that all along.

"All right," she murmured. "I don't want supper to be late on my account. We'll have the fellows over here asking *why*."

"Puh! Like we can't handle them," Laura said as the screen door creaked.

When Deborah swung her feet to the other side of the bunk to face her incoming guests, Phoebe and Laura immediately sat down on either side of her while Rosetta, Christine, and Mattie pulled up the other chairs in the room. The love and concern on their faces touched her.

"Don't go thinking Noah has upset me," she murmured to Mattie. "This was my doing, mostly, and rather than mislead you, I'd better tell you the rest of what happened the other night when the barn burned. That's what Noah and I were discussing, and why we've gone our separate ways."

The women leaned closer, their faces furrowed. Phoebe patted Deborah's arm and Laura grabbed her hand.

"Well, I told you how Isaac shoved me into the ditch and left me," Deborah began in a low voice. "After that, when I'd finally found the paved road, Isaac's buddy Kerry drove up in his car. He offered me a ride home, and even though I knew he was drunk—even though it was wrong for me to ride with him because he's English—I got in. Big mistake."

"You were lost!" Laura protested.

"And you'd been hurt, too," Phoebe pointed out.

"Let Deborah finish," Rosetta suggested gently. "This can't be easy for her."

Deborah looked at the sturdy hands of the stalwart friends

who sat beside her. She tried to take comfort from the girls' insisting that she'd done nothing they wouldn't have done. But would they *really* have been foolish enough to get into Kerry's car? "It seems Kerry wanted me to repay the favor of his ride with—well, *you* know," she murmured. "I said no, but he grabbed hold of me anyway, while he was driving. When I slapped him, the car swerved off the road—"

Her friends sucked in a sudden breath.

"—and then he steered too hard in the other direction and crashed his car into a guardrail," she continued in a rush. "I got away from him—probably because he was more worried about his car than about me—but now he and Isaac both have it in for me. If I hadn't been so stupid—if I hadn't defied the *Ordnung* by getting into an Englisher's car, on top of calling nine-one-one and then snooping in the barn when—"

"But you were trying to save the barn," Christine insisted. "Probably because it had been *ours*."

"*Jah,* that's true. But what was I thinking?" Deborah lamented. "Yet another sin was being so prideful that I believed God had sent Kerry to rescue me. And instead of turning the other cheek, as Jesus taught—instead of trusting that God would take care of me—I fought both of those boys. Is it any wonder that Dat got angry? I'd gone against everything he—and the church—have taught me all my life."

"But what might've happened if you *hadn't* fought them off?" Mattie demanded in a terse whisper. "It was God who gave you the strength to defend yourself, and the sense to *run* when you realized the trouble you were in."

"And you've recognized your mistakes and now you've confessed them," Preacher Amos's voice came through the screen door. "Wherever two or three are gathered in His name, we believe Christ is present. As your preacher, I'm saying your admission is every bit as *gut* as kneeling before the members in church, acknowledging that you've done wrong, Deborah. *Go and sin no more,* Jesus would say. Your sins have been forgiven."

Deborah closed her eyes, awash in a fresh wave of embarrassment that made her face hot. If Amos had been listening outside, Roman and Noah were probably out there, as well. *But now everyone knows the truth, and the truth shall set you free. The Bible says so.*

So why didn't she feel better? Everyone at Promise Lodge was on her side. They all believed her confession.

Yet Deborah felt hollow; as fragile as the bone china cup and saucer Mamma had given her for her birthday. What would her mother say if she knew the whole truth? Would she defend her daughter, or allow Dat's decision to stand? Mamma, like most Old Order wives, had never been one to challenge her husband's opinions or decisions.

Deborah exhaled slowly. "You fellows may as well come in."

The screen door creaked and Preacher Amos entered, followed by Roman and Noah. The little cabin felt crowded. As the three fellows stood behind Mattie, Christine, and Rosetta, Deborah couldn't miss the concern on their faces.

"I um, thought Preacher Amos should know about what Isaac and that Kerry fellow did to you," Noah admitted softly. "I didn't mean to make you feel worse, Deborah. Really I didn't."

"And now that I've heard the story from both you and Noah," Amos said, "I'm even more concerned about what those boys are up to—and why. Isaac's in his *rumspringa,* but that doesn't mean he and his friends can terrorize our young women or destroy property."

"Isaac used to torment Teacher Catherine something awful—left dead mice and other nasty stuff in her desk drawers," Laura recalled. "But she could never catch him at it. And I suspect she didn't want to cross Bishop Obadiah by suggesting his son was a troublemaker."

"I think Isaac's parents spared the rod because he came along so much later than the other Chupp kids," Mattie pointed out in a disapproving tone. "What with already raising ten youngsters, poor Bertha was worn-out by the time Isaac was in school."

"Obadiah kept so busy with his auctions and his duties as the bishop that *he* didn't always know what his youngest was up to, either," Christine said with a shake of her head.

"That's a dangerous way to raise a boy." Preacher Amos draped his arms around Roman and Noah's shoulders. "I'm pleased that you two Schwartzes have already committed your lives to Christ and His church, because I suspect it won't be long before Isaac jumps the fence."

"*Jah,* I've seen him in that Kerry fellow's old car, learning how to drive it," Roman said. "While I know a lot of guys who got drivers' licenses when they were his age, it was a passing fad to them. I figure to see Isaac behind the wheel of a much nicer car than Kerry's someday—"

"But where's he getting his money?" Noah blurted. "I can't think Obadiah pays him much for clerking at the auctions—especially since the two oldest Chupp sons partner with their *dat* and are raising families, needing a steady income."

Deborah had been following this conversation with a heavy heart, hoping something these friends said would make her feel better about her run-in with Isaac. "Do you suppose he's got sticky fingers?" she ventured. "He might not *earn* much, but a lot of money passes through his hands during big livestock auctions. Don't most Amish buyers pay cash?"

The cabin got very quiet.

"I see what you're saying," Preacher Amos murmured. "No one could ever accuse Isaac of being slow, so maybe he's figured out how to slip money out of the till and then adjust the sales records in the ledger."

"Now *that* bothers me," Rosetta muttered. "Isaac clerked at the last couple of benefit auctions we held for the Coldstream school, and a *bunch* of money was raised then. Thousands of dollars."

"We shouldn't assume that Isaac's guilty of such theft," Preacher Amos hastened to say. "With two older brothers and his *dat* managing the auction's operations, I'd think someone would've noticed any discrepancies between the ledger entries and the amount their auction items had sold for—especially if differences occurred more than once or twice."

An uneasy silence settled over them again until Mattie sighed and stood up. "Not much we can do about Isaac's activities except pray over them—and we're grateful to God that Deborah is here safe with us, as well," she added. "Let's have our supper. Tomorrow's a busy day, what with Truman and his tree-trimming crew coming over."

As the women cleared away the dirty dishes after their simple supper of sandwiches and desserts left from their noon meal, Rosetta listened to Preacher Amos with particular interest. He was reading the latest letters they'd received, from folks who wanted to come to Promise Lodge—or at least visit their new settlement to see if it would suit them. He read two from families with young adults looking to marry into fresh bloodlines—a common reason for Plain families to relocate—and then his eyebrows rose as he unfolded another letter.

"The fellow who wrote this one says, 'We believe the Lord is leading us to your new colony, to the new beginnings we've been reading about in your scribe's letters in *The Budget*,'" Amos read aloud in his melodious voice.

Rosetta couldn't help smiling, for she was writing the weekly reports that appeared in *The Budget,* a newspaper that served the Plain population all over the United States.

"It'll be fun to see who shows up to stay, and who decides Promise Lodge won't be their new home," she remarked. "Folks who come here just from reading my letters are either very strong in their faith, or very eager to leave where they've been living, I would think."

"He's Preacher Marlin Kurtz," Amos said as he skimmed the letter. "His family includes a married son named Harley, Harley's wife, Minerva, and Marlin's two teenaged kids named Fannie and Lowell. They live in Iowa, not all that far from here."

"No mention of Marlin's wife?" Mattie asked.

Amos shook his head. "He's a widower, which might explain why he wants to move. Maybe he can't handle living with two kids who need a woman's guidance "

"And a woman to keep the place clean and put meals on the table," Rosetta remarked. She wiggled her eyebrows at Christine. "What do you think about taking on a couple more kids, Sister?"

"Puh! It could just as well be *you* filling that role, Rosetta," Christine shot back.

"I don't think so," Rosetta replied without missing a beat. "If I took up with a preacher, my plans for managing apartments would go out the window in a hurry."

"It's gut that another ordained fellow wants to come here, though," Amos remarked. "We could get our church district organized a lot sooner."

"But don't you wonder why a preacher wants to leave the district he's serving? I'd think he could find a new wife to hitch up with easily enough," Mattie said in a pensive voice. "Unless he's like you, Amos, leaving because he and his bishop don't see eye to eye."

"We can ask him that when they come for a visit next month." Amos stuffed the folded letter back into its envelope and waved a sheet of yellow legal-sized paper at them. Even from across the kitchen, Rosetta could see that the writer of this letter wrote with a firm, decisive hand and used a fine-tipped black marker rather than an ink pen or pencil.

"I saved this one for last because I'm not sure what to make of it," Amos said with a chuckle. "It's from a Bishop Floyd Lehman, who hails from Sugarcreek, Ohio. He intends to bring his wife, Frances, and his daughters, Gloria and Mary Kate, to Promise Lodge because God has told him we need his leadership. They'll arrive as soon as he gets their property in Ohio sold."

"Hmm," Mattie said. "That's a pretty bold statement to make when he's not even met us, or seen the place—"

"And why would *he* be leaving his church district?" Roman asked with raised eyebrows. "Usually it's the bishop who stays to rule the roost while the unsatisfied district members go elsewhere. After all, God decided he would be that district's leader—not ours."

Amos was nodding as he listened to Roman. "Floyd goes on to say that because his district has gotten so populated, folks are splitting off to form a new district—but there's no affordable land nearby. Sugarcreek's got a huge Amish population, so he's probably right about some of his people needing to relocate."

"So Bishop Floyd figures to come to Missouri, along with several other folks, and plant himself here as our leader?" Rosetta asked in a doubtful tone. "How does that work, Amos? He can't just take over Promise Lodge without a drawing of the lot for a bishop—can he?"

"Well, he *could*—bishops serve for life, you know," Amos replied as he refolded the yellow sheet of paper. "But who can tell? Perhaps other bishops will move here, just as we already have Preacher Marlin stating his intention to come. We'll decide on our leaders when we know for sure who's going to live here."

"But what if we don't *like* Floyd Lehman—or anybody

else who wants to live here?" Laura blurted. "Do we have to let them move in?"

"*Jah!* The land belongs to you and our *mamm* and aunts," Phoebe pointed out. "Can you decide you'll not sell them any property?"

Amos smiled as he rose from the table. "We're bound to get folks with viewpoints that are different from ours, and with ideas that might push our buttons," he said. "We must rely upon God to grant us patience, and we'll trust Him to send us new neighbors who want to live in hardworking harmony. Life at Promise Lodge might get a whole lot more interesting than we figured on when we left Coldstream."

When the kitchen was tidy, Rosetta went upstairs to her room, where she wrote her report for *The Budget* each Sunday evening. Composing her column was a good way to review the previous days' happenings as she prepared herself for the coming week, she'd found. As she took out her pen and paper, however, her thoughts hopped like agitated rabbits.

What if Floyd Lehman insisted that it was his God-given right to be their bishop? What if he was as brash and willful in person as he sounded in his letter? What if he believed Amish women shouldn't be managing apartments? What if—

Rosetta exhaled her frustration and looked out the window. Dusk was settling over the woods, and the surface of Rainbow Lake reflected the blue gray of the sky. Beyond the orchard, at the two-story Wickey home, a light came on in an upstairs window.

Is that Truman's room? What if he's gazing in this direction, wondering which room I'm in?

Rosetta knew this was a silly, adolescent thought—but her room was getting dark, so she lit the lantern nearest the window. They were all grateful for the helpful suggestions Truman had given them about clearing away underbrush that had gotten out of control, and Amos was extremely glad to have the Wickey Landscaping crew coming to take down a number of dangerous dead trees.

What should they serve for noon dinner tomorrow? With at least four additional men to feed, she and her sisters needed to overestimate the amount of food they cooked rather than risk running short. Imagining the pies, rolls, and other good things they would bake early tomorrow morning, Rosetta went down the back steps and into the pantry. She gazed into one of the big upright freezers, selecting the largest venison roast along with two packages of ham steaks. When she placed them in the refrigerator to defrost, she realized her heart was beating faster with the anticipation of seeing Truman again.

That's silliness. He's a Mennonite and I'm Amish, Rosetta reminded herself as she returned to her room.

But what was wrong with planning a nice meal—planning for happiness—when their attractive neighbor came over? She and her sisters would be thanking the crew for their labor rather than just entertaining Truman. It wasn't as though she'd be trying for his attention, after all. She was happily single, embarking upon a business path Plain men didn't approve of.

Rosetta laughed at herself as she sat down at her desk again. If she didn't set aside her schoolgirl crush on Truman, she wouldn't get her *Budget* column written. She picked up her pen and positioned her lined tablet.

> *We've spent another busy week transforming this former campground into a new colony. Along with a couple days of soaking rain, we welcomed our dear friend Deborah Peterscheim. We've also met our Mennonite neighbor, Truman Wickey, and we're grateful for his landscaping crew and heavy equipment helping us clear away underbrush and dead trees. The garden plots are popping with rows*

*of green shoots and leaves, the honeysuckle bushes
smell heavenly, and we're receiving letters from
Plain folks all over the country who might want to
make their new homes with us.*

Rosetta paused, thinking of how to finish her account.
The events of the past week had given her plenty of food for
thought—and thinking about Truman had made her stop
fretting about Bishop Floyd Lehman and his attitude. She
would go to bed with a smile on her face, and for that she
was grateful.

Chapter Eleven

That same evening, Deborah borrowed some paper, an envelope, and a stamp from Phoebe and returned to her cabin to write her mother a long overdue letter. She lit the lamp and sat in one of the chairs, gazing at the blank page a long time before the words finally came.

> *Dear Mamma,*
>   *I'm so glad you've talked to Mattie. I'm sorry it's taken me a while to write. I'm sorrier still that I stuck my nose where it didn't belong the night of the fire, and that I've caused you and Dat so much trouble. I hope you can find it in your hearts to forgive me.*

Deborah paused to allow her emotions to settle. After all the talking she'd done today about Isaac and the circumstances of the Bender barn, she felt like a dress in a washing machine, getting agitated and then run through the wringer—yet still not clean. Confessing her story to Noah had brought so many other trespasses to light—so many ways she could have acted differently—even though Laura,

Phoebe, and the three women insisted she'd been right to
defend herself and that she'd done the best she could, considering her circumstances.

She didn't have the strength to write out each and every
incident she'd endured that night, and such an apology
should be made to her parents in person. Deborah wrote only
the main points about getting herself away from Isaac and
then Kerry, and assured Mamma that her clothing had been
lost or torn during her struggles with them.

> *I didn't know what else to do, Mamma. Like I told*
> *you before I left, I'm grateful to God that He helped*
> *me escape Isaac and Kerry before they could do*
> *more than rough me up.*
>
> *How are Lily and Lavern? And Menno and*
> *Johnny? My days here at Promise Lodge have been*
> *very busy because the buildings need paint and*
> *repairs before other families arrive at the new*
> *colony. No amount of hard work can erase how*
> *much I miss you all. I'm grateful that everyone here*
> *has welcomed me and accepted my confession. I*
> *understand that I have no right to return home until*
> *you and Dat believe I'm worthy to live under your*
> *roof again*

As Deborah pictured her four siblings' faces, she wondered what questions they must be asking and what answers
Dat was giving them. At thirteen, Lily and Lavern—her
sister and brother who were twins—were probably the most
aware of what had happened after she'd discovered Isaac
Chupp and his friends in the blazing barn. Menno and
Johnny, who were eleven and eight, would be curious about
where she'd gone. It was a blessing that Lily could help
Mamma with the housework now that school had let out for
the summer, but Deborah's heart still ached because she

wasn't there with her family. At home, she knew her duties and she sat in the same spot at the table she'd occupied all her life. Being sent away had made her feel more displaced than she could ever have imagined. Was this how a baby bird felt when it fell from its nest?

Deborah finished the letter quickly, for the words on the page were yet another reminder of the separation she'd caused by behaving so carelessly. She folded the pages and slipped them into the envelope. As she addressed it to her mother, it occurred to Deborah that she'd written many letters in her lifetime, but she'd never needed to write to Mamma. She'd been her mother's constant companion since the day she'd been born.

Deborah extinguished the lamp, surprised at how late it was. The cry of a distant coyote underscored her loneliness, but she focused on getting ready for bed. She owed it to Rosetta, Mattie, Christine, and the girls to be rested and ready to work in the kitchen, preparing the noon meal for the crew Truman Wickey was bringing.

She knelt beside her bed, resting her head on her folded hands. *Help me be a more obedient servant, Lord, open to Your will instead of so likely to wander from Your way.*

Deborah slipped between the sheets and eventually drifted off. After what seemed like only a few hours of sleep, a steady *ping! ping! ping!* drew her to the window.

In the stillness of dawn, while the sky shone as pale as a pearl and the sun made a glimmering ribbon of light on the horizon, she spotted Noah near the orchard. He was shooting tin cans off the woodpile with rapid-fire precision, as though intent upon stopping hungry coyotes in their tracks.

Or was he releasing his frustration with *her*? He appeared to be firing and making the cans fly as though each one represented a reason he could no longer love her. If he was out there shooting this early in the day, he surely must be in a foul mood. For all she knew, everyone else had found discrepancies in her confession, too, now that they'd slept on it.

The only antidote for this worrisome frame of mind was work, so Deborah got dressed and headed for the lodge to help prepare breakfast.

By noon, Noah was famished and parched from working in the hot sun. While Truman Wickey and his three men had manned their cherry picker and high-powered saws to fell seven dead trees, Noah, Roman, and Amos had used their chain saws and hatchets to cut the branches that had landed on the ground. They were keeping the smaller logs for firewood, and would feed the remainder of the wood to Truman's giant chipper to make mulch.

"Sure makes it easier, having Wickey's equipment to handle most of the work," Preacher Amos remarked when they stopped for dinner. "Think about how long it would've taken the three of us to fell those trees and cut them up."

"*If* we could've gotten around to it," Roman remarked. "Our other projects might've kept us so busy that we would've left those trees for another year."

After the seven of them washed up out at the pump, they headed inside for dinner. They hung their straw hats on pegs Amos had mounted along the dining room wall, planning for when several residents would be taking their meals there. Noah was glad that the nearby maple trees shaded this side of the lodge and lowered the temperature by several degrees. Truman and his men were greeting the ladies, making much of the food that was being set down the center of the table.

"Is that a banana cake I see?" Edgar asked as he looked at the desserts on one of the tables. "And cookies and pie, too? What a feast!"

"Oh, I'm eyeballing that bowl of mashed potatoes with the chunks of bacon," Jay replied, rubbing his hands together.

Toby let out a laugh. "I'm saving room for a *lot* of that shoofly pie."

"Is that a venison roast I smell?" Truman asked as Rosetta set the platter on the table. "Covered with sliced onions and gravy, too. That's a real treat."

Rosetta's cheeks were flushed from working in the hot kitchen, and they burned brighter at Truman's compliment. "Noah's our deer hunter," she remarked. "He's put a lot of meat on our tables over the years."

Noah smiled at his aunt's compliment, but his eyes were on Deborah. She and the other girls were carrying a platter of ham steaks, steaming bowls of sliced carrots, green beans, pickled beets, and a fruit salad from the kitchen. While Laura and her sister happily greeted the workers, Deborah appeared subdued. Downhearted.

Noah sighed. She was probably still upset from telling her story about the Bender barn. What girl *wouldn't* feel the weight of such an ordeal? Although he wasn't ready to ask if he could court her again, he was still her lifelong friend, wasn't he?

He decided that if the weather remained pleasant, he would take her fishing at Rainbow Lake after supper. Maybe in the stillness of evening they could talk some more, and she would reveal what was troubling her.

Wouldn't it be nice to kiss her again? That always made her smile.

After grace, as Noah passed the meat platters and bowls of vegetables, he stole glances at Deborah without trying to engage her attention. He thought ahead to sitting on the grassy bank, baiting the hooks on fishing rods they'd found in one of the sheds, left from the days when Promise Lodge had been a church camp.

"This is the best bread I've eaten in ages," Jay remarked as he smeared butter on his third slice. "Soft and chewy. Bet it would make a great sandwich, too."

Laura slung her arm around Deborah's shoulder. "This

would be our bread baker," she said. "Deborah had the dough rising before I even got to the kitchen this morning!"

"We're mighty glad she's come to visit," Aunt Christine chimed in as she started the vegetable bowls around again. "Her peanut butter cookies are chewy-*gut* and so easy to stir up."

Noah was already planning to devour his share of Deborah's cookies before their guests discovered how wonderful they were. Deborah was smiling politely at these compliments, but the light was missing from her deep green eyes—more incentive for Noah to improve her mood once they could be alone this evening.

"Oh, my," Truman said as he held up a forkful of cake. "This is more than just a banana cake, ain't so? Maybe if I have a second piece I'll figure out what makes it so moist and tasty."

As Noah savored one of Deborah's chewy peanut butter cookies, he couldn't miss how Aunt Rosetta's cheeks bloomed with pink roses—how much younger she looked as she responded to their neighbor.

"Have a third piece—or take some home," she replied. "That's a hummingbird cake, so *jah,* it's got bananas and pineapple in the batter, but I think it's the banana glaze that makes it special."

"A big improvement over the version that has creamed cheese heaped on it," Preacher Amos remarked. "You ladies outdid yourselves today making this dinner."

After the meal, when the men rose from the table, Noah snatched three more peanut butter cookies on his way outside. When he held them up, winking at Deborah, he was pleased to see her smile shining a bit brighter. Thinking about fishing with her later on, just the two of them at Rainbow Lake, made the afternoon's labor seem less intense.

Roman and Wickey's men cut up the tree trunks that lay on the ground, while Noah and Preacher Amos fed those pieces to the chipper. When they finished around five o'clock, a mountain of mulch stood at the edge of the orchard and the woodpile had doubled in size—testimony to what seven men could accomplish when they worked as a team.

Amos paid Truman, and they waved as the four guys took off in his big pickup, hauling the chipper and the cherry picker behind it. Anticipating some time alone with Deborah after she'd finished in the kitchen, Noah took a quick shower. When he sat down at the table, he drank an entire glass of iced tea after their silent grace. This meal was simpler—egg salad and ham sandwiches, along with sliced cheese, and a mixture of the vegetables left over from dinner.

As they were passing what remained of their noon desserts, Noah's mother fetched an envelope from the kitchen. "I got a letter from Alma Peterscheim today," she said. "We thought you fellows might want to see these clippings from the Coldstream paper."

Deborah's cheeks colored as she gazed down at her lap. As his mother unfolded the newspaper articles, Noah could see that a couple of photographs were included—which had probably put Deborah through that tragedy all over again when she and the women had read the articles earlier.

"May I read them aloud so we fellows hear the story all at once?" Preacher Amos asked. "I sure hope the reporter wrote an accurate account, which might convince Bishop Obadiah to follow up with discipline for his son."

Deborah nodded, although she looked as if she'd rather be somewhere else. Once again Noah felt his mission was to cheer her up—to convince her she'd been forgiven for any wrongdoing on the night that had sent her life down a path she hadn't planned to follow.

"'On Tuesday evening Coldstream's emergency dispatcher received a call that the barn on the farm formerly owned by the Walt Bender family was in flames,'" Amos read in his resonant voice. "'Sheriff Curtiss Renfro was the first to arrive on the scene, where tire tracks in the mud suggested that at least three cars and a horse-drawn buggy had been present. No one remained on the premises. The local volunteer fire department doused the flames, but the structure was pronounced a total loss.'"

Amos gazed at Rosetta, Mattie, and Christine. "I'm sorry about this, ladies. These photos look pretty bleak."

Rosetta shrugged, sighing. "I suppose we should be thankful we sold the farm when we did, but I still feel bad for the new owner. Keep reading, Amos—although the article doesn't get much cheerier, I'm afraid."

Amos found his place on the printed page. "'Firefighters and the sheriff noted the presence of several beer bottles, cigarette butts, and two oil lanterns, which might have ignited the hay still stored in the barn. Bishop Obadiah Chupp insisted that any further investigations will be done by the leaders of his church district, as the Amish prefer to handle their own emergencies rather than allowing local law enforcement officers to intrude in their members' lives.'"

Amos looked up from the clipping. "As much as I respect our church policy, I sure hope an investigation won't be glossed over because the sheriff's not in on it," he remarked. "Once again, this gives Chupp the opportunity to cover for his son's involvement—knowing the members in the district probably won't challenge him."

The preacher began reading again. "'The nine-one-one call was traced to the phone on Eli Peterscheim's farm down the road from the barn, but Peterscheim denied knowledge of who had placed the call. "Anybody driving by who saw the barn was afire might have stopped at the phone shanty and called in," he claimed.'"

"If they were in a car, it's more likely they'd call on their cell phone," Noah pointed out. "So the sheriff surely must figure the caller was Plain."

Everyone around the table got quiet, considering this

point. Noah's mother squeezed Deborah's hand. "This is all pretty scary, dear, but you did the right thing by calling," she insisted.

"You were trying to save the place from total destruction, after all," Christine agreed.

Amos, who'd picked up the second clipping, raised his eyebrows. "Here's where push comes to shove. 'Friday morning Eli Peterscheim called the sheriff's office to report that Isaac Chupp, seventeen, of Coldstream along with Kerry Corbett, eighteen, of Eulah, were suspects in the case. When questioned, he did not identify his source of information. The former Bender farm is currently unoccupied, and its new owner could not be reached for comment.'"

"Preacher Eli's in hot water with the bishop *now,*" Roman remarked. "I hope he'll watch over the buildings on *his* place, considering that Isaac'll be none too pleased that his name got into the paper."

As Amos passed the clippings to his brother, Noah considered what he'd just heard. "Well, then, Eli took the same sort of risk Deborah did by reporting what he knew to the sheriff, who could do something about it—knowing Bishop Obadiah would be plenty upset with him," he reasoned aloud. "So while none of us likes it that Eli sent Deborah away . . . maybe he was protecting her as much as punishing her."

"That's not how it seemed to me," Deborah murmured ruefully.

"God will make the best of this whole situation," Rosetta declared staunchly. "We have to keep believing that His justice will be done."

"'Vengeance is mine, saith the Lord,'" Preacher Amos reminded them as he rose from the table. "We'll leave it in His hands to judge, and to carry out His will."

The women and girls began scraping plates while Roman headed outside to start the evening livestock chores. When

Phoebe and Laura had gone into the kitchen with stacks of dishes, Noah took Deborah's elbow. "How about we go fishing this evening?" he asked softly. "It'll be cool and quiet at the lake, with just you and me."

Her eyes widened. "I've not done all that much fishing, you know," she pointed out. "If you're thinking to get a *gut* laugh out of the way I bait a hook—"

"I will *never* laugh at you," Noah declared. He held her gaze, happy to see a spark of interest on her pretty face. "Meet me out on the dock when you're finished with the dishes. I'll help Roman with the chores and have your hooks all baited and ready to go. How's that?"

"All right. I'll be there."

Noah nodded, aware that his heart was beating in double time. He felt almost as excited as when he'd first asked Deborah to ride home with him from a Singing and she'd agreed. He was determined to re-create the fun they'd had back then. Somehow, he'd think of a way to brighten her life again.

Chapter Twelve

Standing beside Noah on the shoreline, Deborah watched attentively as he showed her how to cast her fishing line.

"A sideways cast is easier than an overhead one," he said as he demonstrated. "You press the thumb button and then take the rod behind you—like so. Then you whip it forward and let up on the button at the same time. See?"

As the fishing line whizzed out of the reel, Deborah watched Noah's bobber and hook sail effortlessly across the water. She hoped she wouldn't appear totally clueless and awkward when she tried to follow his example. "Dat takes the boys fishing but not Lily and me," she explained. "He says it's a guy thing."

Noah smiled as he set the handle of his rod into a little tunnel he'd dug in the shoreline mud. "So now it's a me-and-you thing," he replied. "*Jah,* you're holding it just right . . . keep the rod level when you take it behind you, then you throw it forward and let fly with it—*now!*"

Deborah lifted her thumb and watched her red-and-white bobber arc out over the lake. When it plopped into the water even farther out than Noah's bobber, she squealed with delight. "I think I can do this!"

"Of course you can, sweetie. There wouldn't be nearly so many fellows who like to fish all day if it was hard."

Queenie got caught up in Deborah's excitement and let out a few excited woofs as she trotted along the shoreline. Deborah felt a laugh bubbling up from deep inside her. Noah had called her his *sweetie,* the way he had when they'd been courting. The exhilaration of his praise and her first successful cast was a heady sensation.

"Look at that," he whispered, pointing toward the lake. "You've got a nibble already! Crank your reel handle to set the line, like I showed you."

Deborah's heart was pounding as she heard the *click* of the mechanism.

"Now, wait for the bobber to go under—" Noah positioned himself behind her, placing his hands over hers. "There it goes! Now let's jerk back real hard to set the hook!"

As she allowed Noah to assist her, Deborah didn't know if she was more thrilled about the tug of a fish on her line or about how close Noah was standing to her. It felt so good to have his arms around her again. "And now I reel it in?"

"*Jah,* with a slow, steady cranking," he murmured near her ear. "Oh, look at the way your rod's curving down! I think you've got a big one—but don't lose him by dropping your rod or getting in a hurry. Let him wear himself out."

"He's really strong," Deborah breathed. She gripped the handle of the bending rod, watching her line zig and zag in the water as she slowly cranked the reel handle.

"Don't lose him, now. Let me grab the net."

Deborah held her breath as she reeled the fish closer. When she caught sight of it beneath the water's surface, her eyes widened and she hung on even tighter.

Noah planted his feet firmly on the edge of the lake, extending the net toward her incoming fish. "Steady now. Bring him on up here . . . *jah, baby!* Would you look at this nice trout!" he cried as he scooped it out of the water. "This is the biggest fish we've seen since we got here!"

Deborah gaped at the shiny trout as it writhed in Noah's net. "So *now* what do we do?"

"I'll put him on a stringer, and we'll keep him in the lake until we're ready to quit," he replied. "Stick your rod in your tunnel, like mine is. Then hang on to the net."

Deborah hurried to help Noah, tickled at the fish's size and how she had to grasp the net's handle with both hands to keep from dropping it. Noah grabbed the fish's head and slipped the metal end of the stringer through its gill. Then he gripped the hook to twist it out of the trout's silver lip. Deborah wasn't going to say so, but she was glad Noah was doing this part. The fish was watching them with its lidless eye, still flipping and flapping as Noah lifted it out of the net. Queenie came over to sniff at it and shook her head when the trout flipped water in her face.

"He surely must weigh four or five pounds, and lake trout makes mighty fine eating," Noah remarked as he lowered the fish into the water. He stabbed the spike end of the stringer deep into the mud and swished his hands in the water. When he stood up, he was grinning like a little kid. "Wow! Was that fun, or what?"

"*Jah,* it was," Deborah replied. Her breath caught when Noah grabbed her hands and squeezed them. "It's really nice of you to be so patient with me. I—I haven't been any too cheerful lately, and I know some of the stuff I've said hasn't been what you wanted to hear."

Noah's dark eyes softened as he gazed at her. "You must've been scared out of your mind when those guys . . . well, I hope you can put all that fear behind you now, Deborah. You're safe here at Promise Lodge. No matter how they feel about your situation in Coldstream, we all want you here with us."

Deborah's heartbeat stilled. Clearly, Noah now believed

she'd done all she could on the night of the fire, for he wasn't a fellow to waste words. The idea of being safe among the folks here—three hours away from the ordeal and humiliation she'd endured last week—made her feel much better.

"*Denki* for saying that, Noah," she murmured. "It means a lot, coming from you."

He squeezed her hands once more before he eased away. "Looky there—my bobber's moving. You must be my *gut* luck charm, girl."

She watched, enthralled, as Noah set his hook and steadily cranked the reel handle. The clench of his firm jaw . . . the steady in and out of his breathing as he concentrated . . . the flexing of his muscular arms and hands, combined with his fresh, familiar scent hooked Deborah as surely as Noah had latched on to a fish. It felt so good to be near him again, to be in harmony and having fun with him.

"Grab the net and bring it in for me," he said. "Brace your feet real steady. That's the way."

Deborah scooped the net beneath the fish, yelping as it flipped water on her.

"A bass this time," Noah remarked as he set down his reel to help her. "We'll need to restock the lake before a lot of other folks get here, to be sure we've got fish in the future. I think we're catching such nice ones because nobody's fished here for a year or two. *Gut* job with the net. You're a natural at this."

Deborah felt herself glowing. As the evening settled around them and the cicadas began to sing, she felt content to keep casting and watching the bobber, even when she didn't catch a fish each time. While she hoped to let go of her fear and move on, new thoughts were surfacing as she and Noah stood beside each other.

"Maybe you were right about Dat trying to protect me," she murmured. "It didn't seem that way when he was in such a huff, pointing toward the road. But I got *him* into hot water by getting mixed up in this business with the bishop's son, too. I hadn't thought about how my actions that night would affect anybody else."

"You were too busy defending yourself to consider the consequences, by the sound of it. And you had no way of knowing what Isaac might do," Noah pointed out. "He's always been a daredevil. And he'd been drinking."

Deborah considered this as she thought about what might be going on back home. "It's still my word against Isaac's— and with Dat not giving my name, it doesn't leave the sheriff much to go on," she remarked. "I was the only witness likely to tell about what really went on at the Bender barn, after all."

Noah checked the worm on his hook and cast out again. Then he studied her face. "Tell me true now, Deborah," he said softly. "I know how embarrassing this is, but—but if Isaac or Kerry . . . if either one forced you to—I'm going to Coldstream to be sure Sheriff Renfro nails them for—"

Deborah's eyes stung as she grabbed his arm. Noah was trembling with the intensity of his desire to protect her. "Really and truly," she insisted, "they were both hinting at that, but the beer was making them clumsy—and mad at me, when I slapped them and hollered at them."

Noah exhaled. "All right, then. Sorry. I had to ask."

"And now it's God's job to see that justice is done," Deborah reminded him with a somber smile. "If you go back and stir up more trouble, it won't make Dat or the bishop any too happy."

"*Jah,* you're probably right. It's not like I was anywhere near the Bender barn to vouch for what happened that night."

Even as Noah's shift in attitude gratified her, Deborah allowed another silence to settle around them. She cast her line again, thinking carefully about what she wanted to say. If Noah believed her now—trusted her again—did she dare bring up the subject of their broken engagement? Was it too soon to speak of courtship, now that Noah seemed to be in such an agreeable mood?

Deborah gripped her rod, hoping the words sounded right. "I can understand why you might not want to marry such a troublemaker, after all I've stirred up back home," she whispered. "But I *am* sincerely sorry I doubted you and—and tore us apart, Noah."

He focused on her for a long moment in the dusk. "It's high time I forgave you for that, too," he at last replied. "I accept your apology, Deborah and I—I forgive you for ending our engagement."

She swallowed hard, her throat so tight she couldn't speak. Both of them faced the lake, watching bobbers that were becoming harder to see as darkness fell. Deborah realized she'd just received what she'd come to Promise Lodge for, even though their relationship had not yet been fully mended. Noah's forgiveness was a big step forward, however, and she was grateful for it.

"After thinking about *why* you broke up with me," Noah continued in a tight voice, "I'm not going to court you again, Deborah. I'm not making you any promises until I'm sure I can give you a *gut*, steady life—if not here in this new colony, then someplace else. Maybe I *wasn't* ready to be a husband when you walked away from me. No sense in making the same mistake twice."

"I really love it here," Deborah murmured as fear flooded her heart. Had she received Noah's forgiveness only to remain without him? It startled her to hear that Noah might consider breaking away from his family in search of employment that would support a wife and kids. Amish men generally settled near their kin, knowing they could depend upon help when they needed it—just as they would be close by in case their parents or other relatives needed them.

Deborah nipped her lip, praying this new concern wouldn't

make her blurt out unfounded assumptions. Noah seemed calm, however, so Deborah offered what she hoped would be a helpful observation. "I suspect you're not crazy about Promise Lodge because it wasn't *your* idea to come here," she said. "I can see why you'd feel uprooted—unhappy— because you and Roman had figured on staying at your family's farm for the rest of your lives. You've left everything and everyone you've ever known on your *mamm*'s say-so. Not many guys would be wild about doing that," she added with a wry smile.

Noah chuckled softly. "You might be on to something there. I'll think on it."

After they reeled in two more trout, Noah carried their stringer of flopping, wet fish toward the lodge while Deborah handled the rods and the tackle box. Lightning bugs rose from the grass ahead of them, twinkling in the night. As she, Noah, and Queenie headed across the yard to where the lit-up kitchen windows welcomed them, she savored the sheer contentment she'd been missing for so long. She'd really enjoyed learning how to catch fish. And Noah's forgiveness was a welcome gift.

They got a round of applause when they showed their catch to Preacher Amos and Noah's *mamm* and aunts, who sat on the wide lodge porch sipping lemonade. After she helped Noah clean their catch, Deborah entered her little cabin to prepare for bed.

It had been quite a day. When she had prayed and slipped between the sheets, Deborah drifted off to sleep with a smile on her face. Surely God was in this place called Promise Lodge, and surely He was watching over them all.

Chapter Thirteen

Rosetta smoothed the quilt she and Christine had just put on the double bed they'd made up. As she looked around the cabin they'd furnished with pieces that had once been in the Hershbergers' home, she smiled. "These cottages are looking really homey, now that they've been painted and repaired," she said. "How many more do you suppose we should fix up? New residents will probably bring their own furniture, and they might as well use it."

"We'll also have families who come to look us over before they decide whether to move," Christine pointed out. "For now, I think the four cabins we've set up are enough. We have a couple of extra beds in the cellar, if we need to furnish any others."

"We already have four new families ready to build homes. That's so exciting! I suspect they'll start showing up soon, too." Rosetta sighed contentedly as she glanced out the front window. "Won't be long until Deborah and Noah have the rest of the cabins painted and repaired. Maybe they'll tackle some rooms in the lodge after that."

"They seem to be a couple again," Christine remarked with a chuckle. "My girls were hoping Deborah could help them and Mattie out in the gardens more, but Preacher Amos made the right decision. She's a better, faster painter than any of the rest of us."

"*Jah,* I've not seen any speckles of paint on the floor-boards—which is more than I can say when I use a roller." When Queenie began barking excitedly, Rosetta glanced out the window. Preacher Amos was riding through the arched entryway sign on horseback, slowing his mount from a graceful canter to a walk as he approached the lodge. "By the looks of Amos's smile, he found more letters in the post office box. Shall we see who they're from? It's time to finish getting dinner ready anyway."

The grass felt cool to Rosetta's bare feet as she and Christine stepped outside. The old maple trees provided welcome shade on this sunny June day, while out in the sunshine the honeysuckle and trumpet vines whispered in the breeze and spread their sweet perfume. When Amos waved at them, his hand held several envelopes.

"See you inside after I unsaddle Mabel!" he called out. "You've got a letter from Coldstream, Rosetta."

Christine smiled and linked her arm through Rosetta's. "It'll be *gut* to hear from an old friend—maybe someone who misses us," she said. "Meanwhile, Amos will be looking for coffee and a snack of some sort. How about if I slice that cinnamon swirl bread you made and put out the cookies we'll have for dessert while you put the meat loaf and veggies in the oven?"

"I'll boil water to brew iced tea, too," Rosetta replied as they entered the lodge. "Mattie and the girls will be hot after working in the sun all morning."

As she and her sister began preparing the noon meal, Rosetta hummed happily. This kitchen was feeling like home to her, and she looked forward to the day when new residents would be sitting at the dining room tables, getting acquainted and talking about the homes they were building—or the apartments the single ladies wanted to rent—and the businesses they would establish. The back door creaked as Amos came in and removed his straw hat.

"Four new letters today, along with a flyer from the mercantile in Forest Grove. It's a *gut* thing that place carries a wide variety of groceries and hardware, since the business district of Promise isn't much more than the post office and a gas station," he remarked as he pulled out his chair at the table.

After Rosetta put the meat loaf and vegetables in the oven, she grinned with anticipation as she joined Amos in the dining room. "Oh, I've looked forward to hearing from folks in—"

When she saw the return address, her eyebrows rose. "I wasn't figuring to hear from Bertha Chupp, though. She never had much to say to me, until after the folks died. Told me I should be baking pies to entice men to date me—as though I had dozens of single fellows my age to choose from."

Rosetta tore the envelope open and removed two folded sheets of pale blue stationery, which were covered from edge to edge with lines of tight, precise handwriting. She scowled as she skimmed the first page. "My word, this letter's so full of vinegar, I could pour oil on it and dress a salad," she blurted. "Not that anyone would find it fit to eat."

Christine looked up as she set a small plate of cinnamon bread in front of Preacher Amos. "Why would Bertha waste time and paper being snippy—and to *you*, Rosetta? What'd she say?"

Inhaling deeply to settle her nerves, Rosetta debated about whether to read such a mean-spirited message aloud—except it made reference to all of the Bender sisters, not just to her. "All right, here goes," she said in a strained voice. "'Rosetta, I held my tongue when I heard you and your kin were pulling out of Coldstream, but someone needs to point out the error of your ways and set you straight about a few things. How dare you sell your farms to English rather than giving your Amish neighbors a chance at your land? Now the church district has big holes in it—'"

"Well, there's her first mistake," Christine interrupted tersely. "We *asked* if they wanted the land—"

"But the ones I spoke with couldn't come up with enough cash anytime soon," Preacher Amos chimed in as he stirred sugar into his coffee. "Some of the folks in Coldstream are like family to me, but I refused to take a big loss on my property just so somebody local could buy it."

"Same here," Christine said. "Mattie and I were down-right offended at a couple of offers the men living on either side of us made. They thought that because we're widows, we wouldn't know they were undercutting the value of our land and houses."

"Oh, it gets better," Rosetta muttered before she continued reading. "'Not only does your selling out cast a bad light on Obadiah's leadership of the Coldstream church district, but you and your sisters have gone far astray by presuming to start up a new colony without asking his permission—and without having the leadership of a bishop who will guide you in laying the proper groundwork to form a congregation of God's true church.'"

"Never mind that you've got an ordained preacher taking charge of that part," Amos remarked.

"'Not only was Mattie out of line, enticing Preacher Amos to leave the district that God chose him to help lead,'" Rosetta continued in a rising voice, "'but you women have behaved in a sinfully prideful way, taking up your own pursuits rather than marrying, as the Bible says the weaker sex is meant to do.'"

Christine frowned. "*Jah,* I'm getting weaker by the moment listening to Bertha's claptrap, too. What brought this on, I wonder?" she asked as she got the dinner plates from the cupboard. "She rarely strung two sentences together around me while I was a married woman tending my family, but *now*. Mercy."

Preacher Amos sighed as he dunked a cookie into his coffee. "Bertha has incorrectly implied that Mattie lured me away from Coldstream with improper words or behavior—and I resent such a slur on Mattie's character. I made my own decision to leave, for many reasons."

Rosetta, who'd been skimming the remainder of the letter, nearly ripped it into shreds—except she felt Amos and Christine should bear witness to the unsettling words Bertha Chupp had closed with. "'I find it equally disturbing that Deborah Peterscheim has run off rather than facing the consequences of her wayward, improper behavior the night of the fire at your parents' place. I suspect she's hiding herself amongst you liberal, misguided folks, heedless of the havoc she's wreaked upon this town and of the shame she's heaped upon her family.'"

Christine's eyebrows rose. "Let's not forget that Bertha's son played a part in—"

"Oh, she's getting to him," Rosetta said, shaking her head sadly. "'Isaac tells me Deborah broke up with Noah Schwartz a while back, so I also suspect she's worming her way into his good graces again, under false pretenses. My son was appalled when Deborah came around to see him on the sly while she was still engaged to Noah, so here's a word to the wise: she's trouble, that one. Noah—and the rest of you—should take her lies with a grain of salt. Send her home, where she belongs. Deborah should confess her sins before the congregation she has wronged and face the discipline she deserves.'"

A little sob made Rosetta turn toward the doorway. Her heart shriveled. How long had Deborah and Noah been standing in the kitchen? "Oh, kids, I'm so sorry you heard Bertha Chupp's vicious letter," she said ruefully. "Don't think for a second that any of us believe what she's saying."

"But why would Isaac accuse me of sneaking over to see him?" Deborah was struggling to be strong but her voice wavered. "What if he's been telling other lies to folks around Coldstream—maybe that *I* was to blame for the fire and—and that I made that phone call after I set it, to mislead the sheriff? That's how twisted Isaac's thinking gets sometimes."

Rosetta's mouth dropped open. "No one would believe such lies about you, Deborah! Nor do we need to waste any more time considering the falsehoods Bertha's written about the rest of us." She hurried into the kitchen to throw the letter in the trash.

"Don't think for a minute I believe any of Bertha's gossip, either," Noah insisted as he grabbed Deborah's hand. "I'm going back to Coldstream to set those people straight. If the bishop's wife is writing that sort of letter to Rosetta, I don't even want to think about what she's telling everyone there about us."

"I'm calling the Chupps right now!" Christine said as she strode toward the phone in the pantry. "If anyone deserves discipline and needs to confess, it's the bishop's wife—"

"Wait just a moment, folks." Preacher Amos rose from his seat and gazed at them all with his deep brown eyes. "Let's not forget how the Bible warns against lashing out in the heat of the moment. Deborah's *dat* and I have both preached on that passage from the book of James—the one that says we should be quick to hear, but slow to speak and slow to anger because the wrath of man doesn't work toward the righteousness of God."

Rosetta took a deep breath. Everyone else in the room got quiet, considering what Amos had said about reacting in anger. "Truth be told, I can't imagine Bertha spending the time or effort to write me such a letter," she murmured. "It does make me wonder what sort of talk is going around Coldstream, however."

"I was thinking the same thing," Amos replied. "Do any

of you know what her handwriting looks like? Before now, we've not had the occasion to receive letters from anyone in Coldstream."

Rosetta shook her head, wondering what Amos might be thinking. Christine and Deborah indicated that they'd never seen Bertha's writing, either. It wasn't as though the bishop's wife had been one to share recipes or anything else she would have written.

"I'll call Obadiah," Amos said as he walked across the kitchen. "The bishop needs to know about this letter and to ask his wife some questions about it."

Preacher Amos tapped in the number on the wall phone and waited while the Chupps' message machine played its recording. "Obadiah, this is Amos Troyer. We've received a disturbing, rather malicious letter from Bertha, which contains a number of false accusations against Deborah Peterscheim and all of us who sold our property in Coldstream," he said calmly. "If you or your wife have bones to pick with any of us, you're welcome to come to Promise Lodge and discuss these issues with us face-to-face. I felt you should know about this letter because I fear for your wife's soul if she's spreading the same sort of gossip about us around Coldstream. We wish you God's blessings and His peace."

The preacher hung up. "How did I do? It's not our place to make threats, but I will *not* tolerate any further interference from the Chupp family."

Deborah nodded. "If we let Bertha's words rile us up, we're not behaving any better than she did when she wrote them."

"You're right," Rosetta agreed as she went to the silverware drawer. "Promise Lodge is a place of peace. We have no use for such nasty gossip as Bertha's—which convinces me yet again that we did the right thing when we left Coldstream. Let's get on with our day, shall we?"

When Mattie, Laura, Phoebe, and Roman came in for

dinner, Rosetta mentioned the letter she'd received, but she didn't show it to them. What good would come of repeating Bertha Chupp's inflammatory remarks?

"Of all the families we know in Coldstream, why do the Chupps always seem to rub us the wrong way?" Laura asked. She poured glasses of iced tea for everyone before drinking one herself to cool off.

"I'm glad we've got better things to do than responding to Bertha's gossip—and pleased that you called Obadiah to that effect, Amos," Mattie said. When she'd set the platter of meat loaf on the table, they all took their seats. "I'm thankful for the way the rain has made our garden plots grow these past few days, and grateful for *gut*, honest work—and for the family and friends who share these things with me."

"Amen to that," Preacher Amos said. "As we thank God for this wonderful food, let's also put in a word for the Chupps. They're in need of prayer and healing, I believe."

Rosetta bowed her head. *Lord, we are grateful for Your many gifts and for this food. Give us the grace to continue on this path You've led us to at Promise Lodge. I ask Your special blessings on Deborah—and Noah—as she deals with another hurtful message from folks in Coldstream. Deliver us from evil. Thy will be done.*

After everyone ate and the kitchen was cleaned up, the others went back to their tasks in the cabins, the barn, and the garden plots. Rosetta's soap had hardened in a big rectangular pan in the mudroom, so she sharpened a knife and began to cut along the lines she'd scored into the soap's surface after she'd poured it. The fragrance of the mint and lavender oils she'd used lifted her spirits. Even after listening to the letters from more people who planned to come to Promise Lodge, however, she couldn't get Bertha Chupp's words out of her mind. Something told her to retrieve the letter from the wastebasket.

Rosetta wiped some crumbs and splotches off the pale blue paper. The handwriting resembled that of many women she knew, but she still wondered why the bishop's wife had written her such an unsettling letter.

She stuck the folded sheets into the drawer with her soap-making supplies. *Amos and Mattie have it right. Our work and our dreams bless us here, and we shouldn't sink to Bertha's level by answering in a spirit of spitefulness. Promise Lodge is a place of peace. Here, we plan for happiness.*

Rosetta smiled. As she stood each rectangular bar of soap on end on an old window screen to dry completely, she imagined the new friends who would soon be coming to the lodge. She thought about getting better acquainted with Truman Wickey, too, and seeing him again sometime soon. It was best to focus forward and to leave the past behind.

Chapter Fourteen

The next morning, Noah sat between Preacher Amos and Roman on the wagon seat, driving to Forest Grove to fetch lumber and other supplies they needed to build the produce stand. As Buck clip-clopped along the county highway, the breeze made the silver maple leaves shimmer in the morning sunlight. Queenie sat behind them in the wagon, her tongue lolling from her mouth as she watched for squirrels and other animals in the woods. He couldn't recall such a picture-perfect day—at least not since he'd moved to Promise. Or was he feeling better about life, in general, because he'd made his peace with Deborah?

"Noah, it's *gut* to see you smile," Amos remarked. "I was wondering if you'd forgotten how."

Noah's lips twitched. "Deborah and I have talked things through. I told her I'd not be courting her again—not just yet, anyway. But we've mended our fences."

"Ah, forgiveness," the older man said lightly. "The gift that blesses the giver as much as the receiver. Do I have that figured right?"

"*Jah.* You tried to tell me and I finally got it," Noah replied. He tugged on the leather lines to slow the Belgian for an upcoming curve.

"But you're not going to court her? What's the deal with that?" Roman quizzed him. "Once upon a time, the two of you were all but married, planning a home and a family—"

"And that's where it gets sticky," Noah interrupted urgently. "How am I to afford a house now? And the land to build it on? Back in Coldstream, Preacher Eli was taking me on welding jobs and I was building up a trade and a reputation. I don't see that happening out here in the middle of nowhere."

Preacher Amos stroked his silver-shot beard as he considered this. "You and your bride could start out in one of the cabins," he suggested. "The tradition of living with one set of parents or the other for a year probably isn't practical for you, but a cabin would keep you close to us while you save up to build your own house."

Noah sighed. "Deborah and I agreed long ago that we didn't want to live with her family, because the quarters are pretty close in the Peterscheim house," he said. "And now that Mamm doesn't have plans to build another house—well, I've always wanted to provide Deborah a home of her own, anyway. But I can't see how I'll ever earn enough to do that if I stay in Promise."

Roman and Amos exchanged a startled look before focusing on Noah. "Where would you go, then?" his brother demanded. "Back to Coldstream?"

"Maybe you've not been in this area long enough to see the possibilities," Preacher Amos insisted. "We've all been awfully busy since the move, and we haven't really found our way around yet. But I'll tell you this, son," he continued earnestly. "Your *mamm* would be deeply hurt if you went somewhere else to start your family. She'd be lost without you, whether she'd say so or not. She's looking forward to grandkids, too."

"*Jah,* I've heard about that," Noah murmured.

"I have to admit that you've come in handy for rebuilding

some of the dairy equipment and welding the broken water pipes since we've moved," Roman remarked with a chuckle. "There was a time, when we were kids, that I wondered if you'd ever be worth the trouble you caused me, but I've changed my tune. You're a *gut* man to have around, little brother."

Noah let out an exasperated sigh. "But living rent-free and taking my pay in meals won't buy me the home place I'm hoping for," he told his brother. "I need steady work—and soon—or I'll be as old as Amos before I can marry Deborah."

"Hey! Don't go calling me *old,*" the preacher teased, elbowing Noah good-naturedly. "I see your point, though. It was the same for me when I was starting out in carpentry work. A *lot* of fellows could swing a hammer in Coldstream back then, and I had to make my own opportunities . . . branch out into the surrounding towns and get my name and my work known amongst the English."

The preacher was only a few years older than his mother, but Noah still had trouble imagining Amos Troyer as a young man with girlfriends—and a full head of hair. "So, you were dating Mamm back then, right?" he asked, partly to steer the conversation away from himself. "What happened that you didn't marry her?"

A faraway look overtook Amos's weathered face. "It wasn't for lack of *gut* intentions, because I was crazy about Mattie all through school," he murmured. "But your grandfather, Walt Bender, had different aspirations for his eldest daughter, and Marvin Schwartz had already bought the place just down the road from them."

"So Dat won out because he had property?" Roman asked. "What did *Mamm* say about *that*?"

"Not much," Amos replied with a short laugh. "She was an obedient daughter, and her respect for her parents' wishes overrode her feelings for me—which might explain why she's not much for *obeying* any other man these days. Got a mind of her own, Mattie does."

Noah steered the Belgian quickly through the intersection and onto the shoulder of the state highway so the cars behind them could get around the wagon. "See what I'm saying?" he protested. "When we lived in Coldstream, I was thinking to build Deborah a house near the fence between us and the Hershberger farm, so I'd still be on the home place. But now . . ." He let his sentence trail. It did no good to keep complaining about the recent changes in his life.

"Don't give up on it. Keep believing God's got a plan for you, Noah, and your job is to find it and follow it," Amos mused aloud. "Takes some of us two or three tries before we get it right. Nothing would make me happier than to see you and Deborah settling into a place at Promise Lodge. I'll see what I can do to help that happen."

Noah's eyebrows rose. Preacher Amos sounded ready to do more than pray for the home Noah wanted so badly. In his mind he could see Deborah on the front porch of a tidy white house, and he could envision the arched rose trellis she'd always wanted, too. When they'd left for Forest Grove, Deborah had already been up on the ladder painting the inside of cabin eight. She was such a hard worker, kind and gentle—and truth be told, he'd never stopped loving her, even after she'd jilted him.

But he'd decided not to say any more to Deborah about marriage until he could give her the life she deserved. He'd disappointed her during their first courtship, and he hoped never to endure such gut-wrenching heartache again.

Noah steered Buck into the parking lot of the Forest Grove Mercantile. Maybe he could find a simple gift in the store that would put a smile on her pretty face. . . .

* * *

Deborah looked around the cabin's main room, gratified at what a huge improvement a coat of paint made. Mattie and the Hershberger girls were planting peaches-and-cream sweet corn in the farthest plowed plot today, while Christine and Rosetta worked upstairs in the lodge sewing simple curtains for the rooms that would soon become apartments. They had all invited her to help them, but Deborah found a certain satisfaction in rolling paint on the walls, knowing the cabins would be ready for their incoming residents sooner.

Every now and again, a little solitude was soothing. It gave Deborah time to review her recent fishing date with Noah . . . to think about how his attitude had improved now that they were friends again. *She* felt better, too—hopeful, now that they'd salvaged their relationship.

Deborah stopped the rhythmic *swish-swish-swish* of her roller to listen. Had she heard voices? It was too early for the men to be back from their shopping expedition.

She listened again, her roller poised on the partially painted wall. Nothing.

As Deborah spun her roller in the tray to fill it with beige paint, however, a movement outside caught her eye. She froze on the ladder, gripping the roller handle, when one male face and then another appeared at the cabin's open front window.

"Well, well, well," said Isaac Chupp in a sly voice. "Corbett and I watched the men drive off earlier—and the other gals are all real busy right now, working in that old lodge building or waaay out beyond the lake. Is this a *gut* time to talk, Deborah?"

Why didn't Queenie bark? How did Isaac and Kerry know where to—

"Figured we'd find you here," Kerry remarked with a smug laugh. He swung open the screen door and stepped inside, looking taller and stronger than Deborah recalled from her previous encounter with him. "Your old man said he didn't know where you'd run off to, but we didn't buy that for a second."

"*Jah,* we figured you'd come here to Promise to hang out—or hide—where all these other do-gooders would believe whatever you told them and feel sorry for you," Isaac continued coldly. He and Kerry stopped a couple of yards away from her ladder, crossing their arms as they glared at her. "You're really stupid, you know? Maybe too stupid to live."

Deborah's body forgot how to function. And where could she go, even if her legs would move? The boys stood between her and the cabin's only door. Isaac's eyes narrowed as he sneered at her. A malevolent smile lit Kerry's pale, freckled face beneath his shaggy carrot-colored hair.

"Guess you know we've got a score to settle—not only for putting our names in the paper so the sheriff came calling," Isaac said in a hard-edged voice, "but also because you made Kerry wreck his car—"

"None of that was my doing," Deborah rasped. She gripped the ladder, resting her knees against its wooden frame so the boys wouldn't see how badly they were shaking. "You were both really drunk—"

"Shut up! I'm not finished!" Isaac barked. He ran his hand through his blunt-cut blond hair, appearing eager to grab hold of her again. "I *told* you not to breathe a word about finding us in the barn, but no! You had to blab to your *dat* and get the law involved, so now *my* old man's all hot and bothered—"

"And fixing my car would cost more than it's worth," Kerry interrupted in a rising voice. "So now I've got no wheels, all because you wouldn't give me a little payback for taking you home."

"So we'll take what you owe us right now, while there's nobody else around to get in our way." Isaac looked her up and down as though he could see through her paint-splotched dress. "After all these years of wanting a sample of Schwartz's little honey, I'm about to get one. Then Corbett will take his turn. Wonder how Noah will feel about you *then*?"

The hairs on the back of Deborah's neck stood up and every nerve in her body vibrated. *Please, dear Jesus, You've got to help me. Without You, I don't stand a chance.*

"Mostly, though, we want to make sure you don't get any ideas about going back to Coldstream," Isaac said with a nasty laugh. "As long as you're not there shooting off your mouth, Sheriff Renfro has no *proof* of who was in that barn—except for you, of course. I told him to listen to the call the nine-one-one dispatcher took. Told him that was *your* voice on the recording, after you got so smashed while you were sneaking a beer in the barn that you knocked over a lantern," he continued. "Then you felt guilty about starting the fire, so you called them and took off—because you knew you'd be in big trouble with your *dat* if he found out you'd been drinking."

Oh, this is worse than you ever imagined.

Deborah sucked in air, hoping to steady her nerves—trying to sort the truth from the lies Isaac could spin so effortlessly. Had he really given her name to Sheriff Renfro? Would he and Kerry take their revenge, or were they just hazing her? Deborah didn't want to find out. She sensed that the hand-shaped bruise on her neck had been a minor injury compared to the pain they could inflict as a team.

When Isaac stepped toward her, Deborah hurled the paint-saturated roller at him. As it hit him in the face, he and Kerry hollered obscenities and rushed toward her. With every last ounce of strength she had, Deborah jumped from the ladder and swung it at them. The paint tray flew at Kerry, splattering him, while the ladder struck Isaac on the shoulder. She didn't wait around to see how either of them reacted.

Deborah bolted out the screen door, hollering at the top

of her lungs. "Rosetta! Christine!" she cried. She ran toward the lodge, hoping the women heard her through the open windows. "Help me! Isaac's here!"

As she sprinted up the stairs to the lodge porch, Deborah heard the boys' rapid footfalls behind her but she didn't turn around. Spotting the wire basket of eggs Rosetta had gathered earlier, she picked it up.

"Rosetta!" she yelled through the screen door. "Christine, come quick!"

Footsteps thundered on the lobby's wooden staircase as Deborah turned toward Isaac and Kerry. Both boys were splattered with beige paint, still intent on getting their revenge. Deborah began pelting them with eggs, aiming toward their faces. "Don't you touch me!" she cried.

From the direction of the garden, she heard the Hershberger girls and Mattie hollering as they came running toward the lodge. Behind her, Rosetta and Christine rushed out onto the porch.

"Don't think for a minute you're going to get away with this, Isaac Chupp!" Rosetta cried. She had grabbed the scrub bucket they'd used to clean the kitchen floor, and when she flung the dirty water in Isaac's face, he sputtered like an angry cat—but it slowed him down. Christine, who had carried a bolt of blue curtain fabric downstairs, pitched it fiercely at Kerry, making him stumble and slip in the wet grass. When the redhead saw that Mattie, Laura, and Phoebe were rushing at them with their rakes and hoes, he fled down the gravel lane toward the camp entrance.

Isaac seemed to think escape was the better option, as well. He was close on Kerry's heels—until the Hershberger girls launched their garden tools at his feet and tripped him.

"Don't let him get away!" Laura cried as he hit the ground.

"We can do this, girls! We've got him outnumbered," Phoebe said as she and Mattie rushed around to either side of him.

Rosetta hurried over before Isaac could get his feet under him and stuffed the plastic scrub bucket over his head. Deborah and Christine joined the fray, bringing along the partial bolt of fabric, which was coming unwound.

"Roll him up like a rug," Christine muttered. "I think we've got enough fabric here to do the job." She tossed the bolt to the ground and began to unwind it on one side of Isaac while her sisters and daughters pinned his flailing hands to his sides and grabbed his feet. When they had shoved him onto the loose end of the fabric, Deborah tucked the sturdy cotton around him and held it in place. She pushed him from the middle while the others rotated him at the ends, until Isaac's arms were bound close to his sides and he couldn't move his legs. With a look of great satisfaction, Christine removed the last of the fabric from the cardboard center of the bolt.

The bucket had rolled away, revealing Isaac's paint-splotched, egg-smeared face and his saturated blond hair—not to mention his startled expression. Out near the campground entrance, a car engine roared to life. Tires squealed on the blacktop.

"That jerk's driving off in my car!" Isaac protested, struggling frantically to loosen the fabric that was bound around him.

"Silly you, leaving the keys in it. So now you've missed your ride," Laura remarked. "Fair enough, considering how you tried to hurt Deborah *again*."

"Get those bungee cords Amos keeps on the basement shelf," Rosetta suggested. "We can secure the fabric with that and leave him here until the men come—"

"You *won't* get away with this," Isaac muttered as he kicked and wiggled.

"You don't have a leg to stand on, and we're all witnesses to what you've tried to do to Deborah today," Christine replied. She and her sisters and Deborah stood along either side of him, pinning him with their feet while Laura ran to fetch the cords. "So tell me this, Isaac. Was it you who set the barn afire at our place, too?"

Isaac's eyes widened in his eggy, paint-splotched face, but he quickly resumed his defensive attitude. "You've got no proof about any of—"

"Well, *God* knows," Rosetta interrupted him. "And Deborah witnessed your latest escapade, too."

"I'm calling your *dat*," Mattie said. "We'll see how eager the bishop is to come get you after I tell him what you've done." She wrapped an arm around Deborah's shoulders. "Come inside with me, dear. You've gone through enough for one day."

Deborah didn't realize how tightly wound she was until she nearly stumbled trying to keep up with Mattie's stride. Noah's *mamm* slowed her pace then, lowering her voice as they ascended the stairs to the porch. "You're shaking like a scared rabbit, and it's no wonder," she murmured soothingly. "Let's sit you down with a glass of lemonade while I make that phone call."

Deborah nodded mutely, allowing Mattie to steer her through the lobby and the dining hall toward a stool in the kitchen. She was still horrified at how Isaac and Kerry had sneaked up on her—how they had carefully checked everyone else's whereabouts before they'd trapped her. How long had they been at Promise Lodge? Had they made it all the way upstairs without Rosetta and Christine becoming aware of them? Or had they heard the women's voices and continued their search for *her*?

She didn't really want to know. Deborah sipped gratefully at the lemonade Mattie had poured, but she had no appetite for the brownie Noah's *mamm* put in front of her.

Mattie opened a kitchen drawer near the wall phone and pulled out a small directory. "*Gut* thing we brought this with us from Coldstream," she remarked as she thumbed through the pages. "Obadiah's most likely at the auction barn, so I'll call there first."

Resolutely, Mattie gazed at the phone, gathering her thoughts. Then she punched the number buttons and waited.

"*Jah*, Mose, this is Mattie Schwartz," she said brusquely. "Put your *dat* on . . . no, I won't give you a message for him. Get him *now*. Your little brother's in big trouble."

Deborah's eyes widened as she broke off a corner of the brownie. She'd *never* heard Mattie speak in such a sharp tone—and to a man, no less. Mattie squared her shoulders, gripping the receiver. "Obadiah, this is Mattie Schwartz and we've got Isaac here at Promise Lodge," she said. "He came after Deborah, to *hurt* her again—still up to no *gut,* after he set the Bender barn afire. If you're not here by one o'clock to fetch him, we're turning him over to the sheriff." Without waiting for the bishop's response, she hung up.

Deborah let out the breath she'd been holding. "So, what'll we do with Isaac?"

"Leave him right where he is," Mattie replied. "We'll let him sweat it out until his *dat* gets here—or the sheriff comes."

Mattie's shoulders relaxed. She reached for the pitcher of lemonade and another glass. "I hope to *gut*ness Amos and the boys come back before Obadiah arrives," she murmured. The stream of lemonade shimmied as she poured it. "We'll hear no end of the bishop's accusations and threats if it's just us women here. That's a sad thing to say about the leader of our home church district, but it's true."

Nodding, Deborah took a long drink of her lemonade. "I—I was never so glad to see you three sisters and the girls," she murmured. "What's scary is how Isaac and Kerry watched Amos and the boys leave, and then figured out where all the rest of you were, so they found me painting by myself."

"Which tells you how smart Isaac is, but in the wrong

ways. We fixed their wagons, though," Mattie replied with a shaky laugh. "I'm not quite sure how we did it, but the *Gut* Lord was working right alongside us or we'd never have caught Isaac."

Deborah breathed deeply, finally able to believe she was in no further danger today. "Let's take the lemonade and brownies out to the porch. The others have surely worked up a thirst."

Once the six of them had placed the wicker porch chairs around the table where the treats were, they were smiling again.

"This was a fine idea," Laura said as she took a second brownie. "We planted a lot of sweet corn this morning, and it was getting hot out there in the garden."

"Christine and I were making *gut* progress on our curtains, too," Rosetta said.

Deborah sighed as she gazed beyond the bushy trumpet vines toward the line of brown cabins. "I'd better mop up that paint I threw at Isaac and Kerry. It'll be drying on the floor—"

"Phoebe and I can help you with that," Laura insisted. "With some scrub brushes and elbow grease it'll look *gut* as new."

"You were mighty quick-thinking, to slow those boys down with your paint," Christine remarked with a nod. "It's a *gut* thing you hollered for us when you did, too. Out here where we don't know many folks yet—and where we're a distance from the Wickey house—we've got to watch out for each other."

"Hey!" Isaac hollered from his spot in the yard. "I have to *go*."

The women and girls glanced at him. "How's that, again?" Rosetta asked.

Isaac glowered. "I need to use the bathroom."

"Nice try, but we're not about to turn you loose," Phoebe said.

"*Jah,* don't let us stop you," Laura chimed in. "We won't watch, we promise."

When Isaac smarted off in protest, Rosetta stood up to glare at him, placing her hand on her hip. "High time you got a taste of humiliation, even if wet pants aren't *half* of what you and that redheaded friend of yours heaped on Deborah," she said sternly. "Consider this fair warning that we folks at Promise Lodge won't tolerate your lies and wrongdoing."

"Puh!" he replied, struggling against the fabric and the bungee cords. "When my *dat* sees what you've done to me, he'll—"

"He'll be getting a head-on dose of the truth about the trouble you've been stirring up," Mattie informed him in the same tone her sister had used. Then she looked out toward the road. "And here come Preacher Amos and my boys. I'm sure they'll want to hear every detail of your visit."

widened as he took in the ladder on its side, the overturned paint tray in the center of the room, the roller lying a few feet away—and beige paint flung in so many directions, it appeared that Deborah had thrown an entire gallon of it.

"Oh, my," Laura murmured. "I've never known you to be so messy, Deborah."

Noah smiled halfheartedly at his younger cousin's attempt to lighten the impact of the struggle that had taken place in this room. He put his arm around Deborah's shoulders. "I don't know how you kept away from them," he said earnestly, "but so help me, if those guys had gotten hold of you—"

Deborah placed her finger across his lips. Her green eyes were wide, as serene as a shady glen on a summer day. "It's behind us now," she said. "I prayed for Jesus to help me, and He came through. 'God is our refuge and strength, a very present help in trouble.'"

"Can't argue with that," Phoebe remarked. She went down on her knees to sop up the nearest pool of paint with an old towel.

Using steel wool pads, scrub brushes, and lots of water, the four of them made good progress at cleaning up the cabin. As they worked, Noah described the many items for sale at the mercantile. He was answering the girls' questions about other places to shop in Forest Grove when raised voices drifted through the screen door from the yard.

"I don't know what you people think you're doing, holding my boy hostage," Bishop Obadiah said hatefully. "And I will *not* tolerate any more phone messages from you in such a *tone,* Matilda Schwartz. You know better than to address me—"

"You should keep your son at home where he belongs," Preacher Amos countered. "We've seen what the Coldstream paper reported about the fire on the Bender place, and we've heard Deborah's account of what Isaac and his friends were

Chapter Fifteen

As Noah listened to the women's account of how Isaac and Kerry had slipped onto Promise Lodge property, catching Deborah unaware, his heart rose into his throat. It was all he could do not to kick at Isaac as the blond troublemaker lay in the yard wrapped in the wet blue fabric that was secured with three bungee cords. While the chain of events his cousins and aunts had described was almost comical—wrangling Isaac with a scrub bucket, their rakes, and a bolt of fabric—Noah was gravely aware of what would have happened had Deborah not gotten away from the intruders.

Preacher Amos was interrogating Isaac about the Bender barn fire, gazing sternly down at the bishop's son, so Noah joined Deborah, Laura, and Phoebe as they went to clean up the paint-splattered cabin. "All three of us fellows probably shouldn't leave the property at the same time anymore," he remarked. "At least until we're sure Chupp and Corbett won't be back."

"*Jah,* that might be wise," Phoebe replied. "The way we women were all spread out, busy at our projects, it's a wonder we got to Deborah in time to help her."

When Noah stepped inside the cabin, he stopped immediately so he wouldn't step in puddled paint. His eyes doing there that night—and now he's come all the way to Promise Lodge to get his revenge against her. It only confirms the wisdom of breaking away from your district, Obadiah. We pray each day that you'll come to see what's going on right under your nose and *deal* with it, rather than turning a blind eye."

"'Thou shalt not bear false witness against thy neighbor,'" Obadiah intoned as though he were warming up to give a blistering sermon.

"'He that hath ears to hear, let him hear,'" Amos shot back before the bishop could continue.

Noah and the girls stood in the cabin's doorway to watch the conversation, which was escalating into a shouting match. It went against their most basic Old Order beliefs for members to speak to each other this way, to vent frustration and anger rather than showing patience or giving the benefit of the doubt.

But nobody here doubts what has really happened, Noah thought as he felt his muscles tightening. "I've seen enough," he murmured. "It's probably best if you girls stay here until the Chupps have gone."

As Noah started across the yard, it appeared his aunts were agitated enough to break the silence that was expected of women in situations such as these.

"Wait just a moment," Rosetta insisted. "We're not finished talking about false witness until you see the letter your wife wrote, Bishop. I'll fetch it."

"Bertha wrote no such letter!" Obadiah cried as Rosetta hurried up the porch steps and into the lodge.

"Fine. You can tell us who did write it," Noah's mother chimed in. "Somebody from Coldstream wasted stationery and a considerable amount of time telling us how sinfully we've all behaved—"

"And it's a pack of lies," Aunt Christine put in. She crossed her arms, daring to hold Obadiah's angry gaze. "I have an idea who really wrote it, but I want to hear what *you* think, Bishop."

Noah suddenly realized that his mother and aunts had made a good point yesterday, about Bertha Chupp not being the type to write a lengthy letter to women she'd seldom spoken to. And when Isaac stopped squirming in the grass and protesting, Noah wondered if the bishop's son could've written the letter. It seemed unlikely, however, that Isaac could've composed such adult-sounding sentences. And why would he have written to Rosetta instead of to Deborah?

The screen door banged shut behind Rosetta as she returned to the gathering and handed the letter to Obadiah. "Is this your wife's handwriting?"

The bishop sneered as he snatched the pale blue pages from Rosetta's hand, but his eyes widened as he scanned the first page. His graying U-shaped beard fluttered in the breeze beneath his sweat-stained straw hat as he turned the page over and kept reading.

Noah saw a familiar white van parked down by the arched entry sign to the campground. He waved at Dick Mercer, who did a lot of driving for Plain folks around Coldstream, and then he went to stand beside Roman, near the women. Obadiah reached the end of the letter. His *mamm,* his aunts, and Amos remained silent, waiting for the bishop to speak first.

Obadiah cleared his throat. "While my wife and I have discussed our concerns about the way you people left our church district, Bertha would never write such a letter—"

"So who did?" Amos interrupted tersely. "Do you understand now why I called you about these accusations?"

"And why *I* called you to come fetch your son after he attacked Deborah today—*again?*" Noah's mother demanded.

"Maybe we should ask Isaac who wrote it." Aunt Christine stared sternly at the young man who lay on the ground wrapped in her curtain fabric. "Did you listen to your parents' conversations and write down what they've been saying about us—maybe adding in some drama to make us angry?"

"Have you practiced copying your mother's penmanship, to make us believe *she* wrote this letter?" Rosetta asked in a rising voice. "How often have you forged her signature or— maybe you started out when you were still in school with notes to Teacher Catherine, excusing yourself from class, eh?"

Isaac's eyes widened in his paint-splotched face, but he quickly resumed his usual defiant demeanor. "Why would I waste my time writing to an old *maidel* like you when it's Deborah who needs to be set straight about calling the—"

"And how did you know it was addressed to Rosetta?" Preacher Amos interrupted him. "No one has mentioned that—except you."

"Grab his feet," Noah muttered to his brother. "Let's get this show on the road."

Roman nodded. Without a word, the two of them scooped Isaac from the ground, placing their arms beneath his shoulders and his knees. As they walked awkwardly toward the van with Isaac slung between them, Obadiah and the others continued their strained conversation near the lodge. But the bishop had lost some of his bluster.

Isaac gawked at Noah and Roman in disbelief. "You can't believe I wrote that—you've *got* to unfasten these stupid bungee cords and—"

"We don't have to do any such thing," Roman said coolly.

"I figure if your *dat* unwraps you, you can answer his questions about what you were doing way out here in our colony—and maybe about what you really did on the night of the fire," Noah explained. "Don't mess with Deborah again, understand me? Next time we'll deal with you the old-fashioned way—an eye for an eye and a tooth for a tooth."

Isaac stopped his squirming. His eyes narrowed. "Do you really think I can leave her alone?" he asked in a throaty voice. "She's addictive, man. And now that I've had a taste, I'll find a way to come back for more . . . because she wants *me,* too."

"I don't *think* so," Noah retorted. "Not after you grabbed her neck and threw her into that ditch and then *left* her."

"That's what she told you?" Isaac asked with a derisive chuckle. "She's a sly one, Deborah is. She was putting on that innocent act for me, too—until I got into that ditch *with* her. *Jah,* I grabbed her neck, because I had to hang on for dear life."

The pictures running through Noah's mind made him stop breathing. He roughly shifted his grip on Isaac's shoulders as he and Roman lumbered closer to the van. "You are so full of—"

"You think so?" Chupp challenged. "She was crazy for me, Schwartz. Kissing me and calling out my name—but then, I doubt you'll ever be able to bring out that side of her, now that she's been with me." He laughed again, louder this time. "There's only one word for Deborah Peterscheim. *Wildcat.*"

"And the word for you is *dreamer*. Not to mention *liar* and *loser,*" Roman retorted, jostling Isaac as he got a better grip on his bound legs.

Noah focused on the remaining distance between them and the white van, too disturbed to say any more. He was glad to see Dick Mercer hurrying around to open the van's hatchback.

"Here's where the baggage goes," the driver remarked as he folded down the back seats. "No need to get paint on my upholstery. And I hope the Peterscheim girl is doing all right. I was . . . rather concerned when I drove her out here."

"Deborah's stronger than we ever suspected," Noah replied, hoping he sounded more confident than he felt. He shoved Isaac's feet out of the way and shut the hatchback with a loud *whump*. "Give her family our best, will you? Tell them she's making herself right at home in Promise."

"Happy to do that." Dick glanced back toward the lodge, and they saw that the bishop was striding their way, looking none too happy. "You fellows take care. I'm sure it'll be an interesting three hours back to Coldstream."

Obadiah glared at Noah and his brother, got into the front seat, and slammed the van door. As he headed back down the lane with Roman, Noah felt relieved that their uninvited guests were departing. What he'd seen and heard since he'd returned from the mercantile had given him plenty to think about.

"Do you suppose Obadiah's going to make Isaac ride all the way back to Coldstream with those bungee cords around him?" Roman asked as they started back toward the lodge.

"I really don't care," Noah replied. "But if Isaac comes back here, we're calling the sheriff."

He hoped his voice expressed all the disgust and irritation Isaac had inspired, rather than his fears about what the bishop's son claimed he'd done with Deborah. Try as he might, Noah couldn't rid his mind of the images . . . Deborah writhing in the ditch with Isaac, in passion rather than pain—

Are you sure Deborah's making herself at home in Promise? What if she's here only because she has nowhere else to go?

Noah caught sight of Deborah coming out of the cabin she and his cousins had been cleaning. He told himself not to believe what Isaac had insinuated about her. Surely he knew his former fiancée better than Chupp ever would. He'd accused her of being sweet on Isaac earlier, yet that purple handprint on her neck had imprinted her with lingering guilt even as it faded from her skin. Deborah had convinced him with her eyes and her words that she had no feelings—except negative, regretful ones—for the bishop's wayward son.

Hadn't she?

What if her dat *had it right? What if Preacher Eli sent Deborah away because he saw through her sob story— believed that she'd invited the trouble she'd gotten into?*

There's only one word for Deborah Peterscheim. Wildcat.

Noah exhaled loudly. Instead of going back to the lodge with Roman to talk to the others, he headed toward the shed. It felt like a fine time for some target practice.

Ping! Ping! Ping! Ping!

Deborah watched the cans fly off the top of the wood-pile in rapid succession, sensing she should leave Noah alone. It was just as well. Now that the Chupps had left, her legs and arms felt rubbery from the ordeal she'd endured. While she and Laura and Phoebe were helping with supper preparations, Deborah allowed them to carry the conversation—which was mostly about Isaac, Kerry, and the bishop of Coldstream. They were aghast at the sheer *nerve* of the two boys, and at how Obadiah Chupp had refused to acknowledge his son's role in the fire, his attack on Deborah, or as the author of that awful letter.

But Deborah's thoughts remained worrisome. What if she was a magnet for trouble? What if today's surprise visit was only the first, because the two boys didn't feel they'd gotten even with her? Considering all the sheds and animals, and the vegetables that were now growing in straight, green rows, it wouldn't take Isaac and Kerry long to destroy the progress her hardworking friends had made at their new home. Deborah had no trouble imagining Christine's cows and Rosetta's goats being frightened out of the barn—or left inside it after the boys set the hay on fire. Or they could drive a car through the garden plots and lay them waste within minutes, all to get back at *her.*

After everyone sat down to supper and prayed, Preacher Amos smiled at Mattie. "We got lumber today, and your produce stand will be built by the end of the week," he assured her. "Noah's going to make you a sign that'll hold slats, each of them with the name of a vegetable that's for sale on any given day."

"So we can change out the slats as the season moves from the early salad greens into tomatoes, sweet corn, and melons," Noah's mother said as she smiled at Phoebe and Laura. "Now that the gardens are growing so well and the stand's going to be built, I'm getting excited! One of our dreams is about to come true!"

The platter of hamburger patties smothered in fried onions made a second round, along with the bowls of macaroni salad, fruit gelatin, and green beans, but Deborah was still picking at her first serving. Across the table, Noah seemed determined not to make eye contact with her.

What did his change in attitude mean? He'd seemed so talkative—so protective—after he'd returned from town to find that Isaac and Kerry had come after her, yet now he was stewing in the same moody silence she'd witnessed when she'd first arrived at Promise Lodge. Deborah had admired Noah for taking action — for trundling Isaac out to the van while Amos and the others had continued bickering with the bishop.

But after that he'd gone sour. What had happened while he and Roman were carrying Isaac to Dick's van?

Most likely, you'll have to pry the story out of him. Deborah didn't have the energy for that this evening. And she didn't want to bother anyone else with her concerns—not when they were enjoying Christine's fresh apple pie, served with scoops of the ice cream Amos had surprised them with.

"You're awfully quiet, Deborah," Phoebe remarked as they began scraping the plates. The men had gone outside to tend the livestock, so the women had begun talking about tomorrow's meals and the work they needed to do in the garden and around the house.

Deborah shrugged. "I'm just wrung out from our uninvited guests," she said, hoping she sounded convincing. "Everything happened so fast, once Isaac and Kerry came into the cabin. I've had about all the drama I can handle for a while."

"We did have our share of excitement," Christine replied as she carried dirty dishes over to the sink. "But wasn't it wonderful, the way we all came together and handled our emergency without any assistance from the men? I don't feel nearly so helpless now, like I did after Willis died and left the girls and me to fend for ourselves."

"Glad to hear it, Sister," Mattie chimed in. "If nothing else, we've learned a lesson today. Until Isaac's been taken down a peg or two—caught by somebody who can make him behave responsibly—we need to watch out for each other. Especially now that he's got a car."

Deborah made an effort to chat, but when she turned in for the night, her concerns returned. Rosetta had suggested that she should start sleeping in one of the rooms in the lodge, but Deborah didn't want the others hovering over her, feeling sorry for her. Everyone had agreed that Queenie should sleep in the cabin with her, and Deborah felt safer with Noah's alert dog for company.

"But what if those boys come back?" she murmured as she gazed into the Border Collie's bright eyes. Deborah sat on the side of her bed, stroking the dog's soft face. "I know you'll bark if they show up, Queenie, but . . . it'll be my fault if they hurt you or ruin things around here to get back at *me*. That's not fair to these folks, after they've so generously taken me in."

Queenie nuzzled her hand and whimpered sympathetically. Then she curled up on the rag rug, her sigh suggesting that it was time to get some sleep.

Deborah extinguished the lamp and settled into bed. The night songs of crickets and frogs suggested that all was as it should be, that peace had returned to Promise Lodge.

Hearing is one thing, but believing is another, she thought as she tried to find a comfortable position. It took her a long time to fall asleep.

Chapter Sixteen

"I thought you and Noah worked everything out while you were fishing the other night," Rosetta remarked as she shook out a wet magenta dress. "But at breakfast you both looked like you'd been chewing on lemons again."

Deborah smiled in spite of how low she felt. She was helping Rosetta with the laundry while the other women were weeding the gardens. The steady *whack-whack-whack* of hammers out by the road announced the men's progress on the produce stand. "Who can tell what's on Noah's mind?" she murmured as she took a wet green shirt from the laundry basket. "I've given up trying to figure him out."

"Oh, don't throw in the towel!" Rosetta arranged the dress on a plastic hanger so the polyester-blend fabric would dry without wrinkling. Then she hung it on the short clothesline that spanned the end of the porch. "You two are meant for each other—truly—if only you'd keep talking instead of turning your backs when you get miffed about every little thing."

Deborah's eyebrows rose. The main clothesline Amos had rigged up for them extended between the end of the porch and the roof of the chicken house. She cranked its big pulley to send a row of shirts out of her way and bring a clear stretch of line within reach. As she hung the green shirt with wooden clothespins, she considered what Rosetta had said. "Is this the voice of experience I'm hearing? I never knew you to get crossways with anybody, let alone a man."

"That's because you're too young to recall my dating days, before I decided my purpose in life was to look after the folks," Rosetta replied pertly. "Before I got engaged to Tim, I had my eye on Denny Coblentz, and I dated Paul Lapp for a long while, too. But other girls caught their attention, and after Tim died and Mamm got hurt in a buggy accident, I knew where my time and efforts would be better spent."

Deborah took the opportunity to steer the conversation away from herself. She shook out a blue shirt until it snapped. "Were you ever sorry you didn't marry? I mean, not to be nosy or anything—"

"Once I realized that God was showing me the way He wanted me to go, I didn't second-guess Him." Rosetta smoothed a cape over another hanger and hung it beside the dress it matched, smiling as though she had a secret. "That doesn't mean I didn't *look* at men," she clarified. "But it all worked out the way it was supposed to. Now I've got a nice new life here—a dream of providing apartments for other unattached women—and the fellows I once fancied are married with families now."

"Not Truman Wickey."

Rosetta's laughter echoed under the porch roof. "*Jah,* he's a nice guy and he's *gut*-looking, for sure. But I don't see him changing from his Mennonite faith any more than I intend to leave the Old Order," she said with a shrug. "We can be friends, though—just like you and Noah can be friends even if you're not courting again. *Yet.*"

Deborah sighed. She should've guessed Rosetta wouldn't let her off the hook so easily. "I don't know what sort of bee's gotten under Noah's bonnet. But I'm thinking that, for the *gut* of everyone concerned, I should go stay with my cousins in Eulah. I'd thought about going there when Dat put me out, but—"

"And what brought *that* on?" Rosetta demanded. The wet dress she'd picked up puckered in her grip. "We're all *so* glad you're here, Deborah. And it's not only because Noah needs to be near you so he'll come to his senses."

"But what if Isaac and Kerry come back?" Deborah protested. "What if they sneak in to set the barn afire, or— or they drive their car through the produce plots? Just to get back at *me*?"

"Is *that* what you've been stewing over? 'The Lord is my light and my salvation! Whom then shall I fear?'" Rosetta shook the green dress again and hung it on a hanger. "The way Kerry tucked his tail and ran, I doubt we'll be seeing him again—especially because he took off in Isaac's car. And the bishop's boy didn't fare so well, either, did he?"

Recalling how Isaac had squirmed, bound in curtain fabric with paint and egg on his face, made Deborah smile. "But it's not fair to the rest of you that their kind of trouble has followed me here. I—"

"You're forgetting that Kerry lives in Eulah, *jah?*" Rosetta quizzed her. "And how long do you figure to keep moving from place to place? You know what they say—you can run but you can't hide."

Deborah sighed and reached for another wet shirt. Once Rosetta became convinced of something, there was no changing her mind.

"And mark my words," Rosetta continued with a shake of her head. "Somebody *will* catch up to Isaac. How can Obadiah deny his son was up to no *gut,* after having to come all the way out here to fetch him—and after we figured out that Isaac was the one who wrote that letter, imitating his *mamm*'s handwriting?"

Deborah picked up more clothespins. "I just thought—"

"Well, think on *this!*" Rosetta slung her arm around Deborah's shoulders, gesturing toward the vast expanse of yard and plowed plots and buildings. "Look at this glorious garden the Lord's brought us to! Surely God is in this place, and He's led you here to be with us—to be Noah's wife, I believe."

Deborah's breath caught as Rosetta held her gaze with eyes as dark and sweet as molasses. Joy shone on her attractive face. Conviction rang in her voice.

"Adam and Eve went running from the Garden, but we don't have to, Deborah," Rosetta continued earnestly. "*We've done nothing wrong.* Not you, not any of us—at least where Obadiah and his son are concerned. Will you please believe that for me?"

The clothes on the line rippled in the breeze. The sky, dotted with puffy white clouds, was as blue as a morning glory and the lush foliage did resemble a garden, even if some of the underbrush and weeds needed cutting. Out in the center of Rainbow Lake, a fish jumped up and splashed down.

"It *is* beautiful here," Deborah agreed. "And I really like being with you and your sisters and the girls."

"So if Noah's stewing, let him! You're a young woman of faith, Deborah," Rosetta insisted, "and you don't have to be laid low by any man's attitude. Sometime I hope you'll adjust that boy's attitude once and for all, but for now, what's your plan for happiness? Let's work it out while we finish with this laundry."

There it was again, Rosetta's refusal to be sucked into a bad mood. Deborah smiled, because the woman who gripped her by both shoulders wouldn't ease up until they'd concocted a course of action.

"What if we made a cake roll with what's left of the ice cream?" Deborah ventured.

Rosetta's face lit up. "We'll all enjoy that! What else?"

When she noticed another ripple on the water's surface, Deborah felt herself grinning. "What if we took a picnic supper to the lake? And after we eat, we can have a fishing contest?"

"Now you're talking!" Rosetta crowed. "I love to fish but I haven't had the chance to wet a line since I got to Promise. We can add tonight's catch to what you and Noah brought in the other night and have enough for a fish fry this weekend."

Deborah realized she was grinning back at Rosetta then, happy to have a plan—an evening to anticipate instead of a day to dread because she and Noah weren't seeing eye to eye.

No, it's Noah who's bent out of shape, and he's keeping the reason to himself. So what're you going to do about that?

"Shoo, now. I'll hang the rest of these clothes," Rosetta insisted. "Go ask the fellows to get the fishing gear ready— and the worms dug—for this evening." She chuckled then, taking the clothespins from Deborah's hands. "No need to tell them, of course, that we girls will catch more fish than they will."

When Queenie woofed and ran toward the lodge, Noah glanced up in time to catch a grin flickering on Deborah's face as she strode down the lane. She was carrying a plate and a picnic jug—a welcome sight, considering that he and Amos and Roman had spent the morning building the produce stand out in the hot sun. But her expression told him she was up to something. And with the preacher and his brother here, Noah would have no chance to ignore Deborah if she spoke to him—or asked what was bothering him. There was no getting around it: women picked at scabs.

If Deborah doesn't tell you to get over your mood, Amos

will, he reminded himself. *Be nice, even though you wonder if there's any truth to what Isaac said. . . .*

"Deborah! You're a sight for sore eyes and parched tongues," Preacher Amos exclaimed. He rose from the ground, where they'd been bolting the front panel of the produce stand to its sides, reinforcing the corners. "What do you think of our little shack?"

Deborah's green eyes lit up as she looked at the structure, setting her plate, the jug, and some plastic glasses on the wooden countertop. "Looks big enough to hold quite a lot of produce," she remarked. "And I like the way the roof slants down over the front to keep the sun and rain out."

"It'll get plenty warm out here by midsummer," Roman remarked as he helped himself to a brownie. "Once the word gets around, though, I think Mamm and the girls will run a brisk business."

"Because of all the trees here, they'll be in the shade a lot of the time," Amos pointed out as he unscrewed the lid of the jug. "We've put hooks up in the ceiling to hang a couple of fans, too. I'm going to install solar panels on the roof to run those, as well as a small fridge for keeping the eggs and the more perishable produce cool."

"And we're building a couple of rolling racks for the melons and squash and whatever else the girls might want to display closer to the road," Roman said. "When they close up for the day, the racks will fit inside the stand."

Noah let the others talk as he filled a glass with cold water and drank it down. He tried not to look too obvious about watching Deborah as she went inside the little building. It was built in a U shape, and they had already installed sturdy wooden shelves and pull-out bins around its three sides. She was nodding as she checked out these features.

"Maybe I could bake bread and goodies and sell them out

here, too," she murmured. "It would be a way to earn my keep."

Noah felt a pang, not only because Deborah thought she needed to make money but because it sounded like she intended to stick around for a while. Everyone else would think that was a fine idea—

And until yesterday, you did, too. What's your problem?

Noah cupped his hand and poured water into it so Queenie could lap it up. He couldn't miss the hint of mischief in Deborah's grin when she looked up at them again.

"I came out to ask you fellows to get the rods ready—and the worms dug—for a fishing contest this evening," she announced. "Rosetta and I thought that would be something fun to do after we have a picnic by the lake."

"What's the prize for catching the most fish?" Roman teased as he grabbed another brownie.

"Hmm . . . maybe you fellows can come up with ideas—especially since we girls figure to win," Deborah replied pertly. "And meanwhile, Noah, you'd better tell me what's chewing on you before our picnic. I won't spend the evening being ignored."

With that, she flashed him a grin and took off toward the lodge.

"There you have it," Amos said with a laugh. He glanced at Noah as he reached for a lemon-frosted molasses cookie. "I thought you two were all cozy again."

"*Jah,* they were—until Isaac made some crass comments about what he and Deborah did together on the night of the fire," Roman remarked. "All his talk was horse hockey, if you ask me."

"Well, I *didn't,*" Noah retorted before he could stop himself. Didn't his brother realize what vivid mental pictures Isaac's descriptions had planted in his mind?

The preacher's eyebrows rose. "Do you have any reason to believe what Isaac said about her, Noah? Far as I could tell, he and his *dat* were both bearing a lot of false witness yesterday, and not owning up to what Isaac's been doing."

Noah could not—would not—admit that Isaac's words had made him painfully aware of what he'd longed to share with Deborah . . . long kisses and the kind of intimacy he'd looked forward to as her husband. He'd known friends who'd succumbed to sexual temptations before they married, but Noah had kept his desires to himself. It was a matter of honor and respect for Deborah and for their faith. He shook his head, knowing Amos wouldn't accept that as an answer to his question.

"Deborah's a beautiful, capable young woman," Amos continued matter-of-factly. "And if you love her, Noah, marriage would cure what's ailing you—and it would protect her from Isaac, as well," he pointed out. "As long as she's at loose ends, any fellow can cast a line. Somebody else's bait might start looking pretty *gut* if you're always pouting."

Noah's eyes widened. But he didn't challenge the preacher's insinuation that he'd been behaving like a kid—or that he'd wanted Deborah in a physical way. "I guess I've never considered the protection angle," he admitted.

"If you love her, you'd better tell her, son. Before somebody else does." Amos took up his screwdriver again, crouching to finish the produce stand's corner.

"*Jah,* you never know what sort of guys might come to live at Promise Lodge—or might already live around here," Roman said as he grabbed his hammer. "If they spot Deborah working at the roadside stand, they'll want to take her home right along with her brownies."

Noah blinked. Not long ago Roman had been touting the merits of the marriageable *girls* who were moving here, saying he should let Deborah go. His brother's remark struck Noah as way off base—but was it? Noah hadn't thought about Deborah paying attention to anyone else, because even after she'd broken their engagement, he'd still considered her *his* girl. He hadn't wanted to date anyone else, so he'd assumed Deborah wouldn't look around, either.

And that's not so smart, is it?

Noah positioned the ladder and began putting shingles on the produce stand's roof. It was all well and good for Amos and Roman to tell him he should latch on to Deborah sooner rather than later, but such ideas didn't provide him a paying job, did they? It would be easier if he could nail down his future as quickly as he was attaching shingles with his pneumatic staple gun. Maybe he should post notices on the bulletin boards in the Forest Grove stores, and run ads in the local papers. People couldn't hire him if they didn't know about his welding skills. . . .

Above the loud hum of his air compressor, Noah heard a vehicle approaching. Queenie barked when the truck stopped at the roadside, but he remained focused on finishing the produce stand's roof. A door slammed behind him.

"And how're you fellows on this fine day?" a familiar voice called out. "Looks like Mattie and the girls will soon be in the produce business."

"*Jah,* we need to keep them busy or they have too much time to think up more work for *us,*" Amos joked. "How are you, Truman?"

"Fine and dandy. If my memory serves me right, you've got a guy here who's handy with a welding torch."

Noah shot the last two staples into a sheet of shingles before he looked down to see Truman grinning at him. "That would be me," he said. "What's on your mind? Got some repairs at your place?"

"No, it's a landscaping job at a new senior living center south of here." He removed his straw hat to wipe his forehead on his rolled-up shirtsleeve. "They've hired my crew to design the raised flower beds around the grounds. When the director mentioned they'd like some ornamental metal trellises and gates, I thought of you."

Noah's breath caught. "I'd have to get a forge up and running—"

"Promise Lodge will soon be needing a forge anyway, to keep our horses shod and our buggies in *gut* repair," Preacher Amos pointed out.

"—but *jah*, I've done a fair amount of ornamental metal-work." Noah grinned as his spirits rose. "It's a lot more fun than welding pipe joints and sheet metal, too."

"Can you start next week?"

"Well, *jah!*" Noah's head began to spin. Here was an opportunity exactly like he'd been hoping for! "We'd need to get dimensions, and order the supplies and—"

"I'm going onsite Monday to make out the order for our bushes and perennials," Truman said. "If you come along, you can talk to the managers about what they have in mind. We'll shoot them a bid when you've got an idea of what your materials will run—and I'll cover the cost of your equipment and supplies as part of the overall job. How's that sound?"

Noah's jaw dropped. "Well, it doesn't get any better than *that*," he exclaimed. He came down the ladder and stuck out his hand. "You have no idea how much I appreciate this, Truman."

Their neighbor gripped Noah's hand firmly and pumped it. "I think I do," he replied. "I was your age once, just starting out. I'd rather hire an Amish fellow than somebody English any day. I know the job'll get done right."

"You'll not find anyone more conscientious or capable than Noah," Preacher Amos agreed. "We've been trying to convince him that the doors of opportunity would soon swing open, and you've just answered our prayers in a big way."

"Well, now." Truman met their gazes with earnest hazel eyes. "It's been a while since anybody told me that. I knew you folks would make *gut* neighbors!"

Noah's mind was still reeling with his good fortune, but he had a sudden inspiration. "How'd you like to join us for a picnic supper tonight? Followed by a fishing contest?"

"*Jah,* Deborah tells us it's girls against the boys, and we could use another guy on our team," Roman said. "You can keep your catch—"

"Or you can come back when we fry up what we've been accumulating," Amos joined in. "Bring your mother. We'd love to meet her."

Truman slapped his hat against his thigh. "Now that's an offer I can't refuse—more fun than I've had in a long while. Mamm's none too steady on rugged ground, so she won't come this evening, but I'll be there!"

After Truman's big truck had rumbled down the county road, leaving a dust cloud in its wake, Noah was still agog. "What do you think of that? It was like Truman could read my mind—knew what I was concerned about when he pulled up."

"You were in the right place at the right time with the right skills," Amos replied as he began picking up the tools. "*Gut* opportunities don't happen by accident. They're a sure sign that God's got His eye on us and brings us exactly what we need—wouldn't you say?"

Although he'd never been one to talk a lot about matters of faith, Noah couldn't deny that Amos was on to something. "*Jah,* and I'd say He was watching out for us when He told you to come to Promise Lodge with us, too." He glanced up at the roof of the produce stand. "It'll take me about five minutes to finish the shingling, and then I'll tell the cooks we've got company joining us for supper. I'm guessing Rosetta will see that the food's a little fancier than usual, if you get my meaning."

Chapter Seventeen

Deborah paused with her hands on the warm chocolate sheet cake she'd just rolled up in a towel. Through the kitchen window she saw Noah hurrying up the lane, his arms loaded with tools and Queenie circling him exuberantly. Something wonderful must have happened! His step had a bounce to it. His face glowed in the summer sunshine as he gazed toward the lodge, bursting with news he couldn't wait to tell.

Her heartbeat sped up. *Denki, Lord, for whatever You've brought to this man. He hasn't looked this happy since before I broke up with him.*

"Deborah!" he called out as his footsteps thundered on the porch steps. "Deborah, I got a job!"

From over by the sink, Rosetta cheered while Mattie, Christine, and her two girls grabbed each other's hands. Deborah hurried through the dining room, wiping her sugar-dusted palms on her apron. She heard Noah's tools land in one of the wicker porch chairs, and then he rushed inside, letting the screen door bang behind him. Before she knew what was happening, Noah lifted her up and swung her around in the center of the lobby until her laughter rang happily against the high, beamed ceiling.

"I can't believe it! Truman stopped by just now, and he's

got a job lined up for his crew," Noah crowed, "and he wants *me* to make the trellises and gates! I'm going with him on Monday to speak with the managers!"

Deborah squealed as her arms flew around his neck. "What a fine surprise! See there? I *knew* you'd find work—"

"And Rosetta?" Noah called toward the kitchen. "Wickey's coming to our picnic tonight. Thought you'd want to know."

Deborah felt the color rising in her cheeks. Noah set her carefully on the floor and kept his hands at her waist. His brown eyes had the shine of hot coffee, and his gaze made her feel as if she'd gulped two or three cups of it—all jittery and breathless.

He licked his lips, looking nervous. "I'm sorry I've been snippy," he murmured, "but I had no idea—"

"It's okay, Noah. You've had a lot on your mind."

"—how I was going to make a living or—" His face tightened. "And I'm sorry Isaac's stupid lies made me doubt you, when I know you're not the kind of girl to go along with his um, *ideas,*" Noah continued in a rush. "It's me that needs to be forgiven now—again. Heh, *always*."

"Oh, Noah. Isaac's made us all crazy," Deborah murmured. "I was ready to leave Promise Lodge, to keep him from coming back to ruin everything you've all worked so hard for. But that's—"

"That's what Chupp wants," Noah interrupted earnestly. "If he keeps us agitated about the Bender barn burning—or by threatening what he'll do next—then we'll be the blathering sheep and he'll be the wolf, licking his chops. *Enough,* already."

"Amen! Now you've got it right, son!" Mattie said from the dining room doorway.

"You go, Noah!" Rosetta joined in, while Christine nodded her enthusiastic approval.

Laura and Phoebe broke into applause and then rushed over to hug both of them. "It's so *gut* to see you two getting along again," Phoebe said. "Congratulations on your job, Noah."

"And the minute I figured out you were gone," Laura said as she shook a finger at Deborah, "I would've been running the roads until I found you. And I would've brought you back here to be with us! So there!"

A warm sense of belonging filled Deborah's soul. Her nerves settled. Her body relaxed. Standing among her closest friends, with the young man she'd loved for so long, she realized how much she had to be grateful for. "We need to show our appreciation to Truman with some wonderful-*gut* picnic food," she said to the women in the doorway. "He's done us some big favors since we've met him."

"I thought you'd see it that way," Noah agreed. "I'll go check the fishing rods. Some of them are the worse for wear after being stashed in that old shed, but we'll have enough to go around."

"Scrub the grill, too, please," Mattie said. "We've made hamburger patties, and we took a package of Rosetta's sausages from the freezer."

"I'm going to boil some eggs for potato salad and a deviled egg plate," Christine said as she headed back to the kitchen.

"Do we need a pie as well as the ice cream cake Deborah's making?" Phoebe asked. "We've got jars of rhubarb filling in the cellar—and apple, too."

Noah chuckled. "The answer to a pie question is always *yes*," he replied. "Remember how Truman tucked away two pieces when his crew was here?"

"What's missing? Baked beans, maybe?" Mattie thought aloud. "And we've got leaf lettuce and green onions in the garden that would make a nice bowl of wilted lettuce."

"With lots of bacon," Laura suggested as she joined the others who were returning to the kitchen. "This is going to be a feast! And then we girls are going to outfish the guys!"

Deborah remained in the center of the lobby with Noah, savoring a few more moments of his nearness. "We're cooking up quite a celebration—as well we should," she added. "I'm so glad Truman offered you that job, Noah. It's been hard on you, not having steady welding work."

Noah cleared his throat. "Truth be told, I have to submit a bid to the managers at the senior living center before they'll officially hire me," he said softly. "But I can *do* this. If I have sample sketches of trellises and gates ready come Monday, I think it'll be a go."

"I *know* it will, Noah." Deborah smiled at him, daring to place her hands on either side of his tanned, clean-shaven face the way she used to.

"Coming from you, those words mean a lot." He smiled and eased away from her. "I'd better take care of those fishing rods and the grill before you distract me. But don't think for a minute that I'll ignore you this evening. *Denki* for that kick in the pants you gave me, girl."

Noah didn't kiss her, but Deborah knew he wanted to. He gazed at her mouth, his lips parting, before he turned on his heel to head back outside.

She rejoined her friends in the kitchen, invigorated by their excitement over the evening's plans. Phoebe was mixing dough for piecrusts while Christine had set eggs in a pan of water on the stove. Laura was scrubbing potatoes. At another counter, Rosetta and Mattie had dumped two big cans of pork and beans into a baking dish. They were stirring in seasonings and brown sugar as bacon sizzled in a skillet nearby.

"I'll go pick us some lettuce and onions," Deborah said, grabbing a plastic washtub near the back door.

"Spinach, too!" Rosetta called out.

Deborah gave her a thumbs-up as she stepped outside. It was a fine thing when everyone worked in harmony and agreed on a common purpose, whether it be overruling Isaac's treachery or celebrating Noah's job—or repaying Truman Wickey's kindness.

Deborah smiled as her bare feet sank into the warm, damp earth of the recently hoed garden. Tonight would mark a fresh start between her and Noah. She just knew it.

"In the interest of fairness, what with six gals and only four guys," Preacher Amos said as they were finishing their picnic supper, "I think we men should have six fishing rods to share amongst us, so we'll have just as many lines in the water."

Noah watched his mother and aunts nod to each other. "*Jah,* that makes sense. Evens up the numbers."

"I think the guys should stand along one section of the shore while the girls fish from another area," Truman suggested. "Otherwise, our lines will get tangled."

"Which means the girls have to bait their own hooks and string their own fish," Roman pointed out.

Noah nearly choked on the last bite of his rhubarb pie as the females' protests rose.

"I'm not digging worms out of that can of dirt!" Phoebe declared.

"What if I stab myself with the hook?" Mamm asked as she shot a doubtful look at Amos.

"It's impossible to hang on to flipping, flopping, *slimy* fish!" Aunt Christine chimed in.

"Whose idea *was* this fishing contest, anyway?" Laura's voice rose above the others. "I think you guys set it up this way on purpose!"

Silence settled over them as they sat on the old quilts they'd spread near the shoreline.

"The contest was my idea," Deborah replied softly. "Wouldn't it be just as fair if we fished in three or four rounds? For each round, the fellows could get all the hooks baited, and then everyone can stand wherever they want to, and we can set a timer. The folks who catch a fish can wait for the round to end before they put their lines in again."

"So we'd tally the women's catch and the men's catch, and after the men string up the fish we'd start a new round?" Aunt Rosetta clarified.

"You girls are just afraid to get worm guts on your hands," Roman teased.

Noah smiled. After giving Deborah's fishing lesson the other night—recalling her reaction to handling the bait and the live fish—he knew the contest would be called off if the fellows didn't make a few concessions. "I think that's a workable plan," he said. "After all the effort these gals have put into our picnic, would it hurt us to give them a hand with their hooks?"

"I like the sound of that," Preacher Amos chimed in. "We'd be working together instead of taking sides, and everyone would have more fun. If fishing can't be fun, why bother?"

"*Jah,* that's a better idea," Truman agreed. "I'm all for keeping the ladies happy. They feed me too well, and I want to be invited back."

Everyone laughed and finished eating their pie and the ice cream cake roll. While the women gathered the plates and covered the food, the men put worms on all twelve of the hooks and dug little tunnels at intervals along the shoreline to hold their rods. By the time the ladies had taken the perishable food to the fridge and returned to the lake with a kitchen timer, the men had distributed the nets and stringers around the shoreline and everything was ready for the contest to begin.

Noah smiled at the way the spacing worked out. He and Deborah stood near each other, while Amos had gravitated between Mamm and Aunt Christine, and Truman stood an arm's length from Aunt Rosetta. Phoebe and Laura positioned themselves between Wickey and Roman, and Queenie trotted around them all, anticipating the excitement of flopping fish. They made a satisfying group picture, lining a long stretch of Rainbow Lake's shoreline as the sun was inching its way down the western sky.

"We'll set this first round for ten minutes," Deborah announced. She held up the timer, gripping the handle on its numbered face. "On your mark—get set—*go!*"

With a quick twist, she set the timer. Noah watched her, pleased at how Deborah swung her rod sideways with graceful energy, releasing the thumb button at just the right moment. Her bobber plopped onto the lake well beyond the others.

"Nice cast," Noah remarked as his line sailed out over the water.

"*Gut* teacher," Deborah replied without missing a beat.

Noah's heart sped up. He watched with rising excitement as she quickly jerked her line to set the hook.

"I've got one!" she squealed, slowly cranking the handle.

"There's one on my hook, too," Roman called out from down the shoreline. "A sea monster, by the feel of it."

"Help!" Laura squawked. "My bobber went down and my line's racing out!"

Roman quickly stuck the butt of his rod into a tunnel and took his cousin's line. Truman laughed and stepped behind Rosetta to steady her rod when she, too, cried out for help. Aunt Christine stuck her rod into a tunnel and scurried over to grab Roman's. "You've got a lot more going on than I do," she explained when he gave her a quizzical look.

"I've snagged one that's headed to the bottom of the lake!" Preacher Amos called out with a laugh. "It surely must be a whale like the one that swallowed Jonah."

When the timer trilled behind him and Queenie barked

repeatedly, Noah was reeling in a fish, as well. "Bring in all the lines," he said. "Let's count our catch."

Preacher Amos's whale turned out to be a large mass of weeds and muck. Six nice fish were soon flipping on the stringers, however—three for the women and three for the men, because Roman allowed Aunt Christine to count the one on his hook, and Laura said Roman could claim the bass he'd netted for her. Truman had landed Aunt Rosetta's trout as well as a bass from one of the spare lines. Noah was pleased at the way Deborah had slipped the net under her own fish and had then assisted with his catch, as well. He was glad he'd taken the time to show her how to handle fishing equipment, because she was much more adept—and having more fun—than the other gals were.

The second round brought the total catch to thirteen. By the time the third round was under way, no one was keeping track of which team was bringing in the fish. When the timer rang, dusk was fading into darkness.

"I'd better see to the livestock chores," Roman announced. "But I think we fellows won, if you consider how many times we left our lines to help the women."

"We're all winners," Truman countered good-naturedly. "I can't recall a single thing I'd change, or anything lacking in this wonderful evening. I'll help you fellows clean these fish and then get along home to my mother."

"Give her our best," Aunt Rosetta said as she grabbed one of the stringers of fish. "And don't forget—we're going to fry all our fish sometime soon, and you're both invited."

Truman smiled, obviously delighted in the time he'd spent with her. "So happens I've got a nice, deep fish fryer at my place. Why don't you folks come over with those fish, and that way Mamm can join us. She'll be glad for your company."

"Pick a time that suits her and we'll be there," Preacher Amos replied.

Noah followed the various conversations as everyone headed for the lodge carrying the fish, the last cooler, and the old quilts. He took Deborah's hand. "I'm glad we had our fun this evening," he said. "It was *gut* to hear folks laughing, after all the work we've been so intent on these past weeks. And all the *stuff* with Isaac."

"Credit Rosetta for insisting that I set aside my inclination to leave Promise Lodge because—"

"You really were going to leave?" Noah's throat tightened as he tugged Deborah closer. "I thought you just said that in passing. I—I thought you liked it here, sweetie."

"Oh, I do." Deborah's eyes shone in the darkness, inches in front of his face. "But I let Isaac's bluster get to me, thinking he'd come back to cause trouble for the rest of you because he wasn't finished tormenting *me*."

"He'll have to put *me* out of commission first," Noah declared. He kissed her then, first on the cheek and then on the sweet, soft lips he'd missed even more than he'd realized.

Deborah's breath left her. "Noah? Don't lead me where you don't want me to go," she pleaded.

"Wouldn't dream of it," he replied before kissing her again. "Please, will you stay, Deborah? Can you be patient while I establish myself and—and make sure I can provide you a home?"

She closed her eyes. Then she nodded.

"Even if it takes a couple more years?"

Deborah gazed at him straight-on. "For you, Noah, I can be patient this time around."

His heart danced to the music Deborah made when she said his name. Noah hugged her close for a few precious moments and then started toward the lodge. "It's been a big day, a turning point," he whispered gratefully. "With you by my side, I feel like I can move mountains."

"Me too, Noah."

Silently they walked through the damp grass, surrounded

by the reedy *thrum* of cicadas and a distant rumble of thunder. Noah paused before they entered the back door to the lodge. In the lamplight that spilled from the kitchen window, Deborah's honey-brown hair glimmered beneath her pleated white *kapp*. Her flawless skin glowed, crinkling slightly around her eyes when she smiled at him.

"I'm going to help with the dishes and then head for bed," she said.

"And I'll be cleaning fish for a while," Noah said with a smile. "Sweet dreams, Deborah."

Chapter Eighteen

"Here you go, Aunt Rosetta," Noah said as he came through the screen door. "Our buckets are full of fileted fish!"

Rosetta looked up from rinsing out the laundry tub in the mudroom. "Your timing's perfect. I was just getting some freezer containers ready so we can put—Truman! You're still here."

Both men chuckled as they came to stand on either side of her.

"Hated to leave all that smelly work to Noah when I saw Amos heading toward the barn to help Roman with the livestock chores," their neighbor explained. "We've got quite a nice catch here. I'm looking forward to sharing it over at our place sometime soon."

Rosetta prayed that her face didn't display the same schoolgirlish glee that had rung in her voice when she'd blurted Truman's name. *He's just being thoughtful, helping Noah. Don't go hoping he's stayed to see more of you, silly girl.*

"We should set up a time to do that, so we don't get too busy and let summer slip by," Rosetta agreed. "I feel bad that your *mamm* couldn't come and fish with us tonight. Maybe if you bring her over in your truck for dinner at our table sometime—"

"She'd like that, I'm sure. *Denki* for thinking of her, Rosetta."

Noah smiled slyly. "I'll leave you two to tend this fish while I feed Queenie. See you Monday morning, Truman."

"*Jah,* bright and early," he replied. "Looking forward to it."

Rosetta pressed the stopper into the drain of the big laundry sink and ran some cold water. She was acutely aware that Truman Wickey filled the small room with his presence—and that he showed no inclination to go home. He hung his straw hat on a peg near the door, gazing around the mudroom.

"No wonder it smells so nice in here," he remarked as he looked at the cream-colored bars of soap lined up on her worktable. "Who's the soap maker? Not many folks do that anymore."

"That would be me," Rosetta replied. "I use some of the milk from my goats. When our new families arrive I'm going to give them a bar as a welcome gift." She shut off the water and reached for the nearest pail of fish, hoping Truman didn't think she was babbling.

"Let me hold that for you."

Rosetta's breath left her in a rush when Truman's sturdy hands steadied the bucket against the edge of the sink. He was standing so close to her that—*well, it's a gut thing he smells like fish, and now I will, too,* she thought as she began placing the slippery filets in the water.

"I'm glad Deborah suggested that fishing contest—and a picnic at the lake," she said. The sound of their mingled breathing was starting to unnerve her in the otherwise silent room.

"It's been too long since I took time out for fun," Truman agreed. "I really appreciate you folks inviting me to share your evening. All work and no play—well, you know what they say."

"You could never be a dull boy, Truman," Rosetta blurted. She placed a layer of rinsed filets in the plastic bin she'd prepared, shaking her head at herself. "You must think I sound as silly as— "

"Matter of fact, your voice does crazy things to me, Rosetta. Even if we've both agreed not to let such things distract us."

Rosetta swallowed hard. She *was* distracted. "I don't want to give you the idea that I'd abandon my Old Order faith to—"

"Nor do I intend to change my Mennonite ways," Truman insisted gently. "So now that we've reminded each other of our *gut* intentions, we can return to being two purposeful, responsible adults—as opposed to acting like a couple of kids who'd like to find a dark corner and start kissing. Or at least I would."

Rosetta's mouth dropped open as her cheeks flared with heat. She hoped her sisters and nieces weren't still in the kitchen—or eavesdropping on this intensely private conversation from the top of the back stairs.

Truman sighed as he set aside the empty bucket and reached for the other one. "I'm sorry," he murmured. "I didn't mean to embarrass you. And I hope I wasn't out of line when I stood behind you to steady your fishing rod, with my arms around you. No doubt everyone got ideas about *that*."

As the memory of that moment made her tingle, Rosetta smiled wryly. "But we were surrounded by all those chaperones. And I would've lost my fish—maybe broken my line— had you not helped me." She quickly layered the rest of the rinsed fish in the bin and snapped the lid in place.

"No harm done, then?" he asked earnestly.

"None at all."

"*Gut*. I'd never hurt you, Rosetta," Truman added as she

drained the sink and filled it with clean water. "But then, that was also my intention when I was engaged to a nice young lady, and I lost her because she got tired of me having to be *right.* So now you know what a tyrant I can be."

Rosetta stopped placing filets into the water to look up at him. Truman's handsome face was etched with remorse, as though he realized how different his life might be if that young lady had married him. With his sandy hair crushed from wearing his straw hat and his shirt smeared with fish blood, he looked anything but tyrannical.

"Not to worry," Rosetta said. "As a *maidel,* I'm used to having things my way—which is the right way, of course— so you'll not stand a chance when it comes to bossing me around. Now you know what an outspoken, opinionated old biddy I can be."

Truman's hazel eyes held her gaze for a moment. Then he laughed out loud. "Fair enough. All the more reason we shouldn't get tangled up with each other."

"Right," Rosetta agreed, even as his words brought intimate images to mind. "So mark that down. I allowed you to be right, Truman."

"Yes, ma'am, you did," he said with a grin.

After they'd layered the remaining fish in another bin, Truman placed the containers in the deep freeze while Rosetta held its door for him. She was pleased that they'd reached an understanding and had remained on good terms while they'd defused the *awareness* that filled the small mudroom. Or at least they'd tried to.

"Here—you really need to wash up before you leave," Rosetta said as she offered him a round, grainy bar of soap. "Every stray cat in the countryside will follow you home if you don't."

Truman smiled as he lathered his arms and hands. "Mamm would tell me straight out that I stink, so see? You can be very diplomatic rather than just bossy—but what's in this soap? Lemon, maybe?"

"And some orange oil, and the gritty texture comes from cornmeal," Rosetta replied as she accepted the soap and washed her hands with it. "Our men seem to think it gets them clean without making them smell like girls. We women like it for freshening our hands after we've been cutting up onions."

"I suppose you made this soap, too? I like that it's round and it fits my hands while I'm washing."

Rosetta nodded, flushing at his compliment. "I use an oiled length of plastic plumbing pipe to mold it. The towel's hanging at the side of the sink."

As Truman dried with one end of the towel and Rosetta used the other, she smiled up at him. "You've been a big help this evening. I'm going to send a bar of this cornmeal soap home with you—and a bar of the lavender mint for your mother," she added as she opened the cabinet beside the sink. "Tell her we missed meeting her tonight."

Truman nodded, his hazel eyes softening as he accepted her gift. "Walk with me partway? It's an awfully nice night out."

Rosetta nipped her lip. She wanted to walk with him, yet maybe it was best not to encourage any further contact—and Amos, Noah, and Roman were likely to come out of the barn at any moment. They would tease her ceaselessly if they believed she and Truman were . . .

"I'll go as far as the shed—to be sure the goats and chickens are in for the night," she added quickly. "We've heard coyotes coming around."

Truman smiled as though he saw through her excuse. "*Jah,* out here in the countryside, all sorts of critters prowl around in the dark. And then there's me," he teased as he playfully wiggled his eyebrows. He grabbed his hat and then held the door for her.

Rosetta's heart turned handsprings as they stepped out into the moonlit evening. *Years* it had been since she'd enjoyed a man's company so much, yet she reminded herself of the reality of their religious situations—and her dream of managing apartments for other women who wanted a more independent Plain way of life. She inhaled deeply, enjoying the perfume of the honeysuckle bushes on the breeze as they strolled around the side of the lodge. The moonlight shimmered on the rippling lake, where bullfrogs and cicadas sang their evening duet. The night sky, dotted with stars and constellations, spread forever in every direction.

"God really knew what He was doing when He created the heavens and the earth," Rosetta murmured. "I've not traveled much, but I can't think that anywhere else is as pretty as this tract of land."

"No place like home," Truman said softly. "And I'm glad there's light in the windows now when I glance over here at night. I like to think it's your room I see—"

"Praise God and holler hallelujah! I think we found it, Beulah!"

"*Jah,* Ruby, there's lights on so I sure hope somebody's home!"

Rosetta's head swiveled in the direction of the approaching female voices. She hurried toward the front of the lodge, spotting two women who wore floral print calf-length dresses and white *kapps* that glowed in the moonlight as they strode down the lane. Truman jogged toward them, calling out a greeting before he relieved the ladies of their suitcases.

"You look mighty young to be the Preacher Amos mentioned in *The Budget* ad for this place," one of the women remarked.

"Well, he's sure not the Rosetta Bender who writes the weekly column from Promise," her companion said with a laugh. "You smell to high heaven, young man, but I'm sure there's a *gut* reason you've got fish innards smeared on your shirt."

Rosetta's pulse raced as she covered the remaining distance to meet their guests. Could it be that their first potential residents had arrived? She didn't recall any of the letters mentioning a Beulah or a Ruby, but she sensed that these ladies were going to tell more of a story than would fit into a mere letter.

"I'm Rosetta Bender!" she said, holding her hands out to them. "This *young man* is our neighbor, Truman Wickey, and he's helped us clean the fish we caught in our lake this evening. Welcome to Promise Lodge!"

Two sturdy hands gripped hers as two sets of shining eyes gazed at her through identical pairs of wire-rimmed glasses. "I'm Beulah Kuhn and this is my sister Ruby," the taller, stouter woman said. "We couldn't believe our eyes when we read you were setting up apartments for *maidels*—"

"But we hope it's true—and we hope you've got some places left," Ruby cut in eagerly, "because we've packed our bags and run away from home!"

Rosetta stood speechless. She was guessing these sisters were seventysomething, and their print dresses suggested they were Mennonites. Hearing that they'd left where they'd been living after reading her column in *The Budget* stunned her. She glanced over their heads at Truman, who was smiling.

"I'll carry these suitcases into the lobby and let you ladies get acquainted," he said. "Ruby and Beulah, I'm happy to meet you—and next time I won't smell so gamey. You're in *gut* hands if you've come to stay with Rosetta and her sisters."

Rosetta watched Truman spring up the stairs with the luggage, and then gave him a little wave as he strode past them, heading toward the road. She was grateful that Ruby and Beulah had spoken loudly, announcing their arrival before

Truman had said anything more about looking toward her bedroom.

"You might be a *maidel* now, missy," Beulah remarked as they started up the porch stairs.

"But that fellow's got his eye on you," her sister finished crisply. "And you're still of an age to follow your fancy, too—if he's *gut* enough for you. But never *settle*."

"*Jah,* a life well spent alone beats being a man's slave any day. Ruby and I are living proof of that," Beulah added before her laugh rang off the porch ceiling. "But here we are, telling you what to do before we've been here five minutes! We'd have arrived a whole lot sooner if our driver had looked at our road map instead of listening to that newfangled thinga-majig on his dashboard."

"Puh! That woman telling him to turn around while she *recalculated* was every bit as lost as he was," Ruby insisted. As the three of them stepped into the lobby, she looked upward with an expression of sublime awe. "Ohhh!" she murmured excitedly. "Here we are, Sister, and it's even more wonderful than I dared to imagine."

"Sure is," Beulah replied as she grabbed her sister's hand. "I love this place already. Sign us up, Rosetta. And thank You, Jesus, for giving us the gumption to leave our brother's place and come here to find a new home."

"Amen, Sister."

Rosetta gazed at them, deeply touched by their remarks. "My sisters and I felt the same way when we first saw this lodge and the land around it," she said softly. "We've been working very hard to get it ready—"

"And we aim to help in whatever ways you need us to," Ruby assured her. She smiled sweetly, covering a yawn. "But I'm thinking we'd best get to bed so we don't waken every-body. Plenty of time for talk tomorrow."

"*Jah,* it's been a long day. It's not really our way to just show up and expect folks to cater to us," Beulah insisted.

"But we'll be forever grateful if you've got beds and some furniture we can use until—"

Rosetta grasped their hands, adoring these two sisters already. "Just so happens I've made up a couple of rooms," she assured them. "You can decide which ones you'd like for your apartments tomorrow when it's light and you're rested. Welcome home, Ruby and Beulah. We're glad you're here."

"*Gut* morning!" Rosetta called out when Beulah and Ruby came into the kitchen. "You slept well, I hope?"

"Like a rock," Beulah replied.

"*Jah,* it's not nearly this quiet back home, what with Delbert's eight kids kicking up a fuss when they wake up," Ruby explained with a shake of her head. "The oldest twins are eleven, and from there they stair-step downward in age—"

"And our brother's house is feeling so crowded, we figured coming to Promise Lodge would give them another bedroom—"

"And truth be told, we're a little weary of the way Delbert and Claire keep having more kids, figuring we'll be their built-in babysitters," Ruby blurted. "That's probably not a very Christian attitude, is it?"

"And we needed an *adventure* before we got too old to get out of our rut," Beulah added earnestly. "So after we read your columns, we packed our bags and took off without telling anybody. I suppose we should call home this morning so they won't wonder if kidnappers snatched us in the night."

"Puh! Kidnappers would have their hands full dealing with the two of us!" Ruby declared.

Rosetta followed this rapid-fire conversation, smiling at the way the sisters finished each other's sentences without batting an eye. "You can call them anytime you're ready," she said, gesturing toward the phone on the back wall. "My sisters, Mattie and Christine, are out gathering eggs and weeding the gardens until Amos and the boys finish milking Christine's cows. Here—come take a look now that the sun's up."

Ruby and Beulah eagerly preceded her through the lobby and out to the wide porch. Two hummingbirds hovered near the orange blooms of the trumpet vines before darting off as the women approached. Sunlight dappled the grass beneath the tall oaks that shaded the lodge, and out beyond the barn Rosetta's goats grazed alongside the horses. The treetops swayed gently on the breeze, which carried the heady scent of the honeysuckle bushes out by the road. As one, the Kuhn sisters sighed and gazed out over the property, their faces alight with awe.

"Oh, Sister, we've come to the Garden of Eden," Beulah murmured.

"The land of milk and honey," Ruby said as she nodded in agreement. "It's even more wonderful than I'd imagined it from your reports in *The Budget,* Rosetta. And what's that I see beyond the lake? Apple trees?"

"*Jah,* from what we've heard, the area churches that once owned this property sold the apples as a way to fund their camp programs," Rosetta replied, shielding her eyes to get a better look. "Truman has told the fellows he can help them revive the orchard—keeping it mowed this summer and then pruning back the overgrown trees this winter. It'll make a *gut* source of income for somebody in a year or so—"

"And it'll be even more productive with my bees to pollinate the blossoms!" Ruby exclaimed. "We can move my hives here from Versailles and those little bees will think they've landed in heaven, with all the flowers and bushes around to sip from."

"Along with the money from selling Ruby's honey, we've laid by a nice nest egg from our wages at the cheese factory, too," Beulah told Rosetta. "If it would be all right with you folks, we could build a small factory here and make cheese from your cows' milk! Wouldn't take a building any bigger than that shed I see."

"You'd have milk from my dairy goats, too," Rosetta pointed out. Her heart thudded happily at the prospect of adding bees, honey, and a cheese factory to the businesses she and her sisters were running. "Is it difficult to transport your bees without getting stung?"

Ruby chuckled. "I'll be there to oversee the packing, so it'll be a piece of cake. We'll wrap straps around the hives and duct tape the holes late at night, when they're all inside, so they won't escape while we're moving them," she explained. "I know of folks who transport their hives from place to place all over the country, depending on whether it's apples or grapes or almonds that need pollinating. I don't have that big an operation, of course."

"This'll be the perfect new home for your bees," Beulah remarked. "Lots of room for them—"

"*Jah,* they do best with about an acre for each hive of bees," said Ruby.

"—and we won't be hearing any more complaints from Claire about the kids getting stung because they were playing too close to the hives," Beulah continued. The skin around her eyes crinkled as she smiled at Rosetta. "Let us know what your apartments are going for, and we'll advance you several months' rent. We aim to pay our way and earn our keep from the get-go."

"May we have those rooms down the hall in the corner— the two that share a bathroom between them?" Ruby asked with a lift in her voice. "We'd be right at home there. What a blessing that we saw your columns and Amos's ad—"

"And that we hit the road to find this place instead if ignoring God's nudge to get out and do something useful— something *fun!*—with the rest of our lives," Beulah finished.

She slipped a finger beneath her glasses to clear away a tear. "He's never failed us yet, our Jesus. I can't wait to tell Delbert about our new home!"

"They'll never believe what we've gone and done," Ruby agreed. She shielded her eyes with her hand, gazing at a big truck that was rumbling out of the metal building at the Wickey place. "Is that your boyfriend driving that truck, Rosetta?"

Rosetta swatted Ruby's shoulder playfully. "Truman owns a landscaping company. He's a Mennonite, so don't be thinking I'll hitch up with him."

"We're Mennonites, too, you know," Beulah said. "So I hope it's all right if we want to have electricity to run our cheese machines."

"Amos and Roman run the bulk milk tanks with electricity, so if you put your little factory near the barn, you can hook right in," Rosetta replied. "And speaking of our fellows, here they come. Let's get the stove fired up for some sausage and eggs, and you can get acquainted with everyone over breakfast."

"Show me the flour bin and I'll whip up some biscuits," Ruby said as they went back into the lodge.

"I'll be in charge of the gravy—and in appreciation for your wonderful welcome, Ruby and I will cook tonight's supper," Beulah offered.

Rosetta's eyes widened. "I'd be silly to turn down an offer like that."

"Better yet, we'll cook up enough to have for our dinner tomorrow, too, so we'll not be working on Sunday. How's that?"

Rosetta laughed as they entered the kitchen together. "I like the way you girls jump in and make things happen. Something tells me you two and we three Bender sisters will become *gut* friends in a hurry!"

Chapter Nineteen

That afternoon as Rosetta came downstairs, she inhaled appreciatively. Ruby and Beulah had been cooking and baking most of the day and the whole lodge smelled heavenly. Meanwhile, Rosetta had been able to clean the two corner rooms and the bathroom the Kuhn sisters wanted to rent. Deborah had agreed to paint the apartments on Monday, and Amos had bought their requested buttery yellow and pale blue paint—which would soon freshen Rosetta's apartment and her sisters' rooms, as well.

"What smells so wonderful-*gut?*" Rosetta asked as she entered the kitchen. "It's such a treat to have you cooking our supper and tomorrow's dinner."

Beulah checked the three bread pans in the oven and closed the door. "We thought we'd make some of our family's favorites," she replied. "We're having pizza meat loaf, and Ruby's ready to put her creamed potato loaf in the oven—"

"Topped with lots of cheese," Ruby added. When she expertly overturned a loaf pan, Rosetta's eyes widened as a molded block of chunky, creamed potatoes landed in her casserole dish. She unmolded a second loaf beside the first.

"—so along with a couple jars of green beans from your cellar, and a loaf of fresh bread, I don't think anybody'll go away hungry." Beulah nodded with satisfaction. "It's fun to cook for folks who appreciate our efforts."

"And you should see this apricot-cherry slab pie Ruby baked," Laura said from the dining room, where she and her sister were setting the silverware on a long table.

"*Jah,* we're keeping an eye on it to be sure it's still intact come time for supper," Phoebe teased. "Roman and Amos have been eyeballing it all afternoon."

Rosetta laughed. It was such a pleasure to see the Kuhn sisters making themselves at home in the big kitchen. She hoped to see more women offer to share the cooking chores as they moved into her apartments, because that could be a way for them all to become good friends. "And how did your call to your brother go?"

Ruby and Beulah looked at each other a little sheepishly. "Well, Delbert was glad to hear from us, and to know we're safe," Beulah began.

"Until we got to the part about putting our money down on apartments," Ruby continued as she spread a generous amount of shredded cheese on her potato loaves. "Boy howdy, did we catch an earful about that! He started out by informing us that as the man of the family, he wanted us to get ourselves back home where we belonged—"

"And that's all we needed to hear," Beulah added with a sigh. "You know, I really hate to split away from him and Claire and the kids, but Ruby and I both feel called to stay at Promise Lodge, to live our own lives."

"*Jah,* Claire was none too happy about our decision, either," Ruby remarked with a shake of her head. "She came right out and asked how she was supposed to run the household without us taking care of the eight kids—"

"And I told her those kids needed their *mamm* and *dat's* guidance more than they needed ours. God had His reasons for us not marrying nor having kids." Beulah's voice rose with the conviction of her words, even as it quivered a little.

"I felt funny telling Delbert and Claire we weren't going to live with them anymore— because that's the way of it for Plain *maidel* ladies, to stay with whichever man in the family will look after them. I was glad I'd already paid ahead on the rent so I could stand firm about our decision."

"*Jah,* it'll be a whole new life for us, being useful the way *we* want, instead of being at someone else's beck and call," Ruby insisted. "We'll go back on Monday to pack up the rest of our clothes, and I'll get my bees and hives ready to transport. It'll all work out, Rosetta—because we said so!"

Rosetta smiled. "It took courage and faith to insist on living your own lives," she agreed. "But it's not like you're moving clear across the country. Your family can come visit you, or you can go there anytime you please."

"*Jah,* we're only a few hours apart, as I pointed out to Delbert. And I reminded him that the road runs both directions, too," Beulah added. "We'll be tending our bees and making our cheese, so we won't be going back to Versailles at the drop of a hat."

"Your brother probably wasn't expecting you to say that," Rosetta remarked.

"Oh, Delbert heard quite a few surprising statements today," Beulah agreed.

"*Jah,* I smelled smoke coming out of the phone," Ruby added with a chuckle. "But I feel *happy.* I believe Beulah and I will lead more productive—"

"*Fun* lives," her sister finished. "And we have you to thank for that, Rosetta. You've been our inspiration, more than you'll ever know."

Rosetta's eyes widened. Never had she anticipated such a touching remark, and from a woman she'd just met. "What a fine thing to say, Beulah. *Denki* for telling me that," she murmured. She was about to elaborate upon the reasons she and her sisters had sold their farms to come to Promise when Queenie began barking frantically out in the front yard.

Rosetta and the Hershberger girls hurried through the lobby and out onto the porch to see what the ruckus was about. Halfway between the road and the lodge, a Plain man and woman had stopped with their suitcases—and when the man charged at the Border Collie and spoke harshly to her, Rosetta jogged down the steps.

"Say there! I'll be happy to help you if you'll not threaten our dog," Rosetta called out.

The man, who had a bushy graying beard and eyebrows, immediately scowled. "No, let's tell it like it is," he countered. "Your dog's the one doing the threatening, and if it were mine, I'd keep it tied up."

"Queenie, sit!" Laura called out, while Rosetta snapped her fingers at the dog and pointed toward the ground.

Queenie sat down, but she appeared ready to lunge if the man made any suspicious moves.

Rosetta considered this carefully, for Queenie was generally very friendly and curious around strangers. She didn't act aggressive unless she'd been provoked. "What can I do for you folks?" she asked, wondering whether they'd received a letter from these people. "Please believe that Queenie doesn't ordinarily cause any trouble."

The man's eyes narrowed, while the woman appeared wary of the Border Collie who sat gazing so intently at them. "I assume you've gotten my letter, so it should be no surprise that we've arrived. I'm Bishop Floyd Lehman, and this is Frances, my wife."

Ah, yes. The man whom God has already declared our bishop—in the gospel according to Floyd.

Rosetta put on a polite smile, glad to see Amos coming from the barn. "I recall your letter, *jah,* but we weren't expecting you until you sold your place. This is Preacher Amos Troyer," she added as she gestured at him. "Amos, these are the Lehmans from Ohio, who wrote to us a while back. Bishop Floyd and Frances."

Rosetta detected a flicker of Amos's eyebrows as he extended his hand. "So you've already found a buyer for your place and you're moving to Missouri?" he asked as he smiled at Frances. "Sounds like your home was a choice piece of property, priced right."

Frances smiled stiffly. "Truth be told, we wanted to *see* Promise Lodge before we—"

"Several folks in our overcrowded district thought somebody should check this place out before we committed to coming," Floyd cut in. When he slipped an arm around his wife's shoulders, she grimaced at the squeeze of his hand. "They put up some traveling money, and we're here on their behalf. Can't say your dog's welcome has made a *gut* first impression, though. Better lock it up before it bites somebody."

Amos straightened his shoulders. "Queenie keeps the coyotes and other . . . intruders away," he replied firmly. "*Denki* for your observation, but she'll always have the run of Promise Lodge property. Without her, I doubt we'd still have any of our chickens."

Frances's eyes widened. "You've got coyotes? Have you seen wolves and snakes, as well? It does seem rather wild and removed from civilization out here."

Rosetta smiled, suspecting the bishop's wife didn't often get a word in edgewise. "Once houses start going up, some of the wildlife will find other habitats, I'm thinking. My sisters and I love it here, but we do notice how quiet it is. Won't you come in?" she added. "It's nearly time for supper and you've had a long trip."

Amos glanced toward the road. "Where's your driver? He's welcome to come in, as well."

"We rode the bus from Ohio to Kirksville and got a cab from there," Floyd replied. "We'll call for another cab when we've seen what we need to see."

Maybe the Lehmans already wish they were back in that

cab, considering the rocky start we've gotten off to, Rosetta thought as the four of them walked silently toward the lodge. She sensed the Lehmans were studying the cabins, along with the condition of the lodge, the barn, and the other outbuildings—as well they should, if they were here on behalf of members of their congregation.

"We had a fine time fishing at Rainbow Lake last night," Amos said as he pointed toward the water. "Beyond that, you'll see where we'll be selling off tracts of land—"

"I suppose you folks have already claimed the property right here, where the garden plots are planted and there's grass instead of trees and underbrush," Floyd said in a tight voice.

Again Amos's eyebrows flickered, but he kept a smile on his face. "*Jah,* those are the plots where Mattie Schwartz and the Hershberger girls are raising produce to sell at the stand you saw out by the road. Christine Hershberger owns the property where her dairy herd grazes, including the barn. This lot with the cabins and lodge belongs to Rosetta. She's converting the lodge into apartments for—"

"And our first renters arrived yesterday!" Rosetta added. "You'll soon meet them, because they've been cooking our supper."

Floyd dropped his suitcase to stare at her with a raised eyebrow. "You know quite well that Old Order members don't operate inns or other businesses that allow outsiders to share our living space!" he admonished her. "That's a sure path to temptation—a way for English men to lure away our women. And all those bedrooms! What are you *thinking,* woman?"

Rosetta bit back a retort. Bishop Floyd was going to be a challenge. "*Jah,* I'm aware of our church's rules about outsiders staying with us—so the apartments are only for Plain *women,*" she replied firmly. "Widows and *maidels* will live here permanently, rather than bachelors or families—or guests, as would come to an inn."

She gestured toward the row of cabins nestled in the shade of late afternoon. "We've been redding up these cottages for folks who buy property and need a place to stay until their new homes are built," she pointed out. "Sounds better than having to live in a tent, wouldn't you say?"

Frances's lips flickered with a smile, but Floyd wasn't impressed.

"Your apartment idea is totally *unnatural!*" he declared. "Our women are to be sheltered and provided for by the men in their families—"

"Ah, but you see, my two sisters are widowed now and they have no *dat* or brothers to look after them," Rosetta insisted, keeping her voice low but firm. "It was a hardship for them to maintain farms and outbuildings—as it was for me after our parents passed on. We saw this plan as a solution that would benefit other women, as well. We prayed over this long and hard. We feel God led us here to this beautiful land so we could provide homes for other folks, as well."

Floyd exhaled in disbelief, gawking at Amos. "You're a preacher, *jah?*" he demanded. "Why are you allowing these sisters to be in charge of so much property and their own businesses? That's just *wrong.*"

Amos stopped at the bottom of the porch steps, considering his response. Rosetta noted how his jaw tightened, as though he were restraining words that wanted to stampede like agitated horses.

"I've served my Lord as an ordained preacher for nearly twenty years," he replied patiently. "Jesus taught us that he who would lead must be the servant of all, and that the meek would inherit the earth. These three sisters have taken on an enormous mission—starting a new colony with a spirit of peace and service. I'm honored that they've asked me to partner with them."

Rosetta held her breath, pleased to hear Preacher Amos state his convictions. Before their guest could protest further, Amos continued earnestly.

"If our new idea—our untraditional plan—upsets you, Floyd, perhaps Promise Lodge isn't the place you want to call home," he said. "You've done nothing but criticize us since we met you a few moments ago. You've not even given us a chance to show you around—or to introduce Mattie and Christine—yet you're certain we're steeping ourselves in sin and treading the road to ruin.

"When we received your letter, we agreed that God would provide us the right bishop for Promise Lodge," Amos continued earnestly. "He might well guide more than one bishop here and then do the choosing for us, you know."

Floyd's face had turned the color of raw hamburger. The *whump* of the screen door made him turn to see that the Hershberger girls, the two Kuhns, Mattie, Christine, and Deborah had come outside to meet them—and to witness Floyd's flaring temper. Rosetta saw that Roman and Noah were coming from the barn, as well, their expressions alight with interest. Queenie sat down at Rosetta's feet, as though protecting her from this disagreeable newcomer.

"God Himself directed me to come here," Floyd said in a strained voice. "He said I was to lead you as your bishop—"

"Could be He's leaving our options open," Preacher Amos insisted as he crossed his arms. "Could be we'll hold a drawing of the lot when other bishops get here—the same process that determined that you and I were to be leaders in our previous districts. The same process used in biblical times, beginning when Christ's disciples replaced Judas with Matthias."

"Don't get biblical with *me*," Floyd retorted. "You're the ones breaking the rules by allowing women to own this property and to decide—"

"But Jesus gave women the same attention and respect

He gave to men," Mattie spoke up from the porch. "Our bishop in Coldstream didn't follow the Lord's teachings very closely—which was the main reason my sisters and I felt compelled to find a better place. A better life for our families."

"And while we're stating our beliefs," Christine put in, "you should know that Promise Lodge is a place of peace. We'll not tolerate family violence, where a husband believes he can strike his wife or daughters to keep them in line with his way of thinking."

Frances Lehman sucked in her breath, which gave Rosetta the idea that Floyd was accustomed to controlling her, perhaps with a heavy hand. Deborah licked her lips nervously but she seemed pleased to have this stipulation spelled out.

"Who are *you* to be telling me this?" Floyd challenged. "Why do I sense absolutely no respect or humility from anyone I've met here?"

Rosetta's eyes widened. It wasn't the Plain way to speak so contentiously, nor did she and her sisters intentionally stir things up with men. As Mattie and Christine came down the porch steps, she sincerely hoped they could find a way to dispel the ill will that hung over all of them like a dark cloud.

"I'm Mattie Schwartz and this is my sister, Christine Hershberger," Mattie began, offering her hand to the bishop. "I'm truly sorry if we seem brash or even sacrilegious, Bishop. Forgiveness is the Plain way, and I forgive you for hollering at my son's dog and for speaking so harshly—so judgmentally—to Rosetta and Amos. I suspect you're tired after your long trip. I hope you'll feel better after we eat the meal our new residents, Beulah and Ruby Kuhn, have cooked for us."

Floyd looked at Mattie's extended hand as if she'd offered him a branch from a thorn tree. When his gaze shifted to study the women on the porch, Frances cleared her throat.

"*Denki* for inviting us to supper on such short notice," she said tentatively. "Whatever it is smells awfully *gut,* and we'll be pleased to get better acquainted as we all break bread."

The tension eased a bit, and Rosetta was glad to see the Kuhn sisters nodding. Ruby turned to go inside. "If you'll all get washed up now—"

"We'll have supper on the table in two shakes of Queenie's tail," Beulah finished.

"We'll set a couple more places," Deborah said as she and the Hershberger girls followed the Kuhns back to the kitchen.

"I've had my eye on that apricot cherry slab pie, and I'm ready to try it out!" Noah added with a grin. "Come on, Queenie. Let's put some chow in your bowl so I can head in to my own supper."

Rosetta was relieved that Bishop Floyd entered the lodge without any further negative proclamations. She noted how Frances gazed around the lobby with an admiring eye and then hurried into the kitchen to help carry food out to the long table in the dining room. After everyone was seated and a silent prayer had been offered, they passed the platters of seasoned meat loaf, potato loaf, and a bowl of fresh salad from the garden.

Rosetta saw Frances smiling at her occasionally from across the table as Amos was introducing the young adults to keep the conversation flowing. Rosetta returned her smiles, wondering if Frances would want to move here . . . wondering what sort of life she led in Sugarcreek, and what sort of marriage she had—not that it was any of her business.

"If I recall correctly from your letter, Frances, you have a couple of daughters," Rosetta said when there was a break in the conversation. "Will they be coming to Promise Lodge if you decide to make your new home here? Or are they married and staying in Ohio?"

Frances's face lit up at the mention of her girls. Her gaze fluttered in Roman and Noah's direction. "Our Gloria is twenty-two and Mary Kate is eighteen," she replied. "They've both dated a few fellows—"

"As obedient daughters, they'll come with us wherever we decide to relocate," Floyd put in. He looked intently at Roman and Noah. "They're looking for industrious husbands who can provide well for them. What trades are you boys engaged in?"

Noah looked up from his supper. "I'm a welder, and I've just gotten a job with the landscaper who lives up the hill," he replied confidently. "I'm also serious about Deborah, so I won't be dating your girls."

"I manage Aunt Christine's dairy herd, as well as arranging the milk sales and the tankers that come pick it up," Roman said before Floyd could comment. "We've received several letters from families with daughters, so I'll have plenty of opportunities to find a wife after I help my *mamm* and my aunts get Promise Lodge off to a solid start."

Rosetta shared a smile with her sisters. Not so long ago Noah had expressed doubts about coming to Promise Lodge, but he and his brother sounded determined to make the new colony work out now—on their own terms. She was about to ask Frances more about Gloria and Mary Kate when the phone rang.

"I'll get that," Amos said as he rose from the table. "I'm expecting a call from another one of our potential new families. Excuse me."

Floyd watched Amos go through the kitchen and pick up the wall phone's receiver. "Why is your phone inside the house?" he asked sternly. "You know full well that we Amish believe it's too tempting to chatter away the day—"

"We've lived here less than a month, so we haven't had the chance to get a phone company fellow to move the phone line for us," Christine replied.

"There's also a phone upstairs, in the hallway," Rosetta pointed out. "I thought that with several Plain renters sharing that one, it would be much like neighbors sharing a phone shanty."

"We want the new bishop of Promise Lodge to decide whether we should remove this phone," Mattie joined in. "We have a Bender, three Schwartzes, three Hershbergers, and Amos using the one in the kitchen, so it's not like any of us have the luxury of a private line."

"It also serves as the phone for our dairy," Roman remarked. "And it won't be long before the produce stand opens, so we'll be getting calls about our eggs and vegetables."

"We've never shared a phone. We live a ways down the road from our nearest neighbor," Frances remarked quietly.

Floyd glared at his wife, but he held his tongue as Amos returned to the table.

"Sounds like we'll have another family coming for a visit in a week or two," the preacher remarked as he picked up his fork. "With so many folks arriving, you and Frances might want to pick out the cabin you'll stay in while your house is being built. We'll hold it for you—unless you've already decided you don't want to move here."

In the expectant silence that followed, Rosetta's thoughts raced. It wasn't proper to hope the Lehmans would stay in Ohio, even if it seemed clear that Bishop Floyd would constantly find fault with her and her sisters. Should she and Mattie and Christine concoct a policy for not selling land to prospective residents who rubbed them the wrong way?

Lord, forgive me for such an uncharitable thought. We can't exclude Your children from our new colony simply because we disagree with them. As Rosetta carried dessert to the table, Floyd cleared his throat ceremoniously.

"If you've got so many others coming, perhaps Frances and I should stay in one of the rooms here in the lodge," the bishop began. "I have a bad back that requires a firm bed. I doubt the mattresses in the cabins will support it."

"Just so happens we've put a new mattress in number two," Christine spoke up. "Extra firm. And we've hung new curtains at the windows."

"You're also welcome to furnish any of the cabins with your own belongings," Mattie pointed out.

Beulah leaned toward her sister, who sat beside her. "In your own words, Bishop, it might make for a sinfully tempting situation to have a man here in the apartments that are intended for women," she remarked with a straight face. "All those bedrooms, you know."

"Oh, temptingly sinful," Ruby agreed in a serious tone. "We'd no doubt have someone confessing to wayward thoughts after every Sunday service."

Rosetta bit back laughter as she set the slab pie on the table. Noah and Roman were fighting smiles, as well, while Christine's girls and Deborah nipped their lips and blushed. Floyd appeared ready to deliver a sermon, but as he opened his mouth Beulah raised her hand to silence him.

"My sister and I have crossed the line with our flippant talk," she began contritely. "It was rude and improper of me to start such a thread of conversation—"

"And we hope you can forgive the disrespectful way we twisted your earlier words, Bishop," Ruby continued without missing a beat. "It's not our way to have fun at someone else's expense. Honest. We're very sorry."

Floyd's mouth opened and closed, as though he had no idea how to respond to the gray-haired, bespectacled sisters across the table from him. Rosetta began to cut the slab pie into generous squares, wondering how the conversation would continue.

"You know, this brings up another point," Amos said. "Now that we have our first tenants, it's improper for *me* to be living here any longer. I'll shift my belongings into that smallest cabin at the end of the row, right after supper."

Noah kept his eye on the pie Rosetta was slicing, his expression pensive. "I hate to take up another one of the cabins—especially when Deborah would be so close by," he added, "so I'll bunk in the barn loft. Plenty of space up there until we get a load of hay, and windows on either end to catch the breeze, too."

"I'll join you there," Roman said. "As the summer passes, we'll figure out something more permanent—and you'll most likely be building a house soon anyway."

Noah smiled. "Queenie can stay out there, too. Out of everyone's way."

Once again the dining room grew quiet. Everyone looked at Floyd, awaiting his response. Rosetta was proud of her nephews and pleased that their three men had set an example of consideration—sacrificing their personal comfort and convenience to maintain proper decorum now that the Kuhn sisters would be living here. Deep down, Rosetta wondered if Floyd was making up excuses to stay in the lodge, where the rooms were more modern.

"I think it'll be *fun* to stay in a cabin," Frances remarked. "It reminds me of the day we met, Floyd, when our families were holding reunions in the same state park."

Floyd's eyes widened, suggesting he might launch into another rant, but then he exhaled as though he realized he was outnumbered. "All right then, we'll claim the one with the new mattress for now," he agreed as he accepted the plate of pie Rosetta had passed down the table to him. "By the time we head back to Ohio on Monday, I'll let you know whether you need to hold it for us."

Amos nodded. He sat back as Christine picked up his dirty dinner plate, while Deborah and the two other girls began to clear the food from the table. "Any idea how many other families might be coming with you?" he asked. "We've drawn up a rough map of our property, with some lines where a couple of roads might go, along with some possible boundaries for individual plots. Once you look at that, and we show you around, you'll have a better idea if this land is suited for your friends' homes and businesses."

"It'll be exciting to build a new home and establish a new colony with other folks," Frances said quietly. "But Missouri's a long way from Ohio, where we've lived our entire lives. I'll be praying about this a lot in the next day or so—and I hope you'll pray for us, as well, Rosetta. You and your sisters know exactly what it's like to leave your lifelong home and your friends."

Rosetta handed Frances a plate of pie. "Mattie and Christine and I found that leaving our friends has been the hardest part of this venture."

"But not one of us would turn back," Mattie insisted.

"We're in it for the long haul, too," Beulah said, smiling at her sister.

Ruby nodded emphatically. "I keep bees and Beulah plans to open a small cheese factory. What do you folks do?"

Frances cut into her pie before she responded. "The girls and I maintain the household, mostly. It wouldn't be proper for a bishop's wife to operate a business—"

"Don't get any ideas about doing that if we move here, either," Floyd cut in as he eyed Rosetta and the Kuhn sisters with a hint of disapproval. "My brothers and I own a siding and window installation business. Our ride through the countryside around Promise makes me wonder if that trade would be profitable here, however. I didn't see any residential areas nearby that would provide a customer base."

Amos raised his eyebrows. "Seems to me you'd be perfectly positioned to work on new houses here at Promise Lodge," he pointed out. "I build homes and barns, so I plan to be busy at that for a long time as our new residents move in."

"Maybe our neighbor Truman would connect you with some building contractors, Bishop Floyd," Noah suggested. "He runs a landscaping business, and he's the fellow who just hired me to make ornamental gates at one of his work sites."

"It'll all work out," Frances said with quiet conviction. "There's a place for everyone and work for every hand in God's earthly kingdom."

"*Jah,* we never seem to run out of work!" Beulah replied with a laugh. "I predict that life here at Promise Lodge will be anything but boring."

"I can't wait to settle in next week," Ruby chimed in happily. "A place named Promise Lodge just has to be a spot where God makes His promises come true, ain't so?"

Rosetta smiled as she sat down to her own piece of apricot cherry pie. *Ruby's got it right, Lord Jesus. Let it be so for all of Your servants who come here to live.*

Chapter Twenty

Deborah dressed quickly on Sunday morning, thinking Rosetta might want some extra assistance with breakfast. She was glad Bishop Floyd had agreed that today would be a day of rest rather than a morning for church. Somehow, it seemed their guest had already delivered several sermons on their behavior at Promise Lodge, and—petty as it seemed—she was tired of him pointing up faults he found with every little thing.

Forgive me, Lord, for finding fault, as well, she thought as she strode from her cabin to the back door of the lodge building. *It's not my place to—*

Deborah stopped when she saw Preacher Amos, Noah, and Roman standing outside the mudroom door. Noah placed his finger over his lips, signaling for her silence. Even Queenie, her black ears angled upward, seemed intent on listening to something—and then Deborah heard Floyd's voice drifting through the open window.

"I'm telling you, Lester, these people are like sheep gone astray without any inclination to return to the fold," the bishop was saying. "I hesitate to expose my daughters—and yours—to these wayward, freethinking women even as I believe it's my Christian duty to set them all back on the path to righteousness."

Preacher Amos gripped the door handle. He looked ready to burst in on Bishop Floyd's phone conversation, yet intent upon hearing their guest's entire story before he revealed his presence.

"Oh, Frances thinks this place is quaint, and she loves the idea of building a new house," Floyd continued in a rising voice. "But women usually see the world through impractical rose-colored glasses. It doesn't bother her that the three gals who've established this place are inviting *maidels* and widows to live in apartments, or that they're all running businesses instead of households . . . *jah,* you heard me right," Floyd continued with a humorless laugh. "They seem to believe they can prosper without menfolk, and that's not the way God intended for them to live! And the preacher that came here with them is letting them get away with that."

When Deborah looked away, wondering how long Floyd would rant about Promise Lodge, she saw Frances leaving the cabin the Lehmans had slept in. The bishop's wife walked toward the front porch of the lodge, probably planning to help with the preparation of their simple Sunday breakfast. Deborah heard the steady tattoo of her footsteps crossing the hardwood floors of the lobby . . . then entering the dining room, and then the kitchen.

"That's the way I see it, Lester," Floyd continued. "It would be a lot easier to find our own land and establish a colony that'll be run our way from the beginning. If your wife and mine get into the habit of—"

"Floyd Lehman!" Frances cried out. "Not one thing's been readied for breakfast because you're gossiping on the phone and our hostesses are too polite to interrupt you! How very rude!" she exclaimed. "It would serve you right if they were all listening to you right now. They can't help but hear you—I caught every word before I even stepped inside!"

Deborah covered her mouth to keep from laughing out loud. A loud *clack* told them Floyd had hung up the phone, but how would he react to learning he'd had an audience?

"I was not speaking that loudly," the bishop insisted in a slightly quieter voice. "Once again, you exaggerate about—"

"And once again you refuse to admit how hard of hearing you are," Frances interrupted him. "You have no idea how your voice carries, and how you speak in your sermon-giving voice even during a face-to-face conversation. See there?" she went on after a brief pause. "Rosetta and Mattie have been waiting patiently at the top of the stairs."

As Deborah pictured this, she suspected the Kuhn sisters, Christine, and her girls were standing behind Rosetta and Mattie. They were probably wondering—as she was—what would happen next, and what the proper response to Floyd's phone conversation would be.

Preacher Amos cleared his throat and opened the screen door. "There's no pretending that the rest of us didn't hear what you said, either, Floyd," he remarked as he led the way inside. "I'm sorry you've compared us to sheep gone astray—but you can see that having this phone on the kitchen wall is actually a lot less private than allowing folks to use a phone shanty. I think it'll go a long way toward limiting idle chitchat and the hurtful things we say when we believe no one's listening. No one except God, that is."

Deborah quickly stepped around the men to enter the kitchen. When she glanced up the back stairway, she saw Mattie and Rosetta coming down the steps.

"I didn't say a thing that wasn't true," Floyd insisted. "Every one of you knows that Promise Lodge has gone against Old Order ways from the moment you women decided to buy this land. I may be the first man to point that out, but I won't be the last."

"We anticipated some objections to the way we've established our new colony," Amos replied calmly. "And I'll say it again: perhaps Promise Lodge isn't the right place for you and your family to settle. We believe our ways of peace and acceptance are just as right as you believe they're wrong."

"It's up to God to be the judge of right and wrong," Mattie remarked when she'd reached the bottom of the stairway. "So while I won't criticize you for your opinions of us, neither will I allow you to yank us up and toss us aside as though we're weeds in your garden, Bishop Floyd. My sisters and Amos and I own this land. We can refuse to sell to anyone we choose, you know."

Deborah's eyes widened as she opened the silverware drawer. She'd never heard a Plain woman speak out this way—and to a man, no less.

"*Jah,* we've received letters and calls from plenty of other folks," Christine put in. "I'm not a bit worried about my investment in this place being repaid. And if that sounds boastful and proud, that's not my intention."

"You haven't said a thing that wasn't true, Sisters," Rosetta chimed in. She stood on the step behind Mattie, her arms crossed tightly. "But it seems that our truth and what God has told us are different from what the Lord has revealed to you, Bishop Floyd. We believe He loves all of His children equally, whether they wear suspenders or skirts, hats or *kapps.*"

"You've got it right, Rosetta," Beulah said as she came the rest of the way down the narrow stairs.

"And I see no reason to waste any more time on this conversation," Ruby stated from behind her. "We'll all feel better after we eat breakfast and drink some coffee. 'This is the day the Lord has made. Let us rejoice and be glad in it.'"

Noah smiled at Deborah and his cousins when the women had finished redding up the kitchen after breakfast.

"Anybody in the mood for a walk? I don't want to spend this pretty day being cooped up inside."

"I like the sound of that, Noah," Phoebe replied as they hung up their wet towels. "I'm all for getting some fresh air—"

"Oh, that sounds like a lovely idea," Beulah remarked wistfully.

"But we know you young people would rather have your time together without us old ladies along," Ruby said.

As Noah gazed at the Kuhn sisters, the memory of his long-gone grandmothers tugged at his heart. When Roman joined them, the matter was decided.

"Why not take Ruby and Beulah out to the orchard so they can think about where to situate their beehives?" he asked. "Meanwhile, we'll get a better idea about how much clearing we need to do so the trees will produce *gut* apples again."

"I'd like that," Deborah replied as she linked her arms through Beulah and Ruby's. "I haven't been to see the orchard, either."

Noah smiled as the seven of them headed through the lobby and out onto the porch. The breeze made the humming-bird feeders sway beside the trumpet vines, which was loaded with orange blooms in the shape of pointed hats. Queenie greeted them with a *woof,* circling them in her eagerness to join them. When they'd walked several yards away from the lodge, Noah cleared his throat.

"I need a break from the bishop," he admitted in a low voice.

"I didn't know what to think when you fellows were standing outside the mudroom door this morning," Deborah said with a shake of her head. "Floyd surely had to know we could hear him talking on the phone."

"Loud and clear," Beulah agreed. "When I opened my

door, there was no way around eavesdropping on every word he said."

"I was surprised at the way Frances lit into him, too," Ruby said softly. She glanced back toward the lodge as though to be sure the Lehmans weren't out on the porch— or following them to the orchard. "I have to wonder if Floyd will chastise her for that later. And I've had second thoughts about living here if those folks come to Promise Lodge."

"Oh, Ruby! Please don't let him change your mind about staying," Laura protested. "I'm really looking forward to you ladies setting up your cheese factory, and selling your honey in our roadside stand, too."

Ruby stopped walking at the same moment her sister did, and the two Kuhns exchanged a long look. "Are you sure?" Beulah asked hesitantly.

"*Jah,* we understand what a bother a couple of old biddies can be," Ruby said. "We get reminded about that fairly often—maybe not in so many words—"

"But facial expressions tell the tale," Beulah said with a rueful laugh. "We know we're not perking along like spring chickens anymore."

"Puh!" Laura remarked as she turned to face both of them. "None of us here have any grandmas left, and I for one really miss them!

"*Jah!* You can be our adopted grannies!" Phoebe agreed as she clapped her hands together. "And we can help with your honey and cheese making—if you want us to."

Ruby and Beulah grabbed one another's hands, looking as though they might cry. "Well, if that's not the sweetest thing to say—"

"And it makes up for Bishop Floyd's sharp tongue, too," Ruby finished their sentence. She gazed at the overgrown or-chard. Many of the trees had branches that dragged on the ground, and the grass and weeds were growing in long clumps around their trunks. "My little bees could be just

the remedy for these neglected trees—and *gut* for your
vegetable gardens, as well. I think they'll enjoy having fresh
territory to pollinate."

"Look at how pretty the pasture is—and look at those
cute little goats of Rosetta's frolicking around," Beulah said
lightly. "I'm so glad we saw your ad—"

"And that we decided to visit Promise Lodge instead of
just wishing we could," Ruby remarked. "Truth be told, it'll
be nice to have you older kids around. Our nieces and
nephews sometimes tease us . . . slip into our room to change
things around—"

"Because they think we're too old to grab them and apply
our hands to their backsides when they need it—not that
their *mamm* would tolerate us doing that." Beulah shook her
head in frustrated disapproval. "It's not a *gut* idea to spare
the rod and spoil the child. In the end, *everybody* pays for
that mistake."

Noah was listening intently, touched by the tale the Kuhns
were telling between the lines. The roar of an engine made
them all turn to watch a big pickup truck enter the grounds.
"Looks like we've got more company," he said. "Queenie,
you stay right here. No barking and no getting feisty,
hear me?"

The black-and-white dog let out a frustrated *woof* and sat
down at Noah's side.

"Uh-oh," Beulah murmured.

"We should've known," Ruby said with a sigh. "That's
our little brother, Delbert, come to fetch us home, no doubt."

"Well, he's our *younger* brother," Beulah clarified. "Nothing
little about him."

Noah had to agree. The fellow who unfolded himself out
of the cab stood nearly seven feet tall from his boots to the
top of his straw hat. Noah waved and started toward the man,
wondering what he could say to ease the strain Ruby and

Beulah had probably caused by leaving home without any warning.

"Welcome to Promise Lodge," he called out as Roman caught up to him. "You've picked a great day to see the place."

"Well, what I *see* is two sisters who nearly gave me a heart attack when they disappeared," Delbert replied curtly. "What were Claire and I supposed to think when you didn't show up to fix dinner? The kids were crying and worried about somebody breaking in to steal you away."

Although Noah could understand the concern that creased Delbert's weathered face, he felt bad for Ruby and Beulah. They were walking toward their brother with their heads slightly bowed, clutching one another's hand. The happy confidence they'd displayed just moments ago had been replaced by childlike remorse.

"We did call you," Beulah pointed out.

"And we came here because we figured if we got out of your house, Claire would have an easier time of getting the kids ready for school and church in the mornings," Ruby said contritely. "Here, we've each got our own room—"

"And we share a bathroom for just the two of us, instead one for all twelve of us," Beulah reasoned aloud.

When the two ladies stopped in front of him, Delbert placed his hands on his hips. "I've told you I was going to convert that hall closet into a half-bath—"

"And bless your heart, you've had the toilet and sink for that project for as long as I can recall," Ruby said gently. "You're a busy man with a busy family. We truly appreciate the way you've looked after us all these years—"

"—and we saw this as an opportunity to let your young family have more space," Beulah continued with an earnest expression. "We know we get in the way sometimes. And it'll only get more crowded as the kids—and Ruby and I— get older."

Delbert let out an exasperated sigh. "What makes you think you can just take off on your own? How can you afford to pay any rent?"

The sisters looked at each other as though they shared a juicy little secret. "I've been saving up my money from working at the cheese factory," Beulah replied proudly.

"And I've got my honey money," Ruby said. "It's amazing what you can accumulate when you live a simple life—"

"And we thank you for not charging us rent—"

"—although we certainly did our share of cooking and nose-wiping and—

"—diaper changing and laundry and scrubbing floors and—"

"—and now we're going to take care of ourselves in this lovely new colony—"

"—where we're making friends and figuring out where to put Ruby's hives—"

"—and Beulah's going to start up a little cheese factory, using the milk from the Holsteins and the dairy goats that are already here!"

Noah had stepped aside, watching Delbert follow his sisters' conversation with an expression of bewildered disbelief on his tanned face. The big man cleared his throat as though he was about to deliver a speech he'd been practicing during his drive. Instead, he shook his head.

"But it's my responsibility to see to your needs," Delbert insisted. "Claire and I are happy to have you in our home—"

"When the Lord whispered in our ears to come and look this place over," Beulah began.

"We knew it was the answer to our prayers," Ruby went on in a voice that was barely audible. "Please don't think we're ungrateful. We—we just wanted to—"

"—try our hand at living independently, before we got too old and senile to know what we'd been missing." Beulah exhaled slowly. "We're sorry for the worry we've caused you, Delbert. But our minds are made up."

"Our rent's paid for the next six months, too," Ruby pointed out. "We were coming home tomorrow to fetch the bees and the rest of our clothes, and to tell the family more about our new adventure."

Noah sensed the Kuhn family could use some private time, so he glanced at Roman and the girls. "We'll let you folks talk this out," he said. "Feel free to look the place over—and to stay and have dinner with us, Delbert."

Ruby grinned like an excited little kid. "*Jah,* you should see the big dining room, and the rooms where we gals can hold quilting frolics—"

"Come up and see our apartments—which will only be rented to *maidels* and widows, all nice and proper," Beulah added.

"Once you meet the three sisters who started this place, along with Preacher Amos—"

"—you'll feel a whole lot better about us being here," Beulah assured him. "And when you come to visit, the kids can fish in Rainbow Lake, and play with Queenie—"

The dog let out an exuberant *woof* and wagged her tail. Noah was relieved when Delbert laughed and the stiffness left his broad shoulders.

"Well, I've driven all this way, so I might as well take a *gut* look at the place," he said as he gazed at the orchard and the pasture. "It *is* pretty here. But I'm still not happy about the way you two just up and left us. If something bad happened to you, I could never forgive myself."

Noah clasped Deborah's hand and started toward the lake, with his brother and cousins following them. "I have to think Delbert's heart is in the right place, and that he did the responsible thing, coming to fetch his sisters," he said in a low voice. "But I get the feeling he's never seen Ruby's and Beulah's more *adventurous* side."

Deborah chuckled. "I suspect they'll talk circles around him until he gets too dizzy to keep up with them. But I hope they work it out."

"*Jah,* I'd hate to see them have to go back, if they don't really want to," Laura said. "I really do like them."

Roman glanced toward the porch of the lodge, where they could see Preacher Amos, their *mamm,* and their aunts sitting with the Lehmans. "Just as Delbert's doing the right thing, looking after his sisters, Bishop Floyd is standing up for beliefs about women and our religion that have existed for centuries," he pointed out. "We might not like the way he's been talking, but he's right. He'll not be the only man who'll say that Mamm and the aunts have taken too much control and are stepping out of line."

"I'm glad Preacher Amos said they wanted a deposit to hold the cabin the Lehmans are in," Phoebe remarked. "I think Bishop Floyd took it more seriously because a man was asking him for money instead of Aunt Mattie."

"Do you think they'll stay?" Deborah asked. "Frances seems to like it here."

"Floyd impresses me as the type who'll do things his way," Laura chimed in. "When he told that Lester fellow on the phone that they might be better off starting a colony themselves, I got the idea he already had another place in mind."

Noah smiled, relieved that he would be visiting the job site with Truman tomorrow when the Lehmans left for Ohio. "God knows the answers to all our questions," he murmured, "and we'll have to wait until He decides to reveal them."

That evening, after everyone had eaten a light supper, Rosetta walked Ruby and Beulah out to Delbert's truck. Her heart felt heavy. It was clear that Delbert wanted the best for his older sisters, yet she sensed that once the three of them left Promise Lodge, he would put his foot down and make his sisters stay in his home with Claire and the kids. When he passed them in a long-legged stride, carrying their suitcases to the truck, Rosetta slipped her arms around Beulah's and Ruby's shoulders.

"I hope you'll have a peaceful ride back," she said ruefully. "I'm sorry your brother is so upset about you wanting to live here."

"Oh, it's us who's sorry," Beulah replied with a shake of her head.

"*Jah,* we knew Delbert would be peeved at us," Ruby said in a sorrowful voice, "but after we called him to tell him we were okay, I didn't figure on him coming to haul us home."

"It's not over yet," Beulah insisted. "We love it here, Rosetta, and we want you to keep our rent money and hold our apartments for us. We'll figure out a way to change Delbert's mind."

"And if we see that's not going to happen, we'll let you know where to send our money." Ruby reached into her apron pocket and pulled out a rectangular bar of soap. She inhaled its fragrance wistfully. "Awfully nice of you to welcome us with your homemade soap—"

"And to send a fresh bar along for Claire, too," Beulah added. "In the short time we've been at Promise Lodge, we've felt such kindness and compassion. *Denki* for welcoming us so warmly. We wish you and your sisters all the best as more folks come here to build new homes."

"Better get a move on," Delbert called out from the truck's window. "We've got a ways to go."

With a sigh, Ruby and Beulah both hugged Rosetta tightly. She was surprised at how attached she already felt to these ladies. She would miss them a *lot*.

"We'll keep in touch," Beulah said as she eased away.

"Don't give up on us," Ruby insisted. "I still plan to come back with my bees."

Rosetta nodded, her throat so tight she couldn't respond. She watched the ladies clamber into the truck's extended cab, waving until the vehicle rolled beneath the metal entryway sign.

What if they don't come back? What if Delbert—and other men in other families—won't allow their maidel *sisters and widowed* mamms *to live in our apartments? Have I made a really stupid assumption, Lord, dreaming that I could provide homes for other Plain women? Has all the money I've spent been wasted?*

Rosetta sighed and turned to walk back to the lodge. Bishop Floyd's voice drifted out from the porch, where he sat talking to Amos in that holier-than-thou tone she'd already come to resent.

But what if Floyd had a point? What if the other men who built homes here gave her the same sort of grief about how *unnatural* it was for women to live independently?

Rosetta walked over to the fence where her goats stood watching her, chewing on grass. "What do you think, girls?" she murmured as she stroked their flat, bony foreheads. "What am I going to do if I can't earn back the money I've invested in this place? Sure, Mattie and Christine will share their income, but that's not the way we agreed it would work."

Rosetta walked around to the mudroom door so she wouldn't have to deal with the bishop. Up the back stairs she went, and into her apartment. She would really regret it if she couldn't live independently, as she'd planned—but she'd hate it even more if God decided Floyd Lehman was right.

Chapter Twenty-One

Monday morning as Deborah was helping Laura and Phoebe carry the hash browns, fried bell peppers, onions, and crumbled sausage to the table for their haystack breakfast, the phone rang. Christine was the closest, so she answered it.

"Hello?" She turned toward the dining room, where everyone was taking a seat. "Amos is here, *jah*. I'll put him on."

She laid the receiver on the counter and picked up the big bowl of cheese sauce as Amos made his way to the phone. "It's Preacher Eli calling from Coldstream," she said in a low voice. "Sounds important."

Deborah's throat tightened. Why would her father be calling Amos? Dat had been one of the loudest naysayers when Mattie and her sisters had sold their farms to come to Promise—and he'd considered Preacher Amos a traitor and a fool for joining them, too. She took her seat between Laura and Phoebe as Noah and Roman sat down across the table.

Frances turned to Mattie and whispered, "This is one of the preachers from your former settlement, *jah?*"

"It is," Mattie replied. "Eli also happens to be Deborah's

dat—maybe with news about the unfortunate goings-on there," she murmured. "Let's listen."

As everyone kept quiet to hear Amos's side of the conversation, Deborah looked away from Bishop Floyd's piercing gaze. She'd felt fortunate that the story of her run-ins with Isaac hadn't been mentioned during the Lehmans' visit, and she sensed she would soon be subjected to Floyd's nosy questions.

"Hello, Eli. How've you been?" Preacher Amos said cordially. His brow furrowed as he listened. "Oh, my . . . and what did Obadiah say to *that?* If the new owner found Isaac's driver's license in the barn, that's a horse of a whole different color."

Deborah's eyes widened. Across the table, Noah leaned forward to listen more intently.

"Well, you can't blame Sheriff Renfro for doing his job," Amos pointed out. "Sounds to me like he was being more than fair, all things considered . . . *Jah,* that Presley fellow's only asking for what's rightfully his."

"Who's Presley?" Phoebe whispered.

"The English fellow who bought my farm," Rosetta murmured. "Apparently he's ready to move in and—"

"Well, I'll have to think about that," Amos went on in a louder voice. "Roman's got to be here to milk Christine's cows twice a day, and Noah's landed a new job, so he can't come, either," he explained. "Truth be told, after the way Isaac slipped in on us last week, I'm not keen on leaving the women by themselves . . . *Jah,* I'll get back to you on that, Eli. *Gut* to hear from you. Give our best to Alma and the rest of your family."

Amos returned to the table, his lips twitching in an odd smile. "We'd best pray over this fine breakfast while it's hot—and lift up a word for our friends in Coldstream, as well," he added. "Then I'll share that earful of news from Eli."

Deborah's pulse pounded as she bowed her head. It

seemed the drama with Isaac had risen a notch higher. She prayed that Amos's intriguing facial expression meant the situation wouldn't be affecting them here in Promise. It would be a blessing if Amos nipped Floyd's curiosity in the bud, too, but there was no predicting what the bishop might ask. *Please, Lord Jesus, keep me strong in my faith as we hear what Dat had to say.*

"I sure do love a haystack breakfast," Preacher Amos said as he arranged a layer of hash browns on his plate. "And it seems *hay* is a subject of interest in Coldstream, as well. When Keith Presley was checking out the damage to the Bender barn, he found Isaac Chupp's driver's license in a corner that hadn't burned, amongst some of the boys' beer boxes."

"Well, then," Christine said with a decisive nod. "There's no denying Isaac was there. Not that we ever doubted Deborah's story."

"And aren't we glad she called nine-one-one?" Mattie chimed in. "Had the firefighters not put out the flames, that scrap of evidence would've burned up with the rest of the place."

Bishop Floyd's brow furrowed as he gazed across the table at Deborah. "And why did you call the police? Why did you get involved in a situation where boys were drinking beer and—"

"That's a long story, best saved for another time," Noah interrupted impatiently.

"Isaac Chupp is the bishop's son," Mattie said in a purposeful tone. "And Bishop Obadiah's refusal to rein him in was our main reason for leaving Coldstream."

Frances's eyes widened. Deborah was extremely grateful that her longtime neighbors were determined to steer the conversation away from her painful past and concentrate on this morning's new information. She put a small helping of hash browns on her plate, but she'd lost her appetite.

"So what'd Presley do?" Roman asked. He covered his layer of hash browns with peppers and onions. "Seems to me Obadiah's not got a leg to stand on now."

"Presley took the license to Sheriff Renfro, and the two of them paid a visit to the Chupp place," Amos recounted. "Apparently Obadiah had no idea about the driver's license or Isaac's having a car, because Eli said the starch went right out of him. Isaac wasn't home, but the sheriff drove around the back roads and ran across him and Kerry on the blacktop going into Eulah."

Amos grew more serious as he ladled cheese sauce over top of the sausage and vegetable haystack on his plate. "Renfro pulled Isaac over for driving without a license. Took both boys to his office and called Obadiah and Presley in to talk to them."

Deborah's heart thudded. Was it wrong to feel so smug, so vindicated, because Isaac had finally gotten caught by someone who would do something about his behavior? The food on her plate smelled heavenly, but she set down her fork to listen to the rest of this story.

Across the table, Noah appeared pleased. "No way for Obadiah—or Isaac—to wiggle out of *that*."

"Not a very *gut* impression to make on the new neighbors," Mattie said. "I can imagine Mr. Presley was peeved about losing his barn before he moved in."

"Seems Keith Presley's the sort to turn the other cheek," Amos replied in an approving tone. "He said he wouldn't press charges if the barn was replaced with a new one, because he didn't want Isaac to have a black mark on his record for *arson* at such a young age."

"Oh, my," Frances murmured. "That's a very serious offense."

"So they believe Isaac and his buddies set the barn afire on purpose? Just for the fun of it?" Christine demanded.

Deborah suspected Christine wasn't asking about the

Bender barn alone, but about hers, as well. What a mess Isaac had made for these sisters, carousing with his friends and believing he'd get away with it.

"I still have to wonder why a preacher's daughter would be involved with such dubious activities," Floyd remarked as he eyed Deborah. "Why didn't you run the other way and notify the men—"

"Isaac and Kerry both claimed the fire was an accident—said they'd drunk too much beer and didn't see the flames until Deborah and the sirens alerted them," Amos interrupted. Then he smiled kindly at Deborah. "But this wasn't about *you*, dear. The boys—and Bishop Obadiah—are being held responsible. Which is why—"

"No, wait. This *is* about me," Deborah said in a low voice. Her insides quivered at the thought of setting the record straight—of facing up to Bishop Floyd right here and now. But if she didn't state her case, she would feel forever intimidated by his barbed questions and stares. *Please, Jesus, help me say this right. Floyd won't give me a second chance.*

Deborah inhaled deeply to fortify herself. "All of our men were on the far side of the district, too far away to hear the fire bell," she began, "so when I saw my neighbors' barn burning I called the police. *I did the right thing*—but the bishop's son shoved me into a buggy and then shoved me out into a ditch. And then his English friend took over.

"They were getting even because I'd called the cops," she went on in a steadier voice, daring to hold Floyd Lehman's gaze. "When each of them intended to—to *use* me, I prayed to Jesus and fought them off. When I stumbled home at dawn, my *dat* took one look and he judged me. Just like you're doing," she added in a whisper. "And he sent me away because he was ashamed of me and the way I had sinned."

Deborah swallowed hard. The Lehmans were both watching her closely. The kitchen was absolutely quiet and no one was eating. "So here I am at Promise Lodge, safe among these lifelong friends," she continued softly. "I've thanked God every day since the fire that *He delivered me from evil*—not once but twice, because those boys came here last week intending to hurt me again. I sincerely hope that when you or your daughters find yourselves in peril, God will do the same for you. He didn't fail me."

Frances blinked rapidly. Bishop Floyd glanced at his breakfast.

"Amen, Deborah," Rosetta whispered.

"Tell it like it is, girl," Noah murmured as he gazed at her steadfastly. "We're all with you on this. Your faith got you through the fire."

Preacher Amos watched the Lehmans' reactions for a moment and then nodded at Deborah. "You told that better than I would have, and you've cleared the air now. When your *dat* asked if I would come back to Coldstream to be the foreman for the Presleys' barn raising, your welfare—the safety of all you women—was my first concern."

"I can see why you'd hesitate to do that, Amos," Mattie murmured as she forked up a bite of her breakfast. "I'm glad my boys have *gut* reasons not to go back, however. I suppose that sounds hard-hearted and not very Christ-like."

"Actually, Eli called me because he knew Obadiah wouldn't ask for my help," Amos clarified. "He doesn't think the other men will be as cooperative if they don't have an experienced crew leader. He says everyone's getting mighty fed up with the Chupps."

Amos smiled at Noah then. "He also asked me to pass along his best wishes for your new job, son. Then Eli said that if I went back to help with that barn, he suspected several of our friends might want a firsthand account of the prospects at Promise Lodge."

"Too bad it had to come to this, though," Mattie said with a sigh. "Even if Obadiah's acting contrite now, owning up to

Isaac's activities, he's lost his credibility. It's a sad situation when folks can't believe in their bishop."

Frances's cheeks turned pink and she looked away from her husband. "It is, indeed," she murmured. Floyd focused on eating his breakfast, remained silent.

"*Jah*, it is," Amos agreed. "I suppose I could spare them a day or two, to show I'm still their friend—and to see how serious any of them might be about joining us here. And I'd like the new barn to be done right, so Keith Presley will have a better opinion of his new Amish neighbors."

"A commendable attitude," Floyd murmured. "And it speaks well of your leadership despite the way you left the district that God chose you to lead. A preacher has to have a very *gut* reason for doing that."

"I believe I did," Amos replied. "We all did."

But Dat didn't ask about me? As the folks around her dug into their food again, Deborah kept her question to herself. Her father was obviously caught up in the news about Isaac—and eager for Preacher Amos to take charge of the barn raising—so he hadn't given her a thought. Of course, verifying Isaac's guilt didn't mean she was innocent. She had still defied the *Ordnung* by calling 9-1-1 and by getting into Kerry's car that night. . . .

But your plan for happiness is in place, isn't it? she realized as she glanced across the table. *If you'd stayed in Coldstream you couldn't have reconciled with Noah—and you wouldn't be enjoying the company of these friends who love you.*

As he took his final bite of breakfast, Noah stretched his legs beneath the table to catch her feet between his. "I should head out to the road to meet Truman," he said. "Maybe he'll look at the designs I've drawn up and suggest which are the best ones to show the managers at the senior living center.

Or maybe they'll take one look and won't think I'm the right fellow for this welding job."

"I *doubt* that," Deborah said. He looked so eager and excited that she found a smile for him. "Truman wouldn't have mentioned the job if he didn't want you working for him."

"My thoughts exactly," Amos agreed as he spooned up more hash browns to start a second haystack. "Have a great day, Noah. We'll want to hear all about it when you get home tonight."

"I'll walk out with you," Roman said as he rose from his chair. "I spotted a couple of loose boards in the shed where the goats are. Can't have Rosetta's babies escaping—or have the coyotes finding a way inside."

As the Schwartz boys left the table, Deborah made an effort to eat more of her food so the others wouldn't suspect her feelings had been hurt. It was silly to bemoan her father's attitude, however. She'd known all her life that once Eli Peterscheim formed an opinion or made a decision, he didn't change it. And hadn't she made Bishop Floyd stop asking his pesky questions? Indeed, he and his wife had both remained surprisingly quiet since she'd spoken up.

"I'm glad Isaac's being held accountable now, and pleased to see that Obadiah's stopped ignoring his son's wrongdoing," Amos remarked. "And who knows? Maybe Preacher Eli will open his home to his daughter again—although we're glad you're here with us, dear."

"Maybe he will," Deborah murmured. As she gazed at the dear friends around the table, it again occurred to her that if God had led her to Promise in her time of need, He'd had a good reason. "Noah's asked me to wait for him, though—to be patient while he works toward building a home for us. And I've said I would."

"Yay!" Laura cried as she grabbed Deborah's shoulders. "That's what we've been wanting to hear!" Phoebe agreed. "Oh, but I'm glad you're together for the long haul again!"

Preacher Amos winked slyly at Mattie and then focused on Deborah again. "Happy to hear that," he said with a mysterious smile. "*Gut* things come to those who wait, Deborah. Trust me on this."

After breakfast, Bishop Floyd called for a taxi to take him and his wife to the Kirksville bus station. Then he and Amos went for another walk around the grounds. Rosetta ran dishwater while the other women stacked the dirty dishes and the girls put the leftovers in containers. When Frances cleared her throat rather loudly, all of them looked at her.

"Deborah, I'm glad you told your story," she said as she clutched her tea towel. "And I'm grateful to God that you escaped those boys and your situation in Coldstream because—well, Mary Kate, our youngest, wasn't so lucky. She's the real reason we're looking to leave our church district."

Rosetta's eyebrows rose and she turned off the faucet. "I hope you don't mean that Mary Kate ran afoul of some boys—"

"Just one. An English fellow who saw her walking home one evening from helping at a neighbor's house," Frances said in an urgent voice. "He got out of his car and grabbed her. Forced himself upon her in the woods and drove away. If she'd been brave like you, Deborah—if Mary Kate had screamed and put up a fight, we might've heard her, but . . . well, we're devastated. She's only eighteen."

"Oh, Frances, I'm so sorry," Rosetta murmured. As she put her arm around Frances's shoulders, Mattie and Christine and the girls gathered around to express their sympathy, as well. "What's the world coming to when our girls aren't safe in their own neighborhoods?"

Frances blotted her tears with her towel. "I prayed that we could put the incident behind us and be more watchful, but Mary Kate is carrying the baby of a man we know nothing about. You understand, of course, that her being the bishop's daughter adds another layer of . . . *complication* to our family's problem."

"*Jah,* a bishop's family is expected to toe a higher mark," Mattie murmured. "But you're human, like the rest of us. So this is why you and Floyd are leaving Ohio?"

"Before her condition becomes apparent, and before anyone suspects why he felt called to leave his district," Frances confirmed with a nod. "I refused to send Mary Kate away to distant kin, to have her baby in a strange place— knowing folks would only speculate about the reason she'd left all of a sudden."

"*Jah,* that's how people think, unfortunately." Christine squeezed Frances's shoulder. "If you believe Promise Lodge is a *gut* place to start fresh, we want you to come. Every one of us is here because we chose to leave trouble behind."

"You have no idea how relieved I was to meet you ladies— to know right off that we'd be bringing Mary Kate to a place of caring and compassion." A wry smile lit Frances's face. "*Please* don't let on to Floyd that I've told you about this. He's used to having his say, as bishop, and when situations spin out of his control, he doesn't deal with it very well. The truth will become more obvious as the months go by, of course."

Rosetta chuckled softly. "I figured that about him, *jah.* But it's the same for the rest of us, too," she pointed out. "We do our best to follow God's will, so when life takes a turn for the worse, it slaps us in the face pretty hard."

Wiping her eyes a final time, Frances smiled bravely at all of them. "We still have our family. We still have our Lord Jesus," she said in a determined tone. "I believe we'll be re- turning here very soon to get settled with Mary Kate and

Gloria—and to prepare for a baby in December. It just has to seem like *Floyd's* decision that we're coming here."

Mattie smiled. "Oh, some of us know a little about how the man has to be the head of the family."

"But we women are the necks that turn the heads," Christine added.

As they returned to redding up the kitchen, Rosetta turned the conversation to lighter topics by asking about what sort of house Frances was hoping for and where she might want it built. Within an hour, the Lehmans were packed and waiting for the taxi when it pulled up to the lodge for them.

"We'll keep in touch," Bishop Floyd said as he loaded their luggage into the trunk. "We appreciate your showing us around the place, and holding the cabin for us."

"We'll look forward to hearing from you," Preacher Amos replied.

Rosetta and the rest of them waved as the taxi headed for the road. *Just goes to show how we have no idea what crosses other folks have to bear, Lord. Keep reminding us not to judge others—and please grant Your special grace and peace to young Mary Kate.*

"I suspect we'll be seeing the Lehmans again soon," Amos remarked as he handed a check to Mattie. "When I suggested a deposit of five hundred dollars, he gave us a thousand."

"An investment in his family's future," Mattie said. "Something tells me he won't walk away from his money—or his commitments."

Rosetta shared a quick smile with her sisters as they headed back to the lodge. A few moments alone with Frances had shed a whole new light on Floyd's motivations. She sensed that when the bishop returned to Promise Lodge with Mary Kate, he might act a bit more tolerant of their ways here—and show a lot more humility.

Or not, she thought wryly. *With some men, there's no figuring them out.*

Noah strode quickly up the lane that evening, his heart overflowing. When Queenie rushed up to greet him, barking her welcome, he set his rolled-up papers on the ground so he could rub her head between his hands.

"I think we're gonna make it, Queenie-girl," he said gleefully. "It's all gonna fall into place now."

Queenie licked his face, and together they hurried toward the lodge. As he climbed the wooden steps, aromas of grilled beef, gravy, and fresh bread made his stomach rumble.

Smells like home, he thought. When Noah passed through the dining room, where the table was set for supper, the sight of Deborah at the stove made him stop to gaze at her. She was attacking a pan of boiled potatoes with the masher, steam rising around her precious face as her *kapp* strings fluttered with her energetic efforts. It was such an ordinary sight, yet so dear to him, now that it seemed entirely possible that she'd be standing in *their* kitchen cooking his meals someday.

Deborah reached for the milk jug and then noticed he was watching her. Her grin lit up the kitchen. "Noah! How was your day?" she called out. "We got steaks out of the freezer to celebrate your new job!"

His heart fluttered. He realized then that his *mamm*, his aunts, and his cousins were all busy in the kitchen, as well, and that they had planned a wonderful supper before they even knew if his drawings had been approved—because they loved him, and they believed in him. With that sort of acceptance, how could he fail?

Amos carried a large platter of T-bone steaks in from the backyard. The girls placed bowls of creamed peas, fresh green beans, mashed potatoes, and gravy on the table, along with a basket of bread.

Roman brought along two pies piled high with meringue. "Lemon and butterscotch," he said as he placed them on one of the unset tables. "No matter what they told you about your drawings today, we're eating high on the hog."

"*Jah,* we killed the fatted calf," Amos quipped. "So what *did* those managers say about your ideas, son?"

Noah set his rolled-up drawings on the unset table alongside the pies. "They said *yes!*" he crowed. "They liked my sunflower and hummingbird designs for the outside trellises so much, they want matching insets for the patio doors and for some of the interior glass doors, too!"

"So you'll be doing more projects than you first thought?" his *mamm* asked.

"*Jah,* they seemed mighty glad I'd come along," Noah replied. "Even Truman was surprised about the extra projects. He'd told me not to be disappointed if they scaled back on some of my ideas, yet it seems they dug deeper into their budget to pay for *more* rather than less."

"And for that, and our many blessings, we give thanks!" Amos said.

They all took their seats at the table. As they prayed, Noah bowed his head, grinning when he felt Deborah's toes tapping his ankles. He hugged her feet between his. *Lord God, for this wonderful day and my new job, I thank You. Forgive my earlier bad moods when I didn't believe anything positive would come of our move to Promise Lodge.*

Did anything taste better than steaks cooked on the grill? Or mashed potatoes hollowed into a crater to hold Deborah's thick brown gravy? Noah described the facility where he'd be working, and answered a lot of questions while they ate. His steak was juicy and seasoned to perfection, and he enjoyed every bite of the side dishes that had long been his favorites.

While the girls cleared the table, he unrolled his sketches of gates with insets that included the sunflowers, hummingbirds, and swirls of ivy that had earned him such high praise—and good pay—from the managers at the senior living complex.

"Oh, would you look at that sweet little hummer?" Deborah said as she ran a finger over one of the sketches. "Every one of those little birds is a miracle, don't you think?"

Noah held Deborah's hand as she stood beside him, admiring his drawings. Truman had agreed to order enough extra supplies so he could make the trellis she wanted for their new home, and now he knew exactly what sort of design he'd add into it.

"What a blessing, that you can put your talents to use at a place where they're sure to bring the residents joy," Amos remarked as he studied Noah's sketches. "It's God's providence that brought you here so you could do such special welding work, son."

The preacher stroked his silver-shot beard, smiling as he gazed into Noah's eyes. "The root word of *providence* is *provide*," he went on matter-of-factly. "And just as the Lord has given us all so much since we moved here, your *mamm* has decided to provide you a plot of ground, and I will build you and Deborah a home on it. We think it's fitting that yours should be one of the first houses to go up in our Promise Lodge colony—whenever you're ready to marry."

Noah's mouth dropped open. Beside him, Deborah gasped while Laura and Phoebe squealed with delight.

His mother stepped up behind them to place her hands on their shoulders. "I was planning to do this for both you and Roman when the time was right, to make up for moving you from the land you'd figured on sharing someday," she explained.

"And I'll see that you girls have places to build homes, as

well," Christine said as she joined Phoebe and Laura beside the table. "It's important to us to keep our children nearby, and to build this colony as a place for your families to grow. While this doesn't mean you *must* stay, if the men you marry want you to move elsewhere, it's my way of providing what your *dat* would've wanted you to have."

"Ohhh," Deborah said wistfully. "*Denki* so much for taking care of us—*all* of us."

"I wasn't expecting *this* when I came here," Noah murmured as he gazed at Mamm and Amos. "That's very generous, and—well, you've helped my future come together a whole lot faster."

"Take all the time you need to court this young lady," Amos insisted. "When more families arrive, we'll have carpenters and preachers—and maybe more than one bishop joining us, who knows?—so we can start building homes and performing weddings. So you see, son," he added happily, "*everyone's* dreams are coming true."

"I like the sound of that," Noah murmured as he gazed at Deborah. "I like it a lot."

Chapter Twenty-Two

Deborah spent the next few days floating in a euphoric cloud. While Noah was at work, she painted inside two more cabins. As she helped Rosetta prepare the evening meal, she began a list of baking staples to buy at the mercantile in Forest Grove.

"I've been thinking I could sell breads and goodies at the produce stand," she explained. "I can put the money toward things for the house—and that way, I could also work at the stand when Laura and Phoebe need to be in the gardens. Is that a *gut* idea?"

"I've never known you to have a bad idea, Deborah," Rosetta replied. "When word of your goodies gets around, folks will come to the produce stand as much to buy those as to latch on to home-grown veggies and fresh eggs."

"I sure hope Ruby and Beulah come back. Their honey and cheese would be a big draw to the stand, too."

Rosetta's smile dimmed. "I'm waiting for the phone to ring, and for Beulah to say Delbert will let them live here," she admitted. "Something tells me he'll have the last word about that even though his sisters have paid ahead on their rent."

Soon Mattie, Christine, and the girls came in from the

garden to help put the meal on the table and the kitchen filled with their chatter about opening the produce stand. When Amos returned from the Promise post office, he brought Noah in from where Truman had dropped him off at the camp entrance.

"Letters!" he said as he waved a handful of them. "Plain folks are seeing our ads, wanting to join us here. And this one's for you, missy."

Deborah's eyes widened. The neat handwriting on the envelope could only belong to one person. "It's from Mamma," she breathed as she tore it open. "Maybe she's written more details about Isaac and the goings-on with that Presley fellow."

When she unfolded the pieces of lined writing paper, three twenty-dollar bills slid out. Why would Mamma be sending her money? Although the food was on the table and the men were gathering around it, everyone wanted to hear whatever news was in her letter. Deborah slipped the money into her apron pocket and began to read silently.

My dearest Deborah,

I was mighty put out when your dat didn't ask about you during his chat with Amos, but maybe it's just as well. What he needs to say is something you should hear in person, dear daughter, so please, please come home.

Your dat has forgiven you. Now that the sheriff and the new English owner on the Bender place have proven Isaac and Kerry were to blame for the fire, he realizes that you were telling the truth. He's sorry he sent you away without listening more closely to your side of the story.

Deborah swallowed hard, blinking. Here were the words she'd been longing to hear, even if her mother was relating them secondhand. *Your dat has forgiven you. Please, please come home.*

With a sigh, she wished she'd waited until she could be alone to read Mamma's letter, but there was no stopping. Her mother's neat, purposeful penmanship drew her through paragraphs that became progressively harder to bear as she reached the bottom of the first page.

While we're grateful to Mattie and her sisters for taking you in, your dat and I believe you belong in Coldstream. Your sister misses you something awful and the boys keep asking questions we have no answers for, about when you're returning to our family. If our settlement is to survive, we need responsible young people to marry and raise their families here—especially considering that Mattie's and Christine's kids have already left. If we can't balance out troublemakers like Isaac with honest, God-fearing young adults like you, what's to become of our church district?

Please, please come home, Deborah. My days have been so long and lonely without you.

Deborah felt as though one of Amos's vises had clamped her heart. Why had this letter arrived *now*, when she and Noah had made such wonderful plans for their future in Promise? She'd kept herself very busy these past two weeks, purposely thinking about the tasks at hand rather than her family, to keep from missing them so badly. In her mind she pictured Lily and Lavern, Menno and Johnny . . . her mother's careworn face. How she had missed them all—even Dat, despite his stern, indisputable way of handling their family's challenges.

Mamma had sent her money to pay a driver. It had taken a long time to earn sixty dollars selling eggs because her mother wouldn't have asked her father for money. Maybe she hadn't even told Dat she was begging Deborah to come home.

What if Mamma had written of Dat's forgiveness in the hope that if she came home, he *would* forgive her? What if Mamma was wishing for a miracle, praying God's will would go the way she wanted it to, for once? Deborah couldn't imagine her father carrying on to Mamma about forgiveness, after the way he'd taken one look at her and assumed her soul was as tattered as her clothing.

But Deborah *had* received Noah's forgiveness. He wanted her for his wife again. He had a good job and would soon build a home—to share with *her*. After the joy they'd known these past couple of days, how could she even suggest that she wouldn't become Mrs. Noah Schwartz and live in Promise?

Deborah's dilemma became painfully clear: if she said yes to Noah, she would crush her mother's spirit. Deborah suspected the bitter words and strained silences that often filled the Peterscheim household had felt as jagged as shattered glass in her absence. But if she told Noah she wouldn't be living in Promise anymore, where would that leave him and his dreams? She didn't have it in her to break his heart again.

A sob escaped her. Deborah began to cry so hard her whole body shook.

"Oh, honey-bunch, is somebody sick? Is your *mamm* not doing well?" Rosetta asked as she hurried into the kitchen.

"I miss them so much," Deborah rasped. "I—I want to go home! But—but . . ."

When Rosetta embraced her, Deborah lost herself in the warmth of her understanding. "Of course you want to go home," Rosetta murmured. "You've been a brave girl, Deborah, but family is family. I'm sure your *mamm* feels lost without you."

"She wants me to come back." Deborah hiccupped, trying to regain control of her emotions. "She—she says Dat has forgiven me."

"And that's a fine thing," Preacher Amos assured her as he, too, came over to comfort her. "I've decided to go to Coldstream next Monday to help them with the barn raising. If you can wait until then, we can ride together. I'd feel better if you didn't make the trip by yourself."

Deborah wiped her eyes and gave him a grateful smile. "That would be a *gut* idea. *Denki* so much."

She folded Mamma's letter and slipped it into her apron pocket. She took a deep breath to settle her nerves so she wouldn't ruin everyone's supper with her crying. Then Deborah prayed that God's will would be done, that somehow this situation would work out.

But how could she face Noah when she sat down across from him?

Noah's heart sank like a rock. Deborah took her seat, but she wouldn't look at him. Her eyes were pink around the rims, her mood shadowed by the same desperation that had plagued her the day she'd arrived at Promise Lodge. She wouldn't lie to him, but she didn't have to—in the kitchen she'd blurted *I want to go home,* but he had clearly heard *good-bye*.

He'd spent his day sketching full-scale models for the gates, trellises, and door insets for the care center. While his drafting pencil and ruler had occupied his hands, his thoughts had wandered to the house he would soon help Amos design. When Truman had called in the order for the iron—all the posts, hinges, and hardware, including materials for Deborah's trellis—Noah had felt as though he were floating. The pieces he'd been hired to create were a challenge he looked forward to, signposts on the road to his financial security.

But he was earning the money to support Deborah, to build the home he intended to share with her for the rest of his life. If she left, what was the point of any of this? *What profits a man if he gains the whole world but loses his soul?*

And Deborah was his soul. He knew that now.

After supper, Noah waited out on the porch until she'd finished helping with the dishes. Then he grasped her hand. "Let's go for a stroll," he suggested. "You have to tell me about your *mamm*'s letter. That expression on your face when you were reading—well, it scared me *bad*, Deborah."

She clutched his hand as desperation overtook her pale features once again. "Mamma says my *dat* has forgiven me," she whispered. "She begged me to come home."

Noah hoped he didn't sound unbearably impatient or impertinent. "And why *wouldn't* you go back to visit your family?" he asked nervously. "Anyone would—"

"Mamma wants me back to *stay*, Noah. She wants me to—to marry and settle in Coldstream so there will be young families to keep the colony going," Deborah explained with a sigh. "Especially because you Schwartz boys and the Hershberger girls have already left."

Noah's heart clutched at the hopes and dreams he sensed were swirling down the drain. "How can she expect you to— girls marry guys from other towns all the time!" he protested. "Why doesn't she realize that the husband-to-be has a say about—"

"I'm sorry, Noah," she said in a pinched voice. "I didn't see this coming. But here it is. And I don't know what to do."

Deborah stopped walking. She hung her head. Then she looked away from him, across Rainbow Lake, as though hoping an answer would appear in large letters across the western sky. "Whichever place I choose, I'll hurt someone I need and love dearly. It's been so hard for Mamma with me gone because, well—she and Dat aren't always happy."

Noah already knew that about Eli and Alma. He had vowed long ago that when he married Deborah, their relationship would not sink to the level of disparagement and discouragement that shadowed the Peterscheim home—and many other households where the husband ruled with an iron hand and the wife had become little more than a servant. A doormat.

"Please don't leave me, Deborah," Noah whispered. "I *love* you, girl."

"And I love *you,* Noah," she rasped. "But Mamma needs me, too."

With a sigh, Noah left her standing by the lake. He could think of nothing else to say.

Chapter Twenty-Three

"Queenie, what should I do?" Deborah murmured as she stroked the dog's silky ears. "These next few days will be impossibly long before I either go to Coldstream with Amos . . . or I don't."

The Border Collie gazed up at her with soulful brown eyes, wagging her tail and whimpering sympathetically. It was early Thursday morning, not yet dawn, but Deborah had given up all hope of sleeping.

"I could send Mamma a letter, explaining that Noah and I are planning to marry soon," she mused aloud. "But Mamma deserves to hear that news firsthand. If I go with Amos, though—even just for a visit—Noah will worry that I won't come back after the barn's built. He knows how needy Mamma is."

Queenie nuzzled Deborah's hand, demanding more attention.

Deborah chuckled ruefully. "*Jah,* it's all about staying in *touch,*" she remarked as she rubbed the dog's head. "I want to live with Noah, yet I want my family nearby. But with a three-hour car trip separating us . . . I just don't know."

Sitting on the side of the bed wouldn't solve anything, so Deborah got dressed. She planned to bake some breads and desserts for the opening of the Promise Produce Stand on Saturday, so it seemed like a good time to start her project. Often when she baked, ideas came to her—and perhaps while the women, Laura, and Phoebe made breakfast together they could help her, as well.

The last person Deborah expected to see in the kitchen was Noah. He looked as miserable as she felt, breaking off pieces of a cinnamon roll left over from yesterday's breakfast and jamming them into his mouth. His hair stood out in clumps and he hadn't shaved.

"Hey," he said softly.

Deborah stopped a few feet away from him. "You couldn't sleep, either?"

"I—I feel bad about walking away from you last night, and about making it sound like I don't want you to see your family," he murmured. "I'm sorry."

Deborah let out the breath she'd been holding. "I know I upset you when I started crying. Do you want to see Mamma's letter?" she asked as she reached into her apron pocket. "Maybe you'll get a better feel for what's going on. You know how folks sometimes write things one way but their true thoughts might be something different. And my interpretation might be all wrong, too."

Noah took the folded pages. "Maybe I should go to Coldstream with you on Monday," he murmured. "I could talk with your parents, and help Amos with the barn raising—maybe spend some time with your *dat* then."

"But what about your work with Truman? Won't your iron and welding supplies be delivered by then?" It touched Deborah that Noah had changed his attitude toward her dilemma. But she didn't want him to jeopardize his job.

"Truman would understand that your family situation is important enough to be ironed out sooner rather than later," Noah replied.

"That's very thoughtful of you," she murmured.

"I love you, Deborah."

There it was, the phrase that made this situation so difficult. It would be easier to decide in Mamma's favor if Noah continued to act angry instead of sympathizing with her emotional tug-of-war. He had come so far from the young man who couldn't—or wouldn't—express his innermost thoughts.

"I love you, too, Noah," she murmured. "I came over to make some things to sell at the produce stand, because baking can be like praying for me. When my hands are busy making dough or stirring batter, my mind opens to higher thoughts. New ideas God whispers to me."

"*Jah,* the same happens for me when I'm immersed in my work," he replied. He kissed her cheek. "When I was drawing up those sketches for the gates and door insets, I was imagining the house Amos has offered to build us. But I suppose I should put those ideas on hold until . . ."

Sighing, Deborah eased away from him so he could start his chores. It was heartening that she and Noah both found strength and solace in their work, yet his observations only made it more difficult to talk to Mamma. Her mother tended to see the glass as half empty—or nonexistent—rather than half full, and Deborah had usually gone along with her wishes rather than disappoint her. The two of them had often consoled and encouraged each other when Dat had gotten impatient.

Mamma knows, of course, that when I marry I won't be there to run interference with Dat. . . .

Deborah began to combine the ingredients for cinnamon rolls, losing herself in the familiar acts of measuring and stirring. By the time her large bowl of sweet-smelling dough was rising, Rosetta and the others had come into the kitchen to prepare breakfast.

After the meal, Noah caught his ride with Truman. Roman was taking Laura and Phoebe into Forest Grove to post notices on the local bulletin boards about the Promise Produce Stand's opening, but Deborah chose not to go with them. "I'll finish baking and then get back to my painting," she said. "I've only got two cabins left."

It suited Deborah that Amos was replacing a couple of leaky faucets in the lodge that day. Christine and Rosetta were helping Mattie in the garden, picking green beans, peas, and small zucchini, cutting lettuce and spinach, and pulling radishes and green onions to sell at the produce stand. Painting was another job that allowed Deborah to think while her hands were busy with the roller, even though she wasn't finding any solutions to her dilemma.

When she returned to the kitchen to help serve the pot roast they'd put in the oven for their noon dinner, Christine nodded toward the phone.

"I was just ready to come get you, Deborah. You'd better check the message your sister left," she said. "Seems your *mamm*'s had an accident."

Deborah hurried over to punch the button on the message machine. Her heart raced as fast as her worried thoughts. *If Lily made the call—if Mamma was unable to use the phone—*

"Deborah, it's me, Lily," her sister's shrill voice came through the speaker. "Mamma was carrying a box of canning jars down the basement steps and she tripped. She fell the rest of the way down, so I'm home with the boys while Dat's taking her to the emergency room, and—oh, Deborah, how am I supposed to do all the cooking? And there's a pile of laundry we haven't gotten to, because we just picked a couple bushels of green beans that need snapping, so we can put them up in jars and—"

Lily's voice broke off in a sob. "Deborah, please, you've *got* to come home. I don't *care* that Dat sent you away. *He's* not going to be taking care of all the things Mamma can't do now!"

Deborah's breath escaped her as she gripped the edge of the countertop. "Oh, no. Oh, *no*," she rasped. Lily was only thirteen. If their mother was going to be incapacitated for a long time, the poor girl couldn't possibly keep the household running by herself.

She turned toward Christine and her sisters, who wore concerned expressions. "Do you suppose Mamma's got a bunch of broken bones? What if those jars broke and she fell on them? What if she hit her head on the basement floor?"

"Call back," Rosetta suggested as she poured Deborah a glass of lemonade. "If Lily's there, maybe she'll be waiting to hear from you."

"Or Lavern and the younger boys might be out in the yard, near the phone shanty in case you call," Mattie said. "I'm sure they're all worried about your *mamm*."

"If Dat took her to the hospital, it must've been pretty bad," Deborah remarked. "He's not one to put a lot of trust in doctors if he thinks bed rest will do the trick."

Ignoring the lemonade, Deborah dialed her home phone number. It rang and rang, until the answering machine prompted her to leave a message. "This is Deborah, calling back about Mamma," she said, trying to control her voice. Lily was worried enough, without hearing that her big sister was frantic, as well. "*Please* call back and tell me what's happened. I'll see about arranging a ride to Coldstream, but it might take some doing, as I don't know many folks with cars. *Let me know,* okay?"

Deborah hung up and quickly drank her lemonade.

"Truman would drive you there," Rosetta suggested.

"But he and Noah are working on their big job!" Deborah protested. "I can't ask him to miss a day with his crew—especially when the weather's so perfect for planting."

The three sisters nodded glumly.

"And besides," Deborah went on, "I want to be sure of what's actually happened, and how bad Mamma is. Noah's trying to be a *gut* sport about her wanting me to come home, but . . . but I hate to think about how long I might need to stay. I—I just don't know. I want to be *here,* I want to be *there*—"

"It's a *gut* time to remember that verse that says 'be still and know that I am God,'" Mattie murmured. "If we all three pray on it—quiet our minds—we'll be readier for the news about your mother when you get a call back."

Deborah nodded, squeezing her eyes shut.

An immediate answer didn't come to her. Neither did a phone call.

After another rough night of being awake for more hours than she was asleep, Deborah went to the kitchen early Friday morning. The red light was blinking on the message machine.

"Tell Deborah not to come home," her father's voice announced through the speaker. He sounded weary but firm. "We've got it all under control."

So there you have it, she thought ruefully. *He's not telling us anything about Mamma, but he's saying loud and clear that I'm not to show my face. That makes everything a lot simpler.*

But it really didn't.

When Noah replayed Eli Peterscheim's phone message that evening after Deborah had gone to bed, he scowled. Although deep down he was relieved, because he doubted Deborah would defy her father and go home, the preacher's tone made him very uneasy.

Did Eli expect young Lily to manage the household during Alma's recovery? Why did he still consider Deborah so unforgivable? The preacher might believe he had the situation under control, but Noah sensed nothing was *right* at the Peterscheim place.

Noah joined Amos, who was seated at the small table in the kitchen. Deborah had left them a plate of frosted doughnuts after she'd wrapped the rest to sell at the produce stand. He chose one with sprinkles, nodding his thanks as Amos poured him a glass of milk.

"What do you make of Eli's message?" he asked, and before the preacher could answer he blurted his own opinion. "He didn't even address Deborah directly! And he didn't say a thing about Alma, either, knowing she'd be worried sick about her mother."

Amos shook his head. "I've known Eli a long time. Always considered him a little on the hard-boiled side, but his message sounded—"

"Cruel. Downright heartless," Noah interjected. "And when you consider how Alma's letter begged Deborah to come home—to stay in Coldstream and raise her family there—and then Lily sounded absolutely frantic when she left *her* message," he recounted earnestly, "it seems to me the whole family's a mess. Why won't Eli accept Deborah's help? Is he too proud to admit he needs her? Or too hardhearted to forgive her?"

Amos's brown eyes sparkled as he broke off a chunk of his doughnut. "Listen to *you*," he said with a chuckle. "Couldn't pry a word out of you when Deborah first showed up here, and now you're spouting like a geyser. But I'm glad," he added quickly. "You're worried about Deborah instead of being wrapped up in your own little world. You're a better man with her than without her."

Noah savored the cakelike texture of the doughnut and its satiny chocolate frosting, deciding how involved he should become in the Peterscheims' predicament. When he'd returned from work this afternoon, Deborah had looked like a rose dying on the vine. While he believed her when she said she loved him, she loved her family, too. She wouldn't be the same open, affectionate young woman he wanted to marry until she reconciled with her father and saw to her mother's injuries.

"I'm going to ask Truman to drive me to Coldstream on Sunday," Noah stated. "I can visit with Deborah's family. Find out what's really going on."

"Ah, but riding in a car on the Sabbath flies right in the face of the *Ordnung,* son," Amos reminded him gently. "And while I admire your intention to check on the Peterscheims, you need to ask yourself if you'll create more of a problem than you'll be solving."

"Well, I can't go tomorrow!" Noah blurted. "Truman will be finishing another of his landscaping jobs, so he can't give me a ride."

"I've got a driver lined up for early Monday morning," the preacher murmured as he chose another doughnut. "You're welcome to come along, Noah . . . although the barn raising might be the furthest thing from Eli's mind right now, with Alma not being well. Maybe I'd better be sure he still wants me to come."

Amos went to the phone at the far end of the kitchen. He tapped the number pads, looking lost in thought until it was time to leave his message.

"Eli, it's Amos Troyer. Wanted you to know all of us are concerned about Alma's injuries and praying for your family," he said in his resonant voice. "I've made arrangements to come to Coldstream Monday morning to lead the barn raising crew, but if Alma's condition has changed your plans, *let me know,* all right? Let me hear from you one way or the other, friend. The Lord didn't intend for us to bear our burdens alone."

Amos hung up the phone. "Did I sound convincing?"

Noah shrugged. "He's more likely to respond to you than to me. Guess we'll see what he says when he calls back."

Chapter Twenty-Four

Saturday morning, Deborah joined Laura and Phoebe in the Promise Produce Stand bright and early, hoping folks would stop by to purchase the wide array of items they were displaying. Noah had told her that Amos had left a message for her *dat* to call him back, but they'd gotten no response yet. Deborah didn't have much hope of receiving one. She'd sent up prayer after prayer during the night, asking that Mamma receive comfort and healing and that Lily would find the strength to shoulder all the tasks that had fallen to her.

She and the Hershberger girls stood taller when a car slowed down and pulled off the road. A middle-aged couple got out and studied the slats on their sign, which listed all the items they were selling.

"*Gut* morning," Phoebe called out. "Thanks for stopping by our new stand."

"Glad to see you folks taking over this camp," the man remarked. "We live down the road a piece, and we were concerned that the buildings might start to deteriorate—or attract vandals."

"Look at these beautiful vegetables!" the woman said as

she picked up a bunch of radishes. "Get your sacks ready, girls. I love fresh produce but I don't have time to garden."

"We can be your gardeners, then!" Laura replied pertly. "We've got lots more veggies where these came from."

"We'd better take some of these brownies and cinnamon rolls, too. A fellow can't live on produce alone. It's just not healthy!" the man teased. He smiled at Deborah as he chose a plateful of brownies and a tray containing half a dozen cinnamon rolls. "Did you make these?"

"*Jah,* I did," Deborah replied. Her spirits lifted as he also chose a tray of doughnuts.

"I know they're fresh, then—better than anything in the store," he remarked. "Give us a dozen eggs, too."

Another car rolled to a halt alongside the road, and then another. Phoebe continued helping the first couple, while Laura and Deborah assisted the other shoppers. By the time this initial flurry of customers had driven off, they were amazed to have more than a hundred dollars in the cash box—and a noticeable dent in their supply of vegetables.

"My stars!" Laura said as she straightened the remaining bunches of green onions, lettuce, and peas. "I'm glad we bagged up some one-pound bags of the salad greens and green beans beforehand. And look how many trays of goodies *you've* sold, missy!"

Deborah grinned, feeling better than she had in days. Nearly half of her supply had sold already. "*Denki* for letting me try out my idea, girls. If you need to go fetch more bags, or pick more stuff from the garden, I'll stay here."

Phoebe took a quick count of their bagged greens. "We could probably use more onions and radishes, but I think at least two of us ought to be here in case we get several customers at once."

"I know!" Laura piped up. "I'll fetch more bags, and see if Mamm and Aunt Mattie might pick more stuff for us. They'll be amazed at how fast everything's going."

Laura sprinted up the lane, holding her *kapp* to keep it from flying off. Phoebe turned on the two fans Amos had hung on the ceiling. "We need a clock," she said. "We listed our hours on our posters, but we have no way of knowing when it's time to close—not that I'm ready yet!"

Deborah nodded, but she was focused on an approaching white van that seemed awfully familiar. Its turn signal was blinking, and the vehicle was leaving the paved county road to start up the lane to the lodge—but then it stopped. The back door slid open and out jumped her two youngest brothers.

"Deborah, hi!" Menno called out.

"Surprise!" eight-year-old Johnny hollered. "Guess who!"

Deborah rushed out of the produce stand, too stunned to speak. As she grabbed her brothers, Lavern and Lily were hitting the ground, grinning as though they'd come on some grand adventure—as though nothing had gone wrong at home. "What're you all doing here?" Deborah asked in a bewildered voice. "Lily, when you called about Mamma, I figured she might be all banged up, and in the hospital, and—"

"Well, I gave everybody a scare, for sure. But I'll live to see another day now that I'm here with you, Daughter."

Deborah gazed at her mother, and then jogged over to help her out of the van. "Mamma! Mamma, I was so scared when I heard you'd fallen, and—and—"

As her mother wrapped her arms around her, it was all Deborah could do not to burst into tears. "Seems that cardboard box of canning jars I dropped kept me from hitting the concrete floor full-on," Mamma murmured. "And the lid was folded shut, so I didn't get cut. I've got some bruised ribs, and I have to wear this awkward boot for several weeks while I hobble around on crutches. But the doctor says I'll be right as rain after that."

Thank You, Lord, for lots of little miracles. Deborah glanced at the gray contraption that encased her mother's right leg up to her knee, and she noticed a purple bruise on the side of her neck, but otherwise Mamma seemed to be all right. It would do no good to ask why no one had returned their calls. Seeing her mother upright—having her entire family crowded around her—eased most of the worries that had plagued Deborah for the past few days.

Her *dat* chatted with the driver, Dick Mercer, as he paid him. Dat glanced briefly at Deborah, surrounded by her younger brothers and sister, before going over to the produce stand. "Looks like a lot of progress has been made at Promise Lodge already, if you're selling vegetables from your new garden," he remarked.

"*Jah*, we've been busy bees," Phoebe agreed. "It's our first day to be open. We weren't expecting folks to come all the way from Coldstream to shop!"

Deborah was grateful for this lead-in to a possible explanation, because she hadn't dared to ask why her whole family had shown up without letting anybody know. Her father's expression remained unreadable beneath his black straw hat as he gazed at the trees and the arched metal Promise Lodge sign. "Seemed like a *gut* time for a family road trip," he remarked. "Dick's going to drive us to the lodge so Alma won't have to walk—"

"And we won't have to carry all those suitcases!" eleven-year-old Menno blurted.

"Let's you and me *run* up there. It'll be a race!" Johnny exclaimed. He drew a line in the dirt with the toe of his shoe. "On your mark, get set, let's *go!*"

Deborah chuckled at her two youngest brothers' energy, even as she wondered how many suitcases they'd packed—which suggested more than a day's road trip. "I'll ride with you," she murmured as she helped her mother turn around. "Everybody'll be real glad to see you all, and pleased you're doing so well, Mamma."

As Lily and Lavern climbed into the very backseat, behind Deborah and her mother, her *dat* took his place in the front alongside Dick Mercer. Deborah's heart was thumping wildly. Her father hadn't spoken to her—but he wasn't a man to ride for three hours without something other than recreation and visiting on his mind, either.

"Oh, look at the gardens—and all the trees and shade at the lodge building," her mother murmured, clutching Deborah's hand.

"Can we stay in one of those cool little cabins?" Lily asked.

"Can we fish in that lake?" Lavern chimed in. "Oh, here comes Queenie!"

"And there's Laura on the porch with her *mamm* and her aunts," Mamma said as she gazed through the windshield. "They're a sight for sore eyes. Hasn't been the same at home since they left us."

"Roman's still milking the Hershberger herd, then?" her father asked as he gazed toward the red barn.

"*Jah,* he and Noah and Amos are most likely out there now, finishing up some remodeling they've done in the loft," Deborah replied.

She wasn't surprised that when the van stopped, her father waved at the ladies on the porch and headed toward the barn. Queenie was barking, circling Johnny and Menno, while Mattie, Rosetta, and Christine were making much of the two boys. When Dick popped the latch on the van's hatchback, Lavern and Lily squeezed out from behind Deborah's seat and began to unload the luggage.

By the time she'd helped Mamma out of the van, the Bender sisters were surrounding them, exclaiming over their guests.

"Who could've guessed we'd see all you Peterscheims today?" Mattie said.

"This is the answer to our prayers about *your* condition, too, Alma," Rosetta exclaimed as she reached in for a hug.

"You can stay in the cabins Deborah's been painting,"

Christine said as she grabbed hold of Lily and Alma. "We wouldn't be nearly so far along with our preparations for new residents if she hadn't been helping us."

Deborah held her breath. Her mother appeared ready to reveal the reason behind their visit, or to make some other sort of important statement, but then she glanced toward the kids unloading the back of the van. "We've got a lot to say, and you know Eli will want to do the talking," she murmured. "As for me, I'm ever so grateful that you've taken care of my Deborah—"

"Oh, we've been happy to have her!" Christine blurted.

"She's been wonderful-*gut* help!" Rosetta declared.

"My Noah's awfully glad she showed up," Mattie joined in.

Mamma sighed, leaning heavily on her crutches. "I—I wish things at home had gone differently, the day after the fire," she murmured as she clasped Deborah's hand. "But when God closes a door, He opens a window or two. That day turned out to be a real revelation—a sign that important changes were in order."

Mamma glanced toward the barn. "Yesterday, when we learned that Isaac Chupp's been stealing from Obadiah's auction proceeds, Eli said he'd had enough. He hasn't made any final decisions, but here we are."

Noah sat beside his brother on a hay bale, listening in disbelief as Preacher Eli explained what had been happening in Coldstream. While he wasn't surprised to learn that Isaac had been stealing from his *dat,* he certainly hadn't expected to see the entire Peterscheim tribe arriving at Promise.

"It's been all I could do to hold my tongue during this uproar with the bishop's boy," Eli declared with a shake of his head, "but I couldn't *believe* Obadiah and his two oldest boys didn't realize so much money was slipping through the cracks of their business! Where did they think Isaac got the money for a *car,* for crying out loud? Do you suppose they really didn't know he had one, or were they turning a blind eye?"

Seated on the goats' milking stand, Amos shrugged. "We've been speculating about those same possibilities," he murmured. "I'm sorry this whole mess—two barns and Willis Hershberger lost, not to mention Deborah's predicament— might've been prevented, had the bishop been paying closer attention to his reckless son."

"You saw the writing on the wall before I did, Amos. I don't feel *gut* about leaving the bishop God Himself chose for Coldstream, but I don't feel right about my family being at risk there, either," Eli replied. "I suspect our horses got turned out of the barn the other night because Isaac was per- turbed at me for talking to the sheriff. Who knows what else he might do?"

Noah's heart thudded. Did this mean the Peterscheims planned to live at Promise Lodge? Did he dare hope that because Deborah's family would be within daily visiting dis- tance, the young woman of his dreams could wholeheartedly make her home—her life—with him?

"If I pull up roots, I'll be leaving the contractors and other contacts I've earned my living with," Eli continued earnestly. "Promise Lodge looks like a nice place. But will I be able to find welding work? It's awfully remote out here."

As Amos leaned his elbows on his knees, he winked at Noah. "Eli, we were *all* taking that chance when we bought this tract of land," he answered earnestly. "At last count, we have eight other families seriously interested in joining us— which will keep me in carpentry work for a long while, building their homes. Roman's found a buyer for Christine's milk, Mattie and the girls are selling produce, Rosetta's rent- ing out apartments, and Noah just landed a job making decorative metal gates. Your daughter's selling what she bakes, and I expect she'll do quite well at it."

Amos paused, widening his eyes at the preacher from Coldstream. "There's work for every hand, Eli. The folks coming to Promise Lodge will need their buggies repaired, and we'll soon be installing ductwork and plumbing you can work on," he pointed out. "God will look after you and your family the same way He's guided us. You believe that, don't you?"

Noah held his breath. When Amish families moved, it was usually to find affordable land, or so their kids could marry into fresh bloodlines—or because of a disagreement with the leaders of their church district. Preachers, however, tended to stay put because they'd been selected by God to serve their community.

"I—I *have* to have faith," Eli replied somberly. "A man can sell a farm and buy a new one easily enough, but all the money in the world won't keep his family together—or keep his kids safe. We didn't have to think about that until recently."

Noah vividly recalled the desperation on Deborah's face when she'd shown up at Promise Lodge with her suitcase and that purple handprint on her neck. He didn't want to think about what might've happened to her had she remained at home, where Isaac could've found other ways to torment her. Eli didn't seem inclined to confess that he'd misjudged his daughter, but it was a big admission for him to tell Amos that starting the Promise Lodge colony had been the right move.

Best to watch, wait, and listen, he thought. *The pieces to this puzzle will eventually fall into place.*

Chapter Twenty-Five

As they sat down to supper that evening, Deborah smiled to herself. Rosetta and Mattie had grilled a couple of chickens along with the venison steaks they had originally planned to serve. The women had spent the afternoon snapping the green beans Mamma had brought in coolers from Coldstream, so a large bowl of them now graced the table. They'd opened an extra bag of frozen corn and added two quarts of applesauce to the menu, as well. Knowing how much Deborah's *dat* and three brothers could eat, Phoebe had made a cherry slab pie to go with Rosetta's cupcakes so they would have enough dessert to go around.

"This meal's quite a treat, ladies," Preacher Amos said as he took his place at the head of the two tables they'd placed end to end. "But the real blessing is having you Peterscheims join us today. I pray that the Lord will guide you toward His will, as far as whether you'll make Promise Lodge your new home."

As they bowed for their silent prayer, Deborah's pulse thrummed. While she was thrilled to see her family, she was unsure of where she stood with her *dat*. He and her brothers had spent the afternoon with Amos, Noah, and Roman, touring the orchard, the cabin area, and the wooded

acres that would soon be sold to incoming families, so he
still hadn't spoken directly to her.

*Will he really uproot the family? Leave the home where
he—and his parents and grandparents—have always lived?*
she wondered as they began passing the meat and vegetables. Deborah hadn't heard everything her mother had said
about that subject because she'd helped Laura and Phoebe at
the produce stand all afternoon. But Mamma's opinion
wasn't the one that counted.

"Chicken legs!" Johnny crowed as he put two of them on
his plate.

Menno and Lavern held the platter of venison steaks between them, their forks poised as they decided which pieces
to take. "I suppose you shot this deer back home, Noah?"
Lavern asked.

"*Jah,* and I've spotted lots of deer—and quail—around
here, too," Noah replied. "Lately, though, I've been con-
centrating on the coyotes. You'll hear them singing tonight,
no doubt."

Her brothers' eyes widened. Deborah could see they were
eager for the adventure of moving here, where the countryside was wild and unsettled compared to what they were
used to.

"And just think," Noah went on in a speculative tone. "If
your sister hadn't joined us, you wouldn't have the chance to
live so close to a lake you could fish in—or the chance to help
build a new house. Maybe."

Deborah's eyebrows rose. Was Noah casting that line at
her *dat,* fishing for his reaction?

"I'm grateful to God for giving Deborah the *gut* sense to
come here," Mamma said as she passed the corn. "Much
as I've missed her, I was relieved to know she was safe
amongst our friends."

Deborah watched the color rise in her father's face as he
cut his steak. He was seated across the table, all the way

down by Amos, and he hadn't met her eyes since he'd first gotten out of the van.

"I sent Deborah away for the *gut* of all concerned—and to protect her," her father stated.

"Without so much as fare to pay a driver," her mother murmured. "Might as well have sent a little lamb into the woods."

The dining room got painfully quiet.

Deborah stopped chewing for fear she'd choke. Her mother *never* challenged Dat. And now Mamma had made her objections known in front of Preacher Amos and their friends, not to mention the younger kids. The kitchen clock ticked away several tense seconds.

Dat frowned at Mamma from his end of the table. "Did I not keep her name out of the papers, Alma? Did I not defy our bishop and the *Ordnung* by giving information about the fire to Sheriff Renfro?" he countered stiffly. "This isn't the time or the place for questioning the decision I made the night of the fire, when Deborah didn't come home."

Mamma sucked in her breath. "So when is the right time for granting her your forgiveness, Eli?" she asked in a halting voice. "Surely what we've learned about Isaac has tipped the scales in Deborah's favor, yet you've refused to speak of her at home—and now you're acting as though she's not in the room with us," she pointed out. "What sort of example is that to your other children? Why must you keep ignoring her, breaking her heart—and mine?"

Deborah's mouth opened but no sound came out. Her four siblings sat wide-eyed, caught up in this unprecedented contest of wills. Christine took Deborah's hand while Laura slipped a supportive arm around her shoulders.

Across the table, Noah appeared stunned—but not sorry—about the conversation his remark had started. "Forgiveness doesn't come easy," he said, smiling kindly at Deborah. "I had my doubts about Deborah's story when she came here, too, and I still resented the way she'd broken our engagement. But I believe she was the innocent victim of two drunk, out-of-control boys—in the wrong place at the wrong time," he insisted. "I've come to trust her again. I *love* her, matter of fact."

Deborah's breath escaped her in a rush. Once again the room had become extremely quiet, yet she thrummed with strength—and with the joy of Noah's public declaration of his feelings.

Noah set down his utensils to focus on her father. "Forgiving Deborah has made all the difference, Preacher Eli," he continued earnestly. "She's told me she wants to make a home with me here at Promise Lodge, but she feels torn. Deborah wants to live near her family—but even if you Peterscheims move here, that'll be a thorny situation if you're not speaking to her."

Deborah's heart welled up with fierce pride. Imagine Noah speaking out this way, despite her father's objection to the direction this conversation had taken!

"Let's allow Eli to eat his supper," Preacher Amos suggested, encompassing everyone in his gaze. "A man shouldn't be cornered, when it comes to requesting or granting forgiveness. He should act of his own free will, in his own *gut* time.

"But none of us should ignore the opportunity to forgive, either," Amos continued solemnly. "Who knows what tomorrow may bring? It's a church Sunday, so it would be a blessing if all our hearts were free of guilt and worries, ready to worship our Lord."

The meal continued without much further chatter, until the three younger boys expressed their excitement over Phoebe's slab pie and the cupcakes Rosetta had baked. Although Deborah felt prickly, being the indirect cause of such an intense discussion, she was also gratified that Noah and her friends had spoken on her behalf. As she considered what her mother had risked to voice her criticism of Dat's attitude, Deborah sensed that the Peterscheim family had come to a crossroad. They all seemed eager to start fresh in Promise, yet the undercurrent of conflicting wills and opinions wouldn't go away just because Mamma had spoken out. Deborah ached for the resolution of this intense conflict, even as she knew she couldn't bring it about.

When the men and boys went out to tend the livestock, Mattie placed her hands on Mamma's shoulders. "Sit at the kitchen worktable and give that bum foot a rest," she insisted. "We can pass you the silverware to dry. And we can lend an ear—or a shoulder—if you need to release your frustration, too."

Mamma hobbled to the chair Christine had pulled out for her, weariness etched around her eyes. "I don't know what came over me at dinner," she murmured. "I suppose being around you sisters again, seeing the way you've all moved forward, gave me the strength to spell out what's been going on since Eli sent Deborah away. I—I got to feeling so down and out, I had to take her chair away from the table. Couldn't stand to look at it sitting empty during our meals."

"I don't know how I'd get from one day to the next without my girls," Christine agreed quickly. "We're glad you've come, Alma. We've missed you and your family."

"And I could hardly sleep without you being in our room, Deborah," Lily admitted. "I heard every little noise during the night, and well—it was just so lonely."

Deborah hugged her younger sister as her eyes filled with tears. "I'm sorry," she murmured. "I should've called you sooner, Mamma. Should've come home and—"

Mamma's upraised hand silenced her. "No, Deborah, you were obeying your father. It's Eli who's caused this separation within our family, by making a snap judgment," she insisted. "Noah's right. You're a *gut* girl who was caught in the wrong place at the wrong time, and Isaac Chupp and his buddy roughed you up for calling the police. None of this was your fault."

"It's *gut* to be with you, Sister," Lily murmured, resting her head on Deborah's shoulder. "And I'm glad to see you looking so happy, together with Noah again."

"We're all pleased about that," Mattie said. She had a pensive expression on her face as she glanced at her two sisters. "What say we have Noah put up one of the extra beds in Deborah's cabin, so these three Peterscheim gals can catch up with each other?"

Rosetta's eyes sparkled. "And Eli can bunk with Menno, Lavern, and Johnny. We'll have a girls' cabin and a boys', just like when we camp at state parks for family reunions, *jah?*"

"Number ten's probably the best cabin for the fellows, because we've got a couple of beds made up in that one," Mattie mused aloud. She smiled at Mamma. "It's a little ways into the woods, farther away from the lodge—"

"So the fellows will have to make do. They won't have you to choose their clothes or to pick up after them," Christine remarked. "I like it! I'll fetch fresh sheets."

"You and I could probably set up that bed, Rosetta." Deborah felt a grin relieving her previous downhearted mood. "That way, it would be all said and done, with the suitcases put into the two cabins before the guys could fuss about it."

Mamma was chuckling. "Why, this is sounding like a *vacation,* letting Eli tend to the boys. Lily and I will be here bright and early to help with breakfast tomorrow, though. We brought some ripe bananas and a couple of jars of Deborah's favorite plum jam, and we took two pork roasts from the freezer before we left," she added as she gazed around the circle of women. "They're in the cooler, and they should be ready to fix for tomorrow's dinner—if that's all right with *you,* that is."

The three sisters nodded eagerly. "Sounds like we've got

a *gut* start toward a restful, *tasty* Sabbath," Rosetta said. "Deborah, once we set up the other bed in your cabin, why don't you and Lily put on the sheets and take care of the luggage? The rest of us can get the canners and the jars out. We'll make short work of those green beans your *mamm* brought."

After Deborah, her sister, and Rosetta set up the bed in her cabin, Rosetta returned to the lodge. Lily chuckled as she unfolded the bottom sheet and tossed one end of it to Deborah. "It's just like old times, with all the women tending to what needs to be done," she remarked happily. "I sure hope Dat decides we should move here, because . . . well, if you and Noah hitch up, you won't be coming back to Coldstream, ain't so?"

Deborah sighed. If her family remained at their farm three hours away, she'd have some adjusting to do—yet today's terse discussion at the table, when Noah had spoken up in her defense and Dat had remained unmoved, had shifted her loyalties. "*Jah,* that's the way it'll be," she stated gently. "Maybe if you and Mamma come for enough visits and Dat gets left behind to tend his preaching duties and his welding—and the boys—he'll see the move to Promise Lodge as a solution to a lot more problems than Isaac Chupp has caused us."

After she and Lily carried the suitcases to the two cabins, they returned to the lodge. As they stepped onto the porch, Deborah pointed toward Rainbow Lake. "Looks like Preacher Amos and Mattie's boys are showing Dat and our brothers a *gut* time, so maybe—oh, look! Lavern's caught a fish!"

Lily shielded her eyes with her hand, watching as her twin reeled in a fish that Noah caught in a net. "Hmm," she murmured. "The boys love to fish but they don't often get the chance, what with it being an hour's ride to the state park. Could be Lavern's just set another kind of hook."

Deborah laughed at her sister's astute observation. "With

you and me and Mamma praying on it tonight, maybe we'll have our answer soon. Let's help with the canning so it'll go faster."

When they entered the lobby, the steamy scent of boiling green beans filled the air. In the kitchen, large pots of beans were bubbling on the stove while Rosetta and her sisters washed quart Mason jars and set them in the oven to sterilize them. Mamma sat at the worktable placing canning lids into the metal rings that would seal the jars. On each of the two gas stoves, two pressure canners were steaming.

"Here come four more hands!" Phoebe said when she saw Deborah and Lily. "This job's going to go so fast, I bet we'll be finished before—"

The phone jangled and Deborah hurried across the kitchen to answer it. "Hullo? This is Deborah—at Promise Lodge," she added, in case potential new residents were calling.

"Deborah, it's Frances Lehman. It's been nearly a week, so I thought I'd give you an update from our end."

Deborah smiled, raising her eyebrows at the women who were following her conversation. "Frances, it's *gut* to hear from you," she replied. "I hope everything's going well?"

"We've gotten a nice bid on our farm, so we're starting to pack," Frances replied with a delighted chuckle. "It's going to be quite a job, but we believe Floyd's original statement still stands: God is indeed leading us to Promise Lodge, or the pieces wouldn't be falling into place so quickly. We'll be there as soon as we can! Give everyone my best."

Grinning, Deborah hung up the phone. "The Lehmans are coming! They've gotten a bid on their farm."

"I'm so glad that's settled," Mattie said with a nod. "*There's* a family who needs a new beginning."

"Floyd Lehman is a bishop," Christine explained to Mamma, "and his younger daughter had a run-in similar to Deborah's but with a more . . . permanent conclusion."

With a glance at Lily, she silently conveyed the adult nature of the situation. "We'll have lots of ladies—of all ages—here soon."

"And who knows? Maybe another bishop or two will move here and we'll need a drawing of the lot to determine who will lead the Promise Lodge colony," Rosetta remarked. "Let's just say Bishop Floyd's rather outspoken and set in his Old Order ways—not that that's always a bad thing."

Mamma's laughter lifted the lines around her eyes. "Sounds like there'll be no shortage of church leaders—fellows all wanting to do things the way they've always done them in their previous districts, I suspect."

Laughter filled the kitchen as Rosetta carefully carried one of the steaming pots of beans from the burner to the end of the worktable. "But we women are no strangers to managing such men, are we, Alma?"

Deborah smiled as she, her sister, and the Hershberger girls gathered around the pots with cups and wide metal funnels to fill hot jars with beans. *Help us work this out according to Your will, Lord. Forgive us our debts . . . as we forgive our debtors.*

Chapter Twenty-Six

As thunder rumbled on Sunday morning, Rosetta quietly descended the back stairs and entered the kitchen. She set her lamp on the windowsill so its glow would light most of the large room. It was insanely early to be up, but her circling thoughts had made sleeping impossible. She felt unsettled about the Peterscheims' situation—which remained unresolved because Preacher Eli seemed determined to withhold his final decision about leaving Coldstream, not to mention his forgiveness for poor Deborah.

And although Frances Lehman's call had excited her, Rosetta wondered yet again why she hadn't heard from the Kuhns. Last Sunday their chatter had filled the kitchen with their hopeful plans for Ruby's bees and Beulah's cheese, and Rosetta missed them. As she filled the two metal percolators to make coffee, she realized she hadn't even taken down their phone number before Delbert drove them home.

You'll have to be better organized if you're to keep track of your renters, she chided herself. *What if one of them gets ill and you need to contact their—*

When the phone rang, Rosetta nearly dropped the percolator in the sink. She rushed over to answer it before the ringing awakened anybody, wondering who would be calling at this hour. "*Jah?* Hello?" she asked in a loud whisper.

"Rosetta! Didn't mean to startle you, calling so early, but when I saw a light in your kitchen window—well, I couldn't help hoping it would be you."

Rosetta stepped into the mudroom so her voice wouldn't carry up the stairway. "Truman! *Gut* morning," she murmured into the phone. "I'm so glad you're not somebody calling about an emergency, or—"

"Truth be told, I've gone too long without your smile or the sound of your voice," he cut in with a chuckle. "So that feels like an emergency, of sorts. Work has been crazy-busy this week, late into the evenings. It's often that way in the summer. I suppose it's a *gut* problem to have."

Rosetta grinned like a giddy schoolgirl, holding the receiver close and keeping her voice low. She felt better already. Less anxious and more relaxed. "We've been going nonstop here, as well," she replied. "A family from Ohio visited this week—and they've decided to move to Promise Lodge. Then Deborah's family surprised us by showing up yesterday, as well."

"And what about those two gals I met last weekend?" he asked. "One reason for my call was to invite them to our Mennonite church service this morning. My mother and I will be leaving around nine, if they'd like to ride with us."

"That's very thoughtful of you." Rosetta sighed. "Ruby and Beulah put down six months' rent and had big plans for selling their honey and homemade cheese, but their brother took them back home last Sunday. I was just realizing I had no way to contact them when you called."

"Ah." The sound of Truman releasing his breath tickled Rosetta's ear. "Where are they from? I have projects and clients all over northern Missouri, so I might be able to hunt down a phone number."

Rosetta's eyes widened. "Oh, could you? Their brother's name is Delbert—Delbert Kuhn. Hmm . . . I think they live near a place called Versailles, but I have no idea where that is."

"It's south of here quite a ways, near Lake of the Ozarks. Lots of Mennonite folks live in that area, so I'll see what I can find for contact information, all right?"

"That would be wonderful. *Denki* so much, Truman," she replied. "I'm really glad you called."

"Me too. Makes me happy to make you happy."

Once again Rosetta reminded herself not to get caught up in the melody of his voice, or in the way his romantic words made her tingle. Through the window she noticed that the wind had picked up, splattering heavier rain against the glass, yet the dreary weather didn't bother her. "We'll have to set a time for that fish fry soon, or the summer will fly past us. Hard to believe we're more than halfway through June already."

"I'll ask my mother today when she'd like to meet you— and your family and friends, of course," he added quickly. Truman paused. "I hear her walking across the floor above me now, so I should be sure she's off to a steady start. Don't be a stranger, Rosetta."

"You know where to find me."

Rosetta hung up the phone, feeling happier than she had all week. What could possibly be wrong with exchanging some pleasant flirtation with her attractive neighbor? As long as her sisters and the men were around, her friendship with Truman Wickey would remain perfectly safe and proper. None of those *entanglements* he'd mentioned the other night.

You know better than that.

Rosetta returned to the kitchen to finish making the

coffee. This being Sunday, she decided to focus on making the Peterscheims feel at home, and on making the Lord welcome in her heart during church this morning, too . . . even if it was Truman's handsome face she saw in her imagination.

Despite the steady rain and rumbles of thunder that awoke them Sunday morning, Deborah felt hopeful. After she and Lily and Mamma got dressed, she and her sister held umbrellas over their heads while Mamma walked between them on her crutches. "This moisture will make your gardens grow," her mother remarked cheerfully. "How did you girls do at the produce stand yesterday?"

"We had to restock at noon, and we nearly sold out," Deborah replied. "All told, with the veggies, eggs, and my goodies, we brought in nearly four hundred dollars. I could hardly believe it!"

"Wow!" Lily murmured. "Maybe I could make pies to sell at the stand—*if* we move here," she added wistfully.

Deborah smiled. "Your crusts always turn out better than mine, so that might be a *gut* idea. Once word gets around, I think we'll do a steady business. We figure to keep the stand open as long as we've got fresh produce—although we have a couple of other gals who're hoping to sell honey and cheese made from our cows' and goats' milk," she added. "We might be able to stay open later into the fall than Mattie had planned. Pies and breads and goodies will sell no matter what the season."

Queenie raced around them, barking, until Noah opened the back door for them. He smiled as the three of them wiped their feet on the rug. "Did everyone rest well?" he asked, holding Deborah's gaze for an extra moment.

"Snug as a bug in a rug," Lily replied.

"Nothing like the patter of rain on the roof to lull you to sleep," Mamma remarked.

As they entered the kitchen, Deborah's stomach rumbled. They did minimal cooking on Sundays, so breakfast would consist of the banana bread and oatmeal-plum bars she and Lily had baked yesterday evening with a jar of Mamma's plum preserves. Pitchers of milk and boxes of cold cereal sat on the table, as well. The aroma of freshly perked coffee filled the kitchen.

"And how did you fellows like camping in your cabin last night?" Mattie asked as Deborah's *dat* and her three brothers hurried in out of the rain.

Menno and Johnny's hair appeared uncombed and their shirttails stuck out around their suspenders, but they wore wide smiles. "The coyotes sounded so *cool!*" the eight-year-old said.

"And close to our cabin, too," Menno chimed in. "Lavern says he saw a couple of them in the woods, but Dat thought they were probably the neighbors' dogs."

"Needless to say, it was a busy night," Dat remarked as he joined Amos and the Schwartz brothers at the table. "Hope you lock your chickens and goats up tight."

"We do, and Noah's keeping the coyotes in line with his shotgun, too," Amos replied. "Let's have our prayer. Looks like the ladies have outdone themselves baking for us."

Deborah smiled at Lily and bowed her head. It was a pleasure to be around Preacher Amos because he expressed his appreciation for the food they prepared. Like most Amish men, her father tended to compliment the cooks by eating more of what they prepared—*expecting* the pies, breads, and other foods to be made to his liking. He'd told Mamma early in their marriage that he considered store-bought cereal to be a waste of good money, so she wasn't surprised when her father passed those boxes along to

Roman. He crumbled four oatmeal-plum bars in his bowl and doused them with milk.

"Raisin Bran!" Menno exclaimed when the box got to him. He opened it and gleefully filled a bowl.

"And Shredded Wheat with blueberry filling," Johnny said with a grin. "Can we have breakfast here all the time, Dat?"

While most of the folks around the long table chuckled, Deborah noticed that her father's expression remained serious. *Surely he won't lecture Mattie and Rosetta about what they've set out for breakfast,* she hoped. It would be a long day if her father began it on a sour note.

After he'd eaten a large spoonful of his milk-saturated plum bars, however, Dat looked at his two younger sons. "You might get your wish," he replied. "But there's another matter to attend to first."

When her father set down his spoon and gazed directly at her, Deborah's heart thudded. His hair looked shaggy, and he had a red spot beneath his nose where he'd nicked himself shaving. Was it her imagination, or did Dat seem older than when she'd left home a few weeks ago?

"Deborah, when I sent you away after the Bender barn fire, I misjudged the situation. I apologize."

She squeezed her slice of banana bread so tightly that it crumbled to her plate. Everyone around her grew quiet, yet it was a different sort of silence from the one they'd endured during her parents' confrontation at supper last night.

"Seems Noah has gotten *chattier* since he's moved here, and he gave me a pretty stiff earful last night," her father continued. He cleared his throat, still holding her gaze. "I jumped to the wrong conclusion when I saw that your hair was hanging loose and your *kapp* was missing. I hope you can forgive me."

Deborah's throat was so dry it clicked when she swallowed. Although she'd heard her father deliver more Sunday sermons than she could count, she couldn't recall him ever looking so uncertain, as though his salvation—his standing with God—depended upon her response. "I—I can do that, *jah*," she whispered.

"Glory be to God," Mamma murmured. "Our prayers have been answered."

Around the table, their friends nodded their encouragement, but the situation wasn't entirely tidied up. Deborah inhaled deeply, hoping her voice wouldn't crack. "And now you must forgive *me*, Dat," she began nervously. "I went against the *Ordnung* when I called the police that night, and I—I got into an English kid's car, foolishly thinking he would drive me home. I should've run the other way when I first saw those boys drinking in the barn—but I just couldn't let it burn down."

Her father's face remained absolutely still. Unreadable. Once again Deborah felt the clock ticking away untold moments. Was he unable to forgive her mistakes? Would he let her wipe his slate clean without granting her the same gift?

Preacher Amos cleared his throat. "Deborah has already made this confession before us, Eli," he said. "I think it's commendable that she's taking this extra step, so no further barriers remain between the two of you."

Her father closed his eyes. Was he praying—or shutting out the beseeching gazes the others around the table were giving him?

"I appreciate the way you went to the sheriff, Dat," Deborah continued urgently. Her pulse was pounding so loudly she could barely hear what she was saying, but her father deserved a fuller acknowledgment of his sacrifices. "You're the one who had to bear Obadiah's objections to doing that—especially after you'd named Isaac as the one who'd most likely caused the fire. You *did* protect me from the bishop's backlash and the sheriff's interrogation by sending me away," she insisted in a halting voice. "I'm grateful for all you've done for me, Dat . . . grateful to God that everything has worked out, and that we're all safe and together again."

"Amen to that," Mattie whispered.

"God's will be done," Rosetta murmured as she clasped her sisters' hands.

Dat's eyes remained closed. Beneath his dark beard, his jaw clenched and unclenched.

Deborah sighed. Begging Noah's forgiveness for breaking their engagement had been very difficult, but her father's silence hung so heavily, she bowed her head beneath its weight. She'd expressed her appreciation as best she could, yet again the seconds ticked by while she and her friends and family endured this agonizing impasse.

A sob made her glance up.

Dat hastily wiped his eyes on his shirtsleeve and exhaled loudly. "It scared the living *daylights* out of me, Deborah, seeing my little girl with her clothes torn . . . that purple handprint on your neck," he rasped. "I lost all sense of perspective—wanted to *kill* whoever had done that to you. I did what I thought was right at the time—sending you away—but cutting off my own arm with a hacksaw couldn't have hurt me any worse." He yanked his handkerchief from his pocket and blew his nose loudly.

Amos gripped her father's shoulder, nodding. "Had to be one of the most difficult days of your life, Eli."

"*Jah,* but it's behind us now." Dat blinked a few times and then focused on Deborah with pink-rimmed eyes. "I forgive you, Daughter. Let's don't ever go through such a separation again, all right?"

Sweet relief washed over Deborah's soul. It had cost her father a great deal—had humbled him, indeed—to allow his emotions to override his usual stoic control of them. "I plan to stay away from any more of such trouble, *jah*."

"And I figure to help by keeping Deborah with *me*," Noah chimed in. His earnest gaze suggested that he badly wanted to talk to her, sometime when they could be alone.

"If we move to Promise Lodge, we can *all* keep an eye on her!" Johnny crowed. "Let's do it, Dat!"

"*Jah,* you ask us every now and again if we're gonna fish or cut bait," Menno remarked as he snatched another slice of banana bread from the plate. "And the answer's plain as day! There's a lake right here, so what're we waiting for?"

Mamma was chuckling, looking as happy and relieved as the rest of the women at the table. "We're waiting for your *dat* to make that decision, boys," she reminded them. "Let's not pester him about it—even if all of us *do* want to come here to be with Deborah and these *gut* friends we've been missing."

Deborah saw her father fighting a smile. Eli Peterscheim wasn't a man who'd allow outspoken sons or a wishful wife to sway him, yet she sensed his mind had been made up once he'd gotten a look at the Promise Lodge property.

"I had serious reservations when you left Coldstream, Amos, because I believed you were shirking your responsibilities to our church district," Dat said. "But if any *gut*'s to come of Deborah's ordeal with Isaac Chupp, we should see this visit to Promise Lodge as God's taking us by the hand and leading us . . . to our new home."

Christine nodded, smiling at her girls. "That's how we felt when we came here, too, Eli."

"No regrets," Rosetta said firmly.

"You can stake out your property and it'll be waiting for you whenever you're ready to move," Mattie added as she smiled at Mamma and Dat. "We'd be *so* happy to have you folks here!"

The expression on her father's face made Deborah hold her breath. Had Eli Peterscheim ever *beamed* this way? "I'll put the Coldstream farm up for sale when we get back," he stated. "It's time to move our family forward. Thank the Lord we don't have to wander through the wilderness for forty years like the Israelites did, to find where we belong."

Chapter Twenty-Seven

After church—when both Eli and Amos had preached about the blessings of forgiveness—and their simple noon meal, Noah stood on the lodge porch. Once again the grass was dotted with raindrops and the rows of vegetables glowed green against the dark, wet soil of the garden plots. Hummingbirds buzzed around him, darting in to sip the nectar from the trumpet vine flowers. Was there any prettier picture than black-and-white Holsteins grazing in a green pasture beside a red barn?

The clatter of dishes and the women's pleasant chatter drifting through the screen door was interrupted by the ringing of the phone. Noah hoped this call brought more good news. Now that the Peterscheims had resolved their problems, a burden had been lifted from his heart. He was eager to proceed with everyone's plans for Promise Lodge—and his future with Deborah. Aunt Rosetta's happy voice made him smile.

"Ruby Kuhn!" she exclaimed. "Just this morning I was wondering how to call you to . . . oh, my, I'm so sorry . . . but what a blessing that you and Beulah are willing and able to live elsewhere. We're all *so* glad you're coming back to Promise Lodge!"

Noah chuckled. He looked forward to helping the Kuhn sisters set up their beehives and the cheese factory, which would provide an income for others who moved to their colony. He sensed that with Ruby and Beulah around, life at Promise Lodge would never be boring.

"It seems that Delbert had every intention of keeping Ruby and Beulah in Versailles," Rosetta recounted to the others after she'd hung up. "But their youngest sister lost her husband this week, and she'll be moving in with her four kids—which makes a total of a dozen youngsters under their roof. So Delbert will be bringing our friends back—with their bees—in a couple of days."

"Twelve kids and three adults sharing the one bathroom, as I recall," Christine murmured. "Five adults, if Ruby and Beulah stayed there. Oh, my."

"God works out His will in ways we don't always understand," Noah heard his mother respond. "It's a *gut* thing Ruby and Beulah can accommodate their family's need for more space by coming here."

"And what a blessing that you're setting up apartments for *maidels* and widows, Rosetta," Deborah's mother remarked. "I'm sure Delbert would've done right by Beulah and Ruby, but you've saved him the expense of building on to his house on very short notice, it seems."

"They need a couple of those portable toilets like you see in parks," Lily remarked.

Noah chuckled along with the ladies. As he waited patiently on the porch, he saw Amos and Roman walking beyond the orchard with Eli, pointing out the proposed layout of roads and lots. It had been good to hear both preachers leading their worship service this morning. Noah looked forward to living near the Peterscheims again—and to working alongside Eli as a welder in his own right now.

Preacher Eli wasn't as good-natured as Amos, but he was solid in his faith—a leader they could count on as the Promise Lodge colony grew into the future.

At the sound of Deborah's footsteps, Noah turned. She came to stand beside him, smiling sweetly. Now that she and her father had made their peace, her face glowed with an inner beauty he'd always loved. "I'm glad you and your *dat* have settled your differences," he murmured. "I gave him the what-for yesterday—and Amos did, too. Told him if he wanted to see his grandkids, he'd better practice the forgiveness he preaches—"

"You're a wise man, Noah Schwartz," Deborah said. "*Denki* for your patience with him."

"—but I'm putting the cart before the horse," Noah continued in a rush. His pulse pounded with anticipation. "Walk with me, Deborah. I've got something to show you."

Her hand fit perfectly in his, and as they strode toward the barn Noah was glad that he, too, had seen the truth of Deborah's confrontation with Isaac Chupp. He searched for the right words—the perfect way to say them—as he led her to the shed where they kept the tools and outdoor equipment.

Noah felt her pulse thrumming as his grip tightened on her strong, slender hand. Deborah looked eager to see his surprise, yet she was quietly waiting for him to reveal it. How far they both had come since their earlier courting days, when he'd kept his thoughts to himself and she had impulsively blurted her questions and demands.

Noah propped open the shed door with a rock. The sun's rays fell upon his gift and he held his breath as Deborah stepped inside. "For you," he murmured. "I need to paint it white yet, but I—I hope this is what you had in mind."

Deborah hurried toward the trellis. "Oh, Noah, it's *exactly* what I want!" she exclaimed. "And would you look at these hummingbirds? And the way the ivy follows the arched top and—oh, think how pretty this will be with red rose bushes climbing up both sides of it!"

When Deborah hugged him, Noah felt ecstatic. "Marry me, Deborah," he whispered. "Let's make it work this time—*please?* I love you so much."

When she gazed at him, Noah saw himself reflected in her deep green eyes. It was a wonderful place to be, as though he was looking out through the windows of her soul, already at home in her heart.

"You're all I've ever wanted, Noah," Deborah murmured. "It's you and me now, through thick and thin. In sunshine and shadow."

They embraced again, their hearts beating as one. When he thought he could speak coherently, Noah eased away from her. "Shall we pick out the place to put your trellis—and our house?"

Deborah thought for a moment. "It's hard to know where we should live until we see where Dat—or your *mamm*—put their houses."

Noah smiled, not surprised at Deborah's response. She had always placed her family's desires ahead of her own. "No, sweetie, they want *us* to choose—and Mamm has decided to live in the lodge rather than maintain a house," he reminded her gently. "I suspect Amos will keep trying to change her mind about that, however. He says his house will go up right after ours does, and he doesn't intend to live in it alone for long."

Noah led Deborah over to a large piece of paper on the wall. "Here's the sketch Amos and I roughed out, with Truman's suggestions about where to put the roads and the water lines and such. This'll help you picture the colony better, I think."

He watched Deborah's facial expressions as she traced the pencil lines with her finger. "So this row of plots would face the lake . . ."

"We're keeping the space between the lodge, the cabins, and the lake open as common ground for everyone to enjoy," Noah explained as he pointed to these features. "And of course Mamm's produce plots and the orchard will remain intact."

"Could be one of our families will want the orchard as part of their tract—even if Ruby puts her hives there," Deborah murmured. Then she smiled. "What about this plot? Am I right that the apple trees would be the back boundary, and the house could face Rainbow Lake? It seems far enough from the entry road that we wouldn't be bothered by folks coming and going—"

"And this section is big enough to raise hay for our horses, and for a barn," Noah said as he pointed to these spots within the plot's boundaries. "It only totals about fifteen acres—one of the smaller plots—but since I don't intend to farm for a living, that's fine by me. Less fence to maintain. Less mowing, too—although I'd be happy to let Aunt Rosetta pasture her goats with us to save me some labor."

Deborah laughed. "Tell me true, Noah. Is this the spot *you* like the best?"

He grinned as he slipped his arm around her. "And how'd you know that, missy?"

She shrugged, looking very happy. "You're talking about acreage for hay and Rosetta's goats as though you've already figured out where you want the house and your outbuildings."

Noah smiled at her observation. "It helped that your *dat* liked the looks of this place to the south of it. If he puts his forge in this corner, we could build it big enough for both of us to use," he explained. "Amos told him, though, that you and I had first choice. And I want *you* to be happy, Deborah."

"That's quite a nice gift Amos and your *mamm* have given us." She sighed pensively. "When I came here, I never dreamed I'd be—that *we'd* be—picking out a new place that's nowhere near where we would've settled had we married sooner. I love you, Noah. You're so *gut* to me."

Deborah's smile did funny things to Noah's insides. Her tender words made him feel he'd become a man who was truly worthy of her. "Let's have a look, shall we?" he suggested. "You'll get a better feel for this plot if we walk around it instead of deciding by how it looks on paper."

As they left the shed, the sun and clouds shifted, casting an ethereal light over the lodge and the lake, the grassy hills, and the woodlands that rolled farther than they could see in all directions. When they reached the approximate front boundary of the plot they'd discussed, Noah led Deborah to the top of its gentle rise several yards back from where the road would be constructed.

"If we built the house here, we'd catch the breeze," he pointed out. "And we'd be looking out over the lake, toward the lodge and the gardens."

"Better to be within sight of your aunts' places than looking at other families' property, don't you think?" Deborah remarked. She shielded her eyes with her hand, her face aglow in the rays from the setting sun. "Your *mamm* and aunts are right. This place surely must resemble the Garden of Eden, even if some of the trees and underbrush need to be cleared away. And look—a double rainbow!"

Noah's breath caught. Against a backdrop of clouds, two shimmering bands of color seemed to rise out of the lake and arch over the orchard, one above the other. "Wow, it's not often you can distinguish all of the colors. Twice," he whispered as he held her hand tightly.

"It's the sign of God's promise to His people." Deborah gazed at the sight for several seconds, lost in thought. "Maybe He wanted you to take your time while we were courting before, Noah. He might've even used my impatience—our breakup—and Isaac's troublemaking to bring us where He intended for us to live. After all, you don't see the rainbow until you've come through the rain."

Noah smiled, because *he* couldn't see anything except Deborah's gentle smile and shining eyes, and the love that radiated from her face as she gazed at him. He knew he'd recall this moment as the new beginning of their life together. He held her close, kissing her cheek. "There's no place like home," he murmured.

"*Jah,*" Deborah replied. "And here we are."

From the Promise Lodge Kitchen

Rosetta Bender loves to cook, and as she prepares for the opening of the Promise Lodge Apartments, she'll be trying out her favorite recipes for her new friends the way you and I do! In this recipe section, you'll find down-home foods Amish women feed their families, along with some dishes that I've concocted in my own kitchen—because you know what? Amish cooking isn't elaborate. Plain cooks make an astounding number of suppers from whatever's in their pantry and their freezers. They also use convenience foods like Velveeta cheese, cake mixes, and canned soups to feed their large families for less money and investment of their time.

These recipes are also posted on my Web site, www.CharlotteHubbard.com. If you don't find a recipe you want, please e-mail me via my Web site to request it—and to let me know how you liked it!

~Charlotte

Deborah's Peppermint Brownies

No wonder Noah can't resist these moist, chocolaty treats with a surprise burst of mint in the middle! This recipe was originally featured as a Christmas cookie recipe, but why wait for the holidays to enjoy them?

1½ cups butter (3 sticks), melted
3 cups sugar
1 T. vanilla extract
5 eggs
2 cups all-purpose flour
1 cup cocoa powder
1 tsp. baking powder
1 tsp. salt
24 small peppermint patties (1½"), unwrapped

Preheat oven to 350°. Spray a 9" x 13" baking pan with non-stick coating. In a large bowl, stir together the butter, sugar, and vanilla. Add the eggs one at a time and stir until well blended. Stir in the flour, cocoa, baking powder, and salt. Reserve 2 cups of batter.

Spread remaining batter in the prepared pan. Arrange peppermint patties in a single layer over the batter, about ½ inch apart. Carefully spread the reserved batter over the patties. Bake 50–55 minutes, until the center is set. Cool completely in the pan on a wire rack. Cut in 4 columns of 9 rows for 36 brownies. Freezes well.

Kitchen Hint: These brownies can be served as is, or you can make a topping of ½ cup powdered sugar, 2 drops peppermint extract, and enough milk to make a liquid glaze. Drizzle over brownies when cool, before cutting.

Amish No-Bake Peanut Bars

This is a go-to recipe in many Plain households. It resembles other no-bake recipes that use crispy rice cereal, except the peanut butter makes the bars a bit looser and more crumbly—and adds some protein! This will be a hit with peanut butter lovers!

> 1 cup peanut butter
> 2 cups marshmallow cream
> 1 stick butter or margarine
> 1 cup brown sugar
> 1 cup dry roasted peanuts
> 4 cups Cheerios or other toasted oat ring cereal

Melt the peanut butter, marshmallow cream, butter, and brown sugar, stirring until well blended. Stir in the peanuts and dry cereal. Press into a greased/sprayed 9" x 13" pan. Cool and cut into squares.

Kitchen Hint: You can melt the sauce either on the stove or in the microwave. I don't recommend freezing these bars (the cereal will get soggy)—not that you'll have many left over!

Cinnamon Swirl Bread

This is a quick bread that doesn't require yeast, so prep time is short and you don't even need a mixer! As the bread bakes it makes its own cinnamon swirl, and your house will smell heavenly. Might as well double the recipe and make two loaves while you're at it.

Bread Batter

> 1 egg
> 1 cup milk

2 tsp. vanilla extract
⅓ cup plain Greek yogurt or sour cream
2 cups all-purpose flour
1 T. baking powder
½ tsp. salt
½ cup sugar

Swirl

⅓ cup sugar
2 tsp. cinnamon
2 T. butter, melted

Glaze

½ cup powdered sugar
2–3 tsp. cream or milk (more, as needed, for
   drizzle)

Preheat oven to 350° and grease/spray a 9" x 5" glass loaf pan. To make the batter, combine the egg, milk, vanilla, and yogurt or sour cream in a large bowl. Add the flour, baking powder, salt, and sugar and stir everything with a spoon, just until blended. Pour into the prepared loaf pan. To make the swirl, combine the sugar, cinnamon, and butter. Drop by spoonfuls across the batter and use a knife to swirl it into the bread.

Bake for 45–50 minutes or until the center tests done with a toothpick. Cool in the pan on a wire rack for 15 minutes. Remove bread from pan and cool completely on the rack. Stir the glaze ingredients together and drizzle over the top of the bread.

Kitchen Hint: To save some calories and sugar, I don't make the glaze. The bread is so moist and pretty with that cinnamon swirl that nobody misses it. Freezes well.

Hummingbird Cake with Banana Glaze

If you love dense, moist, flavorful cakes, this one's for you!
Because it's chock-full of bananas (I used 5 large bananas,
total), you can serve it with a glass of milk and call it
breakfast!

Cake

  3 cups flour
  2 tsp. baking soda
  1 tsp. salt
  2 cups sugar
  2 T. cinnamon
  3 large eggs
  1 cup vegetable or canola oil
  2 tsp. vanilla
  1 8-oz. can crushed pineapple, undrained
  1 cup chopped pecans
  2½ cups chopped bananas

Banana Glaze

  3 T. butter, softened
  ½ banana, mashed
  2 tsp. vanilla
  2 cups powdered sugar

Preheat the oven to 350° and grease/spray a 9" x 13" baking
pan. In a large bowl, combine the flour, soda, salt, sugar, and
cinnamon. With a fork or spoon, stir in the eggs and oil, just
until dry ingredients are moistened. Stir in the vanilla,
pineapple, pecans, and bananas. Pour batter into the prepared pan and bake for 40–50 minutes, until center of cake
is firm and a toothpick comes out clean. Gently pierce the
cake surface with a fork in several places.

When cake is nearly done, combine the glaze ingredients in a small bowl and mix until smooth. (I was glad I had a hand mixer for this part.) Frost cake while hot from the oven, spreading the glaze that flows toward the edges back onto the center so it will soak in. Cool completely. Freezes well.

Kitchen Hints: When I had chopped the bananas into a measuring cup, I mashed them a bit with a fork so they would incorporate into the batter. Totally mashing them would work fine, as well

If a regular fork is tearing up the hot cake surface, try using a meat fork.

Lemon Shoofly Pie

I confess that shoofly pie is not my favorite—but the lemon in this recipe cuts some of the heavy sweetness of the molasses.

Crumb Topping

1½ cups flour
½ cup sugar
½ cup shortening or softened butter
½ tsp. baking soda

Filling

1 egg
Juice and zest of 2 lemons (strain out seeds)
2 T. flour
½ cup sugar
½ cup molasses
¾ cup boiling water

1 unbaked pie shell

Preheat oven to 350°. In a medium bowl, combine ingredients for crumb topping until you have an even-textured crumb mixture, and set aside. Stir together all filling ingredients until well blended and pour into the pie shell. Sprinkle the crumb topping evenly over the filling. Bake for 45–60 minutes, until center of pie is set.

Molasses Cookies with Lemon Frosting

These soft, spicy cookies are a hit with young and old alike! Easy to make, easy to eat, and they freeze well.

Cookies

> 2 cups sugar
> 1 cup shortening (such as Crisco)
> 2 eggs
> 1 cup molasses
> 1 tsp. vanilla
> 6 cups flour
> 3 tsp. baking soda
> 1 tsp. salt
> 1 T. cinnamon
> 2 tsp. ground ginger
> 2 cups buttermilk
> 1 cup chopped nuts
> 1 cup raisins

Frosting

> 3 cups powdered sugar
> 4 T. butter, softened
> 4 T. lemon juice
> 6 T. milk

Preheat oven to 375°. Line cookie sheets with parchment paper. In a large mixing bowl, cream the sugar and shortening, then add the eggs, molasses, and vanilla and beat well. In a separate bowl, combine the flour, baking soda, salt, cinnamon, and ginger, and add to the sugar mixture alternately with the buttermilk until well combined. Stir in the nuts and raisins. Drop by spoonful on the prepared baking sheets about 2" apart. Bake about 8 minutes, until set but not browned. Allow cookies to cool for a few minutes on baking sheet before removing to a wire rack.

Mix the frosting ingredients until smooth. Spread on cooled cookies.

Kitchen Hints: No buttermilk? Place ¼ cup vinegar in the bottom of a 2-cup measuring cup and add regular milk to equal 2 cups. Stir and allow to sit about 10 minutes, until thick. For extra lemon zing, add the grated peel from one lemon to the frosting before spreading.

Easiest Peanut Butter Cookies Ever

These are fabulous cookies. You can make them on the spur of the moment—and they're gluten-free! Might as well double the batch, because these disappear fast.

  1 cup peanut butter
  1 egg
  1 cup sugar
  Additional sugar

Preheat oven to 350° and prepare a cookie sheet with parchment paper. Stir the first three ingredients with a fork until well blended. Roll dough into balls, roll in additional sugar and place on the cookie sheet. Flatten slightly with a fork to make a crisscross design. Bake about 7 minutes or until firm. Makes 6–8 cookies, depending on size.

Deborah's Best Bread

Here's a wonderful bread that stands up well to slicing, toasting, or any sort of filling you care to put into a sandwich! Amish women would mix this by hand, but using a mixer makes the dough smoother and easier to handle.

    1 cup warm water (110° F)
    1 cup warm milk (110° F)
    1½ T. yeast
    ⅓ cup sugar
    1½ tsp. salt
    ¼ cup olive oil
    5½–6 cups all-purpose flour
    1 egg yolk + 1 T. water to make egg wash
        (optional)
    1 T. butter, melted

In a large mixing bowl, mix the milk, water, sugar, and yeast. Cover for about 5 minutes, allowing yeast to foam. Stir in the salt and olive oil. Using a mixer with a paddle or dough hook, add one cup of flour at a time, mixing well after each addition. Mix until all flour is incorporated. Turn dough onto a lightly floured surface and knead until smooth and elastic. Place in a greased bowl, turning to grease the top of the dough. Cover and let rise in a warm place about an hour or until doubled in size.

Punch down the dough and divide into two equal pieces. Shape into loaves and place in two greased 9" x 5" bread pans. Cover and allow to rise in a warm place for about 30 minutes, or until loaves rise about an inch above the pans. Preheat oven to 350°. With a pastry brush, very carefully brush the tops of the loaves with the egg wash, if using. Bake for 30 minutes. Remove from pans and with a pastry brush, lightly brush melted butter over the tops. Allow to cool completely on a wire rack.

Kitchen Hint: I replace about half the all-purpose flour with white whole wheat flour when I make this recipe—and I increase the yeast to 2 T. Makes the bread a bit more dense, but still chewy-good and healthier!

Pizza Meat Loaf

Who wouldn't love this tasty variation on a favorite comfort food: meat loaf with pizza seasoning and cheese!? It's become a favorite at our house.

    1½ pounds ground meat (hamburger,
        bulk sausage, or a combination)
    8 oz. tomato sauce
    ¼ cup chopped fresh onion (or more!)
    1 egg
    ¾ cup quick oats
    1 T. Worcestershire sauce
    1½ tsp. salt
    ½ tsp. pepper
    2 T. total garlic powder, Italian seasonings, basil,
        oregano
    heaping cup of shredded mozzarella cheese

Preheat oven to 350°. Spray a loaf pan. Combine all ingredients except cheese, and press half the meat mixture into the pan. Sprinkle about ⅔ of the cheese on the meat and then cover with the remaining meat mixture. Bake uncovered for about an hour. Remove from oven and sprinkle with reserved cheese. Allow loaf to sit about 5 minutes before removing from pan to slice it.

Ruby's Potato Loaf

I was intrigued by the loaf "format" of this potato recipe, and delighted by the results—and the fact that you make it ahead. This makes a yummy side dish for any meat!

· 3 T. butter
3 T. flour
1 cup half-and-half (or cream)
salt and pepper to taste
5 medium potatoes, cooked, cooled, and cubed
1 T. parsley
¼ cup chopped green onions (optional)
½ cup (or more!) shredded cheddar cheese

In a large, deep skillet melt butter and gradually stir in flour until blended. Slowly add the half-and-half and simmer until thickened, stirring constantly. Season with salt and pepper. Gently add the potatoes, parsley, and green onions, stir to coat with the sauce, and simmer 2 minutes longer. Spoon this mixture into a well-sprayed bread pan and press down firmly. Chill for several hours or overnight.

About 45 minutes before serving time, preheat oven to 350°. Invert the potato loaf onto an ovenproof pan or serving platter. Bake for 30 minutes, sprinkle with the cheese, and bake for another 10–15 minutes or until cheese is bubbly.

Apricot-Cherry Slab Pie

Here's a way to make the equivalent of about three pies—in a convenient one-pan format! The tangy fruit filling and glaze make this a hit at potlucks, too.

Crust

3 cups flour
1 T. sugar
2 tsp. salt
1¼ cups shortening (such as Crisco)
1 egg
½ cup water
1 T. white vinegar

Fruit Filling

½ cup sugar
3 T. cornstarch
1 14.5-oz. can pitted tart pie cherries, drained
2 15-oz. cans apricot halves, drained and quartered

Glaze

1¼ cup powdered sugar
1 tsp. vanilla
5 tsp. milk (or enough to make drizzling consistency)

To make the crust, combine flour, sugar, and salt in a large bowl. Cut in the shortening with a pastry blender. Beat the egg and mix the vinegar into it, then sprinkle small amounts of the egg mixture over the flour mixture, tossing lightly until all the particles are moistened. Form into a ball, wrap in plastic wrap, and chill. Return to room temperature. Roll slightly more than half the dough on a floured surface and fit it into a 10½" x 15½" jelly roll pan/cookie sheet (with sides) so the pastry hangs over all the edges.

To make the filling, combine the filling ingredients in a medium bowl. Spoon this fruit mixture over the prepared crust. Roll out the remaining pastry and place it over the filling, then fold the bottom pastry up and over the top crust. Seal edges. Prick the top crust with a fork. Bake at 400° for about 20 minutes, until golden. Remove from oven. Stir the glaze ingredients together and drizzle over the top.

<u>Kitchen Hint</u>: To make apple slab pie, use 8 cups of peeled, sliced apples, ½ cup flour, ⅔ cup sugar, and 1 T. cinnamon for the filling instead of the canned fruit.

Don't miss the first of
Charlotte Hubbard's Simple Gifts,

A SIMPLE VOW,

coming this June.

Read on for an introduction to this heartwarming series,
featuring three newcomers to the beloved
Amish community of Willow Ridge.

Edith Riehl stepped out onto the front porch of her new home, bubbling with anticipation. On this beautiful spring morning everyone in Willow Ridge would be attending the wedding of Ira Hooley and Millie Glick, over at the big house on the hill where Nora and Luke Hooley—mother of the bride and brother of the groom—lived. Horse-drawn buggies were already pulling up the driveway and behind the Hooleys' home as guests arrived, and Edith was excited that she and her two sisters would be among them. Loretta and Rosalyn agreed that helping serve the wedding dinner after the ceremony would be a wonderful way to meet their new neighbors on such a special occasion.

As Edith gazed out over the pasture where Bishop Tom Hostetler's dairy cows grazed, beyond the homes and small farms that formed the patchwork of Willow Ridge, her sisters' voices drifted through the upstairs windows. They were trying one last time to convince their father to come with them, but weddings weren't Dat's cup of tea now that Mamm had passed on.

When she heard loud crying, Edith walked to the other end of the porch, wondering where that baby was and why it was fussing. She spotted an enclosed buggy on the side of the road, and behind it two men in Plain clothing and black straw hats were having an agitated conversation.

Don't they realize how they're upsetting that poor wee one? Edith wondered as she hurried down the porch steps. *And where's the mother?*

As she approached the buggy, the men's raised voices became disturbingly clearer.

"What was I supposed to think when I got a phone message from a total stranger, accusing me of—of impregnating his wife?" the taller fellow demanded tersely. He was standing in front of a saddled horse, gripping its reins.

"And how do you think *I* felt when your name was the last thing she uttered before she died?" the other man shot back. "*Tell Asa I'll always love him.* Do you know how those words tore my world to shreds?"

Edith's eyes widened. Clearly, this conversation was none of her business, yet the crying baby compelled her to walk faster. Perhaps she could suggest that these two men speak with Bishop Tom about such a troubling situation—although he was probably already at the Hooley home, preparing for the service that would precede the wedding.

"I'm telling you that I've never so much as *met* your wife, let alone—"

"Shut up! This explains why Molly got so big so fast, and why the twins came two months early!" the man with his back to Edith lashed out. "Not only have I lost my wife, but I've learned that my marriage of seven months was a lie!"

Twins? And their mother's name was Molly—and she died? Edith's thoughts whirled as she stepped up through the buggy's open door. Two tiny infants wiggled in carriers on the backseat as their wails filled the vehicle.

"Oh, look at you," Edith murmured. "Shhh . . . it'll be all right now." She gently scooped the nearest baby, which wore a crocheted yellow cap, into the crook of one arm before lifting its white-capped twin to her other shoulder. It seemed these newborns had no mother and a very distraught father, and they'd been born into a confusing, distressing situation.

As the men's discussion escalated, Edith frowned and stepped carefully down from the buggy. One fellow's voice sounded familiar. She didn't want to believe the scenario he'd been describing, but right now her main concern was for the babies.

"Would you please lower your voices?" she insisted as she came around the buggy. "You've upset these little angels so badly that—Will Gingerich? Are these *your* twins?"

"Edith! Thank God I've found you." The handsome young man to whom her sister Loretta had once been engaged removed his hat to rake his brown hair with his fingers. "*Jah*, I believed they were mine until Molly named this—this *other* dog as their father—"

"I'm trying to get to the bottom of that story," the taller man protested, "but—"

"Stop it, both of you!" Edith insisted in a low voice. "These babies are wet and hungry and upset. Your problems will have to wait until we've taken care of more important matters."

Both men stared at Edith as though she was crazy, and maybe she was. What had possessed her to stick her nose into this business, which sounded more dubious by the moment? She had never seen the taller man with the black hair and riveting eyes, and the last she'd heard of Will Gingerich, he'd married another young woman rather quickly after Dat had called off the engagement between him and Loretta. Edith thought they'd left this heartache behind them when they'd moved away from Roseville to start fresh in Willow Ridge, but it seemed a fresh batch of problems had popped up like a crop of dandelions after they'd left.

"I came to ask you—your family—a huge favor," Will implored her. His Adam's apple bobbed when he swallowed, gazing at her with a desperate expression. "I—I have no idea how to care for these kids, what with Molly dying right after they were born. I was hoping you and your sisters would take them until I can get my life together and—"

Edith's eyes widened. "Is there no one in Molly's family, or—"

"That's just it," Will continued in a desperate whisper. "Molly's *mamm* and grandmother were there at the birthing when she blurted out *this* guy's name—"

"She was no doubt delirious and unaware of what she was saying," Edith suggested.

"—and then when Molly passed on not an hour later, her grandmother had some kind of attack and wound up in the hospital," Will went on doggedly. "Molly's mother isn't speaking to me now. I've had a lot of *stuff* thrown at me these past few days. I trust you Riehl sisters to tend to the twins until I get through the funeral and then figure out, well— what to *do* with them. *Please,* Edith?"

It was indeed quite a favor Will was asking, but how could she refuse? The babies had almost stopped crying. Edith gazed at their red, puckered faces as she swayed from side to side, calming them. By the sound of Will's incredibly sad story, these helpless infants might not have anyone caring for them—for how long? "Of course we'll look after them," she murmured, "but we don't have so much as a diaper or a baby bottle—"

"I brought all that stuff. I was looking for your house when *this* guy"—Will glowered, pointing at the other man— "caught up to me and claimed I'd accused him falsely."

The stranger looked ready to protest again, but instead he crossed his arms, clenching his jaw. Behind him, his black horse nickered and shook its mane.

Edith gestured with her head. "We're in that two-story

white house just down the road. The one with the lilac bushes on either side of the porch steps."

"Hop in. I'll give you a ride."

Before Edith could reply, Will jogged around the buggy and stepped up into the rig. As she followed him, she realized just how scattered his thoughts must be—and how inexperienced he was with babies—because there was no *hopping in* when she was holding an infant in each arm. Gazing into the backseat, Edith was about to ask for Will's help when a strong arm curled around hers.

"Let me hold them, and I'll hand them up after you get in."

Edith blinked, gazing up into the stranger's face. She'd known Will Gingerich—and liked him—for most of her life, so she felt a bit traitorous appreciating help from the man who'd supposedly had *relations* with Molly before she'd married Will. He calmly took one baby and then the other, however, smiling at her as she situated each of them in a carrier.

The buggy lurched and Will drove them down the road without closing the door. "I'm sorry to spring this on you girls," he said ruefully. "Sorry about—well, I just never saw any of this coming."

"I can't imagine," Edith murmured.

"I hope you'll understand if I'd rather not see Loretta—or your *dat*," he added quickly.

Edith smiled sadly. Her sister and Will had been sweethearts all through school, and their broken engagement was still a sore subject. "It's probably best that way, *jah*."

He halted the horse at the end of their lane. While Edith carried a baby basket in each hand, Will followed her to the porch with a large cardboard box. "You're a godsend, Edith—an angel—and I can't thank you enough," he murmured. "I'll come back as soon as I can, after the funeral."

She nodded mutely, wondering how on earth she would explain to her family about the monumental responsibility she'd just taken on. "So, what are the babies' names? Are they boys or girls or—"

"One of each. Leroy and Louisa." Will kept his eyes on her, as though he couldn't bear to look at the children he apparently hadn't fathered. "They were born October tenth, so they'll be six months old tomorrow, and—well, you probably think I'm already a total failure as a father. Give Loretta my best."

As Edith watched Will's rig roll down the road, her mouth fell open. She'd put on her best purple dress to attend the wedding, and now she stood on the porch with two babies and a box of whatever Will had tossed into it. *What were you thinking? What sort of mess have you gotten yourself into? How long will it be before Will comes back—and what if he doesn't?*

Edith's whirling thoughts were interrupted by the tattoo of boots on the porch steps. She turned to find the raven-haired stranger studying her intently with eyes the color of rich, deep molasses. He removed his straw hat.

"My name's Asa Detweiler and I live in Clifford—south of Roseville about ten miles," he said in a low voice. He ducked slightly so that his eyes were level with hers, mere inches away. "I swear to you that I've never met Will's wife—never saw *him* before today, when his phone message accused me of fathering these twins. Do you believe that, Edith?"

She blinked. Asa Detweiler told a compelling story and had the voice and eyes to back it up. But what did she know about any of the stories she'd heard this morning?

Asa smiled wryly. "I admire a woman who doesn't blurt out the first thing that comes to mind—and who has put the needs of these two babies first," he added. "I promise you

I'll get to the bottom of this situation, and I'll be back. Promise me that you'll mother these kids—and that you'll hear me out when I return, all right?"

Edith couldn't help staring into his midnight eyes. Even as she nodded, she sensed that Asa's request, and her unspoken affirmation—such a simple vow—would change her life in ways she couldn't possibly predict.